TESSERACTS

TESSERACTS

EDITED BY
JUDITH MERRIL

Press Porcépic
Victoria • Toronto

This edition is published by Press Porcépic Ltd., 235–560 Johnson Street, Victoria, B.C. V8W 3C3, with the assistance of the Canada Council.

Typeset by The Typeworks in Baskerville 11/13½.
Printed in Canada.

Cover art by Ron Lightburn.

1 2 3 4 88 87 86 85

Canadian Cataloguing in Publication Data

Main entry under title:

Tesseracts

ISBN 0-88878-243-8 (bound). --ISBN
   0-88878-242-X (pbk.)

1. Science fiction, Canadian (English)*   2. Canadian fiction (English) - 20th century.*   I. Merril, Judith, 1923–
PS8323.S3T47 1985   C813'.0876'08   C85–091373-X
PR9197.32.T47 1985

To
the memories of
my friend
Father Arthur Gibson
who challenged a generation of
students at St. Michael's to consider
The Problems of God in Science Fiction
and of
my friend brother lover mentor
Theodore Hamilton Sturgeon
who challenged half a century's
science fiction writers and readers
to
Ask the next question

CONTENTS

Contents

Contents

FOREWORD

I hate writing introductions.

I never read them myself, except perhaps *after* I have read the book: sometimes I like a piece of work enough to want to know more about how/why it came to be; some less loving times, I simply want to find out what justification the author might have had. For those of you who share my prejudice against prejudgements (and therefore are not reading this), I have provided an afterword with my post-editing joys, judgements and (of course) justifications.

One function a foreword can fulfill. For those of you intrigued by title, cover, by-line, back cover and sub-title, but still uncertain, this opening will compose one further essay at getting you to buy/borrow/read the book itself. To that end I offer, not the usual advance gloss, but a form of descriptive glossary.

Tesseracts. A cube is a three-dimensional square. A tesseract is a four-dimensional cube. Since the human eye and brain normally perceive, at most, three dimensions, the tesseract on the cover looks like any other flat-surface representation of a cube. The easiest way to visualize the added dimension is to imagine the cube in motion through *time* (one possible fourth dimension). Or you might conceive of an extra dimension in *space* by remembering

1

that the volume of that cube-shape on the cover is arrived at by multiplying the square on one side by one side of the square—so multiply the cube by one side again, and recognize that the "inside" of the tesseract is enormously more capacious than the outside (as we see it). It is only deceptively easier to opt instead for an additional semantic or symbolic dimension, in which the visible spaces and/or events of "solid reality" acquire a Jarry-esque *pataphysical* enhancement of meaning.

Canadian is both harder and easier to explain. Nobody knows what it is even supposed to be, let far-out-alone what it actually *is*. In this case, the word specifies that the selections in this book were all written in Canada by human beings who make their homes here—all of whom, as it happens, are either Canadian citizens or landed immigrants.

Science fiction is easier than *Canadian* only because it is possible at least to say what it's *not*. (For starters, it is not necessarily either fiction or anything to do with science.) As for what it *is*—

Long ago, and in another country, I sometimes used to stay up till the dawn (not, as mature successful writers do, only for deadlines, sex and taxes, but) in heated discussion and debate in the company of fellow-seekers after science fiction fame and fortune. More often than I'd care to try and count, the topic on the table as the street-lights went out was yet another attempt to agree on a definition of science fiction. Then someone would say, "I may not know what it is, but I know it when I read it!" And we'd make another pot of coffee.

Now, nodding over dawn coffee (with my deadline) I am inspired to set forth a composite of some forty-five years of approximations.

So-called "science fiction" is speculative or extrapolative literature (or sometimes visual art or music) dealing in some way with the idea of *change*—most often changing human responses to the altered, or shifting, environment of some alternative reality. *Most* often, simply, "future fiction."

The key words are *change, environment, alternative*.

If it does not deal with *change*, it is not science fiction. If the human conflict, problem, or experience is not integrally related to some external *environmental* stimulus (which might be simply the process of change) it is not science fiction. Unless the environment posited is not in some way *other* than the familiar assumptions of here-and-now (or past) reality, then it is not science fiction.

Given all these qualifications, it will still not be science fiction, unless the approach to it is either speculative or extrapolative, or both. Definitions aside, the genre demands that every piece in its domain be based on either *What if?*. . . or *If this goes on.* . . .

Well, then, go on—

If you do, look me up at the end of the book.

JUDITH MERRIL
Toronto
July 1985

HOME BY THE SEA

Elisabeth Vonarburg

Translated by Jane Brierley

"Is it a lady, Mommy?"

The small girl looks at me with the innocent insolence of children who say out loud what adults are thinking to themselves. A skinny, pale, fair-haired child of five or six, she already looks so like her mother that I feel sorry for her. The mother gives an embarrassed laugh and lifts the child onto her lap. "Of course it's a lady, Rita." She smiles excuse-her-please, I smile back oh-it's-nothing. Will she take advantage of it to launch into one of those meaningless, ritual conversations whereby neighbours assure each other of their mutual inoffensiveness? To cut her off, I turn towards the window of the compartment and look purposefully at the scenery. Heading to the north the train follows the system of old dike as far as the huge gap breached forty years ago by the Eschatoï in their final madness. The scars left by the explosions have nearly disappeared, and it almost seems as though the dike were meant to stop here and that the waters had been allowed to invade the lowlands as part of some official scheme. We cross the narrows by ferry, and are once more in the train, an ordinary electric train this time, suspended between the two wide sheets of water, to the west rippled by waves, to the east broken by dead trees, old transmission towers, church spires, and caved-in roofs. There is a mist, a whitish breath rising from the waters like a second tide ready to engulf what is left of the man-made land-scape.

Is it a lady? You obviously don't see ladies like me very often in your part of the world, little girl. Cropped hair, boots, army fatigues, a heavy jacket of worn leather; and the way I was sitting, grudgingly corrected when you and your mousy mother came in—a real lady doesn't sprawl like that does she, even when she's by herself. The *lady* actually likes to be comfortable, believe it or not, and in her usual surroundings she doesn't have to worry much about what people think. The lady, little girl, is a re-cuperator.

But she couldn't tell you this; she didn't want to see your big, stupid eyes fill with terror. All the same, you don't get to see a real live bogeywoman every day. I could've taught you a few things. Yes, I know, *If you're not good the Recuperator will get you, and he'll say you're not a real person and put you in his big sack.* As a matter of fact, we don't put human specimens in our big sacks right away, you know; only plants and small animals. Big animals are injected with tracers once they've been put to sleep for preliminary tests. If the Institute researchers discover something especially interesting, they come back for it. I could've told you all this, little girl, you and your mother, who would probably have looked at me with superstitious fear. But who cares what recuperators really do, anyway? They go into the contaminated Zones to bring back hor-rible things that in other times might have been plants, animals, humans. So the recuperators must be contaminated too, mentally if nothing else. No, no one apart from the Recuperation Agency cares what the recuperators really do. And no one, especially not the Institute, wonders who they really are, which suits me just fine.

"Why did they break the dike, Mommy?" asks the small girl. She's sensed that it would be a good idea to change the subject.

"They were crazy," says the mother curtly. Not a bad summing up. Fanatics, they were—but it comes to the same thing. You see, they thought the waters would keep rising, and they wanted to help the process along: *The End of the Damned Human Race.* But the waters stopped. So did the Eschatoï, by the way; it was one of their great collective suicides. But this time there weren't enough of

5

them left to start afresh—nor enough energy in the new generations to be fanatic. The pro-life people have simmered down too.
Even the Institute doesn't believe in its own slogans any more. *The
Rehabilitation of the Marvellous Human Race.* But that's just it: the
human race isn't reproducing itself well or adequately. It probably
wore itself out with its frenetic activity during the Great Tides and
the seismic catastrophes at the end of the last century. Now it's
going downhill, although no one dares say so straight out to the
Institute and its people. True, there are fewer earthquakes, the
sun breaks through the clouds more often, and the waters have
stopped rising, but that's nothing to get excited about; it's not a
human victory. Just a blind, natural phenomenon that peaked by
pure chance before destroying what was left of humanity. And I,
little girl, I who am not human, I collect what the Institute calls
"specimens" in the contaminated Zones—specimens that are also,
in their way, what is left of humanity.

I who am not human. Come on, now, didn't I get over that long
ago? But it's habit, a lapse, a relapse. I could've answered you just
now, little girl, by saying, "The lady is an artifact, and she's going
to see her mother."

But that very word requires so much explaining: *Mother.* At
least I have a navel. A neat little navel, according to the medic who
checked me out before my abortive departure for Australia and
the Institute. The current artifacts have large, clumsily made
navels that the scanner immediately picks up as not being the real
thing. But you, now, it's almost invisible, extraordinary, what
technical skill your. . . . And there he stumbled: *mother, creator,
manufacturer?* He came out of his scientific ecstasy, conscious that
after all someone was listening who hadn't known the truth. None
of the other tests had ever revealed anything. But this Medical
Centre is connected to the Institute, and new detection methods
have been developed that didn't exist when you were, er . . . (he
cleared his throat—he was very embarrassed, poor man) *made.*

Yes, she made me like this so I could pass for a human being.
Almost. In spite of everything I thought then, she surely didn't
foresee that I'd learn about it this way. I probably wasn't meant to
know until the end, with its unmistakable signs. Why? Am I really
going to ask her? Is this why I came? But I'm not really going to

see her. I'm passing by, that's all. I'm going into the Hamburg Zone.

Oh, come on! I know damn well I'll stop at Mahlerzee. I will? I won't? Am I still afraid, then? That cowardice which made me burn all my bridges, swear never to ask her anything when I found out. But it wasn't only cowardice (you see, little girl, the lady always tends to exaggerate, to be too hard on herself). It was a question of survival. It wasn't because I was afraid or desperate that I ran away after the medic's revelations. I didn't want to see the others who were waiting for me outside. Not Rick, especially not Rick. . . . No, if I remember rightly that lady of fifteen years ago was in a fury—and she still is—in spite of everything. A huge fury, a wild, redeeming fury. Surely this was why, on coming out of the Medical Centre, she found herself heading for Colibri Park. It was there that she'd first seen the Walker.

Colibri Park. The first time you go there you wonder why it's not called "Statue Park." Of course, there is the transparent dome in the middle of the main lawn, enclosing its miniature jungle with hummingbirds that flit about on vibrating wings, but what one really sees are the statues. Everywhere, along the alleys, on the lawns, even in the trees, believe it or not. The young lady came there with Rick, her lover, and Yevgheny, the typical street-wise city boy who teaches small-town greenhorns the score. The lady was sixteen. She'd been barely a month in Baïblanca. One of the youngest scholarship students at Kerens University. A future ornament of the Institute. The fledgeling that had fled the nest, slamming the door as she went, so to speak. And on every side, she and her lover were surrounded by the wonders of Baïblanca, the capital of Eurafrica. I could say it was Eldorado for us, but you probably wouldn't know what Eldorado is.

Yevgheny had pointed out, among the people strolling by, the Walker—a man moving slowly, very slowly. He was tall, and could have been handsome had something in his bearing been as imposing as his height. But he walked listlessly, you couldn't even call it sauntering. And then, as he passed them by, that blank face, those eyes that seemed to be looking far off, perhaps sad, perhaps merely empty. . . . He'd been walking like this every day for almost ten years, Yevgheny had said. The sort of thing old men do. . . . That was it, he walked like an old man. But he didn't seem all that old, barely in his thirties. "He was never young, either," said Yevgheny. "He's an artifact."

And I'd never heard the word. How had my *mother* managed to keep me from ever hearing it? At least Rick seemed as stupid as I was. Yevgheny was delighted. "An artifact—an organic work of art. Artificial! Obviously you don't see them running around the streets of Mahlerzee or Broninghe."

This one wasn't doing much running either, Rick remarked. Yevgheny smiled condescendingly; this artifact was at the end of the road, used up, almost finished. He made us go past the Walker and sit on one of the long benches facing the central lawn. Then he launched into a detailed explanation. (I was afraid he would wake the young woman in blue who was dozing at the other end of the bench, one arm resting on the back, the other propped by the elbow to support her head with its heavy black hair, but his brash voice didn't seem to disturb her.) Not many of these artifacts were made nowadays; they'd gone out of fashion, and there had been incidents. During their fully active period they were far more lively than the Walker (who moved slowly, so slowly, towards the bench). Very lively, in fact. And not everyone knew what they were, not even the artifacts themselves. Thirty years earlier the great diversion in the smart circles of Baïblanca was to bet on who among the new favourites in the salon of this or that well-known personality was an artifact, whether or not the artifact knew, whether or not the artifact's "client" knew, whether or not either would find out, and how either would react. Particularly the artifact. There were *Sheep,* and there were *Tigers.* The *Tigers* tended to self-destruct deliberately before their program terminated, sometimes with spectacular violence. A biosculptor had made a fortune in this way. One of his artifacts had reacted by setting out to kill him. There was always some doubt about the precise moment when an artifact stopped working completely, and the biosculptor gambled that his would self-destruct before getting him. He almost lost his bet. Instead he merely lost both arms and half his face. It wasn't serious; the medics made them grow again. After several premature deaths among the elite of Baïblanca in these inopportune explosions, the government put a stop to it.

This didn't keep the biosculptors from continuing for a while. Artifacts popped up now and then, but no more *Tigers* were made; the penalty was too stiff.

Yevgheny rattled all this off with a relish that disgusted the lovers. They didn't know much about Baïblanca yet; they had heard the Judgmentalists fulminating against the "New Sodom," and now they understood why. This decadent society wasn't much better than that of the Eschatoï, the dyke-destroyers whom they'd beaten. Rick and Manou understood each other so well, little girl. They were so pure, the brave new generation. (Oh, what high-flown debates we used to have, late into the night, about what we'd do for this poor, ailing world once we were in the Institute!) With Yevgheny they watched the Walker reach the bench and sit down beside the blue-clad sleeper. Yevgheny began to laugh as he felt the lovers stiffen: the Walker wouldn't do anything to them even if he heard them, which wasn't likely! It was an artifact, an *object*! But didn't he say they automatically exploded? "I told you, they aren't making any more *Tigers*!"

The final moments of the *Sheep* weren't nearly as spectacular. They became less and less mobile, and finally their artorganic material destabilized. And then the artifacts vaporized, or else. . . . Yevgheny rose as he spoke, and went over to the Sleeper in blue. Bending his index finger, he tapped her on the forehead. ". . . or else they turn to stone."

The young woman in blue hadn't moved; neither had the man. He seemed to have seen and heard nothing. He was contemplating the Sleeper.

When Yevgheny, all out of breath, caught up with the lovers, he finished what he was saying. "And you know what they call those two? Tristan and Isolde!"

He nearly killed himself laughing. He probably never understood why we systematically avoided him afterward. We had some moral fibre, Rick and I. Small-town greenhorns are better brought up than Baïblancans.

You see, when you come right down to it, little girl, probably nothing would have happened, or not in the same way, if I hadn't been so much like her, like my *mother*. But of course I was. Oh, not physically. But in character. And typically pig-headed. Reconciliations as tempestuous as our rows. We had a marvellous time, we two. She told me the most extraordinary stories; she knew everything, could do everything, I was convinced of it. And it was true—almost. A man—what for? (Because one day, and you must realize it too, the question of the father will arise.) And at this point I distinctly sensed a wound somewhere deep down, a bitterness, despite her effort to be honest. ("They have their uses," she had said, laughing.) But really the two of us needed no one else; we were happy in the big house by the beach. She took care of everything: lessons, cooking, fixing things; and the toys when I was little, made of cloth, wood, anything! Taïko Orogatsu, you see, was a sculptress. I can picture her now, smudges up to her elbows and even on her face, circling her lump of clay like a panther, talking to herself in Japanese. Of course, I didn't understand any of it. I thought it was magic. She was determined to hold on to her language, but she never taught it to me. It was all that she had left of Japan, where she had never set foot. Her ancestors had emigrated long before the Great Tides and the final submersion. She didn't even have slanted eyes.

But I'm not going to tell you about my memories of that time, little girl. Perhaps they're lies. Real memories? Implanted memories? I don't know. But even if they are implants, she wanted it that way. It must reveal something about her, after all, because I can also remember her faults, her brutal practicality, her impatience, or else the interminable, logical arguments that would cave in beneath a sudden arbitrary decision: and-that's-the-way-it-is-and-you'll-understand-later. My adolescent whining was typical. Another series of implanted memories? Impossible to find out, unless I asked her. Did I really go through the adolescent crisis, I-want-to-live-my-own-life-and-not-yours, or do I merely *think* I walked out slamming the door? Looking back now, however, isn't it really the same thing? That old-fashioned career as a space pilot, did I want it for myself, or to thwart her? So as not to go into biotronics as she wanted me to? Did I really mean it? In the end, when I fled the Medical Centre after the medic's revelation, what really hurt wasn't the loss of a future career destroyed before it even began. I didn't shed any tears about it later, either. I didn't cry at all, in fact. For years. It almost killed me. The young lady who'd just found out she was an artifact was furious. Can you understand that, little girl? Beside herself with fury and hate. The Taïko who had done this, who had done this to me, who had *made* me, she couldn't be the Taïko of my memories! Yes she was. But I couldn't have lived with a monster all those years without even realizing it! Yes I could. She did this to me, so that I would find out like this, go crazy, do dreadful things, anything? But it wasn't possible! Yes it was. A monster. Underneath the Taïko that I thought I remembered. Two contradictory images met in my head, matter/antimatter, with myself in the middle of the disintegrating fire. Infinite emptiness as the pillars of a whole, full life crumble.

In any case, you see, the lady was so gutted that she scarcely remembers the weeks that followed. She dropped deep beneath the civilized surface of Baïblanca, into the submarine current of non-persons. Threw her credentity card into an incinerator! Disappeared, as far as Kerens University was concerned—and the Institute, and the universal data banks. And you know what? It's extraordinarily easy to live underwater once you've given up breathing. The current wasn't fast or cold; the creatures who lived there were so indifferent that it was almost a kindness. I haven't any really coherent memory of it. The shop where no questions were asked. The mechanical work, day in, day out. An empty shell. Automaton. I was never so much an artifact as then. And of course, the nightmares; I was a time bomb ready to explode, and so naturally I had to become an automaton to protect myself. So as not to begin thinking, mainly, and especially not to begin feeling.

But one day, quite by chance, the lady encountered the Walker. For weeks after that she followed him around in horrible fascination. He walked slower and slower, and people turned to look at him—those who didn't realize what he was. And then it happened, in broad daylight. I saw him on the Promenade, walking so, so slowly, as though he were floating in a time bubble. It wasn't his usual hour at all. And there was something about his face, as though he were . . . in a hurry. I followed him to Colibri Park where the Sleeper slept, uncaring, in full sunlight. The Walker halted by the bench, and with impossible slowness he began to seat himself beside the motionless woman; but this time he did not simply sit: he curled up against her, placing his head in the crook of the arm on which the Sleeper was resting her head. He closed his eyes and stopped moving.

And the follower sat down beside the Walker, now at his final destination, and watched his flesh become stone. It was like a slow and ultimate tremor rising from his innermost being, rising to the surface of his skin and then imperceptibly stiffening, while the cells emptied out their sublimated substance and their walls became mineral. The extinction of life, as lightly as the passing shadow of a cloud.

And I . . . I felt as though I were awakening. I stayed there a long time, beginning to think, to feel again. Through the fury, I sensed . . . no, not peace, but a resolve, a certainty, the glimmer of an *emotion.* . . . I didn't know what end had been planned for me—explosion or petrification—but I found I could bear it after all. It wasn't so terrible in the long run. (I was absolutely amazed to find myself thinking this way, but that was all right: astonishment is also an emotion.) It was like one of those incurable illnesses of which the outcome was at once certain, quick, and curiously problematical. You knew it would happen, but not when or how. There were lots of humans who lived like this. So why not me?

Yes, astonishment was the initial emotion. The idea of revenge only came later. *I would not give her the satisfaction of seeing me die before my time.* I would not put on such a performance for her. I would not make a spectacle of myself.

But I still had enough sense of showmanship to join the recuperators.

No. There were two ways of completely covering one's tracks. Either go and live in a Zone, or go and hunt in a Zone. The really theatrical thing to do would be to go and live in a Zone: "I'm a monster, and I'm joining the monsters." Whereas becoming a recuperator. . . .

Well, the lady still had a perverse streak in spite of everything. She was meant to be caught in the net, and instead found herself doing the catching, ready to spring the trap in which she would capture these quasi-humans, these para-animals . . . these specimens. She could have become very cruel. She could have. But she had seen too many sadistic recuperators, fanatic, sick. And then she inevitably recognized herself in her prey. She was teetering on the razor's edge between disgust and compassion. But she came down on the side of compassion; this recuperator was not a bogeywoman after all. On the side of compassion or "by accident," or "because of inadequate programming," or "because I had been properly brought up." It comes to the same thing as far as results are concerned, and that's all that counts.

That's what Brutus thought. The only result that counted for him was that I had opened his cage to let him go. Brutus. He called himself this because the para-leprosy had only affected his face then, giving him a lion's muzzle. Quite handsome, as a matter of fact. One found everything in the recuperators' cages, little girl, and this *specimen* was terribly well-educated. There are still lots of operational infolibraries in the Zones. "The complete programming of artifacts is a myth maintained by the Institute. Actually, it's not as simple as that. Implant memories? Yes, perhaps. But mainly biosculptors insert the faculty of learning, plus a certain number of predispositions that won't all necessarily develop, depending on circumstances—exactly like human beings." How strange, to be discussing the nature of conscience and freedom with a half-man crouching in the moonlight. Because yes, Brutus often came back to see me, little girl, but that's another story.

The lady has kept on being a recuperator since Brutus, however. Not for the sake of delivering specimens to the far-off Institute, but to help them escape. If absolutely necessary, I bring back plants and animals. But not the quasi-, pseudo-, para-, semi-*people*. How long will I be able to go on like this? I suppose that will be another story, too. Perhaps it won't be much of a story, after all. The people at the Institute don't really care. In Australia they're so far away from our old, sick Europe. They work at their research programs like sleepwalkers, and probably don't even know why. They merely keep on with what they're doing; it's a lot simpler.

And as you can see, little girl, the lady has also kept on with what she was already doing. She's been at it for quite some time. Thirty-two years old and no teeth missing, when most known artifacts only last a maximum of twenty years in the active phase. And then one day, having seen how her fellow recuperators thinned out around her—radiation, viruses, accidents or "burnout," as the Agency refers to the madness that overtakes them—she began to doubt whether she really was an artifact. And she had all the tests run again. Not at the Kerens Medical Centre. Naturally. But one of the axioms of Baïblanca was that everything legitimate had its underground counterpart. There were specialized medics among the non-people. In any case, my artifacticity was confirmed. The only reasonable hypothesis was that I wasn't really thirty-two years old and had only fifteen years of actual existence behind me. My birth certificate was false, of course. And all my memories until the time I left home were implants.

And it bothers me. Not only because I must be nearing my "limit of obsolescence," as the second examining medic so elegantly put it while admiring the performance of my biosculptress, just as the first had. But because I wonder why she made me like this, with *these* memories? And so detailed, so exact. I've got a right to be a little curious, after all, since I've made my peace with the inevitable, up to a point. It doesn't matter so much now about not asking her anything. I'll be very calm when I see her. I'm not going there to demand an explanation. It's past history. Fifteen years ago, I might have. But now. . . .

You want to know what the lady's going to do? So do I. See Taïko before she dies, is that all? Because she's old, Taïko is. Fifty-seven is very old; you may not live that long, little girl. The average life-span for you humans is barely sixty, and getting less all the time.

See Taïko. Let her see me? No need to say anything, in fact. Just to satisfy my conscience, liberate it, prove that I've really made my peace with myself. (With her? Despite her?) See her. And show her, to be honest. Show her that I've survived, that she's failed if she built me merely to self-destruct. But she can't have wanted that. The more I think about it the less it fits with what I remember about her—even if the memories are implants. No. She must have wanted a "daughter" of her own making, a creature who'd adore her, not foreseeing the innate unpredictability of any creation, the rebellion, the escape . . . *if* I really did escape. But if this is also a pseudo-memory, what on earth can it *mean*?

Usually, little girl, the lady takes some reading material or music with her when travelling; otherwise she thinks too much. Why didn't I bring along anything to keep me occupied this time? Because I didn't want to be distracted on the way north, to the past? Because I'm trying to work up nostalgia for memories that were probably implanted? Come on, Manou, be serious. I might as well go and have something to drink in the dining car. There's no point keeping on like this, speculating. I'll ask, she'll explain. People don't do what she's done without wanting to explain, surely. Even after all this time.

Perhaps you wonder, little girl, how the lady knows that Taïko Orogatsu is still alive? Well, she took the precaution of checking it out. Without phoning the house, though. Really, is there any point going? It's perhaps another kind of cowardice, going, an admission of something missing somewhere. Do I really need to know why she made me this way? I've made myself, since. And anyway, I'm going into the Hamburg Zone. I'm not *obliged* to stop.

There, the train has finally ground to a halt. Mahlerzee. You see, little girl, the lady's getting off here.

Try to work up nostalgia? Artificial memory or no, it's impossible to avoid clichés: flood-of-memories, changed-yet-unaltered-scenery. tthe wharf completely submerged by the high tide, the avenue of statues almost buried in the sand. The terrace with its old wooden furniture, the varnish peeled off by the salt air. An unfamiliar black and white cat on the mat in front of the double doors, slightly ajar to show the living room beyond. Not a sound. The porcelain vase with its blue dragon, full of freshly cut flowering broom. I should call out, but I can't, the silence oppresses me. Perhaps she won't recognize me. I'll say anything, that I'm a census-taker, that I mistook the house. Or simply go. . . . But, "Hello, Manou." I didn't hear her coming—she's behind me.

Small, so small, diminutive, like a bird. Was she like this? I don't remember her being so frail. The hair is quite white, tousled, she must have been having an afternoon nap. The wrinkles, the flabby cheeks, chin, eyelids. And yet her features seem clearer, as though purified. And the eyes, the eyes haven't changed, big and black, liquid, lively. Try to think: she recognized me, how? Make out her expression . . . I can't, it's been so long that I've lost the habit of reading her face—and it's not the same face. Or it's the same but different. It's her. She's old, she's tired. I look at her, she looks at me, her head thrown back, and I feel huge, a giant, but hollow, fragile. She speaks first: "So you recuperated yourself." Sarcasm or satisfaction? And I say, "I'm going into the Hamburg Zone, I'm catching the six o'clock train," and it's a *retort,* I'm on the defensive. I thought we'd chat about trivialities, embarrassed perhaps, before speaking about. . . . But it's true she never liked beating about the bush, and then when you're old there's no time to lose, right? Well, I haven't any time to lose either! No, I'm not going to get angry in order to stand up to her; I've learned to control that reflex. It kept me alive, but it's not what I need here. I don't, absolutely don't, want to get angry.

She doesn't make it easy for me. "Not married, then, no children?" And while I suffocate in silence she goes on: "You left to live your own life, you should have been consistent, lived to the full. With your gifts, to become a recuperator! You stopped halfway! Really, I didn't bring you up like that."

I can't mistake her tone. She's *reproaching* me, she's *resentful!*

"You didn't make me like that, you mean! But perhaps you didn't make as much of me as you think!" There we go, fighting. It can't be true, I'm dreaming; fifteen years, and it's as though I left last week!

"So you actually took the trouble to find out? If you'd taken a little more trouble, you'd have learned that artifacts are not necessarily sterile. True, the Institute buried the really pertinent data, but with a little effort. . . . But you didn't even try, eh? So sure you were sterile! When I think of the pains I took to make you completely normal!"

I cool down. Suddenly, somewhere, I cross a threshold, and once over it I'm incredulously calm. That's Taïko. Not a goddess, not a monster. Just a woman set in her ways, with her limitations, her goodwill, her unawareness. I hear myself saying almost politely, "Still, I failed their tests."

Apparently she's crossed a threshold of her own at the same time, in the same direction. She sighs. "I should have told you sooner. When you were little. But I kept putting it off. And then it was too late, you were right in the middle of the terrible teens, and I lost my temper. I couldn't tell you just then, you can understand that! Well, yes, I should have; perhaps it would have calmed you down. I was so furious after you left. I expected a phone call, a letter. I said to myself, at least the Institute can't find out about her. And in fact they know nothing. The Kerens medic called me first. A nice person, actually. You'd never said anything, you were a brilliant student that disappeared without a trace. They offered me their sympathy, you know, Kerens and the Institute. Afterward, I tried to have you found. Why didn't you call me, you stubborn mule?"

I'm the one being accused, can you beat that? I stare hard at her. And all of a sudden it's too much. I burst out laughing. So does she.

We're still the same, after all this time.

"But you came, anyway. None too soon, either."

After that, a long silence. Embarrassed, pensive? *She's* pensive. "You ought to try. To have children. There's no guarantee you'll succeed, but it's highly probable. Have you really never tried?"

Does she realize what she's *saying*?!

"What, there's never been anyone?"

(Rick, the first. Yes, and a few others, initially as a challenge, just to see, and after because it didn't really matter what I was, thanks to Brutus. But still!) I retort that knowing you're an artifact doesn't make for particularly harmonious relations with normal humans.

"*Normal humans!* I can't believe my ears! You were born. The fact that it was in the lab down there doesn't change anything. You grew up, you made mistakes and you'll make more. You think, you feel, you choose. What more do you want? You're a normal human being, like all the other so-called artifacts."

Oh yes. Like the Walker and the Sleeper, I suppose? I grit my teeth. She looks me in the eye, impatiently. "Well, what's the matter?" Doesn't even let me try to speak. "There may have been biosculptors who were stupid or crazy, but that's another matter. Of course some artifacts were very limited. The Institute made sure of it by suppressing the necessary data, all Permahlion's research. They made him practically an outlaw, fifty years ago, and after that they did everything to discourage artorganics. But it didn't stop us from carrying on."

I can't understand what she's saying. She must see it, and it gives her fresh cause for annoyance. "Well, what do you think, that you're the only one in the world? There are hundreds of you, silly! Just because the original human race is doomed to disappear sooner or later doesn't mean that all life must end. It was all right for the Eschatoï to think that way."

And suddenly, quietly, sadly, "You really thought I was a monster, didn't you?"

What can I say? I subside onto the sofa and she sits down as well, not too near, slowly, sparing her knees. Yes, she's old, really old. When she becomes animated, the expression in her eyes, her way of talking, her leap-frog sentences are there; but when she's quiet it all flickers out. I look away. After the silence, all I can find to say is, "You made others? Like me?"

The answer is straightforward, almost absentminded. "No. I could have made others, probably, but for me, one baby was already a lot."

"You made me . . . a baby?"

"I wanted you to be as normal as possible. There's nothing to prevent artorganic matter growing as slowly as organic matter. Actually, it's the best way; the personality develops along with it. I wasn't in a hurry."

"But you never made others . . . in the usual way?"

A sad-amused smile. "Come on, Manou. I was sterile, of course. Or rather, my karyotype was so damaged that it was unthinkable to try to have children in the usual way, as you call it."

"And I can."

"Theoretically."

"After working fifteen years in the contaminated Zones."

"Oh, but you're a lot more resistant than we are. The beauty of artorganics is that you can improve on nature. That's the danger as well. But in the long run, it means I was able to give you the chance to adapt yourself better than we could to the world you'd be dealing with after us. Do you remember? You were never sick when you were little."

And I still heal very quickly. Oh yes, the medic in the Kerens Centre pointed that out. That was a constant factor in artifacts. Not a proof, however; there had been a fairly widespread mutation of this kind about a hundred years earlier. "It was from studying this phenomenon, among others, that artorganic matter ended up being created. There are still instances of it among normal humans." It was a parallelism, he emphasized, not a proof. But an indication which, combined with others, added to the presumption.

"I'm telling you"—she's still adamant—" you should try to have children." She's really determined to know whether or not her experiment has worked, is that it?

"Thirty-two is a bit late, don't you think?"

"A bit late? You're in your prime!"

"For how long?"

I'm standing up, fists clenched. I wasn't aware of getting up, I wasn't aware of shaking. If she notices it she gives no sign. She shrugs. "I don't know." And before I can react she smiles the old sarcastic smile: "At least as long as I, in any case. Longer, if I've been successful. But for exactly how long I don't know."

She looks straight at me, screwing up her eyes a little. Suddenly no longer old and tired, she's ageless; so very gently sad, so very wise. "You thought I could tell you. That's why you came."

"You made me, you should know!"

"Someone made me, too. Not in the same way, but someone made me. And I don't know when I'm going to die either." The small, ironic smile comes back. "I'm beginning to get some idea, mind you." The smile disappears. "But I'm not certain, I don't know the date. That's what being human is like, too. Haven't you learned anything in fifteen years? The only way to be sure is to kill yourself, which you didn't. So keep on. You'll still live long enough to forget lots of things and learn them all over again."

And she looks at the old watch that slides around her birdlike wrist. "Two hours before your train. Would you like something to eat?"

"Are you in a hurry for me to leave?"

"For our first time it would be better not to try our luck too far."

"You really think I'll come back?"

Gently, she says, "I *hope* you'll come back." Again the sarcastic smile. "With a belly this big."

I shake my head; I can't take any more. She's right. I rise to get my bag near the door. "I think I'll walk back to the station."

Still, she goes with me onto the terrace and we walk down to the beach together. As we pass one of the statues, she puts a hand on the grey, shapeless stone. "It was his house, Permahlion's. He brought the statues here himself. He liked to scuba-dive when he was young. I was his very last pupil, you know. He made the first artorganic humans, but he didn't call them artifacts. It killed him, what was done to them after him."

As always when the sun finally breaks through the clouds, it gets hot quickly. As I shrug off my jacket, I see her looking at me; she barely reaches my shoulder. It must be a long time since she was in the sun; she's so pale.

I scan the distance for something else to look at. A few hundred yards from the beach there seem to be shapes jumping in the waves. Dolphins? Swimmers? An arm above the water, like a sign. . . .

She shades her eyes. "No, they're Permahlion's mermaids. I call them 'mermaids,' anyway. I don't know why, but they've been coming here for several seasons. They don't talk and they're very shy." At my stupified silence, she remarks acidly, "Don't tell me you've something against humanoids?"

No, of course not, but. . . .

She brushes off my questions, her hands spread in front of her. "I'll look for everything there is about them in the lab. You'll be able to see it. If you ever come back." A cloud seems to pass over her rapidly, and she fades again. "I'm tired, my daughter. The sun isn't good for me these days. I'm going to lie down for a bit."

And she goes, just like that, without another word or gesture, a tiny figure stumbling a little in the sand. I want to watch her go and I can't watch her go, as though it were the last time, because perhaps it is the last time, and "my daughter" has lodged itself in my chest somewhere; it grows, pushing my ribs, and the pressure becomes so strong that I shed my clothes and dive into the green, warm water to swim towards the sea creatures. My first burst of energy exhausted, I turn on my back and look towards the house. The tiny silhouette has stopped on the terrace. I wave an arm, I shout, "I'll come back, Mother!" I laugh, and my tears mingle with the sea.

CHRONOS' CHRISTMAS

Rhea Rose

Any minute, two more kids would be arriving at Daycare. *Two* replacements at once. That was unusual. Normally we arrived one at a time. Two would give us a small advantage over Deemi's Daycare unit, but I'd already decided not to keep them both. I'd give one to Deemi. That would make for fair play, and I figured that this year my unit could still beat Deemi's to Christmas.

Three of us sat in different corners of the large activity room, across from Ceep who filled an entire wall of the pentagonal room. Except for his flashing red eye and the blue glow from his vidscreen, we waited in the dark; it was better for the arrival of the replacements, less of a shock for them.

I could hear Snuks sucking her thumb, and I tried to see where she was hiding. She must have noticed, because she leaned out of the shadows and into the vidscreen's blue glow, looking eerie. Her round eyes made contact with mine.

Ceep's red eye, located at the other end of the room where Geebo waited, became a steady red.

"They're coming," I said to the others.

"Chronos?"

It was Ceep. "Here," I answered.

"Stand by for replacement 1313M and replacement 1315M, both chronological four."

"Double chrono four?" I asked. I thought that was strange. I

21

went over to Ceep and touched him for a pause and repee. He repeated, and I'd heard the computer correctly. Chrono fours, *two* of them. Snuks, Geebo and myself had all arrived when we were five, and as far as I knew the kids at the other unit had all arrived when they were five, too. This Christmas I would be nine and Snuks would be six. This was her first Christmas at Daycare.

"We're ready here, Ceep," I said. Instantly, above our heads, a pink finger-thin laze shot across the room. It was a soothing, hypnotic colour, and I had to look away for a moment. The beam began to pulse, expanding in all directions and filling the room with a warm sleepy glow. A low hum caused vibrations in the floor and walls. I looked over at Snuks. Her hiding place was exposed by the light, and she was really pulling on her thumb. She'd never seen the arrival of new kids.

At the centre of the room appeared a blue dot as big as a fingernail. It hung in mid air, and then another appeared beside the first. They grew simultaneously. Snuks was engrossed by the process, or maybe she was just affected by the light. Whichever the case, she appeared to be watching very carefully. The miniature blue dots started to take shape. The tiny human forms looked like holos suspended just above the floor. They stayed that way for a moment, then quickly grew. The pink light intensified, became brighter, and a sudden white flash blinded us for an instant.

"How long?" I asked.

"Two hours before they are fully awake," Ceep replied.

I heard Geebo set down the gadget he'd been tinkering with while the new kids arrived. He'd been preparing the gadget for Christmas, but now that the replacements were here, he was more interested in them. He began looking the new arrivals over, checking their pockets, cutting the velcro from their clothes and stuffing the strips into his own pockets. Ceep's red light shone in Geebo's hair making it almost the same color as mine. It was the only time Geebo and I ever resembled each other. We were the same age, but he was a head shorter than I. His dark eyes were almost black, while mine were pale, almost colourless. I was the only one at Daycare with freckles.

I could see that Geebo was completely absorbed with the sleeping kids, while Snuks sat back in the shadows like she always did when something was new to her. There was little to do except wait for the arrivals to wake up so that we could orient them to Daycare and Christmas, which would be the next day. Deemi and his unit would be anxious to beat us to it, if they could. But we were ready, too.

"You gotta see these kids, Chronos," Geebo said. He came over to me, brushing his dark hair out of his eyes and exposing a thin, raised white line that ran horizontally across his forehead—a scar from a gadget that had backfired on him when he was younger. Geebo hadn't been much of a talker when he first came to Daycare, and after he was killed the first time, he spoke even less. The only time I'd ever seen him excited was over a new gadget he'd created and now, with these new kids. He tugged my sleeve insistently.

I followed him, and we crouched over the small bodies. He pulled a tube of glow grease out of his pocket, squirted some into his palms, and then rubbed them rapidly together.

Snuks crawled over from her corner. Her long golden hair, curling delicately at the ends, became blue as she passed through the light cast by the vidscreen at her end of the room. Sitting cross-legged, she looked at the sleeping arrivals, then at me. One of her fingers was curled over her nose as she sucked her thumb. Geebo had made her a warm-doll which she held by its head in the crook of her arm. I thought the doll was dumb, with its gaping mouth exposing its large front tooth, but Snuks would fight anyone who tried to take it from her. She took her thumb out of her mouth. "Ith that how I came here?"

"Yeah, 'cept you were a pink dot, not blue," I said.

"Why?"

"'Cause you're a girl."

"Why am I the only girl?" she insisted.

"I asked Ceep about girls once," I told her. She shifted her warm-doll from one arm to the other. "He said that girls used to be a lot more popular, but for a long time now girls haven't been requested as much."

"Why am I here, then?"

"I don't know," I lied.

"Doth Theep know?" She looked from me to Ceep.

23

I was relieved when Ceep didn't say anything. Sometimes he'd give answers and other times he wouldn't, but by that time he'd only told Deemi and me about girls like Snuks. He said that she was a longlifer. All girls were. It's the way the dults wanted them. When she was ready to leave Daycare the dults would eventually trade her to Offworlders. She wouldn't get to be immortal like me and Geebo and the others at Daycare, like the dults. Ceep told me not to tell Snuks just yet. When I asked Ceep who the Offworlders were and why they weren't immortal, he just stayed quiet.

"Look." Geebo elbowed me. He grinned and held a green glowing hand over the face of each replacement. I was surprised to see their faces were identical, and I had a feeling these two would be special. Christmas, and now the replacements, had me excited and a little nervous.

They awoke earlier than Ceep had calculated and sat quietly in the same place they had been deposited. Fair-haired and shy, they looked up at Ceep. He was talking to them, telling them about Daycare.

"Since the skirmishes with the Offworlders first began more than a century ago, it became economically unfeasible to restore Daycare to its original standards. When those in charge of maintenance were destroyed in a particularly violent encounter with the Offworlders, the dults, who long ago lost the ability to nurture their own young, also lost the maintenance knowledge needed to make sure I continued to perform the task for them. Now it is entirely up to me to make the necessary adjustments in both of you if you are to fulfill the role the dults have prescribed for you."

"What adjustments?" one of the replacements asked Ceep.

"Those cannot be determined until you have spent more time at Daycare," he replied.

I knew that Ceep was talking about the times they'd be killed. Any desired abilities they displayed before their first three deaths would be "sharpened" by him.

Ceep continued: "A basic foundation of knowledge is given to all of you before you come to Daycare, but the dults can never be sure, any more, what your pre-Daycare knowledge along with your adjustments and experiences at Daycare will result in. It is during your time in Daycare that your intrinsic abilities will—or will not—manifest."

One of the little kids turned to me. "What do you call him?" he asked.

"Ceep."

"Why do you call him Ceep?"

"He makes a noise that sounds like 'ceep.' But forget him," I said. If these two were going to participate in Christmas, we would have to orient them to Daycare pretty quickly. Officially, Christmas started at 1900 hours, now only a few hours away.

"One of you has to join Deemi's Daycare unit. Now, who wants to go?" I looked from one to the other.

"Does Deemi have one of those?" One of them pointed at Ceep.

"Yeah. His unit's identical to this one, and Ceep is over there, too."

"I'll go," said the one who'd been doing all the talking so far.

"Good. Ceep, has Deemi responded to my message about the new arrivals?"

"Yes. He says that if you want to take Christmas this year, you should keep them both. You need all the help you can get."

I ignored the message. When I first came to Daycare, I arrived at Deemi's unit. He taught me everything he knew about getting Christmas. Together, Deemi and I used to be on the same team; we were invincible. Every year, Christmas was ours. But when he started making his own rules, I left his unit.

I looked over at Geebo, and he seemed to have forgotten the new kids and was completely absorbed with his tinkering. I waved over the kid that had volunteered, and he followed me to the exit.

"Except for Deemi, Geebo and I are the oldest at Daycare," I explained to him. "Deemi's eleven, the oldest and biggest kid Daycare's ever had. He'd never been killed before I took over this unit, but I've killed him three times." I looked him straight in the eye. "And I plan to kill him and whoever gets in the way of me and Christmas." He just looked up at me with an innocent and shy expression. I told him how to get to Deemi's unit, and said that he should follow my directions exactly. If he wandered or dawdled there was a good chance he'd be killed by one of the many traps which both units had spent the rest of the year setting up. I

25

watched him walk down the stairs to the sidewalk. He stopped and looked up at me.

"Bye." He turned and never looked back. I really hoped he made it to Deemi's, and I hoped Deemi liked him. At least this kid wasn't a girl. One of the rules Deemi had decided on, while I was still with him, was no girls. Once he was sent a girl, and he killed her himself. What a waste. He never even tried to use any of her abilities for Christmas. Every time Ceep restored her, Deemi'd just kill her again until after the fourth time Ceep never brought her back. No one came back to Daycare after the fourth death. I thought it was really a shame; I felt sorry for the girl. No one *wants* to leave Daycare. I've never traded a girl to Deemi's unit, and I don't think Ceep's ever sent him another one.

When the new replacement was out of sight, I looked up at the light dome high overhead. It was the ceiling to the walls that enclosed the one and a half square kilometres of Daycare. Ceep had the overcast filters up.

I went back to the activity room, and my knee started aching. I'd been killed three times, twice by Deemi, and my knee hadn't been repaired properly. It usually started bothering me around this time, when I was worrying about Christmas. Ceep said there was nothing the matter with it, but I knew he had to be wrong.

When I walked into the activity room, I saw Geebo watching the remaining kid, who was standing on a stool and halfway inside Ceep. The vidscreen light was out and the screen was off and *on the floor*. Geebo gave me a worried look, but the kid kept working. "Ceep, are you still there?" It made me nervous, seeing him in pieces on the floor.

"I'm here, Chronos," he answered. He sounded different. His voice was the same, but there was something different. By this time the blond kid was looking at me. He smiled.

"Geebo, what's he doing? *You* know Ceep's off limits. We all know that," I said. Snuks sat in the corner, her face painted white. She was about to apply more colours. At least someone was getting ready for Christmas.

"I gave that new kid a name," Snuks said. "Teb."

"Ceep asked Teb to do this," Geebo said.

"Do what?" I asked.

"Fixth him," Snuks answered. She went back to colouring her face. Teb still worked on Ceep.

"Is that true, Ceep?" I asked, half expecting him not to answer.

"Yes, Chronos."

"But why Teb? Why not Geebo? You know how he loves to do that kind of thing. And why now with only one hour until Christmas? We've got to be ready. Deemi will be ready."

"Geebo wasn't bred for this kind of job, Chronos. I couldn't let him work on me."

I recalled the one time Geebo had attempted to tinker with Ceep. Geebo hadn't been here too long, and Ceep had zapped him so badly that I thought he'd been killed for sure, but he hadn't.

"Geebo would have changed me. He would have made me something more—or less."

"I wouldn't," Geebo protested.

"Yes, you would have. Don't feel bad, Geebo. That is your specialty. It has become more and more obvious. Your creativity is greatly needed and desired."

Ceep was absolutely right. Geebo's genius had come in handy more than once and would be greatly desired in less than an hour.

"Besides," Ceep continued, "Geebo's hands are too large for this procedure. I could not be sure that Teb or the other replacement would survive this Christmas, and this adjustment could not wait much longer. Do not worry about being prepared for Christmas. You are prepared."

By the time Ceep had finished explaining, Teb had completed what he was doing, and Geebo replaced the vidscreen and turned it back on. We always kept the vidscreen on. That way it felt like Ceep was really there.

"Teb, have you looked at Ceep's Christmas catalogues and given him your list?" I asked. His blond head nodded. It was strange talking to him when I felt like I had just said goodbye to him a moment earlier. "Snuks will help outfit you. Geebo and I have to get ready, too. Remember, it's only fifteen minutes to Christmas." Snuks looked nervous. I was nervous. But Geebo didn't look worried at all. "We've got fifteen blocks to cover by tomorrow, but then so does Deemi," I said.

We gathered on the concrete stairs outside of our unit. We looked at each other, admiring the faces we had painted on ourselves. Geebo and I snickered at Teb. He'd allowed Snuks to apply his paint to him, and she'd given him a clown's face, just like the ones she'd seen in Ceep's catalogues. Teb's nose and mouth were red, and his eyebrows arched into the blond bangs on his forehead. He looked like he'd been surprised by Deemi himself. He didn't seem to mind us laughing at him. Snuks wore a tight, black, stretchy outfit. Her hair was tied back and fastened down with a thong that looped around her neck.

"Watch this," Geebo said. He slipped off something that he had slung over his shoulder, then moved down the stairs and away from us. It was a flat chrome disc tied to the end of a plastic string. He held it out to one side. With a few twists of his wrist he had the disc spinning, and then he released it. Slicing through the air, the silver disc cut two branches from a nearby bush before it was stopped by a clump of twigs. Not until it had become lodged did we realize that the razor-disc was still attached to the string Geebo held. He flicked the string and the disc dislodged and came spinning back to him, stopping just short of his hand. He grinned, looking delighted with himself.

Geebo had other gadgets hooked to his belt. I recognized his grease gun and a few other things. Snuks wore her pellet shooter around her neck like a necklace. She blew through it a couple of times then tucked it down the front of her top. A small pouch of pellets hung by her hip. When she was ready, she slipped her thumb into her mouth and sat on the top step.

I was ready too, but I wasn't sure about Teb. I had no idea what his capabilities were. He probably wouldn't make it all the way through Christmas, but I was going to make sure we got as much use out of him as possible, at least until Deemi or one of his gang got him.

"Message from Deemi." Ceep's voice came through the com by the door.

"I'll come inside to take it." I didn't want to take Deemi's message while the others were listening. It might disturb them.

I left Geebo bragging to Teb about some gadget he'd created and walked into the silent activity room. Ceep was quiet.

Ceep was quiet!

That was it. Teb had fixed Ceep so that he no longer made the hissing sound we'd named him after. I stood in the silence and wondered what Deemi could possibly have to say just before Christmas. I decided that it was probably some kind of trick and was ready to walk back outside when Ceep spoke.

"Shall I communicate Deemi's message?" he asked.

"No." I really didn't want to hear it.

"I would like to talk with you before you go."

"There's not much time, Ceep." I felt uncomfortable.

"I have always considered your development, and the others at Daycare, my most important task, but until now, the way your time has been spent here has never been completely under my control."

"You've done everything for us," I said, wondering what Ceep was getting at.

"No. The dults neglected Daycare and were afraid of the children that were coming out of here because the children were violent. Conditions here demand that you be tough. I do what I can to ensure that you will survive once you leave here. The dults don't know how to stop Daycare, and at one time hoped it would break down completely—until they saw how they could take advantage of the children. They need you to defend them from the Offworlders. The dults introduced Christmas to Daycare to ensure the violence would continue—a motivating agent. They've been preparing you, the others and many before you to fight for them, to die for them—"

"But you won't let us die."

"You will be beyond my range once you leave Daycare," he said.

I felt cold.

"The dults who do not fight the Offworlders are not mine. They didn't come from Daycare. But you and others *are* mine. Especially you, Chronos."

"Me?"

"Yes. You love the other Daycare children, even those in the other unit. You even loved Deemi once, but you especially care for Snuks—"

"I'll be sorry to see her go," I mumbled.

"She will be traded to the Offworlders. You may kill her one day, or she you."

"Why does Snuks have to go there?"

"The Offworlders threaten to destroy the dults. They want the dults' secret to immortality. Unfortunately the remaining dults don't have that information. It was lost long before the first Offworlder skirmishes. The immortality gene was bred into you and the others—except for Snuks. Her offspring will be longlifers, and all females like her are traded to the Offworlders in order to keep the Offworlders from carrying out their threat. This trade appeases them for awhile."

"Can *you* give the Offworders the information they want?"

"No. I've lost large batches of information as a result of the degeneration that has taken place in Daycare and the outside world. Your immortality was already present in your gene pool."

"You don't think I'm going to survive this Christmas, do you, Ceep?"

"I did consider that possibility. I have reissued your genetic pool, Chronos, and have designed the two new replacements after you. Yet they are also significantly different from you."

There was a long silence.

"Are you finished?" I asked.

"Yes."

"I have to get back to the others."

"Goodbye, Chronos."

I stepped outside not wanting to think about why Ceep told me this. I just wanted to win Christmas.

"Let's get Christmas," I said, and we began.

We jogged down the street on which our Daycare unit was stationed. Snuks and Teb followed me with Geebo bringing up the rear. We moved in single file towards the centre of Daycare.

Skirting potholes and debris from other Christmases, we travelled north. Daycare had been a small grassy park surrounded by many city blocks. The park was battered and worn from years of battle, but there were still patches of yellow grass to be found at the outskirts. The old tenament buildings that still stood were now empty shells. Some old street lamps still worked, and Ceep usually turned them on for Christmas.

We didn't move straight down the middle of the park but drifted west where the park foliage was heavier. Here, some of the trees were still real and alive, but most were imitations. None of us were even sure which were the real ones, though Ceep assured us that there were still originals. We had planted many of our own traps here and were able to move through the area in relative security.

The buildings on the outskirts were a kind of no-man's land where both groups, Deemi's and mine, tried not to become trapped. The roads there did not lead to Christmas, but the buildings could provide cover from an attack.

It was getting cooler out. My breath came out in cloudy bursts, but it seemed too early for Ceep to be lowering the temperature. We came to the treed area, and I jogged to the base of a tree with low branches. Linking my fingers together, I formed a cup with my hands. Snuks ran as hard as her legs could go, stepped briefly into my hands and leaped upward. With the momentum gained from the leap, she swung her body around the branch, straddled it and was able to reach the rest of the branches to clamber high into the tree.

In a moment she was rapidly climbing down the tree. As she came to the last branch she leaped, confident that I would catch her.

"They're coming, three of them. They're just over the hill. Run!"

Our only chance was to head west towards the empty buildings and hide there. Snuks was ahead of me, her small legs pumping so fast that I couldn't keep up with her. I couldn't figure out why Deemi had deviated so drastically from the course that would take him to Christmas. Snuks headed for an old house. She took the steps two at a time and disappeared through a doorway. I followed her and, in the distance, could hear Deemi calling my name. I ran faster. Glancing over my shoulder, I saw his gang take cover behind a bush.

In the dim light, inside the house, I saw Snuks in a corner. From the window I saw the dome lights fade. For a moment Daycare was dark. The street lamps that still worked came on. Ceep even brought out a few stars and a moon. Snuks came over to the window and stood beside me. The moonlight sparkled in her eyes.

"Are you afraid to leave Daycare?" she whispered. I looked down at her. She seemed very small. I nodded.

"Why?"

"Because I don't know what's out there," I said.

"Deemi'th out there."

I scanned the street looking for some sign of Deemi. It seemed quiet, and I wondered why he'd called my name.

"Why do we need Chrithmath?"

"Because."

"Becauth why?"

"Because it's important. What else is there? I mean don't you like the idea of getting all those presents every year?"

"Yeah."

"That's why," I said.

"But why don't we share Chrithmath? Then we wouldn't have to kill each other, and then we could alwayth be at Daycare."

She had a point, but it wasn't the time to explain that Deemi would never agree to a truce; besides, before now, Ceep always encouraged us to compete for Christmas.

"Are you afraid of Deemi?" she asked.

"No. Just the dults."

"I'm afraid of Chrithmath. If Deemi killth you, you won't be back. I don't want you to go away, or Geebo."

I didn't know what to tell her, so I took her hand and held it.

Without warning, Deemi burst through the door. Snuks had time to pierce his cheek with one pellet. Then she jumped up onto the window ledge, somersaulted through it and landed safely outside. She ran towards the street. "Run!" I yelled after her. A member of Deemi's gang stepped out from behind a lamp post and caught her.

"Why didn't you answer my message?" Deemi said. He was holding his left cheek, blood oozing through his fingers.

"You mean back at Daycare?" I watched him carefully. I was at a disadvantage. I couldn't get to the door or window without fighting Deemi.

"That kid you sent to me never showed," he said.

I glanced out the window. Snuks struggled with a captor, much bigger than herself. "Damn."

"You should have got rid of her a long time ago." Deemi walked over to the window. His back was to me. I should've tried to kill him then, but I saw something whiz out from one of the shelled houses across the street. It struck Snuk's captor in the neck. He let her go and grabbed his own neck with both hands.

"Those replacements are missing. What's going on with them?" he asked.

"What?"

"The replacement you sent over to my unit—it never showed. Those new kids—they've done something to Ceep."

"How do you mean?" I tried to stall.

"Ceep's making the weather cold sooner than last Christmas. The night's come too soon, and I think it's those new kids."

Deemi was afraid. He leaned on one arm against the window frame, blocking my exit. When I looked for Snuks, she was gone. Her captor was on his knees with a red glistening stream spurting from between his fingers.

"Where's your new kid?" He glanced suspiciously around the room.

"He's not here."

Deemi was volatile and unpredictable. He gave me a violent shove against the wall and then grabbed me. "We've got to find them." He was desperate.

"You find them," I said and jammed two knuckles into his throat. He let go, and I jumped out the window and ran for the cover of the trees. I ran past the body of Snuks' captor and saw someone hiding in the bush ahead of me. It was Geebo. He motioned for me to follow him, and he led me to one of the traps we had set for Deemi's unit. He pointed to the strip of laze-eyes he had placed along one side of the trunk of a tree.

The trap had been tampered with. It should have let any one from my Daycare unit pass through it without harm, but no one from Deemi's. It had been dismantled, and Geebo couldn't figure out how it had been done.

"Did you see Snuks or Teb?" I asked him.

"Snuks got away." Geebo patted his blood-stained razor-disc. "But I haven't seen Teb since we left the unit."

I was relieved to hear that Snuks had got away. We left the trap and decided to try to make our way to Christmas.

We moved cautiously, encountering no difficulties. This unnerved us even more than if we had been attacked or injured by Deemi's gang or their traps. We walked through his territory as if he had never been expecting us. We found that Deemi's traps were dismantled, too.

We weren't far from Christmas when we heard a noise. I climbed a tree and was barely up and hidden when two shadowy forms came from opposite directions to converge on Geebo. He decided to stay and fight it out. Besides he couldn't follow me because he had too much junk strapped to himself. He had his grease gun out and sprayed the stuff all over, but they got him. He never made a sound. His body was heaped awkwardly on the ground, a dark silhouette against the soft green glow of the grease.

They tried to climb the tree after me but were covered with the slippery glow grease, and even when they tried to hide, the thick foliage couldn't completely conceal their glow. They waited for me, so I couldn't climb down. I remembered a group of trees in this part of Daycare that were clumped together. Crawling through the tree, I hoped the neighbouring one would be close enough for me to jump across to it.

Not knowing if the tree I was in was real or not, I moved out onto the branch as far as I dared. There was a good chance that the small branch of a real tree would not hold my weight. Flat on my belly, pulling my feet under me until I crouched, I got ready to jump to the next tree. Suddenly, my knee started to ache.

When the pain subsided a little, I leaped. My knee cramped just as I took off, and I knew in mid air that I did not have enough force to make the branch.

I crashed through the branches, grasping at twigs that tore the skin from my hands. Everything blurred as I plummeted and hit.

I'd been out for a while, but I wasn't sure how long. It was very dark out, and a light snow was falling, covering the ground. I was cold, but more worried that I had lost Christmas.

I took a few things from Geebo's body, things that I thought I might need in case Christmas wasn't over. Carefully, I wiped off my footpads and followed a small trail through the brush. It was against all the rules for members of opposite Daycares to break away and form their own team, and I was beginning to suspect the new kids.

I came to the north gate where Christmas normally took place and didn't find anyone. I climbed another tree and waited there. Perched high in a branch, I could see someone hiding in a bush below. Christmas wasn't over yet!

A portion of the north wall began to change colour. Normally grey, it became a bright orange. Only a small section of the wall changed colour and began to sink into the ground. When it had disappeared, a gush of air and mist blew into Daycare, then quickly dissipated. The black space left in the wall reminded me of the gap left in Geebo's grin when he'd lost his front tooth.

They entered Daycare cautiously and looked the way they had last year, tall, taller even than Deemi. They wore bulky white clothing, their heads helmeted. Their weapons were holstered, but their hands rested on them. More dults followed them. They brought Christmas into Daycare. Some had their arms full of presents while others carried glitter and lights. Another brought a tree.

They placed the parcels and packages on the ground and decorated a small area around the gifts. The tree was raised and powered up. It was a magnificent tree which rotated at the base with the centre section slowly rotating in the opposite direction. The branches shone, blinking on and off in many colours. More and more gifts were brought in, until the area in front of the wall gate was nearly covered. The presents that didn't give off their own light reflected those of the Christmas tree.

Some of the tree ornaments played soft music which drifted upward, to me. The tree smelled fresh, too. Everything was beautiful, better than the light shows Ceep would put on to entertain us. It was a warm, enticing scene and before I realized what I had done, I was down from the tree and wading knee-deep among the presents. I wanted to hold one, feel the smoothness of its wrapping and the crispness of a bow. I picked up a small package that glowed softly. It was wrapped in gold and trimmed with a pink ribbon and bow. I could smell the newness of it and felt whatever was inside slip and slide around. As I turned it over, the small identification tag lit up. It was for Snuks.

"Put that present down. It's not yours yet."

It was Deemi. I dropped the gift and ran towards a bush, trampling gifts as I went. I could hear Deemi right behind me as I dove for the bush. To my surprise Snuks had been hiding there all along, and she sprung at Deemi. I watched them tumble among the gifts and reached in my pocket for one of the velcro bombs I'd taken from Geebo. She was no match for Deemi, but she'd taken him by surprise. At last Snuks fell away from him, but when I stood to throw, I had a severe pain in my ribs. I couldn't throw the small explosive without risking the chance that it would miss Deemi and cling to Snuks. Suddenly, two of the dults were keeping Snuks and Deemi apart with the threat of their weapons.

They threatened to blast all the gifts if Deemi and Snuks didn't stop fighting immediately. They stopped, and Snuks walked back towards me. Someone touched me from behind.

It was the two new kids.

"I found them taking apart all the trapth in Daycare," Snuks said. "They don't want to fight for Chrithmath all the time."

"Geebo's dead." I looked at them. Snuks started to cry quietly. "Teb." I waited until one of the kids looked at me so that I could identify Teb, whose clown face had been wiped off. "What did you do to Ceep back at the unit?"

"Just adjusted the problem that caused him to make that funny noise. It would have eventually caused severe problems," he said.

"They fixthed Theep. Now he doth everything on time, like thnow for Chrithmath," Snuks said.

"That's all. You just fixed him?"

The kids looked at each other, and I had this sick feeling there was more.

"We did some security bypasses," Teb said.

"It was all done at Ceep's request, which was made before we arrived at Daycare," the other one added.

"What does all that mean?" I asked.

"Geebo won't be back," Teb answered.

"Geebo only died twith. He'll be back," Snuks said.

"None of the kids killed this Christmas will be back," Teb told her.

There was a commotion beyond the tree. We turned to see Deemi jump onto the dult guard who had separated him and Snuks. A second dult guard was on his way over. While Deemi struggled with the first guard, I saw my opportunity to win Christmas. Except for the kid who never actually joined his side, Deemi seemed to be the only survivor from his Daycare unit. Once I got rid of him, Christmas would be ours. And Deemi would be gone for good.

The second guard slowly weaved his way through the gifts, weapon ready. Then it happened—my chance came. The first guard, weaponless, broke away from Deemi. I ran from the tree for Deemi, tackled him and struggled for the weapon he'd taken. The next thing I knew Snuks was yelling at me.

"Stop it, Chronos. Stop. Ceep can't bring you back if you die. He can't hold any of us any more."

I let go of Deemi and shoved her away. "Go back!" I screamed.

The second guard grabbed Snuks' arm. "No!" I started after him, but he brought his weapon to her face. I stopped and watched him drag her, screaming, backwards through the gifts.

Behind me I could hear Deemi laughing, and I turned to face him. He had the weapon he'd taken from the first guard aimed at me.

"You lose," he said. And in that instant a hole burned through Deemi's neck as another guard shot him from behind. I thought I would be next but the guard walked away, following the one that carried Snuks. I watched the two dults take her out. Then they all left Daycare and Christmas.

"They won't be coming back," a voice beside me said. It was Teb. "Ceep's gonna let you decide what should happen at Daycare."

I saw the small parcel I'd seen earlier, the one tagged for Snuks. It was crushed; the lighting mechanism on the tag had gone out. I kicked it away. Ceep didn't want any more Christmases—not like this one. That was why he'd brought Teb and the other kid. I supposed it was the only way he could stop it. "Ceep!" I yelled up at the trees. "I don't want any more, either." There was silence.

Behind us the wall began to hum and change colour. The gate slowly sank into the ground, and the two small kids held my hands as we slowly approached the opening. There were no dults anywhere. I thought about Ceep, but he'd already said goodbye. So the three of us walked through the opening and never looked back.

A STRANGE VISITOR

Robert Zend

The outer space intelligence
who hovered over my desk,
a glowing vibrating sphere,
one foot in diameter,
asked me endless questions, for instance:
"What were you doing before I appeared?"
and "Why?" and "For what reason?"
to which I replied I was reading the newspaper
to be informed about what was going on
in the world, and explained the nature
of money and economics and capitalism and communism
and inflation and crises and wars and nations
and borders and territorial expansion and history—
Then he asked me what the other creature
(my two-year old daughter) was doing.
I said she was playing on the broadloom,
talking to her dolls and herself—
Well, this outer space intelligence rather disappointed me,
for after my succinct answers
he asked such a stupid question
that I suspected he hadn't understood anything at all,
the question being: "How many years does it take
for a wrinkled, wrought-up human baby
like you behind a desk, to shrink into a happy,
light-hearted being like the one on the rug?"

THE BYRDS

Michael G. Coney

Gran started it all.

Late one afternoon in the hottest summer in living memory, she took off all her clothes, carefully painted red around her eyes and down her cheeks, chin and throat, painted the rest of her body a contrasting black with the exception of her armpits and the inside of her wrists which she painted white, strapped on her new anti-gravity belt, flapped her arms and rose into the nearest tree, a garry oak, where she perched.

She informed us that, as of now, she was Rufous-necked Hornbill, of India.

"She always wanted to visit India," Gramps told us.

Gran said no more, for the logical reason that Hornbills are not talking birds.

"Come down, Gran!" called Mother. "You'll catch your death of cold."

Gran remained silent. She stretched her neck and gazed at the horizon.

"She's crazy," said Father. "She's crazy. I always said she was. I'll call the asylum."

"You'll do no such thing!" Mother was always very sensitive about Gran's occasional peculiarities. "She'll be down soon. The evenings are drawing in. She'll get cold."

"What's an old fool her age doing with an antigravity unit any-way, that's what I want to know," said Father.

The Water Department was restricting supply and the weath-erman was predicting floods. The Energy Department was warn-ing of depleted stocks, the Department of Rest had announced that the population must fall by one-point-eight per cent by November or else, the Mailgift was spewing out a deluge of appli-cation forms, tax forms and final reminders, the Tidy Mice were malfunctioning so that the house stank. . . .

And now this.

It was humiliating and embarrassing, Gran up a tree, naked and painted. She stayed there all evening, and I knew that my girl-friend Pandora would be dropping by soon and would be sure to ask questions.

Humanity was at that point in the morality cycle when nudity was considered indecent. Gran was probably thirty years before her time. There was something lonely and anachronistic about her, perched there, balancing unsteadily in a squatting position, occasionally grabbing at the trunk for support then flapping her arms to re-establish the birdlike impression. She looked like some horrible mutation. Her resemblance to a Rufous-necked Hornbill was slight.

"Talk her down, Gramps," said Father.

"She'll come down when she's hungry."

He was wrong. Late in the evening Gran winged her way to a vacant lot where an ancient tree stood. She began to eat un-sterilized apples, juice flowing down her chin. It was a grotesque sight.

"She'll be poisoned!" cried Mother.

"So, she's made her choice at last," said Father.

He was referring to Your Choice for Peace, the brochure which Gran and Gramps received monthly from the Department of Rest. Accompanying the brochure is a six-page form on which senior citizens describe all that is good about their life, and a few of the things which bug them. At the end of the form is a box in which the oldster indicates his preference for Life or Peace. If he does not check the box, or if he fails to complete the form, it is assumed that he has chosen Peace, and they send the Wagon for him.

Now Gran was cutting a picturesque silhouette against the pale blue of the evening sky as she circled the rooftops uttering harsh cries. She flew with arms outstretched, legs trailing, and we all had to admit to the beauty of the sight; that is, until a flock of starlings began to mob her. Losing directional control she spiralled downwards, recovered, levelled out and skimmed towards us, outpacing the starlings and regaining her perch in the garry oak. She made preening motions and settled down for the night. The family Pesterminator, zapping bugs with its tiny laser, considered her electronically for a second but held its fire.

We were indoors by the time Pandora arrived. She was nervous, complaining that there was a huge mutation in the tree outside, and it had cawed at her.

Mother said quickly, "It's only a Rufous-necked Hornbill."

"A rare visitor to these shores," added Father.

"Why couldn't she have been a sparrow?" asked Mother. "Or something else inconspicuous." Things were not going well for her. The little robot Tidy Mice still sulked behind the wainscoting and she'd had to clean the house by hand.

The garish Gran shone like a beacon in the morning sunlight. There was no concealing the family's degradation. A small growd had gathered and people were trying to tempt Gran down with breadcrumbs. She looked none the worse for her night out, and was greeting the morning with shrill yells.

Gramps was strapping on an antigravity belt. "I'm going up to fetch her down. This has gone far enough."

I said, "Be careful. She may attack you."

"Don't be a damned fool." Nevertheless Gramps went into the toolshed, later emerging nude and freshly painted. Mother uttered a small scream of distress, suspecting that Gramps, too, had become involved in the conspiracy to diminish the family's social standing.

I reassured her. "She's more likely to listen to one of her own kind."

"Has everyone gone totally insane?" asked Mother.

Gramps rose gracefully into the garry oak, hovered, then settled beside Gran. He spoke to her quietly for a moment and she listened, head cocked attentively.

Then she made low gobbling noises and leaned against him.

He called down, "This may take longer than I thought."

"Oh, my God," said Mother.

"That does it," said Father. "I'm calling the shrink."

Dr. Pratt was tall and dignified, and he took in the situation at a glance. "Has your mother exhibited birdish tendencies before?"

Father answered for Mother. "No more than anyone else. Although, in many other ways, she was—"

"Gran has always been the soul of conformity," said Mother quickly, beginning to weep. "If our neighbours have been saying otherwise I'll remind them of the slander laws. No—she did it to shame us. She always said she hated the colours we painted the house—she said it looked like a strutting peacock."

"Rutting peacock," said Father. "She said rutting peacock. Those were her exact words."

"Peacock, eh?" Dr. Pratt looked thoughtful. There was a definite avian thread running through this. "So you feel she may be acting in retaliation. She thinks you have made a public spectacle of the house in which she lives, so now she is going to make a public spectacle of you."

"Makes sense," said Father.

"Gran!" called Dr. Pratt. She looked down at us, beady little eyes ringed with red. "I have the personal undertaking of your daughter and son-in-law that the house will be repainted in colours of your own choosing." He spoke on for a few minutes in soothing tones. "That should do it," he said to us finally, picking up his bag. "Put her to bed and keep her off berries, seeds, anything like that. And don't leave any antigravity belts lying around. They can arouse all kinds of prurient interests in older people."

"She still isn't coming down," said Father. "I don't think she understood."

"Then I advise you to fell the tree," said Dr. Pratt coldly, his patience evaporated. "She's a disgusting old exhibitionist who needs to be taught a lesson. Just because she chooses to act out her fantasies in an unusual way doesn't make her any different from anyone else. And what's *he* doing up there, anyway? Does he resent the house paint as well?"

"He *chose* the paint. He's there to bring her down."

We watched them in perplexity. The pair huddled together on the branch, engaged in mutual grooming. The crowd outside the gate had swollen to over a hundred.

On the following morning Gran and Gramps greeted the dawn with a cacophony of gobbling and screeching.

I heard Father throw open his bedroom window and threaten to blast them right out of that goddamned tree and into the hereafter if they didn't keep it down. I heard the metallic click as he cocked his twelvebore. I heard Mother squeal with apprehension, and the muffled thumping of a physical struggle in the next room.

I was saddened by the strain it puts on marriages when inlaws live in the house—or, in our case, outside the window.

The crowds gathered early and it was quickly apparent that Gramps was through with trying to talk Gran down; in fact, he was through with talking altogether. He perched beside his mate in spry fashion, jerking his head this way and that as he scanned the sky for hawks, cocking an eye at the crowd, shuddering suddenly as though shaking feathers into position.

Dr. Pratt arrived at noon, shortly before the media.

"A classic case of regression to the childlike state," he told us. "The signs are all there: the unashamed nakedness, the bright colours, the speechlessness, the favourite toy, in this case the antigravity belt. I have brought a surrogate toy which I think will solve our problem. Try luring them down with this."

He handed Mother a bright red plastic baby's rattle.

Gran fastened a beady eye on it, shuffled her arms, then launched herself from the tree in a swooping glide. As Mother ducked in alarm, Gran caught the rattle neatly in her bony old toes, wheeled and flapped back to her perch. Heads close, she and Gramps examined the toy.

We waited breathlessly.

Then Gran stomped it against the branch and the shattered remnants fell to the ground.

The crowd applauded. For the first time we noticed the Newspocket van, and the crew with cameras. The effect on Dr. Pratt was instantaneous. He strode towards them and introduced himself to a red-haired woman with a microphone.

"Tell me, Dr. Pratt, to what do you attribute this phenomenon?"

"The manifestation of birdishness in the elderly is a subject which has received very little study up to the present date. Indeed, I would say that it has been virtually ignored. Apart from my own paper—still in draft form—you could search the psychiatric archives in vain for mention of Pratt's Syndrome."

"And why is that, Dr. Pratt?"

"Basically, fear. The fear in each and every one of us of admitting that something primitive and atavistic can lurk within our very genes. For what is more primitive than a bird, the only survivor of the age of dinosaurs?"

"What indeed, Dr. Pratt?"

"You see in that tree two pathetic human creatures who have reverted to a state which existed long before Man took his first step on Earth, a state which can only have been passed on as a tiny coded message in their very flesh and the flesh of their ancestors, through a million years of Time."

"And how long do you expect their condition to last, Dr. Pratt?"

"Until the fall. The winters in these parts are hard, and they'll be out of that tree come the first frost, if they've got any sense left at all."

"Well, thank you, Dr.—"

A raucous screaming cut her short. A group of shapes appeared in the eastern sky, low over the rooftops. They were too big for birds, yet too small for aircraft, and there was a moment's shocked incomprehension before we recognized them for what they were. Then they wheeled over the Newspocket van with a bedlam of yells and revealed themselves as teenagers of both sexes, unclothed, but painted a simple black semi-matt exterior latex. There were nine of them.

In the weeks following, we came to know them as the Crows.

They flew overhead, circled, then settled all over the garry oak and the roof of our house.

They made no attempt to harass Gran or Gramps. Indeed, they seemed almost reverential in their attitude towards the old people.

It seemed that Gran had unlocked some kind of floodgate in the human unconscious, and people took to the air in increasing numbers. The manufacturers of antigravity belts became millionaires overnight, and the skies became a bright tapestry of wheeling, screeching figures in rainbow colours and startling nakedness.

The media named them the Byrds.

"I view it as a protest against today's moral code," said Dr. Pratt, who spent most of his time on panels or giving interviews. "For more years than I care to remember, people have been repressed, their honest desires cloaked in conformity just as tightly as their bodies have been swathed in concealing garb. Now, suddenly, people are saying they've had enough. They're pleasing themselves. It shouldn't surprise us. It's heathy. It's good."

It was curious, the way the doctor had become pro-Byrd. These days he seemed to be acting in the capacity of press-agent for Gran—who herself had become a cult-figure. In addition, he was working on his learned paper, The Origins and Spread of Avian Tendencies in Humans.

Pandora and I reckoned he was in the pay of the belt people.

"But it's fun to be in the centre of things," she said one evening, as the Crows came in to roost, and the garry oak creaked under the weight of a flock of Glaucous Gulls, come to pay homage to Gran. "It's put the town on the map—and your family too." She took my hand, smiling at me proudly.

There were the Pelicans, who specialized in high dives into the sea, deactivating their belts in mid-air, then reactivating them underwater to rocket Polaris-like from the depths. They rarely caught fish, though; and frequently had to be treated for an ailment known as Pelicans' Balloon, caused by travelling through water at speed with open mouth.

There were the Darwin's Tree Finches, a retiring sect whose existence went unsuspected for some weeks, because they spent so much time in the depths of forests with cactus spines held between their teeth, trying to extract bugs from holes in dead trees. They were a brooding and introspective group.

Virtually every species of bird was represented. And because every cult must have it lunatic fringe, there were the Pigeons. They flocked to the downtown city streets and mingled with the crowds hurrying to and fro. From the shoulders up they looked much like anyone else, only greyer, and with a curious habit of jerking their heads while walking. Bodily, though, they were like any other Byrd: proudly unclothed.

Their roosting habits triggered the first open clash between Byrds and Man. There were complaints that they kept people awake at night, and fouled the rooftops. People began to string electrified wires around their ridges and guttering, and to put poison out.

The Pigeons' retaliation took place early one evening, when the commuting crowds jammed the streets. It was simple and graphic, and well-coordinated. Afterwards, people referred to it obliquely as the Great Deluge, because it was not the kind of event which is discussed openly, in proper society.

There were other sects, many of them; and perhaps the strangest was a group who eschewed the use of antigravity belts altogether. From time to time we would catch sight of them sitting on the concrete abutments of abandoned motorways, searching one another for parasites. Their bodies were painted a uniform brown except for their private parts, which were a luminous red. They called themselves Hamadryas Baboons.

People thought they had missed the point of the whole thing, somehow.

Inevitably when there are large numbers of people involved, there are tragedies. Sometimes an elderly Byrd would succumb to cardiac arrest in mid-air, and drift away on the winds. Others would suffer belt malfunctions and plummet to the ground. As the first chill nights began to grip the country, some of the older Byrds died of exposure and fell from their perches. Courageously

Michael G. Coney

they maintained their role until the end, and when daylight came they would be found in the ritualistic "Dead Byrd" posture, on their backs with legs in the air.

"All good things come to an end," said Dr. Pratt one evening as the russet leaves drifted from the trees. It had been a busy day, dozens of groups having come to pay homage to Gran. There was a sense of wrapping up, of things coming to a climax. "We will stage a mass rally," said Dr. Pratt to the Newspocket reporter. "There will be such a gathering of Byrds as the country has never known. Gran will address the multitude at the Great Coming Down."

Mother said, "So long as it's soon. I don't think Gran can take any more frosts."

I went to invite Pandora to the Great Coming Down, but she was not at home. I was about to return when I caught sight of a monstrous thing sitting on the backyard fence. It was bright green except around the eyes, which were grey, and the hair, which was a vivid yellow. It looked at me. It blinked in oddly reptilian fashion. It was Pandora.

She said, "Who's a pretty boy, then?"

The very next day Gran swooped down from the garry oak and seized Mother's scarf with her toes, and a grim tug-of-war ensued.

"Let go, you crazy old fool!" shouted Mother.

Gran cranked her belt up to maximum lift and took a quick twist of the scarf around her ankles. The other end was wrapped snugly around Mother's neck and tucked into her heavy winter coat. Mother left the ground, feet kicking. Her shouts degenerated into strangled grunts.

Father got a grip of Mother's knees as she passed overhead and Gran, with a harsh screech of frustration, found herself descending again; whereupon Gramps, having observed the scene with bright interest, came winging in and took hold of her, adding the power of his belt to hers.

Father's feet left the ground.

Mother by now had assumed the basic hanging attitude: arms dangling limply, head lolling, tongue protruding, face empur-

48

pled. I jumped and got hold of Father's ankles. There was a short, sharp rending sound and we fell back to earth in a heap, Mother on top. Gran and Gramps flew back to the garry oak with their half of the scarf, and began to pull it apart with their teeth. Father pried the other half away from Mother's neck. She was still breathing.

"Most fascinating," said Dr. Pratt.

"My wife nearly strangled by those goddamned brutes and he calls it fascinating?"

"No—look at the Hornbills."

"So they're eating the scarf. So they're crazy. What's new?"

"They're not eating it. If you will observe closely, you will see them shredding it. And see—the female is working the strands around that clump of twigs. It's crystal clear what they're doing, of course. This is a classic example of nest-building."

The effect on Father was instantaneous. He jumped up, seized Dr. Pratt by the throat and, shaking him back and forth, shouted, "Any fool knows birds only nest in the spring!" He was overwrought, of course. He apologized the next day.

By that time the Byrds were nesting all over town. They used a variety of materials and in many instances their craftsmanship was pretty to see. The local Newspocket station ran a competition for The Nest I Would Be Happiest To Join My Mate In, treating the matter as a great joke; although some of the inhabitants who had been forcibly undressed in the street thought otherwise. The Byrds wasted nothing. Their nests were intricately-woven collections of whatever could be stolen from below: overcoats, shirts, pants, clothesline, undergarments, hearing-aids, wigs.

"The nesting phenomenon has a two-fold significance," Dr. Pratt informed the media. "'On the one hand, we have the desire of the Byrds to emulate the instinctive behavioural patterns of their avian counterparts. On the other hand, there is undoubtedly a suggestion of—how can I say it?—aggression towards the earthbound folk. The Byrds are saying, in their own way: join us. Be natural. Take your clothes off. Otherwise we'll do it for you."

"You don't think they're, uh, sexually *warped?*" asked the reporter.

"Sexually liberated," insisted Dr. Pratt.

The Byrds proved his point the next day, when they began to copulate all over the sky.

It was the biggest sensation since the Great Deluge. Writhing figures filled the heavens and parents locked their children indoors and drew the drapes. It was a fine day for love; the sun glinted on sweat-bedewed flesh, and in the unseasonable warmth the still air rang with cries of delight. The Byrds looped and zoomed and chased one another, and when they met they coupled. Artificial barriers of species were cast aside and Eagle mated with Chaffinch, Robin with Albatross.

"Clearly a visual parable," said Dr. Pratt. "The—"

"Shut up," said Mother. "Shut up, shut up, shut *up!*"

In the garry oak, Rufous-necked Hornbill mated with Rufous-necked Hornbill, then with Crow; then, rising joyously into the sky, with Skua, with Lark, and finally with Hamadryas Baboon, who had at last realized what it was all about and strapped on a belt.

"She's eighty-six years old! What is she thinking of?"

"She's an Earth Mother to them," said Dr. Pratt.

"Earth Mother my ass," said Father. "She's stark, staring mad, and it's about time we faced up to it."

"It's true, it's true!" wailed Mother, a broken woman. "She's crazy! She's been crazy for years! She's old and useless, and yet she keeps filling in all that stuff on her Peace form, instead of forgetting, like any normal old woman!"

"Winter is coming," said Dr. Pratt, "and we are witnessing the symbolic Preservation of the Species. Look at that nice young Tern up there. Tomorrow they must come back to earth, but in the wombs of the females the memory of this glorious September will live on!"

"She's senile and filthy! I've seen her eating roots from out of the ground, and do you know what she did to the Everattentive Waiter? She cross-wired it with the Mailgift chute and filled the kitchen with self-adhesive cookies!"

"She did?"

And the first shadow of doubt crossed Dr. Pratt's face. The leader of the Byrds crazy?

"And one day a Gameshow called on the visiphone and asked her a skill-testing question which would have set us all up for life—and she did the most disgusting thing, and it went out live and the whole town saw it!"

"I'm sure she has sound psychological reasons for her behaviour," said Dr. Pratt desperately.

"She doesn't! She's insane! She walks to town rather than fill out a Busquest form! She brews wine in a horrible jar under the bed! She was once sentenced to one week's community service for indecent exposure! She trespasses in the Department of Agriculture's fields! You want to know why the house stinks? She programmed the Pesterminator to zap the Tidy Mice!"

"But I thought. . . . Why didn't you tell me before? My God, when I think of the things I've said on Newspocket! If this comes out, my reputation, all I've worked for, all. . . . " He was becoming incoherent. "Why didn't you tell me?" he asked again.

"Well, Jesus Christ, it's obvious, isn't it?" snapped Father. "Look at her. She's up in the sky mating with a Hamadryas Baboon, or something very much like one. Now, that's what I call crazy."

"But it's a *Movement*. . . . It's free and vibrant and so basic, so—"

"A nut cult," said Father. "Started by a loonie and encouraged by a quack. Nothing more, nothing less. And the forecast for tonight is twenty below. It'll wipe out the whole lot of them. You'd better get them all down, Pratt, or you'll have a few thousand deaths on your conscience."

But the Byrds came down of their own accord, later that day. As though sensing the end of the Indian summer and the bitter nights to come, they drifted out of the sky in groups, heading for earth, heading for us. Gran alighted in the garry oak with whirling arms, followed by Gramps. They sat close together on their accustomed branch, gobbling quietly to each other. More Byrds came; the Crows, the Pelicans. They filled the tree, spread along the ridge of the roof and squatted on the guttering. They began to perch on fences and posts, even on the ground, all species intermingled. They were all around us, converging, covering the neighbouring roofs and trees, a great final gathering of humans who, just for a few weeks, had gone a little silly. They looked happy although tired, and a few were shivering as the afternoon shortened into evening. They made a great noise at first, a rustling and screeching and fluid piping, but after a while they quietened down. I saw Pandora amidst them, painted and pretty, but her gaze passed right through me. They were still Byrds, playing their role until the end.

And they all faced Gran.

They were awaiting the word to Come Down, but Gran remained silent, living every last moment.

It was like standing in the centre of a vast amphitheatre, with all those heads turned towards us, all those beady eyes watching us. The Newspocket crew were nowhere to be seen; they probably couldn't get through the crowd.

Finally Dr. Pratt strode forward. He was in the grip of a great despondency. He was going to come clean.

"Fools!" he shouted. A murmur of birdlike sounds arose, but soon died. "All through history there have been fools like you, and they've caused wars and disasters and misery. Fools without minds of their own, who follow their leader without thought, without stopping to ask if their leader knows what he is doing. Leaders like Genghis Khan, like Starbusch, like Hitler, leaders who manipulate their followers like puppets in pursuit of their own crazy ends. Crazy leaders drunk with power. Leaders like Gran here.

"Yes, Gran is crazy! I mean certifiably crazy, ready for Peace. Irrational and insane and a burden to the State and to herself. She had me fooled at first." He uttered a short, bitter laugh, not unlike the mating cry of Forster's Tern. "I thought I found logic in what she did. Such was the cunning nature of her madness. It was only recently, when I investigated Gran's past record, that I unmasked her for what she is: a mentally unbalanced old woman with marked antisocial tendencies. I could give you chapter and verse of Gran's past misdemeanors—and I can tell you right now, this isn't the first time she's taken her clothes off in public—but I will refrain, out of consideration for her family, who have suffered enough.

"It will suffice to say that I have recommended her committal and the Peace Wagon is on its way. The whole affair is best forgotten. Now, come down out of those trees and scrub off, and go home to your families, all of you."

He turned away, shoulders drooping. It was nothing like the Great Coming Down he'd pictured. It was a slinking thing, a creeping home, an abashed admission of stupidity.

Except that the Byrds weren't coming down.

They sat silently on their perches, awaiting the word from Gran.

All through Dr. Pratt's oration she'd been quiet, staring fixedly at the sky. Now, at last, she looked around. Her eyes were bright, but it was an almost-human brightness, a different thing from the beady stare of the past weeks. And she half-smiled through the paint, but she didn't utter a word.

She activated her belt and, flapping her arms, rose into the darkening sky.

And the Byrds rose after her.

They filled the sky, a vast multitude of rising figures, and Pandora was with them. Gran led, Gramps close behind, and then came Coot and Skua and Hawk, and the whole thousand-strong mob. They wheeled once over the town and filled the evening with a great and lonely cry. Then they headed off in V-formations, loose flocks, tight echelons, a pattern of dwindling black forms against the pale duck-egg blue of nightfall.

"Where in hell are they going?" shouted Dr. Pratt as I emerged from the shed, naked and painted. It was cold, but I would soon get used to it.

"South," I said.

"Why the hell south? What's wrong with here, for God's sake?"

"It's warmer, south. We're migrating."

So I activated my belt and lifted into the air, and watched the house fall away below me, and the tiny bolts of light as the Pesterminator hunted things. The sky seemed empty now but there was still a pink glow to the west. Hurrying south, I saw something winking like a red star and, before long, I was homing in on the gleaming hindquarters of a Hamadryas Baboon.

REPORT ON
THE EARTH-AIR ADDICTS

Robert Priest

It is said that Earth-Air is at once the sweetest and the most addictive scent there is. That is why Earth has been declared off limits to all our Fair Captains. We have lost too many of them—one scent of it and they abandon everything for the mindless comforts below.

Those who are addicted to Earth-Air often stroll. To stroll is to travel aimlessly—for "pleasure" as they put it. It doesn't matter to the Earth-Air addict—just a change of scenery is enough. For, yes, most of the time the Earth-Air addicts just sit around staring. Just staring and breathing and sighing, examining with intense and seemingly durable curiosity such "fabulous" items as sand, stone, grass or wave.

To be an Earth-Air addict is to abandon the Star-search. It is to willfully glut the senses—to bathe incessantly in emanations. Just to go on breathing is enough—just to go on strolling. What a waste of life it is to become just a bag—a bellows for this detestable Earth-Air. Yet, whenever our Fair Captains are missing we always find them standing on mountain peaks breathing in the Earth-Air. The wind blows and they are insane. They never want to leave. They want to run down into the valleys and breathe. They want to breathe all the different scents of Earth-Air there are. The famed Captain Zenon, for instance, was found, finally, perched over something called a Daffodil, his mind gone, his nostrils flared. Captain Arbox was located in ambergris just rolling and rolling, raving about the "aroma" taking great breasty gusts of it deep into his lungs and then expelling it with long "musical" sighs that were terrible to hear.

JOHNNY APPLESEED
ON THE NEW WORLD

Candas Jane Dorsey

I think the winds terrify me. There is no logic in the sand. There is no reason in the shifting world which covers up everything we have done. Slowly all that we have built is becoming nothing. Slowly the tendrils of sand erase it. The others are angry. My imagination sees a power behind it; my reason says no god abhors us. The result is only fury, a simple emotion hanging like a knot, like a stone, in the centre of my body.

Lesje, the partner with whom I share a shelter, is concerned. She doesn't know whether I am sick or crazy or both. The new world is alien. It has done something to every one of us. She can't figure out what it has done to me. She goes out every morning grumbling, comes back apprehensive, wondering if I've done something stupid.

I have chosen, instead of my regular work, to mend the membranes when they wear thin. She thinks maybe I will neglect this job? She thinks I want the sand in my mouth, while I sleep?

The pod is small, only seven of us living here. The walls were once transparent so we lived among the land, separated only by a membrane. Now the skin is scoured to opacity, so that all we see of outside is dark and light and, when the sand blows, vague shadows shifting above, around. Thin patches on the membrane show shiny and grainy as silk. I go around with a container of membrane material, smoothing it onto the thin bits with a brush, like an ancient House Painter. The brush is made of our hair, recycled. We had to do something with it.

In the old stories we would go crazy, the seven of us cooped up in this planetbound space capsule. Or else we would have been chosen by psychological screening and a bad apple would have got in by accident.

I think I would like to taste an apple. We are supposed to grow them here, the trees were begun on the journey, from the cryonically preserved seeds or cells or some such. That was Heather's business. On the journey, and when we were first here, she was the laughing outward one of us.

Now she stays in her research area a great deal, trying to keep the hydroponics healthy without enough natural light. Of course, they were all designed for this sun, and the shade of the scrubbed dome is too much shade, and our lamps are solthree wavelengths.

Lesje worries because I am not able to do my work.

She worries because I have decided to patch the tent instead. She thinks I don't get enough exercise.

Outside the tent the wind is blowing.

I remember when we first came here, there was a brilliant light on the silver sand beaches, something like the light of Greece. (On Earth now, Greece is part of the History Preserves, to ensure that nothing will further erode the ancient broken marble. Even the gentle wind wore away too much; the energon coating was being put on the Parthenon as we flew away.)

We all remember the journey differently, but it isn't the journey that is important. All the decisions had been made on Earth, and all the action would be made on the new world, so we amused ourselves, on holiday from the universe.

We came here in the spring, when the light was white and bright and cool. We had the long summer to build, the long autumn to rest. Now it is winter.

And the wind blows all the time.

Well, never mind. That's my mantra: oh well, never mind, I repeat to myself. It helps. I find a place in the membrane where the striations are so deep, so close to our side of the tent, that I can see the landscape again. The sand has drifted around the space-grown, firm-planted fruit trees, and among the trees the outside workers ("the husbands" we call them jokingly) are walking ponderously in their membrane suits, only their heads showing through because we replace the helmets regularly. The bodies of the suits are opaque like the tent, and for the same reason.

I crouch there, looking out the tiny peephole, for a long time. Finally I paint on the coating of membrane. The air is not so warm these days, so the patch takes longer to harden. The thickness distorts the image through the tiny strip of light, removes the camera effect. To get back the transparent quality, I would have to paint the other side as well, smooth it off.

I think it is time for an uprising, a change.

We have divided the work along lines of capability. Four go out to tend the garden. Heather, Sam and I work inside. The three of us do housework.

I agreed to the division at the time, even chose the factions and gave the teams their foolish names. Though we are only seven, it was a useful way to order the winter's activities.

Now I think it is time we wives got out of the kitchen, so to speak. That smug metaphor keeps me chuckling until the husbands come home. Mine, that is, Lesje, looks at me as if I'm strange.

Well, I am. We all are. The secret of compatability on a long space voyage and subsequent settlement, I propound to myself (painting the dome and making the most of every stray idea), is to put a randomly chosen assortment of tolerant weirdos and expert improvisors into a membrane shell and accelerate them off to the stars. It isn't necessary even to hope for the best. Whatever happens, happens. After a while the planners drop in, riding a more conventional craft with a conventional crew chosen carefully for their stability and thus with the usual assortment of crazies and a psychotic locked up in the brig since maybe Arcturus when s/he broke a few important things and some heads, and marvel at their intelligent choice of pioneers, wishing only that the upstart offspring swarming around would show more of the proper respect and attitude. (Unfortunately, their parents have taught them that the idiots who sent them off to live in a membrane and plant apple trees, like some kiddie mythological figure, on an unsuitable planet are just that, idiots, and don't even deserve the free lunch they're being served, but it's in the contract.)

So. We have got this far in the scenario; we have arrived.

There are no offspring yet. We haven't had a chance to un-freeze any seed. Just apple trees, drifting over with sand.

These are the thoughts with which I occupy myself as I pull my brush back and forth, meditating on beginnings and voyages and solutions, finally thinking only of the slow and rewarding stroke of the membrane material, smooth under the spreading bristles of hair.

I turn suddenly and there is a figure behind me. One of the others? No. Long robe with hood, long face within the hood. Dimly seen, maybe young, hard to tell, the face is shadowed. Smiling, not menacing, but still, a stranger.

On a world where there are no strangers.

I have decided to go back to my own job. I start with Heather in her hydroponics lab.

"Don't you feel like getting outside?" I say.

"How do you like these low-light hybrids?" she counters. "I'm breeding them with tough bark, like the apple trees, and maybe I can get them out next winter."

"How long is it until spring?" says Samuel, coming in with her carving tool in one hand, a carefully-worked piece of apple wood in the other.

She shows it to us. Heather nods approvingly, familiarly. I take the carving in my hands. It is a tender and meticulous rendition of a hooded person, face smooth and smiling, folds of robe carefully carved. She has been polishing it until it has a patina.

"I see another gardener most days now," says Heather quietly.

"Am I the last one to twig to this?" I ask. I pick up a branch of one of the hybrids; a thorn scrapes my finger. Irritated, I say, "What in the world are they doing out there, anyway?"

Heather grins. I peel a piece of membrane material off my finger. Under it the skin is clean and healthy; the scratch stops where the membrane material began.

At dinner Lesje is irritable. "They're not going to last until spring," she says snappishly to Heather. "Look at this." The apple branch is scoured clean of bark on one side only, polished to almost a shine. The broken end is rough. The gnarls of the grain look like the folds of a robe. Heather shrugs, shakes her head.

"Another suit filter went today," says Anna. "No spares until the supply ship comes in the spring."

"Tanj," swears Lesje furiously.

"I was right," I say.

"They've held up this long," says Jed. "The winter's just been longer and tougher than we expected."

"What, the trees or the filters?" asks Lesje.

"Either."

Pfui."

Nihio says, "The settlers who took over my part of the world in ancient history used to get crazy in the winter. Too much of the same thing. Bushed, they called it."

I don't mention the figure to the husbands. No one is talking. Sam has put her carving into my hand. "I thought I was getting a taste of that kind of crazy, at first," she says.

I was the last of us to see it. I wonder what Lesje and Jed, Nihio and Anna see, outside all day.

"Tomorrow I think we should take over the outside detail," I say, and the discussion about that lasts until midnight. Finally the decision is made, though Lesje is reluctant.

"You don't know that orchard like we do," she says.

"All the better," says Jed, and Lesje casts him an angry look, but in the end agrees to trade jobs with Heather.

In the morning, the husbands crowd around us as we put on the three worn suits with the clear helmets. I have taken a container of energon and one of the recycled-hair brushes. Heather has a few of her new plants. Samuel has her wood-collecting bag. She used to send it out with Nihio, so he could get driftwood for her. Windfalls.

As our four figures go into the airlock, Heather holds back the door until the fourth one's robe has cleared the door-track. She makes sure her hands don't touch the soft folds. We don't look for a reaction in the four we leave inside. None of us really wants to know yet.

The first day I paint three trees with energon on the windward side. Some sand is trapped in the coating as it dries, but that shouldn't matter. Looking back at the dome I see suddenly why the whole tent surface is scoured. The membrane is, accidentally, a perfect airfoil shape, wide end into the wind, so that the sand is drawn across the whole surface before blowing away behind. I flew sailplanes above the Parthenon; I remember drifting supported by that white, hot light.

The second day Lesje and Nihio agree to turn the tent against the wind. I paint four trees with membrane material, to test whether a more flexible coat will let them grow better.

The third day, I paint the downwind side of the tent from the outside while Lesje paints the inside. As our strokes cross, we become clear to each other, she with her face set and unsmiling, wielding the brush like a windstorm.

The fourth day, Lesje puts on the defective suit, comes out at midday and shovels the drifted sand away from the new window. She and Jed have moved the hydroponics to the window area. I have stopped sleeping in the shelter with her and that night I put my pallet under the leaves near the window side of the tent. In the night, I wake to see the figure sitting nearby, hood back, looking out into the orchard. When I move, the calm face looks over at me, a hand raises slightly. I turn over and sleep again.

After a few days' activity outside, Lesje is coughing intermittently, but to Jed's concern she snaps, "Never mind, I'm fine. No one ever got black lung disease and died in this short a time. The bedouins lived in this stuff all their lives, and they didn't have all this fancy technology."

"Well, put your robes across your noses tomorrow and come out," says Heather, "because I think the trees are budding."

"When winter comes can spring be far behind?" says Anna, then laughs his hearty laugh.

Lesje even smiles.

The blossoms are battered by a few spring storms, but gradually the sand slows and stops and we can shovel the drifts away for good, and paint the tent clear. We leave the airlock open as we do it, though the air is cooler than complete comfort, and run in and out with our paintbrushes, making our winter womb into a window again.

"Okay, Yanni," Lesje says to me one day, her hand caressing a branch, "okay. But I wish I'd thought of it."

The blossoms scent the air for a while, then fall away. The eight of us work among the trees, clearing the last of the sand dunes, checking the results of the energon and the membrane tests, finding the membrane worn and cracked but the trees healthier than the three energon-protected ones. I had only painted the upwind sides of any tree, so we can take a rigid and perfectly detailed tree-print in energon from the three test trees, leaving them to grow in health. I stand the energon castings in the middle of the tent, and call the triangle they encircle the art gallery. Samuel hangs her carvings on the transparent half-branches.

Tht fruit begins to ripen, turns from green to tentative red to a deep shine. We decide that when we find the first windfall, that day will be the beginning of the harvest.

The light is white and clear and brilliant as I walk out among the orchard and find, fallen in the thick grass that has grown across the sand beneath the trees, a ripe red apple. I pick it up and take a bite. The fruit is slightly pink, veined with red, and the taste is strange and intense. It is the first apple I have ever held in my hand like this, have ever touched or tasted. To stand under our own trees with the breeze in my face and bite deeply into the fruit of our long year's work—I came a long way to this. I hand the rest of the apple to my companion, who is walking with the hood of the robe pushed back so the wind gently lifts the thin strands of dark hair.

The long brown fingers grasp the alien fruit and the hand takes it slowly to a smiling mouth. Our new companion takes a bite, chews and swallows.

"It's sweet," I say.

The smile is sweet that answers me.

LETTER FROM MARS-DOME # 1

Eileen Kernaghan

We are the unborn.
In this glass egg
glistening
with our hot-house breath
we are indefinitely
sustained.
This place has no time, no
seasons, no geography;
is Plath's bell-jar made
by science—large enough
for all of us.

Recall these words, these myths—
storm
    sunlight
rain
    the sea
Remember snow: a gift
delicate as the blurred
shadows of the stars. . . .

The air clots in our mouths
sour as spoiled milk.
Our bones ache.
This place is shrinking,
flattening
under the dead weight of
the universe.
How long until
the walls crack apart
and let the night in,
the black wind
and terrible ranks of stars?

HINTERLANDS

William Gibson

When Hiro hit the switch, I was dreaming of Paris, dreaming of wet, dark streets in winter. The pain came oscillating up from the floor of my skull, exploding behind my eyes in a wall of blue neon; I jackknifed up out of the mesh hammock, screaming. I always scream; I make a point of it. Feedback raged in my skull. The pain switch is an auxiliary circuit in the bonephone implant, patched directly into the pain centres, just the thing for cutting through a surrogate's barbiturate fog. It took a few seconds for my life to fall together, icebergs of biography looming through the fog: who I was, where I was, what I was doing there, who was waking me.

Hiro's voice came crackling into my head through the bone-conduction implant. "Damn, Toby. Know what it does to my ears, you scream like that?"

"Know how much I care about your *ears*, Dr. Nagashima? I care about them as much as — "

"No time for the litany of love, boy. We've got business. But what is it with these fifty-millivolt spike waves off your temporals, hey? Mixing something with the downers to give it a little colour?"

"Your EEG's screwed, Hiro. You're crazy. I just want my sleep. . . . " I collapsed into the hammock and tried to pull the darkness over me, but his voice was still there.

"Sorry, my man, but you're working today. We got a ship back,

64

an hour ago. Air-lock gang are out there right now, sawing the reaction engine off so she'll just about fit through the door."

"Who is it?"

"Leni Hofmannstahl, Toby, physical chemist, citizen of the Federal Republic of Germany." He waited until I quit groaning. "It's a confirmed meatshot."

Lovely workaday terminology we've developed out here. He meant a returning ship with active medical telemetry, contents one (1) body, warm, psychological status as yet unconfirmed. I shut my eyes and swung there in the dark.

"Looks like you're her surrogate, Toby. Her profile syncs with Taylor's, but he's on leave."

I knew all about Taylor's "leave." He was out in the agricultural canisters, ripped on amytriptyline, doing aerobic exercises to counter his latest bout with clinical depression. One of the occupational hazards of being a surrogate. Taylor and I don't get along. Funny how you usually don't, if the guy's psychosexual profile is too much like your own.

"Hey, Toby, where *are* you getting all that dope?" The question was ritual. "From Charmian?"

"From your mom, Hiro." He knows it's Charmian as well as I do.

"Thanks, Toby. Get up here to the Heavenside elevator in five minutes or I'll send those Russian nurses down to help you. The male ones."

I just swung there in my hammock and played the game called Toby Halpert's Place in the Universe. No egotist, I put the sun in the centre, the luminary, the orb of day. Around it, I swung tidy planets, our cozy home system. But just *here,* at a fixed point about an eighth of the way out toward the orbit of Mars, I hung a fat alloy cylinder, like a quarter-scale model of Tsiolkovsky 1, the Worker's Paradise back at L-5. Tsiolkovsky 1 is fixed at the liberation point between Earth's gravity and the moon's, but we need a lightsail to hold us here, twenty tons of aluminum spun into a hexagon, ten kilometres from side to side. That sail towed us out from Earth orbit, and now it's our anchor. We use it to tack against the photon stream, hanging here beside the thing—the point, the singularity—we call the Highway.

The French call it *le Métro*, the Subway, and the Russians call it the River, but Subway won't carry the distance, and River, for Americans, can't carry quite the same loneliness. Call it the Tovyevski Anomaly Coordinates if you don't mind bringing Olga into it. Olga Tovyevski, Our Lady of Singularities, Patron Saint of the Highway.

Hiro didn't trust me to get up on my own. Just before the Russian orderlies came in, he turned the lights on in my cubicle, by remote control, and let them strobe and stutter for a few seconds before they fell as a steady glare across the pictures of St. Olga that Charmian had taped up on the bulkhead. Dozens of them, her face repeated in newsprint, in magazine glossy. Our Lady of the Highway.

Lieutenant Colonel Olga Tovyevski, youngest woman of her rank in the Soviet space effort, was en route to Mars, solo, in a modified Alyut 6. The modifications allowed her to carry the prototype of a new airscrubber that was to be tested in the USSR's four-man Martian orbital lab. They could just as easily have handled the Alyut by remote, from Tsiolkovsky, but Olga wanted to log mission time. They made sure she kept busy, though; they stuck her with a series of routine hydrogen-band radio-flare experiments, the tail end of a low-priority Soviet-Australian scientific exchange. Olga knew that her role in the experiments could have been handled by a standard household timer. But she was a diligent officer; she'd press the buttons at precisely the correct intervals.

With her brown hair drawn back and caught in a net, she must have looked like some idealized *Pravda* cameo of the Worker in Space, easily the most photogenic cosmonaut of either gender. She checked the Alyut's chonometer again and poised her hand above the buttons that would trigger the first of her flares. Colonel Tovyevski had no way of knowing that she was nearing the point in space that would eventually be known as the Highway.

As she punched the six-button triggering sequence, the Alyut crossed those final kilometres and emitted the flare, a sustained burst of radio energy at 1420 megahertz, broadcast frequency of the hydrogen atom. Tsiolkovsky's radio telescope was tracking, relaying the signal to geosynchronous comsats that bounced it down to stations in the southern Urals and New South Wales. For 3.8 seconds the Alyut's radio image was obscured by the afterimage of the flare.

When the afterimage faded from Earth's monitor screens, the Alyut was gone.

In the Urals a middle-aged Georgian technician bit through the stem of his favourite meerschaum. In New South Wales a young physicist began to slam the side of his monitor, like an enraged pinball finalist protesting TILT.

The elevator that waited to take me up to Heaven looked like Hollywood's best shot at a Bauhaus mummy case—a narrow, upright sarcophagus with a clear acrylic lid. Behind it, rows of identical consoles receded like a textbook illustration of vanishing perspective. The usual crowd of technicians in yellow paper clown suits were milling purposefully around. I spotted Hiro in blue denim, his pearl-buttoned cowboy shirt open over a faded UCLA sweatshirt. Engrossed in the figures cascading down the face of a monitor screen, he didn't notice me. Neither did anyone else.

So I just stood there and stared up at the ceiling, at the bottom of the floor of Heaven. It didn't look like much. Our fat cylinder is actually two cylinders, one inside the other. Down here in the outer one—we make our own "down" with axial rotation—are all the more mundane aspects of our operation: dormitories, cafeterias, the air-lock deck, where we haul in returning boats, Communications—and Wards, where I'm careful never to go.

Heaven, the inner cylinder, the unlikely green heart of this place, is the ripe Disney dream of homecoming, the ravenous ear of an information-hungry global economy. A constant stream of raw data goes pulsing home to Earth, a flood of rumours, whispers, hints of transgalactic traffic. I used to lie rigid in my hammock and feel the pressure of all that data, feel it snaking through the lines I imagined behind the bulkhead, lines like sinews, strapped and bulging, ready to spasm, ready to crush me. Then Charmian moved in with me, and after I told her about the Fear, she made magic against it and put up her icons of St. Olga. And the pressure receded, fell away.

"Patching you in with a translator, Toby. You may need German this morning." His voice was sand in my skull, a dry modulation of static. "Hillary—"

"On line, Dr. Nagashima," said a BBC voice, clear as ice crystal. "You do have French, do you, Toby? Hofmannstahl has French and English."

"You stay the hell out of my hair, Hillary. Speak when you're bloody spoken to, got it?" Her silence became another layer in the complex, continual sizzle of static. Hiro shot me a dirty look across two dozen consoles. I grinned.

It was starting to happen: the elation, the adrenalin rush. I could feel it through the last wisps of barbiturate. A kid with a surfer's smooth, blond face was helping me into a jump suit. It smelled; it was new-old, carefully battered, soaked with synthetic sweat and customized pheromones. Both sleeves were plastered from wrist to shoulder with embroidered patches, mostly corporate logos, subsidiary backers of an imaginary Highway expedition, with the main backer's much larger trademark stitched across my shoulders—the firm that was supposed to have sent HALPERT, TOBY out to his rendezvous with the stars. At least my name was real, embroidered in scarlet nylon capitals just above my heart.

The surfer boy had the kind of standard-issue good looks I associate with junior partners in the CIA, but his name tape said NEVSKY and repeated itself in Cyrillic. KGB, then. He was no *tsiolnik;* he didn't have that loose-jointed style conferred by twenty years in their L-5 habitat. The kid was pure Moscow, a polite clipboard ticker who probably knew eight ways to kill with a rolled newspaper. Now we began the ritual of drugs and pockets; he tucked a microsyringe, loaded with one of the new euphorohallucinogens, into the pocket on my left wrist, took a step back, then ticked it off on his clipboard. The printed outline of a jump-suited surrogate on his special pad looked like a handgun target. He took a five-gram vial of opium from the case he wore chained to his waist and found the pocket for that. Tick. Fourteen pockets. The cocaine was last.

Hiro came over just as the Russian was finishing. "Maybe she has some hard data, Toby; she's a physical chemist, remember." It was strange to hear him acoustically, not as bone vibration from the implant.

"Everything's hard up there, Hiro."

"Don't I know it?" He was feeling it, too, that special buzz. We couldn't quite seem to make eye contact. Before the awkwardness could deepen, he turned and gave one of the yellow clowns the thumbs up.

Two of them helped me into the Bauhaus coffin and stepped back as the lid hissed down like a giant's faceplate. I began my ascent to Heaven and the homecoming of a stranger named Leni Hofmannstahl. A short trip, but it seems to take forever.

Olga, who was our first hitchhiker, the first one to stick out her thumb on the wavelength of hydrogen, made it home in two years. At Tyuratam, in Kazakhstan, one gray winter morning, they recorded her return on eighteen centimetres of magnetic tape.

If a religious man—one with a back-ground in film technology—had been watching the point in space where her Alyut had vanished two years before, it might have seemed to him that God had butt-spliced footage of empty space with footage of Olga's ship. She blipped back into our space-time like some amateur's atrocious special effect. A week later and they might never have reached her in time; Earth would have spun on its way and left her drifting toward the sun. Fifty-three hours after her return a nervous volunteer named Kurtz, wearing an armoured work suit, climbed through the Alyut's hatch. He was an East German specialist in space medicine, and American cigarettes were his secret vice; he wanted one very badly as he negotiated the air lock, wedged his way past a rectangular mass of air-scrubber core, and chinned his helmet lights. The Alyut, even after two years, seemed to be full of breathable air. In the twin beams from the massive helmet, he saw tiny globules of blood and vomit swinging slowly past, swirling in his wake, as he edged the bulky suit out of the crawlway and entered the command module. Then he found her.

She was drifting above the navigational display, naked,

cramped in a rigid fetal knot. Her eyes were open, but fixed on something Kurtz would never see. Her fists were bloody, clenched like stone, and her brown hair, loose now, drifted around her face like seaweed. Very slowly, very carefully, he swung himself across the white keyboards of the command console and secured his suit to the navigational display. She'd gone after the ship's communications gear with her bare hands, he decided. He deactivated the work suit's right claw; it unfolded automatically, like two pairs of vise-grip pliers pretending they were a flower. He extended his hand, still sealed in a pressurized grey surgical glove.

Then, as gently as he could, he pried open the fingers of her left hand. Nothing.

But when he opened her right fist, something spun free and tumbled in slow motion a few centimetres from the synthetic quartz of his faceplate. It looked like a seashell.

Olga came home, but she never came back to life behind those blue eyes. They tried, of course, but the more they tried, the more tenuous she became, and, in their hunger to know, they spread her thinner and thinner until she came, in her martyrdom, to fill whole libraries with frozen aisles of precious relics. No saint was ever pared so fine: at the Plesetsk laboratories alone, she was represented by more than two million tissue slides, racked and numbered in the subbasement of a bombproof biological complex.

They had better luck with the seashell. Exobiology suddenly found itself standing on unnervingly solid ground: one and seven tenths grams of highly organized biological information, definitely extraterrestrial. Olga's seashell generated an entire subbranch of the science, devoted exclusively to the study of . . . Olga's seashell.

The initial findings on the shell made two things clear. It was the product of no known terrestrial biosphere, and as there were no other known biospheres in the solar system, it had come from another star. Olga had either visited the place of its origin or come into contact, however distantly, with something that was, or had once been, capable of making the trip.

They sent a Major Grosz out to the Tovyevski Coordinates in a specially fitted Alyut 9. Another ship followed him. He was on the last of his twenty hydrogen flares when his ship vanished. They recorded his departure and waited. Two hundred thirty-four days later he returned. In the meantime they had probed the area constantly, desperate for anything that might become the specific anomaly, the irritant around which a theory might grow. There was nothing: only Grosz's ship, tumbling out of control. He committed suicide before they could reach him, the Highway's second victim.

When they towed the Alyut back to Tsiolkovsky, they found that the elaborate recording gear was blank. All of it was in perfect working order; none of it had functioned. Grosz was flash-frozen and put on the first shuttle down to Plesetsk, where bulldozers were already excavating for a new subbasement.

Three years later, the morning after they lost their seventh cosmonaut, a telephone rang in Moscow. The caller introduced himself. He was the director of the Central Intelligence Agency of the United States of America. He was authorized, he said, to make a certain offer. Under certain very specific conditions, the Soviet Union might avail itself of the best minds in Western psychiatry. It was the understanding of his agency, he continued, that such help might currently be very welcome.

His Russian was excellent.

The bonephone static was a subliminal sandstorm. The elevator slid up into its narrow shaft through the floor of Heaven. I counted blue lights at two-metre intervals. After the fifth light, darkness and cessation.

Hidden in the hollow command console of the dummy Highway boat, I waited in the elevator, like the secret behind the gimmicked bookcase in a children's mystery story. The boat was a prop, a set piece, like the Bavarian cottage glued to the plaster alp in some amusement park—a nice touch, but one that wasn't quite necessary. If the returnees accept us at all, they take us for granted; our cover stories and props don't seem to make much difference.

"All clear," Hiro said. "No customers hanging around." I reflexively massaged the scar behind my left ear, where they'd gone in to plant the bonephone. The side of the dummy console swung open and let in the grey dawn light of Heaven. The fake boat's interior was familiar and strange at the same time, like your own apartment when you haven't seen it for a week. One of those new Brazilian vines had snaked its way across the left viewport since my last time up, but that seemed to be the only change in the whole scene.

Big fights over those vines at the biotecture meetings, American ecologists screaming about possible nitrogen shortfalls. The Russians have been touchy about biodesign ever since they had to borrow Americans to help them with the biotic program back at Tsiolkovsky 1. Nasty problem with the rot eating the hydroponic wheat; all that superfine Soviet engineering, and they still couldn't establish a functional ecosystem. Doesn't help that that initial debacle paved the way for us to be out here with them now. It irritates them; so they insist on the Brazilian vines, whatever— anything that gives them a chance to argue. But I like those vines: the leaves are heart-shaped, and if you rub one between your hands, it smells like cinnamon.

I stood at the port and watched the clearing take shape, as reflected sunlight entered Heaven. Heaven runs on Greenwich Standard; big Mylar mirrors were swiveling somewhere, out in bright vacuum, on schedule for a Greenwich Standard dawn. The recorded bird songs began back in the trees. Birds have a very hard time in the absence of true gravity. We can't have real ones, because they go crazy trying to make do with centrifugal force.

The first time you see it, Heaven lives up to its name, lush and cool and bright, the long grass dappled with wild flowers. It helps if you don't know that most of the trees are artificial, or the amount of care required to maintain something like the optimal balance between blue-green algae and diatom algae in the ponds. Charmian says she expects Bambi to come gambolling out of the woods, and Hiro claims he knows exactly how many Disney engineers were sworn to secrecy under the National Security Act.

"We're getting fragments from Hofmannstahl," Hiro said. He might almost have been talking to himself; the handler-surrogate gestalt was going into effect, and soon we'd cease to be aware of each other. The adrenalin edge was tapering off. "Nothing very coherent. 'Schöne Maschine' something . . . 'Beautiful machine'. . . . Hillary thinks she sounds pretty calm, but right out of it."

"Don't tell me about it. No expectations, right? Let's go in loose." I opened the hatch and took a breath of Heaven's air; it was like cool white wine. "Where's Charmian?"

He sighed, a soft gust of static. "Charmian should be in Clearing Five, taking care of a Chilean who's three days home, but she's not, because she heard you were coming. So she's waiting for you by the carp pond. Stubborn bitch," he added.

Charmian was flicking pebbles at the Chinese bighead carp. She had a cluster of white flowers tucked behind one ear, a wilted Marlboro behind the other. Her feet were bare and muddy, and she'd hacked the legs off her jump suit at mid-thigh. Her black hair was drawn back in a ponytail.

We'd met for the first time at a party out in one of the welding shops, drunken voices clanging in the hollow of the alloy sphere, homemade vodka in zero gravity. Someone had a bag of water for a chaser, squeezed out a double handful, and flipped it expertly into a rolling, floppy ball of surface tension. Old jokes about passing water. But I'm graceless in zero g. I put my hand through it when it came my way. Shook a thousand silvery little balls from my hair, batting at them, tumbling, and the woman beside me was laughing, turning slow somersaults, long, thin girl with black hair. She wore those baggy drawstring pants that tourists take home from Tsiolkovsky and a faded NASA T-shirt three sizes too big. A minute later she was telling me about hang-gliding with the teen *tsiolniki* and about how proud they'd been of the weak pot they grew in one of the corn canisters. I didn't realize she was another surrogate until Hiro clicked in to tell us the party was over. She moved in with me a week later.

"A minute, okay?" Hiro gritted his teeth, a horrible sound. "One. *Uno.*" Then he was gone, off the circuit entirely, maybe not even listening.

"How's tricks in Clearing Five?" I squatted beside her and found some pebbles of my own.

"Not so hot. I had to get away from him for a while, shot him up with hypnotics. My translator told me you were on your way up."

She has the kind of Texas accent that makes *ice* sound like *ass*.

"Thought you spoke Spanish. Guy's Chilean, isn't he?" I tossed one of my pebbles into the pond.

"I speak Mexican. The culture vultures said he wouldn't like my accent. Good thing, too. I can't follow him when he talks fast." One of her pebbles followed mine, rings spreading on the surface as it sank. "Which is constantly," she added. A bighead swam over to see whether her pebble was good to eat. "He isn't going to make it." She wasn't looking at me. Her tone was perfectly neutral. "Little Jorge is definitely not making it."

I chose the flattest of my pebbles and tried to skip it across the pond, but it sank. The less I knew about Chilean Jorge, the better. I knew he was a live one, one of the ten per cent. Our DOA count runs at twenty per cent. Suicide. Seventy per cent of the meatshots are automatic candidates for Wards: the diaper cases, mumblers, totally gone. Charmian and I are surrogates for that final ten per cent.

If the first ones to come back had only returned with seashells, I doubt that Heaven would be out here. Heaven was built after a dead Frenchman returned with a twelve-centimetre ring of magnetically coded steel locked in his cold hand, black parody of the lucky kid who wins the free ride on the merry-go-round. We may never find out where or how he got it, but that ring was the Rosetta Stone for cancer. So now it's cargo cult time for the human race. We can pick things up out there that we might not stumble across in research in a thousand years. Charmian says we're like those poor suckers on their islands, who spend all their time building landing strips to make the big silver birds come back. Charmian says that contact with "superior" civilizations is something you don't wish on your worst enemy.

"Ever wonder how they thought this scam up, Toby?" She was squinting into the sunlight, east, down the length of our cylindrical country, horizonless and green. "They must've had all the heavies in, the shrink elite, scattered down a long slab of genuine imitation rosewood, standard Pentagon issue. Each one got a clean notepad and a brand-new pencil, specially sharpened for the occasion Everybody was there: Freudians, Jungians, Adlerians, Skinner rat men, you name it. And every one of those bastards knew in his heart that it was time to play his best hand. As a profession, not just as representatives of a given faction. There they are, Western psychiatry incarnate. And nothing's happening! People are popping back off the Highway dead, or else they come back drooling, singing nursery rhymes. The live ones last about three days, won't say a goddamned thing, then shoot themselves· or go catatonic." She took a small flashlight from her belt and casually cracked its plastic shell, extracting the parabolic reflector. "Kremlin's screaming. CIA's going nuts. And worst of all, the multinationals who want to back the show are getting cold feet. 'Dead spacemen? No data? No deal, friends.' So they're getting nervous, all those supershrinks, until some flake, some grinning weirdo from Berkeley maybe, he says," and her drawl sank to parody stoned mellowness, "'Like, hey, why don't we just put these people into a real *nice* place with a lotta *good* dope and somebody they can really *relate* to, hey?'" She laughed, shook her head. She was using the reflector to light her cigarette, concentrating the sunlight. They don't give us matches; fires screw up the oxygen-carbon dioxide balance. A tiny curl of grey smoke twisted away from the white-hot focal point.

"Okay," Hiro said, "that's your minute." I checked my watch; it was more like three minutes.

"Good luck, baby," she said softly, pretending to be intent on her cigarette. "Godspeed."

The promise of pain. It's there each time. You know what will happen, but you don't know when, or exactly how. You try to hold on to them; you rock them in the dark. But if you brace for the pain, you can't function. That poem Hiro quotes, *Teach us to care and not to care.*

We're like intelligent houseflies wandering through an international airport; some of us actually manage to blunder onto flights to London or Rio, maybe even survive the trip and make it back. "Hey," say the other flies, "what's happening on the other side of that door? What do they know that we don't?" At the edge of the Highway every human language unravels in your hands—except, perhaps, the language of the shaman, of the cabalist, the language of the mystic intent on mapping hierarchies of demons, angels, saints.

But the Highway is governed by rules, and we've learned a few of them. That gives us something to cling to.

Rule One: One entity per ride; no teams, no couples.

Rule Two: No artificial intelligences; whatever's out there won't stop for a smart machine, at least not the kind we know how to build.

Rule Three: Recording instruments are a waste of space; they always come back blank.

Dozens of new schools of physics have sprung up in St. Olga's wake, ever more bizarre and more elegant heresies, each one hoping to shoulder its way to the inside track. One by one, they all fall down. In the whispering quiet of Heaven's nights, you imagine you can hear the paradigms shatter, shards of theory tinkling into brilliant dust as the lifework of some corporate think tank is reduced to the tersest historical footnote, and all in the time it takes your damaged traveller to mutter some fragment in the dark.

Flies in an airport, hitching rides. Flies are advised not to ask too many questions; flies are advised not to try for the Big Picture. Repeated attempts in that direction invariably lead to the slow, relentless flowering of paranoia, your mind projecting huge, dark patterns on the walls of night, patterns that have a way of solidifying, becoming madness, becoming religion. Smart flies stick with Black Box theory; Black Box is the sanctioned metaphor, the Highway remaining x in every sane equation. We aren't supposed to worry about what the Highway is, or who put it there. Instead, we concentrate on what we put into the Box and what we get back out of it. There are things we send down the Highway (a woman named Olga, her ship, so many more who've followed) and things that come to us (a madwoman, a seashell, artifacts, fragments of alien technologies). The Black Box theorists assure us that our primary concern is to optimize this exchange. We're out here to see that our species gets its money's worth. Still, certain things become increasingly evident; one of them is that we aren't the only flies who've found their way into an airport. We've collected artifacts from at least half a dozen wildly divergent cultures.

"More hicks," Charmian calls them. We're like packrats in the hold of a freighter, trading little pretties with rats from other ports. Dreaming of the bright lights, the big city . . . .

Keep it simple, a matter of In and Out. Leni Hofmannstahl: Out.

We staged the homecoming of Leni Hofmannstahl in Clearing Three, also known as Elysium. I crouched in a stand of meticulous reproductions of young vine maples and studied her ship. It had originally looked like a wingless dragonfly, a slender, ten-metre abdomen housing the reaction engine. Now, with the engine removed, it looked like a matte-white pupa, larval eye bulges stuffed with the traditional useless array of sensors and probes. It lay on a gentle rise in the centre of the clearing, a specially designed hillock sculpted to support a variety of vessel formats. The newer boats are smaller, like Grand Prix washing machines, minimalist pods with no pretense to being exploratory vessels. Modules for meatshots.

"I don't like it," Hiro said. "I don't like this one. It doesn't feel right. . . . " He might have been talking to himself; he might almost have been *me* talking to myself, which meant the handler-surrogate gestalt was almost operational. Locked into my role, I'm no longer the point man for Heaven's hungry ear, a specialized probe radio-linked with an even more specialized psychiatrist; when the gestalt clicks, Hiro and I meld into something else, something we can never admit to each other, not when it isn't happening. Our relationship would give a classical Freudian nightmares. But I knew that he was right; something felt terribly wrong this time.

The clearing was roughly circular. It had to be; it was actually a fifteen-metre round cut through the floor of Heaven, a circular elevator disguised as an Alpine minimeadow. They'd sawed Leni's engine off, hauled her boat into the outer cylinder, lowered the clearing to the air-lock deck, then lifted her to Heaven on a giant pie plate landscaped with grass and wild flowers. They blanked her sensors with broadcast overrides and sealed her ports and hatch; Heaven is supposed to be a surprise to the newly arrived.

I found myself wondering whether Charmian was back with

Jorge yet. Maybe she'd be cooking something for him, one of the fish we "catch" as they're released into our hands from cages on the pool bottoms. I imagined the smell of frying fish, closed my eyes, and imagined Charmian wading in the shallow water, bright drops beading on her thighs, long-legged girl in a fishpond in Heaven.

"Move, Toby! In now!"

My skull rang with the volume; training and the gestalt reflex already had me half-way across the clearing. "Goddamn, Goddamn, Goddamn . . . " Hiro's mantra, and I knew it had managed to go *all* wrong, then. Hillary the translator was a shrill undertone, BBC ice cracking as she rattled something out at top speed, something about anatomical charts. Hiro must have used the remotes to unseal the hatch, but he didn't wait for it to unscrew itself. He triggered six explosive bolts built into the hull and blew the whole hatch mechanism out intact. It barely missed me. I had instinctively swerved out of its way. Then I was scrambling up the boat's smooth side, grabbing for the honeycomb struts just inside the entranceway; the hatch mechanism had taken the alloy ladder with it.

And I froze there, crouching in the smell of *plastique* from the bolts, because that was when the Fear found me, really found me, for the first time.

I'd felt it before, the Fear, but only the fringes, the least edge. Now it was vast, the very hollow of night, an emptiness cold and implacable. It was last words, deep space, every long goodbye in the history of our species. It made me cringe, whining. I was shaking, groveling, crying. They lecture us on it, warn us, try to explain it away as a kind of temporary agoraphobia endemic to our work. But we know what it is; surrogates know and handlers can't. No explanation has ever even come close.

It's the Fear. It's the long finger of Big Night, the darkness that feeds the muttering damned to the gentle white maw of Wards. Olga knew it first, St. Olga. She tried to hide us from it, clawing at her radio gear, bloodying her hands to destroy her ship's broadcast capacity, praying Earth would lose her, let her die. . . .

Hiro was frantic, but he must have understood, and he knew what to do.

He hit me with the pain switch. Hard. Over and over, like a cattle prod. He drove me into the boat. He drove me through the Fear.

Beyond the Fear, there was a room. Silence, and a stranger's smell, a woman's.

The cramped module was worn, almost homelike, the tired plastic of the acceleration couch patched with peeling strips of silver tape. But it all seemed to mold itself around an absence. She wasn't there. Then I saw the insane frieze of ball-point scratchings, crabbed symbols, thousands of tiny, crooked oblongs locking and over-lapping. Thumb-smudged, pathetic, it covered most of the rear bulkhead.

Hiro was static, whispering, pleading. *Find her, Toby, now, please, Toby, find her, find her, find —*

I found her in the surgical bay, a narrow alcove off the crawlway. Above her, the *Schöne* Maschine, the surgical manipulator, glittering, its bright, thin arms neatly folded, chromed limbs of a spider crab, tipped with hemostats, forceps, laser scalpel. Hillary was hysterical, half-lost on some faint channel, something about the anatomy of the human arm, the tendons, the arteries, basic taxonomy. Hillary was screaming.

There was no blood at all. The manipulator is a clean machine, able to do a no-mess job in zero g, vacuuming the blood away. She'd died just before Hiro had blown the hatch, her right arm spread out across the white plastic work surface like a medieval drawing, flayed, muscles and other tissues tacked out in a neat symmetrical display, held with a dozen stainless steel dissecting pins. She bled to death. A surgical manipulator is carefully programmed against suicides, but it can double as a robot dissector, preparing biologicals for storage.

She'd found a way to fool it. You usually can, with machines, given time. She'd had eight years.

She lay there in a collapsible framework, a thing like the fossil skeleton of a dentist's chair; through it, I could see the faded embroidery across the back of her jump suit, the trademark of a West German electronics conglomerate. I tried to tell her. I said, "Please, you're dead. Forgive us, we came to try to help, Hiro and I. Understand? He *knows* you, see, Hiro, he's here in my head.

79

He's read your dossier, your sexual profile, your favorite colours; he knows your childhood fears, first lover, name of a teacher you liked. And I've got just the right pheromones, and I'm a walking arsenal of drugs, something here you're bound to like. And we can lie, Hiro and I; we're ace liars. Please. You've got to see. Perfect strangers, but Hiro and I, for you, we make up the *perfect stranger*, Leni."

She was a small woman, blonde, her smooth, straight hair streaked with premature grey. I touched her hair, once, and went out into the clearing. As I stood there, the long grass shuddered, the wild flowers began to shake, and we began our descent, the boat centred on its landscaped round of elevator. The clearing slid down out of Heaven, and the sunlight was lost in the glare of huge vapour arcs that threw hard shadows across the broad deck of the air lock. Figures in red suits, running. A red Dinky Toy did a U-turn on fat rubber wheels, getting out of our way.

Nevsky, the KGB surfer, was waiting at the foot of the gangway that they wheeled to the edge of the clearing. I didn't see him until I reached the bottom.

"I must take the drugs now, Mr. Halpert."

I stood there, swaying, blinking tears from my eyes. He reached out to steady me. I wondered whether he even knew why he was down here in the lock deck, a yellow suit in red territory. But he probably didn't mind; he didn't seem to mind anything very much; he had his clipboard ready.

"I must take them, Mr. Halpert."

I stripped out of the suit, bundled it, and handed it to him. He stuffed it into a plastic Ziploc, put the Ziploc in a case manacled to his left wrist, and spun the combination.

"Don't take them all at once, kid," I said. Then I fainted.

Late that night Charmian brought a special kind of darkness down to my cubicle, individual doses sealed in heavy foil. It was nothing like the darkness of Big Night, that sentient, hunting dark that waits to drag the hitchhikers down to Wards, that dark that incubates the Fear. It was a darkness like the shadows moving in the backseat of your parents' car, on a rainy night when you're five years old, warm and secure. Charmian's a lot slicker than I am when it comes to getting past the clipboard tickers, the ones like Nevsky.

I didn't ask her why she was back from Heaven, or what had happened to Jorge. She didn't ask me anything about Leni.

Hiro was gone, off the air entirely. I'd seen him at the debriefing that afternoon; as usual, our eyes didn't meet. It didn't matter. I knew he'd be back. It had been business as usual, really. A bad day in Heaven, but it's neaver easy. It's hard when you feel the Fear for the first time, but I've always known it was there, waiting. They talked about Leni's diagrams and about her ballpoint sketches of molecular chains that shift on command. Molecules that can function as switches, logic elements, even a kind of wiring, built up in layers into a single very large molecule, a very small computer. We'll probably never know what she met out there; we'll probably never know the details of the transaction. We might be sorry if we ever found out. We aren't the only hinterland tribe, the only ones looking for scraps.

Damn Leni, damn that Frenchman, damn all the ones who bring things home, who bring cancer cures, seashells, things without names—who keep us here waiting, who fill Wards, who bring us the Fear. But cling to this dark, warm and close, to Charmian's slow breathing, to the rhythm of the sea. You get high enough out here; you'll hear the sea, deep down behind the constant conchshell static of the bonephone. It's something we carry with us, no matter how far from home.

Charmian stirred beside me, muttered a stranger's name, the name of some broken traveller long gone down to Wards. She holds the current record; she kept a man alive for two weeks, until he put his eyes out with his thumbs. She screamed all the way down, broke her nails on the elevator's plastic lid. Then they sedated her.

We both have the drive, though, that special need, that freak dynamic that lets us keep going back to Heaven. We both got it the same way, lay out there in our little boats for weeks, waiting for the Highway to take us. And when our last flare was gone, we were hauled back here by tugs. Some people just aren't taken, and nobody knows why. And you'll never get a second chance. They say it's too expensive, but what they really mean, as they eye the bandages on your wrists, is that now you're too valuable, too much use to them as a potential surrogate. Don't worry about the suicide attempt, they'll tell you; happens all the time. Perfectly understandable: feeling of profound rejection. But I'd wanted to go, wanted it so bad. Charmian, too. She tried with pills. But they worked on us, twisted us a little, aligned our drives, planted the bonephones, paired us with handlers.

Olga must have known, must have seen it all, somehow; she was trying to keep us from finding our way out there, where she'd been. She knew that if we found her, we'd have to go. Even now, knowing what I know, I still want to go. I never will. But we can swing here in this dark that towers way above us, Charmian's hand in mine. Between our palms the drug's torn foil wrapper. And St. Olga smiles out at us from the walls; you can feel her, all those prints from the same publicity shot, torn and taped across the walls of night, her white smile, forever.

82

POINTS IN TIME

Christopher Dewdney

Two points stabilize two-dimensional space. Three points stabilize a three-dimensional object. Four points stabilize four-dimensional space. A point is one dimension.

A point in motion is a line. A line in motion is a plane. A plane in motion is a solid. A solid in motion is time.

The quantum theory applies to time, which progresses in small pulses of very short duration. The universe exists as a phantom between pulses. The power of the phenomena existing in one pulse is enough to generate itself through the gap, the interval of non-being, into existence in the next pulse. An event or phenomenon loses a small parcel of energy each time it is propagated through the gap.

The universe exists and does not exist in regular, rapid succession.

A fixed point in time, or one quantum, stabilizes the continuum, which is how everything happens at once.

STARDUST BOULEVARD

Daniel Sernine

Translated by Jane Brierley

Morning. Fountain Place. The square is in shadow and will remain so for long hours yet, because buildings border it on three sides. As I sit in the shade looking up at a boundless blue sky, the fresh morning air soothes the fevers of the night.

The Place is deserted. It couldn't be otherwise: the morning calm, the morning mood implies solitude. I'd be startled to see someone else here. I wonder—was it possible to find yourself alone like this, to *feel* alone, at peace, in the days when there were billions of people on this planet?

My cough reverberates sharply between the façades.

It's so vast here, the wind blows so freely I find it hard to imagine that it was once unbearably crowded; perhaps not in this neighbourhood of tall buildings and esplanades.

The concrete rim I'm sitting on is still cool from the night. I don't remember deciding to sit down. That's one of the benefits of being stoned: you don't have to decide what you'll do or say; some apparently independent mental mechanism looks after it.

Running water. The soft gurgle is that of city water rather than a brook. It rises within a thin glass wall and streams down the outer surface. With a little imagination it might be a curtain of water. From one level to another it has been cascading for decades, polishing the surfaces and rounding off the rough edges.

I can't find it in my heart to resent the person who dreamt up these concrete blocks, these rectilinear falls and square pools, a century ago. They have a beauty of their own.

The tall façades are lifeless. Just as well. The only time I saw them in motion they were bending over to grab me. Very unpleasant. Now they are empty, deserted. Not a face at any of the windows, not a curtain fluttering; there must be apartments that no one's gone into for decades. I don't know whether the architect who created this apartment complex had imagined it fully occupied; it can't ever have been the case, anyway, since that was around the time of the Big Sweep. Now only the last two or three floors are lived in. And sometimes one of the unoccupied apartments—when teenagers from the lower town feel like a change of scene.

Well, what do you know. I'm not alone any more. Someone is coming down from one of the top floors by a rope fastened to a balcony. Maher Stelson, of course, unless someone else has had the same idea. He could use the elevator to do his shopping and take his daily exercise, but the rope is . . . more fitting.

Except that one of these days he's going to go splat on the esplanade. Blood and brains all over the place. That'll keep us amused for a while. Nice of him.

In the meantime I'm going in. I'm no longer alone with my morning.

Caught up in a farandole, a great motley caterpillar that gets longer with every wriggle. I was stoned before I came, and here I am on Stardust Boulevard cavorting under the Carnival lanterns without really meaning to.

Cavorting. . . . Perhaps finding. . . .

It isn't very crowded—it never is, even if nearly the whole town is here—but the blare of the loudspeakers is deafening: music, laughter and exclamations, excited voices. You get used to the contradiction of hearing the noise of a lively crowd when there isn't one; anybody not in the know would put it down to being stoned.

A little hand, tepid, soft, slightly limp, takes mine on the left. I turn and see a small woman behind me, a girl perhaps. She's simply dressed: fringed jacket over a flowered blouse. Curly, blond locks over a white face and a sad smile. Deep, shadowed eyes that look elsewhere.

The hand holding my right is icy. The woman is tall and slender; greendelight has turned her into a double-jointed marionette. I see her capering about, pliable bones going every which way. She seems to be able to do anything with her body and still hold together by some miracle. Her face is mauve underneath the pink frizz, three green ovals surround her mouth and eyes. I can't see her costume clearly; lots of veils and feathers, a train streaming out behind her as she rushes along. But her eyes . . . her eyes when she turns around and looks right through me, laughing wildly . . . I break the chain and leave the farandole.

I begin working my way against the flow of the parade. I'll be able to see everyone this way. And perhaps I'll find what I'm looking for.

Image after image. I don't see them come, I don't see them go. I live only in a very finished present that excludes all continuity. To keep it that way, I light up another joint.

The pageant goes on. Characters the size of elephants, escaped from a vial of greendelight. Floating in front of a brilliantly lit UFO, a large alien advances, toga white, hair silver, face blue with an enigmatic beauty. Around him little green men dance in a circle.

Here comes a grotesque lunar excursion module made of balsa wood and silver paper, supported by two trotting legs emerging from its blast pipe. Half a dozen ungainly midgets in space suits bounce around it with the comic slow-motion of astronauts.

A huge, silky dove, washbasin white, skims the ground. I pass under one of its stiff, slowly beating wings, coming out with my hair covered in confetti-sequins thrown by the Priestesses of Peace, their eyes perpetually turned heavenward.

Here is Christ. On his big cardboard cross he's laughing his head off while some skinheads in orange togas prance around him with cymbal and fife.

The balloons have passed by. I watch them go, then turn to find myself face to face with a dragon.

It undulates, a thing of crepe paper and streamers with a fabulous head —a real oriental demon. It spits fire and people draw back, shrieking, excited.

A woman surges forward, twirling in the space cleared by the dragon's breath. It's the junkie I just left, the green and mauve one. Her laughter is demented, her eyes more glittering than ever. The long veils swirl around her, and the rosy hair looks as though electrified by a Van de Graaff generator.

People fall silent and watch. A reeling drunk bumps into the nearest loudspeaker stand and knocks it over. A resonant sputter: the music, laughter and exclamations drop a tone.

She dances, dances, a whirling dervish, twisting and turning, an eddy of colour.

In front of the dragon's head.

That stops its progress and undulates where it stands.

It's ferocious eyes trained on her.

She dances, spins.

Throws herself down on her knees, back arched, arms thrown wide, throat proffered beneath the smoking muzzle.

With a roar of flame, it blasts.

I'm hazy about the time, but there's no mistaking the sun's noonday glare. I would have thought I'd sleep longer, and yet here I am outdoors again, still stoned, but coughing a little less.

Beneath the burning sun the city stretches out in lawns and esplanades, its harmonious buildings rising almost everywhere. All these uninhabited architects' challenges, these sculptural dwellings of glass and concrete, have become monuments. Or memorials?

Their pinnacles pierce the clear sky like blades.

On the esplanade—which one? they have names, I think—Chris and Maryse are seated on the concrete border of an immense square flower bed in the full sunlight.

Should I go up to them? They don't seem to be arguing—even that is too much.

I move forward.

As I walk towards them they remain motionless, apparently silent, looking vaguely at the horizon.

Something is placed between them. What? A candle.

Maryse becomes aware of my presence and recognizes me. A smile—tender? knowing?—lights her thin, angular face.

I draw near.

The candle is lit. In full sunlight. This mania for messages! I don't think I'll stay long.

Stardust Boulevard. The Carnival plays on. The cafés are on a parallel artery, Bloomgarden Street. Why this name? The only things blooming are the café terraces and, behind heavy doors at the foot of staircases, the dens.

No festoons of lights over the street here, only lamps on the café walls.

I come out of Life on Mars. *I'd only found John, Guy and Cornelius, all three already half-stoned. We talked for a bit, with long pauses, like old buddies. Then I left them.*

Moonlight Café. *Faces I've seen before, a few I actually know. I pick a small table on the second terrace, the one overlooking the street on the corner of the Carouseway.*

O'Reilly's doublewhammy. Nothing better for my cough. The first shotglass still makes me wince. But the others slide down easily, and their heat decongests my lungs.

The Carnival music penetrates even here, of course. And the laughter, the exclamations, the excited voices. Powerful loudspeakers.

Now and then the sound of a firecracker, the faint whiff of laughing-gas. Occasionally, bubblelights go by, chased by children shrill with fatigue. It's late.

The Carouseway is not lit. At the end of this dark trench I can see a slice of Stardust Boulevard. Like a stage set from the very back of the theatre. Brilliantly lighted.

Sarabandes. A cavalcade. But there is more noise than there are people. I muse on what Carnivals must have been like before the Big Sweep, when there were millions and millions of people in the cities. New Orleans! Venice! Quebec! Nice! Trinidad! Rio! It must have been delirious. I've never seen anything like that; it's hard to imagine. . . . But it must have been hell to make them come to that decision. I'm not one to complain about the Big Sweep, anyway. How could you —how did you —merely survive in this city when there were a thousand times more people? It's beyond comprehension, like trying to picture the immensity of the galaxy. In any case, no one complains about the Big Sweep these days, not even old people; they're just glad to be able to breathe freely.

The thing is, if the Big Sweep had really succeeded there'd be no Earthlings left.

"Munchies, mister?"

Why not? The boy is perhaps twelve, thirteen. Dark-haired, pretty. His made-up eyes have an equivocal look. He carries his munchies in a basket like a flower girl her roses. I select a yellow one.

"Munchies? Munchies?"

He moves off, threading his way between the tables. I look away.

Well, now. There's a face I've seen recently. On the first terrace, the one at street level. Beside the wrought-iron railing. Alone at a table.

The blond from the farandole.

That mop of hair like pale seaweed gathered on the shore. Bizarre: one long, curled strand; one long, frizzed strand; one curled; one frizzed. Two panels of alternating threads drape a pale, so pale, face.

Dark, unfathomable eyes.

Something strange. I can't put my finger on it.

Flickering. The girl and her table are flickering like a candle flame in a draft. The munchy is working.

I look towards the Boulevard. The lighted scene stands out like a series of frames on a film strip.

More inflatable allegories. A large, rotund tree. Then another and another, prancing along. Next a cohort of flowers, their faces indistinguishable at the centre of their corollas.

Now I see only one frame at a time. The receding ones fade out behind one another, away from the present. The coming images are still blurred, transparent, ahead of reality.

Everything radiates gold. The golden gleam of the torches. The golden lightbulbs in the illuminated wreaths. The gold lamé of some of the costumes. The sousaphones and tubas of a brass band.

My camera eye reverts to the terrace. The pale-faced little blond has left. Is that her disappearing down Bloomgarden Street? Too bad.

The munchy is already losing its potency. It's just candy.

Another shot of doublewhammy and I'll be off to the Straynight Cabaret.

The sky has changed. No, not the sky: it has stayed blue, limpid. But what must be a wind of very high altitude is pushing big white clouds along. It creates an atmosphere, a very special light, a continual contrast between chiaroscuro and full sun. I don't like this weather; the light is too harsh, too brusque in its variations, and I feel threatened, uncomfortable. Such days put me in a very odd mood. Not really depressive, a sort of aggravated consciousness. Of time fleeting. Time wasted. Of dabblings leading nowhere. Of the inanity of doing anything.

Uptown, where the daring but empty buildings are—empty,

but carefully maintained for aesthetic reasons—robot-sweepers stream along the esplanades and automatic mowers whirr in the parks. On the lawns the idlers flourish. In Century Park I catch sight of Philip underneath the great trees.

Philip passes the time making art objects.

They're fine. You can't deny the things he does are fine. They're difficult to describe. Sculpture? They're more like three-dimensional collages. Stained glass and precious stones assembled on delicate metal frames.

He's just finished one and is showing it in the park. Standing on its granite pedestal it looks to me like a cylinder in shades of sapphire, amethyst and garnet, set in silver. Apparently it's supposed to sing as well, at dawn and dusk. Rapid variations of light and heat activate chords memorized in the very structure of crystal and gems.

I stop beside the artist in front of the pedestal.

"Has it got a title?"

"I'm open to suggestion."

He's almost bald, with a greying beard. And yet he's not so old. But burnt out. Why? Because he's put too much of himself into his works? They're stale as dregs. Or so it seems to me. But perhaps that's the way he's made. Who am I to judge?

"So—what do you suggest?"

I think of the candle in full sun.

"Leisure Society."

I don't think he appreciates it. I move away.

Seated on the edge of the man-made lake, a little girl searches gravely in her bag of marbles. She's having fun. Is she having fun? Perhaps; she's too young to be bored. She's having fun throwing them in the pond to make circles.

Passing close to her I notice that the marbles are jewels. Emeralds, diamonds, rubies, roughly cut.

They make a very ordinary plop as they hit the water.

The dens.
Smoky, sewer-dark.
Syncopated flashes above the sweaty, gleaming torsos, dancing, dancing.

The music is a solid block. And a powerful rhythm, making the room a monstrous, engorged heart.

But it's a trick: the room is tiny, the walls covered with mirrors. The crowding is an illusion, a few dozen seem like several hundred. Sometimes you find that after fifteen minutes of ardent looks, the face you're eyeing is your own. Cruising yourself: the height of narcissism! Or just schizo.

In the dens the looks are heavy, the hands insistent. Here is a woman — or is it? Here is a man — or is it? Doubt blossoms in the shadows. The couples that form and leave give rise to the wildest speculation. For many, the doubt continues until they're in bed. And even after.

I haven't found what I'm looking for.

Haven't even been able to get near the bar to have a drink.

I saw the little munchy-vendor, but someone carried him off. Too bad.

An eddy among the surrounding people brings me face to face with an Erymaean — well, I'm not sure whether he's an Atropian, a Psychaean, a Dissident or God knows what. I've never been able to figure out all these parties. But in general you can recognize Erymaeans by their subtly tragic expression, by their air of purposefulness. They haven't that vacuous look we Earthlings get from being idle. But it's something very subtle, something you feel rather than see.

This one really looks the part. There are people like that; Philip, for instance. They really have — or else they contrive to have, consciously or not — the face that corresponds to their calling or station. The stereotype.

He's clothed in black with simple silver embroidery. Some Erymaeans like sombre colours. And he is sombre: black hair greying at the temples; serious eyes surrounded by a network of fine lines; thin, pale lips from having smiled too little; a lean face with something aristocratic in its features.

I wonder what he's doing here? I wouldn't have thought that Erymaeans frequented dens. But no doubt he's here for a reason.

He's already behind me, out of my line of vision.

I'm leaving because the smoke really isn't helping my cough.

The air in the street seems cold, making me shiver. This isn't very healthy either. The night closes behind me, peopled with furtive shadows.

Probing hands in the den have given me a furious desire to screw. Let's go to the woods.

In the azure sky the moon is in its first quarter. Its texture by day is not at all the same as by night: this crescent, this demi-circle, looks as insubstantial as mist. Hard to believe it's a globe of rock, especially the part you can't see—invisible, therefore transparent?—and yet it's tangible. But you see the clear blue of the sky where you know the other half of the globe exists. Come to think of it, do you *know*? Doesn't its existence depend on the light it receives—and if not lighted, then non-existent? If the blue of the sky were *behind* the moon, you'd see a white crescent and the rest of the globe in black. Therefore the blue of the sky is *in front* of the moon: but that's also an illusion, merely the effect of light and optics. Everything is illusion, Philip would say. Except that he deludes himself with words. I've tried to deceive myself with empty arguments, tried to make them dizzingly metaphysical, but it doesn't work: the moon is still there, concrete, whole, I *know* it. Even when smoking I'm not able to make reality abstract, to escape.

Amusing to think that the people of Argus are perhaps behind the transparent, immaterial portion of the moon; a tiny dot in the blue sky, to the left of the first quarter.

Now why did I think of Argus? Is the city still inhabited? They haven't anything left to observe: the Earthlings are so quiet, so inoffensive, since becoming a mere handful, no longer obliged to fight over land and resources. Are the underground halls of Argus deserted? Or are they haunted too, like our cities, by a few people whom leisure has rendered hollow, shallow, without ties—mere party balloons. Has boredom overtaken the Erymaeans? What a joke: to be condemned to idleness by Peace on Earth, their *raison d'être* since time immemorial.

A hand touches my arm before I reach Stardust Boulevard. I turn my head: the Erymaean of a moment ago. A Psychaean, I now observe; the breeze has lifted a lock of hair from his temple, revealing the small triangular interface.

He scrutinizes me intently, as though to scan not my mind but my soul, if in fact I have one.

I submit to his scrutiny without flinching, and, funny thing, I imagine the contrast between the black diamonds of his hard, piercing eyes with their clear-cut irises, and my own as they must be at the moment: washed-out blue seeping into the rosy-veined whites, as though melting in the water that constantly bathes my eyes.

Everything about him seems clear cut: his elegant but sober costume, his precise way of speaking, his intensity. It's the intensity, I think, that I envy; I feel I'm always . . . blurred, vague.

"Are you happy?"

What's he getting at? And that almost solicitous air, as though he really cared about my happiness, about the happiness of us Earthlings. They've always been concerned about us.

Just curiosity? More than that. Is he conducting a sociological survey? His question seems more like a heartfelt cry.

"I'm okay," I answer. "I can't complain."

"But still—don't you sense . . . something missing, some uneasiness?"

Some uneasiness! I should ask him to spend a few days inside my head; then he'd see. Some uneasiness. . . . Yes, perhaps: to live is an uneasiness. But I'm not about to unburden my soul to him in the midst of the thronging Carnival crowd—we've reached the Boulevard and its merrymaking. I answer by telling him what I'm missing most.

"Right now what I want most is a good screw."

"There must be something else. . . ."

"So long, buddy. At least try to have a little fun."

I think I've disappointed him. No, not really disappointed. Hurt. He carries a burden of hurt that I've made a bit heavier, just a bit. But he could have stopped anyone in the street and got the same sort of answer, or an even more curt retort. For a moment I think of turning back and saying, "You shouldn't worry about us; we're okay like this, I suppose. There's no way we'd want to live like they did in the last century."

I look behind me. He's standing where I left him, scanning the merrymakers with a sombre eye. He's not going to interrogate anyone else. It was just something that came over him all of a sudden; he spotted me — perhaps I also look very much the part.

Poor guy. I'd rather be me than you, with all those gloomy thoughts festering in your head. Is it remorse? You should have a fix of green-delight; it'd do you good, make you forget.

A cortège of inflatable myths hides him from view: great country bumpkins swollen to bursting, girls in peasant skirts and ankle-boots, pink with health. I bump into someone—I should look where I'm going—and then a really clever juggler by the roadside makes me forget all about the Erymaean.

Not really, though; who can forget the Erymaeans?

I've lost the moon and here I am, alone again, between two long buildings that form an artificial canyon. The shade is cool at the end of the day.

This is the silence I like. I don't think anyone lives here.

The slice of sky is blue, with a few fast-moving, grey-bellied clouds. I stop and look up. I like it when there are clouds. You'd think the tops of the buildings were moving against a steady background of sky. Like standing at the bowsprit of a ship. Dizzying, even when you haven't had anything. When you're stoned, it's better to stretch out on the concrete; it creates the perfect illusion.

Time passes unnoticed.

Children's voices. I turn to look, propping myself up on one elbow.

Over there in the square. Two or three kids on low-slung tricycles, the ones with a huge front wheel and gears. The fun is in skidding around corners, but at those speeds it's dangerous. The kids are helmeted and swathed in elbow guards and kneepads.

One of them heads in my direction.

I watch him coming the length of the canyon.

Quite effective.

He jams on the pedals, braking at my feet. I've risen.

"Come and see, mister. Aeros."

He turns on a dime; look at the way he handles that cycle! And off he goes. I run after him, feeling like a teenager with my beat-up running shoes, my jeans and T-shirt. I feel the wind in my long hair—a bit stiff; I'll have to see about washing it.

I pass the little guy, but by the time he catches up with me on the square I'm doubled over with a coughing fit. The other kids—are there four?—watch me without a word.

"How old are you?" finally asks a little girl with yellow ribbons.

It's not the one with the jewels. This one's even younger.

"Twenty-two, I think."

I look up at the sky: two aeros. Who had talked of going up?

Charles, I think. And the girl who was with him last time . . .Vonda? It doesn't matter, anyway. Their aeros are high up, you can't hear them. It's mainly the vapour trail that shows they're there. They make patterns, arabesques. Symbols? I'm not stoned enough to read anything into it.

I find they're delaying, dragging out the show. The children have already started pedalling and shouting.

"How old are you?"

It's the same kid.

"I just told you."

"Have you a mom?"

"Everyone has."

"And a dad?"

"Must have."

"And a little brother?"

"Yes."

The crafts have stopped their somersaults.

"How old is he?"

"He's dead."

"How old was he?"

I really think they're getting ready for the grand finale.

"How old was he?"

"Sixteen."

Yes, there they go, letting off all the remaining smoke charges. Red, as it should be.

"How did he die?"

Two thick red lines converge on a huge field of azure.

"How did he die?"

I raise my arm and point.

"Like that."

Short and sharp. Head on.

Did I *see* the aeros break up a fraction of a second before the explosion? Bravo! Not surprising their somersaults were a bit slow, with a payload like that.

The flash has tinged the cloud-bellies pink, hundreds of metres above. Pink, green, a hint of silver in the falling debris. A beautiful combination.

The smoke lasts for quite some time, white as a real cloud but with a glow underneath.

I'll have to find out if that was Charles. I didn't think he was up to such a good performance.

A Carnival night without fireworks wouldn't be the same. Pyrotechnics have certainly improved since the ancient Chinese, but I don't think the ritual of exclamations has changed. The oohs! and ahs! of the spectators are those of my grandparents on public holidays. I don't think you ever get tired of it. Except that fireworks can't fill your whole life.

In Century Park at the end of Stardust Boulevard I find a good place to look up at the sky. I should have taken two munchies from the little vendor just now in the Moonlight Café. *They're best when you're watching fireworks.*

Among the heads lit up by the explosions I see a light gold one. The girl with the curly-frizzy-curly hair. Her head is lowered, her pale face in shadow. And her eyes are two wells of darkness.

Still the same sad, fixed smile.

I realize that unconsciously I've been looking for her.

She manoeuvres her way between the people and animated sculptures, walking purposefully towards the park woods. She's taken off her sandals and lets her feet drag on the grass. Waves of whistling rockets—the kind that don't go very high and form a curtain of colours—silhouette her against the light, a frail outline on a luminous ground, her head a fluffy halo.

I stay a moment to watch the sprays, the showers of gold, the bursts of colour, the fleeting comets, the small, blinding suns.

Then I climb the gentle slope as far as the woods.

The echo of Carnival fades as you go beyond the first line of trees. Even the explosions are somewhat subdued. The flashes filter through the young leaves, lighting the scene in snatches. People leaning against the trees, or strolling, hands in their pockets.

As you penetrate the wood, the human density increases. There are almost as many people as on the Boulevard. They scrutinize each other as they pass, but the darkness only allows them an impression. Guys? Girls? Men? Women? Everything is in the way they walk, linger, turn their heads to look intently at one another.

Hands furtively probing to check or make contact. Hands gently pushed away, or grasped and held.

Murmurs. Friends meet, recognize each other, light up a joint, part to continue the round.

From the thickets come whispers, sighs, raucous breathing.

In the heart of the woods is where it happens. In couples. Leaning against trees, stretched out beside a bush or one kneeling while the other stands. In clusters on the grass, confused movements, soft slitherings, glimpses of white skin when a flash lights up the sky. Passersby meld, separate, in incessant rotation.

Gasps, sucks, hisses.

I don't enter into the orgy, not for now, at any rate. You can't always control what's happening; my anus is still sore from being buggered yesterday evening because I was too stoned to get myself out of a tangle of arms and legs.

I go back to the less thriving section.

And there, in front of me, is the little blond again.

Perhaps she's what I'm looking for?

She looks at me steadily, deeply. The fixed smile on her pale face makes me uncomfortable.

My hand seeks hers. Slim and warm. Soft, slightly limp. Like in the farandole.

Almost blindly we reach a bank and lie down on it.

That pathetic smile, that unmoving face. . . .

I bring mine close to hers.

With a rapid movement she lifts hers off.

Her mask.

My lips touch hers before I've had time to see her real face. My fingers find it slim, angular, firm-skinned. And the eyes that open when I open mine are the black holes that I wanted to sink into.

Her blouse opens on slight breasts. How old is she, then?

Awkward rubbings and squirmings. Our jeans are off at last, our legs find each other, entwine, our bodies roll.

The damp triangle is not blond. I look up, see a dark head with short hair. The wig is on the grass, near my T-shirt rolled up in a ball. The fireworks have stopped.

The rest happens as usual. Even stoned, I come right away—the hands in the den really turned me on—but I keep it up until she shudders and lies quiet.

I've heard those stifled little cries before.

We go on for a moment, giving pleasure to our bodies that came here for this purpose. But it isn't as if the little blond were . . . what she seemed.

But just what am I looking for? It's pathetic: I don't even have a clear idea. And when I find it, if there is anything to find, it will be vague, uncertain. Am I actually looking for someone? *That would be too easy: I might end up finding someone, there aren't that many of us. A mirage, then, that will always elude my grasp just when I think I've caught it?*

I'm asking too many questions. There are times like this, especially after making love, when my mind becomes cruelly lucid despite the smoke I inhale.

It doesn't last, fortunately, and the next day I take up where I left off.

The girl and I get dressed. She puts her wig back on, but not her mask. We head towards the edge of the woods.

Her hand feels for mine. I take it. Soft and warm, but now her clasp is firm.

A little before reaching the open area of the Park, those vast lawns planted with singing sculptures, we stop for a last kiss. Passionate, as is often the case here, expressing the tacit closeness, the almost pathetic moment of great tenderness, the complicity of two absurd lives that, for the space of an embrace, have sought to reach something together.

Already our bodies move away from each other. Her hand grasps mine hard, and I return the pressure. Then we drop hands and, without looking back, I walk towards Stardust Boulevard where the Carnival hasn't yet run out of steam.

I think that was Maryse.

At twilight people stroll on the promenade overlooking the lower town. If we were in a seaside resort this would be the boardwalk along the ocean front, with bonfires on the dunes, cocktails on the villa patios, with poets, actors and artists.

Here there are also poets, actors and artists, and this evening most of them will go down to Stardust Boulevard to play among the Carnival characters, masked and music-making, to recite their verses on the café terraces, to dance and show their fine bodies in the dens.

I lean on the balustrade, my head swimming a little, my stomach churning.

The Boulevard is lighting up for the Carnival, but all I can see are the images of this day. The aeros and Charles, my little sixteen-year-old brother. Chris and his candle lighted in full sun.

Maher Stelson is dead. I saw him sprawled on the concrete when I went home just now to shower and change. Blood and brains splattered all over the place, as I'd pictured. Greendelight sometimes gives you premonitions. Too bad he did it when I wasn't around. In fact, it seems that no one saw it happen: the body was lying alone, still warm. Poor Stelson. Climbing up and down his rope every day for months on end—it was a good idea—and then to flub his exit line like that. . . .

There's a planetary show tonight. Before going down to the Carnival I'll stay on the promenade for a while and watch, since it's beginning in a minute.

And not a munchy vendor in sight.

The ships have all lit up at once. There must be at least twenty in translunar orbit.

They form a four-pronged star. That pulses and fades. Hey, look at that! They make a line that must stretch halfway across the sky. A vast, synchronized movement, from east to west, like a bow drawn across the firmament. Then the ships close up.

What speeds they must be doing!

Energy beams! From one ship to another, a line of bluish, vibrating lights. A good start, if they're going to stay up for an hour.

It might have been an interesting job. Astronaut. Of course, it's no big deal, just entertainment for idlers. But all the same, to see good old Earth from up there. Now it's done by remote control and they don't need pilots. They wouldn't have picked me anyway; my health isn't good enough.

I'm impatient to see the Northern Lights. Nothing beats it, whatever else they try. Especially when one doesn't have to live up north to see it.

Strange how the best things never last and leave you feeling let down. . . . Yesterday it was that little blond with the sad smile who succeeded in making herself desirable simply by appearing here and there during my trip. The planetary show just now; unforgettable, yes. But I'm already off my high.

Broadgate Street, and no one's going uptown. We're all going in the same direction, towards Stardust Boulevard, towards the cafés and the dens. In little groups, in couples, and alone; there's something to look at and enjoy, in any case.

Tonight again I'll search among the masks and costumes, among the inflatable myths. Beneath the festoons of light, the torches and Chinese lanterns, the bubblelights.

The loudspeakers are already broadcasting music, laughter and exclamations, excited voices.

A particularly violent coughing fit brings my supper up. Just as well, I won't have anything on my stomach. I'd better go by the Moonlight Café *early, though, and have a shot of O'Reilly's doublewhammy.*

The people going down talk of nothing but the planetary show.

"That Catherine Wheel!"

"And the laser battle!"

True, it was a success.

Trainers cross the street with enormous tigers on leashes. Those eyes! Those green eyes! Awesome!

Small circles of four dancers form, chasing each other like links from a broken necklace. A circle opens for me. I stick my joint between my lips and take the two proffered hands.

Tonight again I'll search among the café terraces and in the smoke of the dens. On the grass and among the trees of Century Park.

On Stardust Boulevard the Carnival plays on.

LAST WILL AND TESTAMENT OF THE UNKNOWN EARTHMAN LOST IN THE SECOND VEGAN CAMPAIGN

D.M. Price

You are the one
Solid the spaces lean on, envious.
> Sylvia Plath, "Nick and the Candlestick"

Sum of yellow
Blue total
A black fraction

He's a bruise on time's trajectory, a drop
Of a few years generated here to there, homing
His thin thread past the facets deep
Into this diamond's dark
Cornered heart

Dead astronaut, taut solid, he's the very brink
Of the line he travels, bent
On a hunt for himself, falling

Introduced, open
Mouthed, he's the current star
Boarder in coma's bright house, aging
Alien, a god
Though in the germ

What are his sad recognitions?
A flicker of earth in a golden shaft, topaz
Belt of river sky the kingfisher never leaves
Ignored red brook that, drying
Babbles earth's patriotisms
Into strange dusts, his legacy
Of the one

Green able moment
A wave in your night
My love
Farewell

Radiating passage
He splits the veil in the rift
Of us

Crystal cataract, Antares' eye, he leaves
The three gifts of a bitten god

You. Me. A wasp at the window

THE WOMAN WHO IS
THE MIDNIGHT WIND

Terence M. Green

Juturna, 20-4-3

I really should have started a journal seasons ago. Probably when I first arrived on Juturna. Or at least when Jacques died.

But I did not.

I am starting one now.

I am hoping, I guess, that this may shape my life, however weakly. This is, of course, a mild delusion of grandeur. Just mild though. Nevertheless, if I choose to delude myself, very well, then I choose to delude myself. In this, I feel akin to the rest of my species.

20-4-7

Knowledge that a woman who has injured you is aging is, indeed, a constant vengeance.

Since I am no longer a young woman, this observation strikes me pointedly. Being one of Juturna's original colonists, I have been here twenty J-years. I have forgotten the formula that I knew when we immigrated, but I think that I am now about fifty Terran years old. I stopped worrying about it—mostly after Jacques died.

Note the irony that I am the woman who has injured me—many times, in many ways. I am not sure that reflecting upon my aging can ever be adequate vengeance for my various follies.

Am I a woman more sinned against than sinning?
Most often I think not.

20-4-9

I think of Jacques often.

He was too good for me. No politician, Jacques. No language but the language of the heart.

Who would have guessed that I would outlive him?

I, who connived to marry him, to have a mate to light out to the stars with. . . . In his innocence, he wedded me, took me unto him, as they might say classically, and together we leapt the stars to Juturna.

This journal turns increasingly inward. I had no idea of what it might evolve into, but I think I'm surprising myself. Perhaps I am no longer young enough for the guile needed merely to catalogue the events of each day. Indeed, my days are seldom different from one another any more. Three days a week I do volunteer work at the hospital. Such work is desperately needed.

I am the one who needs it.

20-4-10

Juturna—why here?

Jacques' work, of course. He loved the idea of being one of the top engineers on a Colony World; he was also idealistic and romantic enough to want the challenge.

Challenge. The word seems alien to me now.

As a Class-A World, we are fully equipped with high-tech via the Lightships that come down on the Big Continent weekly.

I am no scientist, but I know the basics about my world. I know that Juturna is about 420 light-years from Earth in the direction of Ursa Major. I know that Juturna is the only habitable planet in our system of eight planets. I know that our sun is a K2 star, slightly cooler and redder than Sol, that Juturna is similar in size to Earth (a bit larger, actually), that the seasons are longer, that we rotate rapidly enough to stimulate a cyclone-breeding Coriolis force, so that our weather is usually quite awful. And wet.

What else do I remember? Let me see. That our sun is not up to Sol in mass or luminosity, that we are quite close to our sun (the closest planet, in fact), that it's a good ol' star, about five billion years old and counting. . . .

I am cataloguing at last. Is this what my journal will be?

Somehow, I do not think that it is enough.

20-4-12

I am endeavouring to treat the subject of myself best. But many questions arise.

Should I treat the days objectively? Or should I subjectively treat my emotional reactions to the days as they pass?

Can I indulge in a stream-of-consciousness style? Can I be all things to myself? Will I be fully honest? Or is that last the stance of a fool?

In truth, I know that I am writing this because I am no longer young (such an understatement!). Perhaps I see this as my testament to posterity, my feeble attempt to live beyond my physical years. In my more idealistic moments, I see it as a chance to record and comment on the atomic particles of truth that I have stumbled across in my voyage through both the chronological and the light-years. In my more cynical moments, I see it as a form of therapy. It is probably, in small measure, both.

My hands are arthritic as I write this; the dampness of the day seizes my right knee with pain. I cannot totally escape my physical self as I sit here, but perhaps I can peer further inward, down the funnel of my ego.

Perhaps.

Today at the hospital, for instance, I spent time with a woman who was suffering horribly from a blood disorder that is causing epidermal purpura, and swelling of the joints. She is a young woman, recently arrived with her husband. The doctors say that it is an allergic reaction to something, but they cannot pin it down.

And how could they pin it down? Man has known Juturna for such a brief span. Adaptation of a species to an environment, as we know it, swallows aeons. Yet the Juturnans adapt to their environment daily, and prior to our arrival there was no such thing as "species"—just "Juturnans."

The Juturnans themselves are products of specific evolution, are they not? In this great, damp world, they are awesome in their alienness, profound in their similarity to us. The closest Terran composite would be a reptile-human, though of course they are neither reptile nor human, but merely Juturnan (can I use this word to describe a complexity?). The rain, the wetness, the vast seas—all have contributed to the evolution of these solemn creatures.

Jacques had found them—the Juturnans—fascinating.

And what had he known of anthropology? An engineer, supervising road-building, bridge-building. . . . He had often sat on one of his river projects and watched a lone, grey-skinned shape emerge from the undergrowth, study him and his crew with curious and perplexing eyes, then fade unassumingly back into the omnipresent greenery. There was an undefined concept of *laissez-faire* that permeated relations between us and them.

Jacques had said many times that he should make notes of their behaviour patterns—for those who could better interpret them.

But that was before the mudslide.

That was before I was left here alone.

20-4-14

Today I stayed at home all morning, venturing out only in the afternoon for exercise and some shopping.

I am tired.

I ache.

Tomorrow I will go to the hospital to try to forget my own pains. Such irony.

Tonight, as I sit in bed, I will read a story or two from the works of the Irish writer Liam O'Flaherty. I have worked my way through Hemingway, Faulkner, Poe, Lawrence, Joyce in the last five seasons. O'Flaherty is a concise *evocateur* of landscapes and emotions. His descriptions of the awesomely desolate Aran Islands of his birthplace remind me in many ways of our settlement on Juturna. There is the same mixture of beauty and ugliness.

Juturna has yet to produce a Literature. How long does it take, I wonder? Who will capture this place for future generations?

Perhaps we are too busy surviving as yet to afford the luxury of creating our own art. We must import it still.

My hands are cold. I fold them one in the other as I sit here in the evening.

20-4-15

I must catalogue an event.

Today, at the hospital, a Silent Child was born.

It has never happened before in Egerton—although such creatures have been born in two of the larger cities on the Big Continent. The entire community is unsettled; word-of-mouth has spread the news like cell-division.

I, myself, am unable to comprehend the bizarre nature of the incident. I focus on the mother. Why would she do it?

I would have aborted.

But then, I would never have had intercourse with a Juturnan in the first place.

Why would she?

Why would *anybody*?

We are strange creatures, we humans. We are often as alien to one another as we are to an "alien" species.

With whom are we to relate?

I once read, while browsing through some old books on rhetoric at the library, something that Winston Churchill observed in a radio broadcast early in the twentieth century: ". . . we learn that we are spirits, not animals, and that something is going on in space and time, which, whether we like it or not, spells duty."

If I could only be certain of what this duty is. Churchill seemed so sure. But then, it was the strength of his convictions, the strength of his personality, that forged for him his place in history.

Something is definitely "going on in space and time."

But what duty does it describe?

20-4-17

The first sign, they say, occurs when the doctor pulls the child from its mother's womb, anticipating the cry of life that should ensue. But the Silent Child does not cry out. Nor does it breathe, speak, laugh or cry as it grows.

Yet it lives.

It is half human, half Juturnan.

And just as we fail to understand what it is to be human most of the time, we definitely fail to grasp what it must be to be Juturnan.

Juturnans, as we know from rare autopsies performed upon

cadavers stumbled upon through accident (or fortuitous circumstances, if you wish), are silent; they have no larynges. More importantly, they are changing rapidly, coverging with *Homo sapiens* almost before our eyes. They have adapted fully to their wet world, surely evolving from their seas as we did from ours, but with this new evolutionary wrinkle. The only constant from generation to generation seems to be the ability to survive for long periods of time without breathing. The popular theory is that they extract oxygen through the mucous membranes of their pharynges and cloaca, and probably through their skin as well. In this, they are not unlike Terran turtles. There is another school of thought that believes Juturnans can dispense with respiration completely, deriving energy from an oxygenless breakdown of glycogen.

Whatever. They are one of the universe's magnificent complexities, and there is much for us to learn yet . . . as indicated by the fact that cross-breeding is indeed a reality, if not a pleasant one.

But what drove this woman to such a demeaning act?

Why would she bring such a creature into the world?

All my reservations convince me that it would be best for all if the doctors did not allow them to live after birth. Perhaps simply tell the mother that it had been still-born.

My curiosity is scudding along like the night-clouds. To have this happen right here in Egerton! It is astounding.

This is a rupture in the colonial fabric which represents the casting aside of the ultimate taboo. This miscegenation has no context, other than mythology. But this is no myth—no minotaur or Pan. This is a reality. And therein lies its horror, its fascination.

What will the mother do?

Others, apparently, gave their Silent Children up for adoption, in all cases, and all re-emigrated, with full governmental cooperation.

And the Children?

Well, strange as they are, they do live and thrive; and they do breathe, but in the manner of Juturnans—that is, almost intermittently, and without concern for the process.

They learn, and seem to understand much. Yet we do not understand them.

20-4-19

Today I visited the mother. My curiosity was overpowering, and I do have access as a "charitable volunteer." The doctors thought that I might do some good.

She is young—so young. A mere girl. Not more than fifteen or sixteen J-years old. I know now why she did not abort. She had not the sense nor the knowledge.

She was propped in bed watching video, eating candy and combing her hair—which is dark and stringy. She is not attractive. The poor child has an acne problem and is slightly overweight. Her eyes are hazel, quick, darting and shallow. She said to call her Marie—a lovely name.

I came prepared—for what? For disgust? For morbid voyeurism? Whatever it was that I had anticipated melted away during the course of my stay with Marie. She does not have full comprehension of either her act or its consequences. In truth, kindly put, she is not very bright.

We chatted for a while about how she felt, and all her responses were concerned solely with her physical pains, her bodily functions. The Child, she told me quietly, and with a faraway look in her eyes, would be given up for adoption. She and her family could either re-emigrate or re-locate on the Big Continent. Her father, a farmer, apparently favoured the latter, feeling there would be sufficient anonymity for them all there.

For their sakes, I hope that he is right.

I asked her if she had seen it. The Child.

She said "no", adding that she did not want to see it either. Her eyes became distant again, then hardened like marbles. Her mouth compressed tightly.

I dropped the subject.

She returned to her juggling of pastimes: watching video, combing her hair, and selecting another sugar-coated pacifier.

I said that I would visit her again, if she wished. She smiled, but did not indicate "yes" or "no".

"I don't want to move away," she said, finally. "All my friends are here. But I guess I'll have to."

She was chewing nonchalantly as I left.

20-4-22

I went to see it today. The Child. It is a male. To my surprise, bewilderment even, he looked no different from other infants in the nursery, except for a dark, grey-green pigmentation, and his stillness.

He was awake but silent.

I was prepare to be repelled, frightened, sickened. I was none of these. He is just a baby. As I looked upon him, I confounded myself by feeling slightly moved. *This* I was not prepared for.

His gaze suddenly locked onto my own. Can he see me? I wondered. What does he know, if anything?

For five minutes or more I let him play upon the scale of my emotions.

Then, scarcely aware that I was doing it, I lifted him gently, held him as one would any infant, while we stared into, and perhaps through one another.

I am a woman, and today, despite his strangeness, the Child comforted me.

I have learned something here. Not about aliens. About myself.

I must sort it out. Carefully.

20-4-24

Women: wiser than men?

A woman understands the importance of her femininity; a man never seems to grasp his masculinity. The explosiveness of the male life-force has always struck me as so frenzied, that it must preclude any true self-evaluation. I have always entertained the wonderful conceit that my woman's slower rhythms keep me more truly in touch with the more harmonious elements of the universe.

Even here on Juturna, where the soil is powder-grey when dry, more often mud when wet; where the daytime skies are wildly crimson, and the nights are haunted by a midnight wind . . . even here, I try to place myself, however roughly, in space and time. . . .

Since Jacques died, there have been others. And as much as they felt any seduction was theirs, I knew that it was mine.

I see them, and I see myself, swirling in gaseous clouds, and I sense the tides of my planet; I become a part of it. They are always separate.

It is true.

I do not know why the wind blows at night here on Juturna, but I know this: the wind is a woman.

I tended my garden today, pulling a few weeds from among the blueyes. But the more I separated the weeds from the delicate domestics, the less certain I became as to which was the intruder. My decision to groom the totality appeared suddenly presumptuous.

I am lying in bed tonight, writing this, aware of the arbitrariness of casual living.

Outside, it is black, and the wind is singing.

20-4-26

I cannot keep myself from the child. When I should be visiting the bed-ridden, as I have promised to do, I go instead to him. I sit beside him, and allow his hand to squeeze my index finger. The contact is becoming more important than I could ever have dreamed.

Louisa, the nurse whose hours coincide with mine, watched curiously at first; but today she could contain herself no longer.

"You know," she began, with no little hostility, "what that thing is—what it means."

We were sorting and folding linens—the white for the third floor, blue for the second.

"I don't know what you mean," I said.

"They say that those things have been modifying and transmogrifying for ages—that they are the only species here because they consume everything else."

"You're talking about the Silent Child?" I knew what she was talking about.

"I'm talking about that thing in there—that thing that's taken

111

your fancy." Her tone was just shy of scorn now.

"It's only a baby, Louisa."

"From what I've read," she continued, "the Juturnan sperm—or whatever it is—consumes the ovum and extracts all the genetic information from it. It's just the opposite of human conception."

She straightened, folded a blue pillowcase, looked at me sternly. "It's as if *they* are devouring *us*." She set the pillowcase aside to add emphasis, sighed, then added: "I'm at a total loss as to how you can be at ease with that thing the way you are. I think the whole thing is creepy."

I did not respond. Louisa said no more, perhaps out of embarrassment. She had said what she felt needed saying.

I am having strange thoughts of late. I am having even more trouble recording them here, since they do not flow smoothly or logically. They spring from a deep well, bubble forth for brief instants, then seep back quietly, as if into soft loam.

Words will not carry them forth.

They will not catalogue.

20-4-28

I wonder where my daughter is, what she is doing now? Is she still on Earth, or has she too, like so many others her age, lighted to the stars to seek a grail?

I was a terrible mother to Genevieve. But then my first marriage was terrible—terrible in its brevity and futility. Pierre took Genevieve after the divorce, and I did nothing to contest it.

Jacques . . . he was the ship that was leaving port, and I set sail on him. He was holed on a reef, sank rapidly, ungracefully, beneath the mud of Juturna. I am marooned.

I did not count on this.

On Juturna, the clouds move more swiftly than on Earth. When I sit in the afternoon and watch them race across the crimson skies, I feel a part of some frantic movement. I must breathe deeply to relax.

My thoughts, of late, excite me as the clouds do.

One can gaze directly at the sun here, and then contemplate the blurry outline of shadows that it casts so feebly.

The shadows are my thoughts.

20-4-29

When I taught Earth history to children here on Juturna, before my arthritis demanded that I cease, my life was busy enough to prevent me from reflecting on it too deeply. These days that I have free now, and my sojourns at the hospital, have altered this. My life passes through the sieve of my mind, and that which remains is insufficient.

The tide in my affairs is at the flood. I can ride it out, or I can remain marooned.

The child.

I see him again tomorrow.

20-4-30

I have spoken to Dr. Van Huizen. We had a lengthy discussion. I feel that he understands.

I will not write more today. I cannot. I must feel it first. I am on the edge.

I think I have decided. Finally I have something of sufficient import about which to make a decision. Perhaps I understand my Churchillian "duty" better.

20-4-31

At any rate, it is done.

More tomorrow.

I cannot write. My thoughts are swollen, like my heart.

20-5-6

The recent days have left me unable to either journalize or speculate articulately. I can take time now, to try. There was no problem really. In fact, they were quite happy to have the matter resolved so neatly.

There are few who will take a Silent Child. Although I am not well, I will manage, since he will require so much less care than a normal child. The Council cannot afford to be overly fussy; we have, after all, Colony conditions of population and parochialism.

Are the Silent Children the first generation of new Juturnans—the adaptation of *Homo sapiens* to the environment? Perhaps they can communicate in ways that we cannot yet grasp.

The universe is, after all, large, and there is much more silence than noise, much more void than matter. Perhaps we are the aberration, not the Juturnans. These Children, in many senses, belong here; they will blend perfectly.

As Jacques has blended. Into the powder-grey soil. Into silence.

As I will blend.

Even as Genevieve, my flesh, exists, tacitly, among the stars, a memory.

The gaps exist.

The silence drowns the wawling of birth.

Jacques spoke of Challenge. I think I finally understand.

I feel at peace with myself tonight as I sit here with Yves, the child, his tiny fingers clenched on my thumb. The woman who is the midnight wind is singing and, for me alone, the planet is rotating fiercely.

INSTINCT

Dorothy Corbett Gentleman

As the earth tips over
into the crater of space,
I say to myself:
I am alive,
I am the driver
of these springs and wheels
basted with blood,
I am the operator
in command of my being.

Sounds of the mountains
breaking into sand,
the violent wash of oceans,
the shattering of glass,
are all muted and distant
as the music of an ending parade.

In the dead gap of sky
I am lashed tight to this moment,
breathing instinctively
above the tilted earth.

CEE

Gerry Truscott

I am making shapes and statues in the snow: an angel, a dragon, a snow bunny, a holo-musshan. The holo-musshan takes the longest. I make the face fat like a panda's and the body like a heap of soft ice cream, using Mom's little gardening shovel to etch the grooves. Then I push in large steelies for the eyes and shape the snout really long until it's ready to break off.

When I'm finished I stand back and admire it. To me it looks just like the real thing; I wish Cee were here so I could show him. A cat balances on our fence. I wonder if it's Cee, but he says no from somewhere above and I automatically look up to the attic window of our big old house. There he is, a shadow on the glass.

Come on out and play, Cee. Come look at what I've made.

The shadow moves. *Impressive work,* he says. *I can't come out right now, but I'll see you later.*

The shadow disappears. Cee has been busy the past few days preparing to go home.

I build a termite hill a little way away from the other statues. Cee told me how much he liked termites when he was in Africa visiting a boy who is like me. Cee showed me what a termite hill looks like inside and out. He admires the way termites work together. I dig through the snow to the garden and rub dirt over the termite mound so it looks real.

Dad gets home just before dark with a Christmas tree tied to the top of the car. I run to meet him as he unties the tree. "Dad, it's beautiful."

He crouches and hugs me. His whiskers scratch my cheek. "How's my little girl," he says, and picks me up with a grunt.

"Are we going to put it up tonight?" I like decorating the tree almost as much as Christmas itself. And this year I am twice as excited because Cee is going to help.

"We sure are. Hey, what have you been making?"

"Come and see."

He carries me half way to the statues, then puts me down and says, "You're not so little any more."

"What do you think," I say when we are standing in front of them.

"Hey, you're a regular sculptor." He looks at the holo-musshan. "What an imagination! What is it supposed to be?"

"Whatever it looks like," I say. That's what Cee said when he first showed one to me.

Dad examines it a little closer, then shrugs. "Let's go in for dinner." He's saying to himself that maybe I'll be an artist when I grow up. I can hear him inside, almost as clearly as I can hear Cee's voice. I've been able to hear Mom's and Dad's thoughts since Cee taught me how to listen with my mind. But only sometimes: some thoughts are just easier to hear than others, especially if they are about me.

After dinner Mom says I have to do my homework before we can start to put up the tree. I hate homework even more since Cee's been here. He won't even help me; he says I have to think for myself. But since he showed me how to think better, homework has been much easier.

Between arithmetic and vocabulary, I call him. *Cee, are you there?*

I'm here, he answers, and that's all.

I finish my homework quickly. Most of the words in the vocabulary exercise I know without having to look them up.

"Already?" Mom says when I come downstairs again.

"Yup. Want to see it?"

"I'll look at it later," she says. She hasn't got used to me being smarter than I was.

Dad is reading a magazine on the couch. I grab his arm and pull. "Come on Dad. You have to set up the tree." He scowls at first, then gives in with a smile.

Dad sets up the tree in front of the living room window. Mom and I sort out the bulbs and the ornaments while he strings the lights. All the time I'm calling for Cee. I begin to worry that he left sooner than he had planned.

Then, in a pile of decorations, I see a little Santa made out of red and white felt. Its funny smile reaches out from beneath the reindeers and angels. As I hang it on a branch its tiny felt hand reaches up to its mouth.

Cee! I almost say it out loud. *I thought it was you.*

Your perception is better than ever, he says, *though I detected some surprise.*

Isn't this fun? I say. *Look how beautiful it is.*

I step back and admire the tree with all its coloured lights and sparkling bulbs. Cee shares my eyes. *It's very pretty,* he says.

Dad hands me some tinsel and says, "You take the low branches and I'll take the high ones."

You just wait till we're finished, I tell Cee.

Mom takes pictures while Dad and I hang the tinsel. The room is warm and sparkling. The tree makes it so cozy. Cee is still with me. He says nothing, but I know he's impressed. Later, when I start to get tired, Cee quietly slips away.

Before I go upstairs to bed, Dad says, "Maybe Santa will drop off some early presents tonight."

"Oh, Dad." He says that every year. I'm too old to believe in Santa Claus, but he doesn't like to admit it.

As I'm lying in bed, Cee speaks to me. *Connie, I enjoyed your tree decorating ceremony very much.*

I wish you would stay for Christmas.

The decorated tree reminded me of a ceremony at home. Would you like to see it?

I say yes, of course, and close my eyes. Cee shows me a forest in the early morning. The tree tops stick up from a thick pearly-coloured mist. The sky is purplish and the mist looks bruised in places.

Then the sun appears on the horizon, very small and red. The bruises in the mist bulge and burst upward, making me jump. I open my eyes and for a moment I'm back in my dark bedroom. Cee chuckles softly and I close my eyes again.

Thousands of coloured bubbles fill the air, silently rising above the tree tops. They're like soap bubbles with rainbows swirling on their surfaces, but I can't see inside them. The bubbles are filling the air with wonderful voices.

Cee moves us through the rising balls towards the sunrise. We pass so close to some that I can hear individual voices. The balls are all about the same size, but each one is coloured differently. One bubble passes very close in front of me and I see a dark shape inside. It rolls upward with its song. Farther away, two bubbles bump and melt into a single red blob which falls back into the mist. Though I can't hear the difference I know that the chorus is less two voices. But this happens only a few times. The rest of the bubbles continue upward into the brightening sky. I feel like singing with them. But soon they are far above me and heading towards a brighter, bluish light high in the sky.

Cee returns me to my bedroom, humming a different, though similar, song. When he finishes he says, *We're very much the same, aren't we?*

I say yes, of course. *Oh yes,* and drift off to sleep.

The day Cee has to leave is the last day of school before Christmas. Everybody at school is excited about Christmas holidays, but I am sad. I try not to let it show. At recess I play in the snow with the other kids. I try to show them how to make a holo-musshan, but all they want to make is a stupid snowman.

After school I rush home to play with Cee. Mom asks me if I want to go grocery shopping with her and help her pick out the turkey. I tell her I want to write a letter to Nanna and Papa, so it gets to them before Christmas. She has been meaning to ask me to write to them, but kept forgetting.

The attic is our meeting place. I sit in the middle of the floor with my toys sitting all around me on boxes and old pieces of furniture. I brought the toys up as decoys so Mom and Dad would think I was playing with them instead of Cee: a parcheesee game, dominoes, my favourite rag doll, my outer-space creatures and lots of stuffed animals.

I close my eyes and call, *Cee are you there?*

I am here.

I opened my eyes and there he is, a little spider swinging on a web in front of my nose. I giggle and remember the first time he came as a spider.

It was when he'd only been here a week or so. He swung in front of me as a big orange spider. He frightened me a little, but I soon got used to his appearance. Then he asked me if I wanted to see what I look like from a spider's eyes. I said okay. Suddenly, I was looking at a huge grey nose covered with little holes all filled with dirt. The nose swung back and forth in front of me. On the far swing, giant lips appeared below it, dark and lumpy, like melted plastic. I wanted to scream. The lips opened to a gigantic hole filled with dirty cracked teeth. Then, with a terrible roar, the face swung away. Everything went blurry and I felt like I was falling.

When I had my own eyes back, Cee was not in front of me.

Below, he said, and scurried into a knot hole in the floor.

Later that night, when I was in bed, Cee apologized. *I should have warned you.*

Am I really full of dirty holes? I asked him.

He explained about the pores in my skin and how everything looks big to a spider. He said that I would understand better if I read about Gulliver in the land of Brobdingnag. Just the same, I got up and scrubbed my face. And I've kept very clean ever since that day.

Cee laughs at the memory, too. *We won't do that again,* he says.

I keep very still and look down at him cross-eyed. He bounces lightly on the tip of my nose. *What are we going to do today?*

This is our last chance to practise reaching, says Cee the spider.

I try to concentrate, but thoughts leak out: *Don't go, Cee. I wish you could stay. . . .*

Push outward with your mind, says Cee.

I push, imagining myself rising higher and higher above the house and being able to see farther and farther on all sides. The first time we tried it, Cee flew up as a bird and let me share his eyes. Gradually, we shifted from seeing with his eyes to seeing, or listening, with our minds together. Now I can do it by myself; Cee helps me reach farther out each time.

I hear mumblings as I always do at first, like voices from a radio in another room. Cee tells me to pay no attention to the mumbles. *Search for the clear sounds of a mind like yours.*

He and I know I won't find one today. Cee told me that there are others like me all over the world. Many of them are trying to reach me, too, and one day we'll meet. Then, together, we'll be able to call Cee back.

I push out farther than ever before. I am a bubble rising higher, higher towards a bright blue light. I reach out in all directions, push the horizon back. Cee has to stop me before I strain myself. I guess I was thinking that if I could reach another kid like me, Cee would stay. I feel a bit dizzy.

Keep practising, says Cee the spider. *But be careful not to push too hard.*

The front door slams and Mom calls. "Connie, I need some help please."

Tears fill my eyes. Cee says, *I'll see you one more time. After dinner.* He drops to the cedar chest and skitters over the side.

After dinner Mom and Dad say they want to talk to me about school. I know what they're going to say; I want to rush upstairs before they have a chance to speak, but Dad starts talking before I finish dessert.

He says that he and Mom are very proud of me for doing so well in school lately. "Your marks have improved very much in the last month or so. We're both very pleased." He tries to be casual about it, but he's thinking that my improvement is incredible and he wants to hug me. He says he can't understand it because a few months ago I wasn't interested in school at all.

"Mrs. Holdsworth said that your attitude has improved tremendously," says Mom. "Why the sudden change?"

"I don't know," I say. "School work is just easier now."

I wish I could tell them about Cee. But I gave him my solemn oath of secrecy. *I am on a secret mission*, Cee said to me the first day I saw him. He came to me as a bird: a sparrow. He flew into the attic through a vent. I heard the fluttering and twittering from my room and went upstairs to check. There he was, dusting himself off on one of the old boxes. When Cee first talked to me I thought it was someone calling from far away. Gradually his voice became clearer until I knew it came from the sparrow.

He said that he came from a far away place to learn about me and to teach me how to speak and listen with my mind. He had visited other parts of the world where he met children who have the same talent that I have. He said I should keep my talent a secret until the time is right. I wonder if he will leave as a bird.

"Dad and I have been talking about your improvement," says Mom, "and we've decided that you should take advantage of this spurt of interest in learning. You've been doing your homework so fast—"

"—and almost perfectly," Dad says.

Mom nods. "After Christmas holidays Mrs. Holdsworth is going to give you more homework every night. We want you to do a minimum of one hour's work. How does that sound to you?"

"Okay, I guess." I stare into the swirls of ice-cream colours in my bowl. I feel sick. It's one thing to know what someone is going to say—and another to hear it. The only reason I did my homework fast was so I'd have more time to play with Cee. After he's gone it won't matter.

"We'll try to make it as much fun as possible," says Dad. "We're very proud of you."

At least I won't have to do homework over the Christmas holidays.

Later, I meet Cee in the attic for the last time. He does appear as a bird, not a sparrow but an osprey. I almost start crying.

I am ready to leave now, he says. *I enjoyed my stay here and I've learned very much.*

I hold back tears. *You taught me lots too, Cee.*

Keep practising. Even if you think you will never reach another with the talent. They are there, and eventually you'll meet them.

It won't be as much fun without you.

The osprey cocks his head. *Nevertheless, you must keep pushing out. And be patient.*

He looks at me with one eye. I see a sparkle in there and I know that he'll never really leave me, as long as I have the talent. But when he flutters his wings I burst into tears.

We'll meet again, Connie.

He hops up onto an old dusty box next to the window. The window opens. A cold draft from the darkness makes me shiver.

Mom and Dad are giving me more homework, I say, hoping to keep him a little longer.

Good, says Cee the osprey. *Exercising all parts of the mind is important.* He hops to the window and flies away.

The attic is suddenly a lonely place. I run to the window and find Cee's bird shape over the neighbour's roof.

Cee, I won't be able to do it without you.

All I've done is awaken your talent. You are using more of your mind now than ever before. Keep practising. You'll grow even stronger. As long as you keep your mind open you will learn.

His bird silhouette shrinks to a black dot and disappears in the moonlit grey clouds.

Goodbye, Cee.

Goodbye, Connie, says Cee from far away.

The window creaks when I close it. Alone in the attic, I feel so empty. I sit among my toys, crying for a long time.

Later in bed I call out. *Cee, are you there?* No answer.

Christmas is only a few days away, but I am not excited about it. Mom notices and asks me if I'm feeling sick. I tell her I'm just bored. She doesn't believe me, of course. She thinks I might be depressed about having more homework, but she decides to wait and see how I am after Christmas.

As the presents pile up under the tree, the magic of Christmas overcomes my sadness. When Christmas morning finally arrives, I run down the stairs and wake Mom and Dad. After breakfast we rush to the tree.

Dad gives out the presents. We take turns opening them, but I always get more than Mom and Dad so I open two at a time. From Mom I get lots of books (she wants me to read more), and Grandma gives me an electronic arcade game. Dad gets a sheepskin coat from Mom. He gives her a sparkling gold necklace and matching bracelet. I open a big box from Nanna filled with stuffed animals for my collection, and Dad gives me a soccer ball. "We'll kick it around when the snow disappears," he says.

I give Mom a glass sculpture of a unicorn, and Dad a sixteen-piece socket set. They both say, "How did you know I wanted this?" I just smile. Dad hands me a present wrapped in flowery paper. "It says, 'From Santa Claus.'" He shrugs.

"That's wedding shower paper," Mom says, and she laughs uneasily. "It must be from one of your grandmothers."

I tear off the wrapping and recognize the old shoe box that I keep my space creatures in. My own writing is on the top: STARSHIP.

I open it and pull out a stuffed animal. It feels like soft leather. I don't recognize it until the long snout flops up and touches my face. A holo-musshan!

I hear Cee's voice inside. *I have left a few thoughts behind, Connie, to help you practise while I am gone.*

Mom and Dad study it closely. "What is it?" Mom says.

Dad looks closer and his eyes brighten in recognition for a second, then he looks puzzled again. "Whatever it looks like. Right, Connie?"

I just nod. I can't speak. My face is wet, pushed into the soft skin of the holo-musshan.

ON THE PLANET GRAFOOL

Benjamin Freedman

On the planet Grafool, the inhabitants never take medicine when they are sick. Some, though by no means all, take medicine when they are well.

They reason like this:

"If you are sick, you are not healthy. Medicine is something which is designed for health, not for sickness. What would be the point of getting sick if you're going to take medicine to become healthy? Why would anybody get sick in the first place? That's logic."

Some people feel that the inhabitants of the planet Grafool are not problem-oriented.

On the planet Grafool, they never read books. Many times they have been asked why they don't read books. Surely, many advantages could be gained thereby. And what could one possibly do for entertainment without books? Their answer is always the same: "Who knows what will happen tomorrow?" This always frustrates the questioner. Questioners on the planet Grafool are far more frustrated than are the residents of the planet Grafool.

On the planet Earth, girls can wear skirts or pants, whichever they prefer; boys can only wear pants. On the planet Grafool, boys are only allowed to wear skirts and girls are only allowed to wear pants. Any deviation from this is grounds for denial of pudding. This seems terribly unfair; no explanation is ever offered.

On the planet Grafool, the inhabitants don't own any mirrors and refuse to look into the mirrors that visitors bring. They reason as follows:

"When you look into a mirror you see yourself, or other things around you (depending on the angle). You don't see the mirror itself. When you look into a mirror the mirror must see itself; it could not see you or the things around you. The mirror would not see you at all. There are easier ways to commit suicide."

If there are, I haven't heard of any. One of the major principles of the planet Grafool is that there is no such thing as a one-way street. Another one is that you can never get something from nothing.

The people on the planet Grafool look exactly like the people of Earth. Close observation, however, reveals some differences. Nobody on the planet Grafool has any freckles, no matter how long they stay out in the sun. And everybody on the planet Grafool, without an exception, is double-jointed. They can stretch their thumbs way back until they touch their forearms. This achievement, so uncommon on the planet Earth, poses no difficulty at all for the people of Grafool. They are very proud of this, and do it constantly (at least in the presence of visitors).

The family unit on the planet Grafool is very strong. All the members of a family, no matter where they work or where they are during the day, are expected to sleep with the family at night. This point has been raised to the level of a moral principle on the planet Grafool, and anybody who disobeys this commandment is a transgressor.

The adults on the planet Grafool sleep in chairs at the kitchen table. Wealthy Grafoolians sleep at the dining-room table. All infants and the smaller children sleep in specially-designed teacups.

An overnight visitor to the planet Grafool can expect to see a whole family of Grafoolians slumped over the table, around the table, snoring. They always choose straight-backed chairs. They claim that this is better for the posture and prevents backache. It appears that other planets may be picking this up as a fad. It is no fad on the planet Grafool.

Children on the planet Grafool are highly respected, and can often be found occupying important positions in commerce and government. They hold these positions by design, not default, though it is true that adult Grafoolians tend to shun responsibility or any other kind of labour. The adults, when questioned about child labour, say it is important that everyone be given the opportunity to learn from his or her own mistakes. This, they feel, is a duty, not a privilege.

Still, children are children everywhere. Children on Grafool enjoy pictures about them: on their walls, and on their skirts (if they are boys) or their pants (if they are girls). Children on the planet Earth like to have pictures of flowers, animals and other little children. Children on Grafool, curiously, favour pictures of lamps. Pictures of all sorts of lamps can be found everywhere: tall and short lamps, straight and goose-necked lamps, lamps with incandescent bulbs, and high-intensity Tensor lamps.

If asked about death, Grafoolians claim that nobody ever "dies" on the planet Grafool. "Dying" is against their religion, they say. Some feel that "dying" would be a form of sleeping away from the family and, therefore, would be a transgression.

No dead people have ever been observed on the planet Grafool.

Religion on the planet Grafool is a form of mathematics. This is a culmination of a long evolutionary process. The inhabitants were entranced by numbers; it seemed that anything could be done with mathematics, which offered no resistance to any manipulation, no matter how bizarre. Ignoring the constraints of all possible worlds, the mathematicians of Grafool revelled in their powers of fantasy.

Ultimately mathematics became entirely mysterious. First its content, then its form, withered away, leaving only a subjective experience of appreciation. It found a natural partner in religion. The merger is so complete that Grafoolians are puzzled by questions concerning the relationship of the two.

To an outside observer, the inhabitants of Grafool leave the impression of a happy and serene people. Content with their homilies, peaceful in obedience to their simple principles, comforted by their imaginations, they remain a stable island in a tormented and outraged cosmos.

TAUF ALEPH

Phyllis Gotlieb

Samuel Zohar ben Reuven Begelman lived to a great age in the colony Pardes on Tau Ceti IV and in his last years he sent the same message with his annual request for supplies to Galactic Federation Central: *Kindly send one mourner/gravedigger so I can die in peace respectfully.*

And Sol III replied through GalFed Central with the unvarying answer: *Regret cannot find one Jew yours faithfully.*

Because there was not one other identifiable Jew in the known universe, for with the opening of space the people had scattered and intermarried, and though their descendants were as numerous, in the fulfillment of God's promise, as the sands on the shore and the stars in the heavens, there was not one called Jew, nor any other who could speak Hebrew and pray for the dead. The home of the ancestors was emptied: it was now a museum where perfect simulacra performed 7500 years of history in hundreds of languages for tourists from the breadth of the Galaxy.

In Central, Hrsipliy the Xiploid said to Castro-Ibanez the Sol-three, "It is a pity we cannot spare one person to help that poor *juddar*." She meant by this term: body/breath/spirit/sonofabitch, being a woman with three tender hearts.

Castro-Ibanez, who had one kind heart and one hard head, answered, "How can we? He is the last colonist on that world and

refuses to be moved; we keep him alive at great expense already."
He considered for some time and added, "I think perhaps we
might send him a robot. One that can dig and speak recorded
prayers. Not one of the new expensive ones. We ought to have
some old machine good enough for last rites."

O/G5/842 had been resting in a very dark corner of Stores for
324 years, his four coiled arms retracted and his four hinged ones
resting on his four wheeled feet. Two of his arms terminated in
huge scoop shovels, for he had been an ore miner, and he was also
fitted with treads and sucker-pods. He was very great in size; they
made giant machines in those days. New technologies had left him
useless; he was not even worthy of being dismantled for parts.

It happened that this machine was wheeled into the light,
scoured of rust and lubricated. His ore-scoops were replaced with
small ones retrieved from Stores and suitable for gravedigging,
but in respect to Sam Begelman he was not given a recording: he
was rewired and supplemented with an almost new logic and
given orders and permission to go and learn. Once he had done so
to the best of his judgment he would travel out with Begelman's
supplies and land. This took great expense, but less than an irre-
placeable person or a new machine; it fulfilled the Galactic-
Colonial contract. O/G would not return, Begelman would rest in
peace, no one would recolonize Tau Ceti IV.

O/G5/842 emerged from his corner. In the Library he caused
little more stir than the seven members of the Khagodi embassy
(650 kilos apiece) who were searching out a legal point of intra-
Galactic law. He was too broad to occupy a cubicle, and let himself
be stationed in a basement exhibit room where techs wired him to
sensors, sockets, inlets, outlets, screens and tapes. Current flowed,
light came, and he said, LET ME KNOW SAMUEL ZOHAR BEN REUVEN
BEGELMAN DOCTOR OF MEDICINE AND WHAT IT MEANS THAT HE IS A
JEW.

He recorded the life of Sam Begelman; he absorbed Hebrew,
Aramaic, Greek; he learned Torah, which is Law: day one. He
learned Writings, Prophets, and then Mishna, which is the first
exegesis of Law: day the second. He learned Talmud (Palestinian

and Babylonian), which is the completion of Law, and Tosefta, which are ancillary writings and divergent opinions in Law: day the third. He read 3500 years of Commentary and Responsa: day the fourth. He learned Syriac, Arabic, Latin, Yiddish, French, English, Italian, Spanish, Dutch. At the point of learning Chinese he experienced, for the first time, a synapse. For the sake of reading marginally relevant writings by fewer than ten Sino-Japanese Judaic poets it was not worth learning their vast languages; this gave him pause: two nanoseconds:day the fifth. Then he plunged, day the sixth, into the literatures written in the languages he had absorbed. Like all machines, he did not sleep, but on the seventh day he unhooked himself from Library equipment, gave up his space, and returned to his corner. In this place he turned down all motor and afferent circuits and indexed, concordanced, cross-referenced. He developed synapses exponentially to complete and fulfill his logic. Then he shut it down and knew nothing.

But Galactic Federation said, O/G5/842, AROUSE YOURSELF AND BOARD THE SHIP *Aleksandr Nevskii* AT LOADING DOCK 377 BOUND FOR TAU CETI IV.

At the loading dock, Flight Admissions said, YOUR SPACE HAS BEEN PRE—EMPTED FOR SHIPMENT 20 TONNES *Nutrivol* POWDERED DRINKS (39 FLAVOURS) TO DESERT WORLDS TAU CETI II AND III.

O/G knew nothing of such matters and said, I HAVE NOT BEEN INSTRUCTED SO. He called Galactic Federation and said, MOD 0885 THE SPACE ASSIGNED FOR ME IS NOT PERMITTED. IT HAS BEEN PRE—EMPTED BY A BEING CALLED *Nutrivol* SENDING POWDERED DRINKS TO TAU CETI INNER WORLDS.

Mod 0885 said, I AM CHECKING. YES. THAT COMPANY WENT INTO RECEIVERSHIP ONE STANDARD YEAR AGO. I SUSPECT SMUGGLING AND BRIBERY. I WILL WARN.

THE SHIP WILL BE GONE BY THEN MOD 08 WHAT AM I TO DO?

INVESTIGATE, MOD 842.

HOW AM I TO DO THAT?

USE YOUR LOGIC, said Mod 0885 and signed off.

O/G went to the loading dock and stood in the way. The beings ordering the loading mechs said, "You are blocking this shipment! Get out of the way, you old pile of scrap!"

O/G said in his speaking voice, "I am not in the way. I am to board ship for Pardes and it is against the law for this cargo to take my place." He extruded a limb in gesture towards the stacked cartons; but he had forgotten his strength (for he had been an ore miner) and his new scoop smashed five cartons at one blow; the foam packing parted and white crystals poured from the break. O/G regretted this very greatly for one fraction of a second before he remembered how those beings who managed the mines behaved in the freezing darkness of lonely worlds and moons. He extended his chemical sensor and dipping it into the crystal stream said, "Are fruit drinks for desert worlds now made without fructose but with dextroamphetamine sulfate, diacetylmorphine, 2-acetyl-tetrahydrocannabinol—"

Some of the beings at the loading gate cried out curses and many machines began to push and beat at him. But O/G pulled in his limbs and planted his sucker-pods and did not stir. He had been built to work in many gravities near absolute zero under rains of avalanches. He would not be moved.

Presently uniformed officials came and took away those beings and their cargo, and said to O/G, "You too must come and answer questions."

But he said, "I was ordered by Galactic Federation to board this ship for Tau Ceti IV, and you may consult the legal department of Colonial Relations, but I will not be moved."

Because they had no power great enough to move him they consulted among themselves and with the legal department and said, "You may pass."

Then O/G took his assigned place in the cargo hold of the *Aleksandr Nevskii* and after the ship lifted for Pardes he turned down his logic because he had been ordered to think for himself for the first time and this confused him very much.

The word *pardes* is "orchard" but the world Pardes was a bog of mud, foul gases and shifting terrains, where attempts at terraforming failed again and again until colonists left in disgust and many lawsuits plagued the courts of Interworld Colonies at

GalFed. O/G landed there in a stripped shuttle which served as a glider. It was not meant to rise again and it broke and sank in the marshes, but O/G plowed mud, scooping the way before him, and rode on treads, dragging the supplies behind him on a sledge, for 120 kilometres before he came within sight of the colony.

Fierce creatures many times his size, with serpentine necks and terrible fangs, tried to prey on him. He wished to appease them, and offered greetings in many languages, but they would only break their teeth on him. He stunned one with a blow to the head, killed another by snapping its neck, and they left him alone.

The colony centre was a concrete dome surrounded by a force-field that gave out sparks, hissing and crackling. Around it he found many much smaller creatures splashing in pools and scrambling to and fro at the mercy of one of the giants who held a small being writhing in its jaws.

O/G cried in a loud voice, "Go away you savage creature!" and the serpent beast dropped its mouthful, but seeing no great danger dipped its neck to pick it up again. So O/G extended his four hinged limbs to their greatest length and, running behind the monster, seized the pillars of its rear legs, heaving up and out until its spine broke and it fell flattened in mud, thrashing the head on the long neck until it drove it into the ground and smothered.

The small beings surrounded O/G without fear, though he was very great to them, and cried in their thin voices, "Shalom-shalom, Saviour!"

O/G was astonished to hear these strangers speaking clear He-brew. He had not known a great many kinds of living persons during his experience, but among those displayed in the corridors of the Library basement these most resembled walruses. "I am not a saviour, men of Pardes," he said in the same language. "Are you speaking your native tongue?"

"No, Redeemer. We are Cnidori and we spoke Cnidri before we reached this place in our wanderings, but we learned the language of Rav Zohar because he cared for us when we were lost and starving."

"Now Zohar has put up a barrier and shut you out—and I am not a redeemer—but what has happened to that man?"

"He became very ill and shut himself away because he said he was not fit to look upon. The food he helped us store is eaten and the Unds are ravaging us."

"There are some here that will ravage you no longer. Do you eat the flesh of these ones?"

"No, master. Only what grows from the ground."

He saw that beneath the draggling gray moustaches their teeth were the incisors and molars of herbivores. "I am not your master. See if there is food to gather here and I will try to reach Zohar."

"First we will skin one of these to make tents for shelter. It rains every hour." They rose on their haunches in the bog, and he discovered that though their rear limbs were flippers like those of aquatic animals, their forelimbs bore three webbed fingers apiece and each Cnidor had a small shell knife slung over one shoulder. All, moreover, had what appeared to be one mammalian teat and one male generative organ ranged vertically on their bellies, and they began to seem less and less like walruses to O/G. The prime Cnidor continued, "Tell us what name pleases you if you offended by the ways we address you."

"I have no name but a designation: O/G5/842. I am only a machine."

"You are a machine of deliverance and so we will call you Golem."

In courtesy O/G accepted the term. "This forcefield is so noisy it probably has a malfunction. It is not wise to touch it."

"No, we are afraid of it."

Golem scooped mud from the ground and cast it at the forcefield; great lightnings and hissings issued where it landed. "I doubt even radio would cross that."

"Then how can we reach Zohar, Golem, even if he is still alive?"

"I will cry out, Cnidori. Go to a distance and cover your ears, because my voice can pierce a mountain of lead ore."

They did not know what that was, but they removed themselves, and Golem turned his volume to its highest and called in a mighty voice, "*Samuel Zohar ben Reuven Begelman turn off your forcefield for I have come from Galactic Federation to help you!!!*"

Even the forcefield buckled for one second at the sound of his voice.

After a long silence, Golem thought he heard a whimper, from a great distance. "I believe he is alive, but cannot reach the control."

A Cnidor said, trembling, "The Unds have surely heard you, because they are coming back again."

And they did indeed come back, bellowing, hooting and striking with their long necks. Golem tied one great snake neck in a knot and cried again, *"Let us in, Zohar, or the Unds will destroy all of your people!!!"*

The forcefield vanished, and the Cnidori scuttled over its border beneath the sheltering arms of Golem, who cracked several fanged heads like nutshells with his scoops.

"Now put up your shield!!!" And the people were saved.

When Golem numbered them and they declared that only two were missing among forty he said, "Wait here and feed yourselves."

The great outer doorway for working machines was open, but the hangar and store-rooms were empty of them; they had been removed by departing colonists. None had been as huge as Golem, and here he removed his scoops and unhinged his outer carapace with its armour, weapons and storage compartments, for he wished to break no more doorways than necessary. Behind him he pulled the sledge with the supplies.

When his heat sensor identified the locked door behind which Zohar was to be found, he removed the doorway as gently as he could.

"I want to die in peace and you are killing me with noise," said a weak voice out of the darkness.

By infrared Golem saw the old man crumpled on the floor by the bed, filthy and half naked, with the shield control resting near his hand. He turned on light. The old man was nearly bald, wasted and yellow-skinned, wrinkled, his rough beard tangled and clotted with blood.

"Zohar?"

Sam Begelman opened his eyes and saw a tremendous machine, multi-armed and with wheels and treads, wound with coiling tubes and wires, studded with dials. At its top was a dome banded with sensor lenses, and it turned this way and that to survey the room. "What are you?" he whispered in terror. "Where is my kaddish?"

He spoke in *lingua*, but O/G replied in Hebrew. "You know you are the last Jew in the known universe, Rav Zohar. There is no one but me to say prayers for you."

"Then let me die without peace," said Begelman, and closed his eyes.

But Golem knew the plan of the station, and within five minutes he reordered the bed in cleanliness, placed the old man on it, set up an i.v., cleansed him, and injected him with the drugs prepared for him. The old man's hands pushed at him and pushed at him, uselessly. "You are only a machine," he croaked. "Can't you understand that a machine can't pray?"

"Yes, master. I would have told that to Galactic Federation, but they would not believe me, not being Jews."

"I am not your master. Why truly did you come?"

"I was made new again and given orders. My growth in logic now allows me to understand that I cannot be of use to you in exactly the way Galactic Federation wished, but I can still make you more comfortable."

"I don't care!" Begelman snarled. "Who needs a machine!"

"The Cnidori needed me to save them from the Unds when you shut them out, and they tried to call me Saviour, Redeemer, master; I refused because I *am* a machine, but I let them call me Golem because I am a machine of deliverance."

Begelman sniffed. But the sick yellow of his skin was gone; his face was faintly pink and already younger by a few years.

"Shmuel Zohar ben Reuven Begelman, why do you allow those helpless ones to call you Rav Zohar and speak in your language?"

"You nudnik of a machine, my name is not Samuel and certainly not Shmuel! It is Zohar, and I let myself be called Sam because *zohar* is 'splendour' and you can't go through life as Splendour Begelman! I taught those Cnidori the Law and the Prophets to hear my own language spoken because my children are gone and my wife is dead. That is why they call me Teacher. And I shut them out so that they would be forced to make their own way in life before they began to call *me* Redeemer! What do you call yourself, Golem?"

"My designation is O/G5/842."

"Ah. Og the giant King of Bashan. That seems suitable."

"Yes, Zohar. That one your Rabbi Moshe killed in the land of Kana'an with all his people for no great provocation. But O is the height of my oxygen tolerance in Solthree terms; I cannot work at gravities of less than five newtons, and eight four two is my model number. Now Zohar, if you demand it I will turn myself off and be no more. But the people are within your gate; some of them have been killed and they must still be cared for."

Zohar sighed, but he smiled a little as well. Yet he spoke slowly because he was very ill. "Og ha-Golem, before you learn how to tune an argument too fine remember that Master of the Word is one of the names of Satan. Moshe Rabbenu was a bad-tembered man, but he did very greatly, and I am no kind of warrior. Take care of the people, and me too if your . . . logic demands it—and I will consider how to conduct myself off the world properly."

"I am sure your spirit will free itself in peace, Zohar. As for me, my shuttle is broken, I am wanted nowhere else, and I will rust in Pardes."

Og ha-Golem went out of the presence of the old man but it seemed to him as if there were some mild dysfunction in his circuits, for he was mindful—if that is the term—of Begelman's concept of the Satan, Baal Davar, and he did not know for certain if what he had done by the prompting of his logic was right action. How can I know? he asked himself. By what harms and what saves, he answered. By what seems to harm and what seems to save, says the Master of the Word.

Yet he continued by the letter of his instructions from Galactic Federation, and these were to give the old man comfort. For the Cnidori he helped construct tents, because they liked water under their bellies but not pouring on their heads. With his own implements he flensed the bodies of the dead Unds, cleaned their skins and burned their flesh; it was not kosher for Begelman and attracted bothersome scavengers. He did this while Rav Zohar was sleeping and spoke to the people in his language; they had missed it when he was ill. "Zohar believes you must learn to take care of yourselves, against the Unds and on your world, because you cannot now depend on him."

"We would do that, Golem, but we would also like to give comfort to our Teacher."

Og ha-Golem was disturbed once again by the ideas that pieced themselves together in his logic and said to Begelman, "Zohar, you have taught the Cnidori so well that now they are capable of saying the prayers you long for so greatly. Is there a way in which that can be made permissible?"

The old man folded his hands and looked about the bare and cracking walls of the room, as Golem had first done, and then back at him. "In this place?" he whispered. "Do you know what you are saying?"

"Yes, Zohar."

"How they may be made *Jews?*"

"They are sentient beings. What is there to prevent it?"

Begelman's face became red and Og checked his blood-pressure monitor. "Prevent it! What is there to them that would make Jews? Everything they eat is neutral, neither kosher nor tref, so what use is the law of Kashrut? They live in mud—where are the rules of bathing and cleanliness? They had never had any kind of god or any thought of one, as far as they tell me—what does prayer mean? Do you know how they procreate? Could you imagine? They are so completely hermaphroditic the word is meaningless. They pair long enough to raise children together, but only until the children grow teeth and can forage. What you see that looks like a penis is really an ovipositor: each Cnidor who is ready deposits eggs in the pouch of another, and an enzyme of the eggs stimulates the semen glands inside, and when one or two eggs become fertilized the pouch seals until the fetus is of a size to make the fluid pressure around it break the seal, and the young crawls up the belly of the parent to suckle on the teat. Even if one or two among twenty are born incomplete, not one is anything you might call male or female! So tell me, what do you do with all the laws of marriage and divorce, sexual behaviour, the duties of the man at prayer and the woman with the child?"

He was becoming out of breath and Og checked oxygen and heart monitors. "I am not a man or woman either and though I know the Law I am ignorant in experience. I was thinking merely of prayers that God might listen to in charity or appreciation.

I did not mean to upset you. I am not fulfilling my duties."

"Leave me."

Og turned an eyecell to the dripping of the i.v. and removed catheter and urine bag. "You are nearly ready to rise from your bed and feed yourself, Zohar. Perhaps when you feel more of a man you may reconsider."

"Just go away." He added, snarling, "God doesn't need any more Jews!"

"Yes, they would look ridiculous in skullcaps and prayer shawls with all those fringes dragging in mud. . . . "

Zohar, was that why you drove them out into the wild?

Og gathered brushwood and made a great fire. He cut woody vines and burnt them into heaps of charcoal. He gathered and baked clay into blocks and built a kiln. Then he pulled his sledge for 120 kilometres, and dug until he found enough pieces of the glider for his uses. He fired the kiln to a great heat, softened the fragments, and reshaped them into the huge scoops he had been deprived of. They were not as fine and strong as the originals, but very nearly as exact.

He consulted maps of Pardes, which lay near the sea. He began digging channels and heaping breakwaters to divert a number of streams and drain some of the marshes of Pardes, and to keep the sea from washing over it during storms, and this left pools of fresher water for the Cnidori.

Sometimes the sun shone. On a day that was brighter and dryer than usual Begelman came outside the station, supporting himself on canes, and watched the great Golem at work. He had never seen Og in full armour with his scoops. During its renewal his exterior had been bonded with a coating that retarded rust; this was dull grey and the machine had no beauty in the eyes of a Solthree, but he worked with an economy of movement that lent him grace. He was surrounded by Cnidori with shovels of a size they could use, and they seemed to Begelman like little children playing in mud piles, getting in the way while the towering machine worked in silence without harming the small creatures or allowing them to annoy him.

Og, swiveling the beam of his eyecell, saw an old white-bearded

Solthree with a homely face of some dignity; he looked weak but not ill. His hair was neatly trimmed, he wore a blue velvet skullcap worked with silver threads, black trousers and zippered jacket, below which showed the fringes of his *tallith katan*. He matched approximately the thousands of drawings, paintings and photographs of dignified old Jews stored in Og's memory: Og had dressed him to match.

Begelman said, "What are you doing?"

"I am stabilizing the land in order to grow crops of oilseed, lugwort and greenpleat, which are nourishing both to you and the Cnidori. I doubt Galactic Federation is going to give us anything more, and I also wish to store supplies. If other wandering tribes of Cnidori cross this territory it is better to share our plenty than fight over scarcity."

"You're too good to be true," Begelman muttered.

Og had learned something of both wit and sarcasm from Begelman but did not give himself the right to use them on the old man. His logic told him that he, the machine, had nothing to fear from a Satan who was not even a concept in the mainstream of Jewish belief, but that Zohar was doing battle with the common human evil in his own spirit. He said, "Zohar, these Cnidori have decided to take Hebrew names, and they are calling themselves by letters: Aleph, Bet, Gimmel, and when those end at Tauf, by numbers: Echod, Shtaim, Sholosh. This does not seem correct to me but they will not take my word for it. Will you help them?"

Begelman's mouth worked for a moment, twisting as if to say, What have these to do with such names? But Cnidori crowded round him and their black eyes reflected very small lights in the dim sun; they were people of neither fur nor feather, but scales that resembled both: leaf-shaped plates the size of a thumb with central ridges and branching radials; these were very fine in texture and refracted rainbow colours on brighter days.

The old man sighed and said, "Dear people, if you wish to take names in Hebrew you must take the names of human beings like those in Law and Prophets. The names of the Fathers: Avraham, Yitzhak, Yaakov; the Tribes: Yehuda, Shimon, Binyamin; or if you prefer female names, the Mothers: Sarai, Rivkah, Rakhael,

Leah. Whichever seems good to you." The Cnidori thanked him with pleasure and went away content.

Begelman said to Og, "Next thing you know they will want a Temple." Og suspected what they would ask for next, but said, "I believe we must redesign the forcefield to keep the Unds out of the cultivated areas. Perhaps we have enough components in Stores or I can learn to make them."

He had been scouting for Unds every fourth or fifth day and knew their movements. They had been avoiding the station in fear of Og and the malfunctioning forcefield but he believed that they would attack again when the place was quiet, and they did so on the night of that day when the Cnidori took names. The field had been repaired and withstood their battering without shocking them; their cries were terrible to hear, and sometimes their bones cracked against the force. They fell back after many hours, leaving Og with earthworks to repair and two of their bodies to destroy.

In the morning when he had finished doing this he found Begelman lying on a couch in the Common Room, a book of prayers on his lap, faced by a group of ten Cnidori. All eleven spoke at once, Begelman with crackling anger in his voice, the Cnidori softly but with insistence.

Begelman cried out when he saw Og, "Now they tell me they must have surnames!"

"I expected so, Zohar. They know that you are ben Reuven and they have accepted your language and the names of your people. Is this not reasonable?"

"I have no authority to make Jews of them!"

"You are the only authority left. You have taught them."

"Damn you! You have been pushing for this!"

"I have pushed for nothing except to make you well. I taught nothing." Within him the Master of the Word spoke: This is true, but is it right?

Begelman in anger clapped shut his book, but it was very old and its spine cracked slightly; he lifted and kissed it in repentence. He spoke in a low voice, "What does it matter now? There is no surname they can be given except the name of convert, which is

141

ben Avraham or bat Avraham, according to the gender of the first name. And how can they be converts when they can keep no Law and do not even know God? And what does it matter now?" He threw up his hands. "Let them be b'nei Avraham!"

But the Cnidori prime, who had taken the name Binyamin—that is, Son of the Right Hand—said, "We do not wish to be b'nei Avraham, but b'nei Zohar, because we say to you, Og ha-Golem, and to you, Rav Zohar, that because Zohar has been as a father to us we feel as sons to him."

Og feared that the old man might now become truly ill with rage, and indeed his hands trembled on the book, but he said quietly enough, "My children, Jews do not behave so. Converts must become Jews in the ways allowed to them. If you do not understand, I have not taught you well enough, and I am too old to teach more. I have yielded too much already to a people who do not worship God, and I am not even a Rabbi with such small authority as is given to one."

"Rav Zohar, we have come to tell you that we have sworn to worship your God."

"But you must not worship me."

"But we may worship the God who created such a man as you, and such teachings as you have taught us, and those men who made the great Golem." They went away quickly and quietly without speaking further.

"They will be back again," Begelman said. "And again and again. Why did I ever let you in? Lord God King of the Universe, what am I to do?"

It *is* right, Og told the Master of the Word. "You are more alive and healthy than you have long been, Zohar," he said. "And you have people who love you. Can you not let them do so?"

He sought out Binyamin. "Do not trouble Rav Zohar with demands he cannot fulfill, no matter how much you desire to honour him. Later I will ask him to think if there is a way he can do as you wish, within the Law."

"We will do whatever you advise, Golem."

Og continued with his work, but while he was digging he turned up a strange artifact and he had a foreboding. At times he had discovered potsherds which were the remnants of clay vessels the

Cnidori had made to cook vegetables they could not digest raw, and this discovery was an almost whole cylinder of the same texture, color, and markings; one of its end rims was blackened by burn marks, and dark streaks ran up its sides. He did not know what it was, but it seemed sinister to him; in conscience he had no choice but to show it to Zohar.

"It does not seem like a cooking vessel," he said.

"No," said Begelman. "It does not." He pointed to a place inside where there was a leaf-shaped Cnidori scale, blackened, clinging to its wall, and to two other burn marks of the same shape. Strangely, to Og, his eyes filled with tears.

"Perhaps it is a casing in which they dispose of their dead," Og said.

Zohar wiped his eyes and said, "No. It is a casing in which they make them dead. Many were killed by Unds, and some have starved, and the rest die of age. All those they weight and sink into the marshes. This is a sacrifice. They have a god, and its name is Baal." He shook his head. "My children." He wept for a moment again and said, "Take this away and smash it until there is not a piece to recognize."

Og did so, but Zohar locked himself into his room and would not answer to anyone.

Og did not know what to do now. He was again as helpless as he had been on the loading dock where he had first learned to use his logic.

The Cnidori came to inquire of Golem and he told them what had happened. They said, "It is true that our ancestors worshipped a Being and made sacrifices, but none of that was done after Zohar gave us help. We were afraid he and his God would hold us in contempt."

"Both Zohar and his God have done imperfect acts. But now I will leave him alone, because he is very troubled."

"But it is a great sin in his eyes," said Binyamin sorrowfully. "I doubt that he will ever care for us again."

And Og continued with his work, but he thought his logic had failed him, in accordance with Zohar's taunts.

In the evening a Cnidor called Elyahu came writhing towards him along the ground in great distress. "Come quickly!" he called.

"Binyamin is doing *nidset!*"

"What is that?"

"Only come quickly!" Elyahu turned back in haste. Og unclipped his scoops and followed, overtaking the small creature and bearing him forward in his arms. They found Binyamin and other Cnidori in a grove of ferns. They had built a smoky fire and were placing upon it a fresh cylinder: a network of withy branches had been woven into the bottom of it.

"No, no!" cried Og, but they did not regard him; the cylinder was set on the fire and smoke came out of its top. Then the Cnidori helped Binyamin climb over its edge and he dropped inward, into the smoke.

"No!" Og cried again, and he toppled the vessel from the fire, but without violence so that Binyamin would not be harmed. *"You shall make no sacrifices!"* Then he tapped it so that it split, and the Cnidor lay in its halves, trembling.

"That is *nidset,* Golem," said Elyahu.

But Golem plucked up the whimpering Cnidor. "Why were you doing such a terrible thing, Binyamin?"

'We thought," Binyamin said in a quavering voice, "we thought that all of the gods were angry with us—our old god for leaving him and our new one for having worshipped the old—and that a sacrifice would take away the anger of all."

"That confounds my logic somewhat." Og set down Binyamin, beat out the fire, and cast the pieces of the cylinder far away. "All gods are One, and the One forgives whoever asks. Now come. I believe I hear the Unds again, and we need shelter close to home until we can build a wider one."

Then the Cnidori raised a babble of voices. "No! What good is such a God if even Zohar does not listen to Him and forgive us?"

It seemed to Og for one moment as if the Cnidori felt themselves cheated of a sacrifice; he put this thought aside. "The man is sick and old, and he is not thinking clearly either, while you have demanded much of him."

"Then, Golem, we will demand no more, but die among the Unds!" The shrieking of the beasts grew louder on the night winds but the Cnidori drew their little knives and would not stir.

"Truly you are an outrageous people," said Golem. "But I am

only a machine." He extended his four hinged arms and his four coil arms and bearing them up in their tens raced with them on treads and wheels until they were within the safety of the forcefield.

But when he set them down they grouped together closely near the field and would not say one word.

Og considered the stubborn Zohar on the one side, and the stubborn b'nei Avraham on the other, and he thought that perhaps it was time for him to cease his being. A great storm of lightning and thunder broke out; the Unds did not approach and within the forcefield there was stillness.

He disarmed himself and stood before Zohar's door. He considered the sacrifice of Yitzhak, and the Golden Calf, and how Moshe Rabbenu had broken the Tables, and many other excellent examples, and he spoke quietly.

"Zohar, you need not answer, but you must listen. Your people tell me they have made no sacrifices since they knew you. But Binyamin, who longs to call himself your son, has tried to sacrifice himself to placate whatever gods may forgive his people, and would have died if I had not prevented him. After that they were ready to let the Unds kill them. I prevented that also, but they will not speak to me, or to you if you do not forgive them. I cannot do any more here and I have nothing further to say to you. Goodbye."

He turned from the door without waiting, but heard it open, and Zohar's voice cried out, "Og, where are you going?"

"To the store-room, to turn myself off. I have always said I was no more than a machine, and now I have reached the limit of my logic and my usefulness."

"No Golem, wait! Don't take everything from me!" The old man was standing with hands clasped and hair awry. "There must be some end to foolishness," he whispered. "Where are they?"

"Out by the field near the entrance," Og said. "You will see them when the lightning flashes."

The Holy One, blessed be His Name, gave Zohar one more year, and in that time Og ha-Golem built and planted, and in this he was helped by the b'nei Avraham. They made lamps from their vegetable oils and lit them on Sabbaths and the Holy Days calcu-lated by Zohar. In season they mated and their bellies swelled. Zohar tended them when his strength allowed, as in old days, and when Elyahu died of brain hemorrhage and Yitzhak of a swift-growing tumour which nothing could stop, he led the mourners in prayer for their length of days. One baby was stillborn, but ten came from the womb in good health; they were grey-pink, tooth-less, and squalled fearfully, but Zohar fondled and praised them. "These people were twelve when I found them," he said to Og. "Now there are forty-six and I have known them for five genera-tions." He told the Cnidori, "Children of Avraham, Jews have converted, and Jews have adopted, but never children of a differ-ent species, so there is no precedent I can find to let any one of you call yourself a child of Zohar, but as a community I see no reason why you cannot call yourselves b'nei Zohar, my children, collectively,"

The people were wise enough by now to accept this decision without argument. They saw that the old man's time of renewed strength was done and he was becoming frailer every day; they learned to make decisions for themselves. Og too helped him now only when he asked. Zohar seemed content, although sometimes he appeared about to speak and remained silent. The people noticed these moods and spoke to Og of them occasionally, but Og said, "He must tend to his spirit for himself, b'nei Avraham. My work is done."

He had cleared the land in many areas around the station, and protected them with forcefields whose antennas he had made with forges he had built. The Unds were driven back into their wilds of cave and valley; they were great and terrible, but magnificent life-forms of their own kind and he wished to kill no more. He had only to wait for the day when Zohar would die in peace.

Once a day Og visited him in the Common Room where he spent most of his time reading or with his hands on his book and his eyes to the distance. One peaceful day when they were alone he said to Og, "I must tell you this while my head is still clear. And I can tell only you." He gathered his thoughts for a moment. "It took me a long time to realize that I was the last Jew, though Galactic Federation kept saying so. I had been long alone, but that realization made me fiercely, hideously lonely. Perhaps you don't understand. I think you do. And then my loneliness turned itself inside out and I grew myself a kind of perverse pride. The last! The last! I would close the Book that was opened those thousands of years before, as great in a way as the first had been . . . but I had found the Cnidori, and they were a people to talk with and keep from going mad in loneliness—but Jews! They were ugly and filthy and the opposite of everything I saw as human. I despised them. Almost, I hated them . . . that was what wanted to be Jews! And I had started it by teaching them, because I was so lonely—and I had no way to stop it except to destroy them, and I nearly did that! And you—" He began to weep with the weak passion of age.

"Zohar, do not weep. You will make yourself ill."

"My soul is sick! It is like a boil that needs lancing, and it hurts so much! Who will forgive me?" He reached out and grasped one of Og's arms. "Who?"

"*They* will forgive you anything—but if you ask you will only hurt yourself more deeply. And I make no judgments."

"But I must be judged!" Zohar cried. "Let me have a little peace to die with!"

"If I must, then Zohar, I judge you a member of humanity who has saved more people than would be alive without him. I think you could not wish better."

Zohar said weakly, "You knew all the time, didn't you?"

"Yes," said Og. "I believe I did."

But Zohar did not hear, for he had fainted.

He woke in his bed and when his eyes opened he saw Og beside him. "What are you?" he said, and Og stared with his unwinking eye; he thought Zohar's mind had left him.

Then Zohar laughed. "My mind is not gone yet. But what are you, really, Og? You cannot answer. Ah well . . . would you ask my people to come here now, so I can say goodbye? I doubt it will be long; they raise all kinds of uproar, but at least they can't cry."

Og brought the people, and Zohar blessed them all and each; they were silent, in awe of him. He seemed to fade while he spoke, as if he were being enveloped in mist. "I have no advice for you," he whispered at last. "I have taught all I know and that is little enough because I am not very wise, but you will find the wise among yourselves. Now, whoever remembers, let him recite me a psalm. Not the twenty-third. I want the hundred and fourth, and leave out that stupid part at the end where the sinners are consumed from the earth."

But it was only Og who remembered that psalm in its entirety, and spoke the words describing the world Zohar had come from an unmeasurable time ago.

O Lord my God You are very great!
You are clothed with honour and majesty,
Who covers Yourself with light as with a garment,
Who has stretched out the heavens like a tent,
Who has laid the beams of Your chambers on the waters,
Who makes the clouds Your chariot,
Who rides on the wings of the wind,
Who makes the winds Your messengers,
fire and flame Your ministers . . .

When he was finished, Zohar said the *Shema*, which tells that God is One, and died. And Og thought that he must be pleased with his dying.

Og removed himself. He let the b'nei Avraham prepare the body, wrap it in the prayer shawl and bury it. He waited during the days in which the people sat in mourning, and when they had got up he said, "Surely my time is come." He travelled once about the domains he had created for their inhabitants and returned to say goodbye in fewer words than Zohar had done.

But the people cried, "No, Golem, no! How can you leave us now when we need you so greatly?"

"You are not children. Zohar told you that you must manage for yourselves."

"But we have so much to learn. We do not know how to use the radio, and we want to tell Galactic Federation that Zohar is dead, and of all he and you have done for us."

"I doubt that Galactic Federation is interested," said Og.

"Nevertheless we will learn!"

They were a stubborn people. Og said, "I will stay for that, but no longer."

Then Og discovered he must teach them enough *lingua* to make themselves understood by Galactic Federation. All were determined learners, and a few had a gift for languages. When he had satisfied himself that they were capable, he said, "Now."

And they said, "Og ha-Golem, why must you waste yourself? We have so much to discover about the God we worship and the men who have worshipped Him!"

"Zohar taught you all he knew, and that was a great deal."

"Indeed he taught us the Law and the Prophets, but he did not teach us the tongues of Aramaic or Greek, or Writings, or Mishna, or Talmud (Palestinian and Babylonian), or Tosefta, or Commentary, or—"

"But why must you learn all that?"

"To keep it for others who may wish to know it when we are dead."

So Og surrounded himself with them, the sons and daughters of Avraham and their children, who now took surnames of their own from womb parents—and all of them b'nei Zohar—and he began: "Here is Mishna, given by word of mouth from Scribe to Scribe for a thousand years. Fifth Division, *Nezikin*, which is Damages; *Baba Metzia:* the Middle Gate: 'If two took hold of a garment and one said, 'I found it,' and the other said, '*I* found it,' or one said, 'I bought it,' and the other said, '*I* bought it,' each takes an oath that he claims not less than half and they divide it. . . .'"

In this manner Og ha-Golem, who had endless patience, lived a thousand and twenty years. By radio the Galaxy heard of the strange work of strange creatures, and over hundreds of years colonists who wished to call themselves b'nei Avraham drifted inward to re-create the world Pardes. They were not great in number, but they made a world. From *pardes* is derived "Paradise." but in the humble world of Pardes the peoples drained more of the swamps and planted fruitful orchards and pleasant gardens. All of these were named for their creators, except one.

When Og discovered that his functions were deteriorating he

refused replacement parts and directed that when he stopped, all of his components must be dismantled and scattered to the ends of the earth, for fear of idolatry. But a garden was named for him, may his spirit rest in justice and his carapace rust in peace, and the one being who had no organic life is remembered with love among living things.

Here the people live, doing good and evil, contending with God and arguing with each other as usual, and all keep the Tradition as well as they can. Only the descendants of the aboriginal inhabitants, once called Cnidori, jealously guard for themselves the privilege of the name b'nei Zohar, and they are considered by the others to be snobbish, clannish, and stiff-necked.

ANTHROPOLOGY 101

Gary Eikenberry

And so I return. My proper body is strange to me. Everything about Home feels a single degree off centre. The universe seems odd. Even the organs of perception feel alien. The burrows of Home have a strangeness about them.

Through a significant expanse of time, I *zi-am* Ellen Cumberland, a surface dwelling creature from a far-off, inconceivably alien world. But this welcome place is Home, and the closeness of the burrows of Home feels good. A time of Tribute is a time of joy. The joy wells up in me, filling in the spaces around the oppressive strangeness of the world of Ellen Cumberland. The joy is not lessened by the regret that I have very little of substance to report to the commissioners of the Entropy Probe.

ENTROPY PROBE 101 :: Vreeselle, researcher :: Sol III

As with other events in the Entropy Probe series, the PURPOSE of this event is to explore the relationships between the subject beings and the world they inhabit, paying particular attention to any cultural manifestations with implications for the goals of the Entropy Project.

The METHOD follows the accepted standard of *integrated participatory observation.*

The SELECTION of this particular world is due to the fact that the subject beings exhibit a high degree of vitality. They boldly change the physical attributes of the surface of their world with great frequency. As Home, itself, is a fading world, we must explore the possibility that elements contributing to the vitality of these beings are significant to the goals of this project.

"I know it's hard, Ellen, but you have to try—"

"I'll be fine, Vince. It's just. . . ."

"Do you want me to stay for a while longer?"

"It's just that everything reminds me of her. She was here helping me with the curtains just a few days ago. Now she's gone. I keep expecting the phone to ring and it'll be her."

"She's dead, Ellen, gone forever. You have to accept that."

"I know she died. I can accept her *death,* but not that she's *gone forever.* Remember what I was saying last night? What if all those memories were tangible? What if they were more than just in my head?"

"Ellen, don't do this to yourself. We've been through this already. Have you talked about this with Dr. Spellman? I really think you should. You can't go on like this. It's been almost a month now."

ENTROPY PROBE 101 :: Vreeselle, researcher :: Report 101:1

Very little about the subject world resembles Home. Much of the strangeness of these creatures and their ways is attributed to the fact that they are surface dwellers.

The specific subject I inhabit is Ellen Cumberland. She is a complex being and prefers to surround herself with vast, open spaces which serve no purpose. This is common among all subject beings. The living space allotted to a single one of these creatures is more vast than the greatest Grand Council Chamber in all of Home and could easily contain as many as seventy of these enigmatic beings.

Theirs is a culture of taboos and irrationalities much too various and complex to describe. They are peculiarly unevolved for a species spanning such a length of time, but much of this may be attributed to their preference for living on the surface of their world. Perhaps the vulnerability of surface dwelling explains their constant, frenetic activity and their tendency to expend tremendous amounts of energy transforming the matter of their world into perversely unnatural objects. Religious implications related to the pressures of surface dwelling may explain this level of activity.

SPECIAL COMMUNICATION 101 : 1 :: TO Vreeselle

The fading of Ssooulian, Maker of Vreeselle, achieves precedence. Home summons Vreeselle for Ssooulian's Tribute.

It makes me glad to be within Home, but this time of Ssooulian's Tribute is difficult. So much of the surface dweller's world remains with me. Home, itself, seems almost alien. I attempt to cleanse myself of these alien accumulations, but this dreadful feeling of dislocation remains, even within Home.

These perverse cultural traits, a quirk of the unfortunate surface dwellers' evolution, are clearly maladaptive within Home and must be cast off.

ENTROPY PROBE 101 :: Vreeselle, researcher :: Report 101:1

It is now clear that the subjects suffer from an inability to transcend the linear time mode. This temporal paralysis results in their peculiar way of dividing events into three catagories: *past, present,* and *future.* Their term *present* appears to approximate our own *now,* while *past,* and *future* appear to represent two forms of the *zi-now.*

Their critical misperception of reality is clearly attributable to the congenital temporal paralysis which afflicts all but a minute number of their species. They are, quite literally, utterly helpless in time. Their temporal movement is limited to uncontrollable drifting *in a single direction.* Past represents time vectors to which they *cannot return;* future represents time vectors which they *cannot experience out of sequence.* Theirs is a truly dismal existence.

I am struggling to understand the multitude of other terms and distinctions they apply to the *zi-now.*

Another significant trait they exhibit is a tendency to categorize things in their world into what they refer to as *opposites.* Opposites are not easily explained. The common thing/*zi-thing* distinction does not apply here. Opposites appear to be arbitrary points along any and every continuum. These arbitrary points are seen as differing from each other to the greatest extent conceivable. Examples of opposites are up vs. down, in vs. out, red vs. green, good vs. boring and hot vs. cold. This concept of opposites is difficult to understand given the fact that the subjects clearly recognize the absolute multiplicity of points along any continuum. I can only conclude a curious cultural propensity towards these arbitrary absolutes over our more subtle distinctions of degree. This propensity may have some relationship to a general inclination towards duality attributable to the extraordinary means of reproduction peculiar to most of the higher lifeforms inhabiting the subject world. Reproduction here requires the participation of two members (direct participation is limited to two) of the species of different physical characteristics, described as *male* and *female.* A more detailed analysis of this phenomenon is contained in my biological report.

I am in my own body. I am sensing the soothing burrows of Home in my own way, not confined by the sensory or temporal limitations of the surface dweller, Ellen Cumberland. I am in intimate contact with those who give my life its deepest meaning. And yet, I am experiencing a feeling towards the fading of Ssoulian, which is not my own feeling. This is *sadness,* which Ellen

Cumberland feels towards the subject being she calls her *mother*. Ellen Cumberland perceives her mother as *dead*. She does so with great sadness. Dead appears to mean isolation in the totally inaccessible past.

"You were telling me about this 'other way of seeing things,' Ellen."

"When you say it like that you make it sound like they're delusions or something."

"I'm sorry if that's the way it seems to you. I certainly don't intend to be judgmental. Try not to worry so much about people thinking you're crazy, Ellen. You're not."

"Then what *is* wrong with me?"

"Why do you think the death of your mother has affected you so strongly?"

"I don't know . . . it's the finality. I mean, one minute you're, well, taking someone for granted, and then the next minute she's gone—it's just, well, so hard to deal with someone just *never ever* being there again."

"You feel as if your mother abandoned you?"

"I don't think so."

"What would you do if she were still alive? What is it you never had a chance to do?"

"I don't think I'd do anything differently. It's so hard to explain. . . . It's just that in the past she isn't really dead. Do you see what I mean?"

'But we can't live in the past, can we, Ellen?"

The surface dwellers refer to this unpleasant sensation as *remembering*. Remembering is a way of projecting the mind, alone, *without sensory support,* into that portion of the *zi-now* which they call the past. It is as if the body and its senses are filtered out. It is very unsettling, this remembering. I *remember* Sssooulian. I *zi-am* with Sssooulian—I am only remembering. Remembering makes Sssooulian distant and inaccessible. It is a terrible thing.

I worry that I am performing very poorly on this assignment by becoming involved with the subject in an inexplicably complex way.

ENTROPY PROBE 101 :: Vreeselle, researcher :: Report 101:2

The great vitality of these surface dwellers seems to be rooted in their lack of temporal freedom. While these beings often experience extreme discomfort if confined spatially, they seem quite content to have their temporal mobility restricted along a single, linear continuum. I believe that they are not only content with this restriction, but that their entire existence and sense of being is based on it.

What appears to be vitality is, in reality, nothing more than extremely rapid temporal movement. The surface dwellers have no control over the rate or direction of this movement. Such uncontrolled motion should not be confused with true progress.

The phenomenon they call past can best be described as the isolation of objects, individuals, events, et cetera, in a location in time which is beyond the reach of direct sensing. Its opposite, future, is the particular form of *zi-now* that compels these beings to alter the surface of their world and create artificial objects.

I am unable to recommend future as a viable solution to our entropy crisis.

THE TRAIN

Marc Sévigny

Translated by Frances Morgan

For your information, my name is Loïc. I'll be twenty in ten days. Soon I'll have been living on this train for twenty years. If that surprises you, that must mean you're no longer one of us or else you belong to the world outside, which I know nothing about. You must understand. This isn't a train that stops at stations, picking up and unloading passengers at stops along the track. On our train, no one gets on, no one gets off. You're here, you stay.

Our caravan has been on the move constantly. Looking out the filthy windows (how can they be washed on the outside if no one is allowed out?), we always see the same countryside: miles of sand, chalky rock, once in a while a scrawny tree, sometimes a leafless bush, but never another living soul. Maybe we're going around in circles; who knows? Everything outside is the same and unbelievably boring. Inside, no one talks, no one wants to talk. If you have the misfortune to be a blue, that is, someone who was born on board, you'll never know anything about the world before. I'm a blue. There are quite a few of us in this category, but for some time now, regulations have kept the birth rate near zero. A question of necessity, it seems; the train is getting crowded.

After a childhood spent in cramped cars, life seemed dull enough already, but when I started to ask questions and came up against a wall of silence all around me, it became unbearable.

And yet, there's no lack of people to teach me. There are those we call "the elders," "the old people," but so far they refuse to break their stubborn silence. They hardly ever mix with the young people anyway; and when they do condescend to join us they're extremely careful to avoid our questions. Their age gives them a tranquil authority that no one dreams of challenging. Over the years (that pass with an oppressive slowness), they've formed a separate world in reserved cars where no blues are allowed.

There are also those we call "middlemen"; they make up an intermediate class between absolute blues and the elders. At the time of the confinement on the train, the middlemen were still children. They've kept vague memories of the world before, but like the elders, they jealously guard them for themselves. The middlemen are the ones who in fact organize our "community life" here. In my opinion, it's more like organized solitude.

I don't know my father or my mother, but that's not unusual. A sense of family, in these quarters, would never survive the terrible lack of privacy. In the blues' section, we live one on top of the other. I don't really know how many passengers there are in the other compartments. To count them, you'd have to be able to visit the train from one end to the other, which, given the rules prohibiting entry to certain cars, is hardly possible for a blue like me.

On the unanimous recommendation of the middlemen, children are separated from their parents at a very early age and handed over to the community. What that means, *grosso modo,* is that the raising and education of children is taken care of on an annual basis. Teaching is mostly oral. Books are rare on the train, and those that could be used are scrupulously kept in the area reserved for the elders. However, handwritten texts, prepared by the most experienced teachers, are circulated for the purposes of instruction. This instruction generally applies only to the necessities of life on board the train, and even then, necessities have been reduced to the bare minimum. Speak (if the very rare occasion should arise), read (if you can find anything to read), write (graffiti in the washrooms) and count (zero, I repeat, zero equals zero).

Learning games is by far the most useful educational tool. Let me explain. The soul of the train, or what's left of its soul, is games. Elders, middlemen and blues meet at card tables and at backgammon, checkers and chess games, confronting each other with a silent but vital passion. In a way, games keep the imprisoned passengers from losing their minds day in and day out. As proof, the cars that have been turned into games rooms are so busy they had to install a rotation system to let all the passengers have their turn.

I adore playing games. That's how I met my only friend Noemie. Fifteen. A blue. A terrific backgammon player.

The train, apart from playing, eating and sleeping (copulation forbidden), isn't exactly a hive of activity. As far as sleeping goes, it's out of the question for a blue in my category to even dream of having a sleeping compartment. They're occupied permanently by the elders and a few worthy middlemen. We, the blues, sleep right on the coach seats. For eating, there's the dining-car, and when I'm not at a backgammon table, that's where you'll find me. Naturally, the blues have to do a number of maintenance jobs, but they're periodic and divided equally among those old enough to work for the community. In particular, it's our job to keep the cars clean. Fear of disease on the train leads to a sense of hygiene that borders on the hysterical.

Of course an epidemic would mean mass fatality, especially since there are no facilities to fight it; medicine here has become a matter of expediency. Anyone found with a contagious disease is thrown off the train, *ipso facto*. This rule might seem ruthless, and undoubtedly it is, but everyone accepts it nevertheless in the interest of the collectivity. These "clean-up" operations are carried out promptly by the middlemen duty officers, easily recognized by their caps as they patrol the aisles from one end of the train to the other. The same Draconian treatment is given to the dying, the depressed, the hyperactive and the mentally ill.

I keep wondering how they throw them out.

The dining-car is an excellent place to kill time. There's always a lot of activity at the counter and at the arborite tables around the huge compartment. With a little luck, you might overhear a conversation, usually banal, above the shouts of the customers and the waiters who do their utmost to make the cook hear their orders. Stress is a way of life for the dining-car employees; they've all got a greenish complexion because of it. But they wouldn't change jobs for anything in the world. For them, time passes quickly, and they're never bored like the rest of the passengers. Naturally, their jobs are the envy of all.

There's always a steady stream of people coming and going and the waiters often have trouble making their way to the tables. Whenever I can, I sit in the back, order a coffee and observe the passengers pushing and shoving in the aisle. I examine faces for an answer. Who are we, where did we come from, where are we going? And systematically, eyes are averted, because of my reputation for asking questions.

Gradually, I've learned how to be like everyone else, that is, to be quiet and wander aimlessly from car to car, stifling the cry inside me. If I had the courage to let it go, it might wake up this crowd of dreary sleepwalkers.

And what about me, Loïc, aren't I half asleep? Yes, I slept, I slept my fill, until I met Noemie. Noemie. Looking out the soot-black window, I tell myself that maybe she's there, somewhere outside, and then I cup my hands over my eyes and squint to try to see out beyond, when I know perfectly well that beyond there's only the smooth sand of the desert. Noemie is dead, I repeat to myself without really believing it. She died because she couldn't stay silent. She couldn't sleep like the rest.

Noemie had a trick. She could control the dice. There was no one like her for rolling double sixes at just the right time. In backgammon, that can often be fatal for the opponent. With one quick glance, she could size up the game and make her moves. The rapidity, confidence and the accuracy of her plays made me lose my concentration. Invariably, I made mistakes and then I'd tell myself that luck was against me. I must admit, I have a persecution complex that's easily aroused. In fact, I was furious at her luck and she . . . she would just laugh.

"Better luck next time."

I lost my temper. I thought I was good at that game. I jumped up and left the table, throwing her my blackest look. That only made her laugh harder, which infuriated me. I didn't expect to see her again.

But I did. In the dining-car. I saw her coming towards me and this time, I looked at her carefully. Noemie was neither beautiful nor ugly; she had a freckled, baby face, a little turned up nose, sparkling eyes and the gangling manner of a scatterbrain. She was the image of the way she played backgammon: energetic and formidable. Quite unexpectedly, she came right up and sat beside me at my table in the back. It took a certain amount of courage on her part to approach me so boldly in this car full of hostile middlemen; on our train, relations between blue males and blue females are frowned upon. As for me, I was nervous and kept looking around me as if I were in real danger. She didn't take any notice and stared at me boldly.

"What's your name, poor loser?"

"Loïc."

"Mine's Noemie. Are you still mad at me?"

"I'm not mad, but we shouldn't be talking. Even at the games tables, personal conversations are discouraged."

I was stammering. She laughed; it was indecent. I wanted to melt away and disappear. Half the restaurant was looking our way. Sooner or later, someone would intervene.

"I've got a plan."

Now her voice became a barely audible whisper.

"A way of getting into the elders' area without being seen."

My whole being was willing her to be quiet. I was dying of fear. Finally, she realized and stood up, much to my relief. But still she whispered:

"Come back here tonight."

I was trembling, pretending to look elsewhere, not to hear her. Then she disappeared among the tables where the disapproval was growing. An authoritative voice growled over my shoulder. A duty officer, his cap half-covering his eyes, loomed over my table, where a crowd of curious onlookers had gathered.

"I'm warning you, blue. Don't let me catch you with that girl again, or else you'll be in for it. Understand?"

I nodded obediently, sinking down in my chair. With that, the officer left, breaking up the crowd.

What would I do if she came back? She had arranged a secret meeting—illegal and obviously dangerous—and yet . . . and yet, I wanted to see her again. I was obsessed with her proposal. Visit the elders' quarters! It could only be a bad joke. But if I didn't take the chance with her, I'd still in the same boat: alone, ignorant and unhappy.

So I remained at my table in the dining-car until late that night. Outside, the desolation of the desert had disappeared with nightfall. The waiters, as greenish-looking as ever, were getting ready to close. Finally I decided not to wait for Noemie any longer but to go back to my seat and sleep.

As I started down the aisle, the door of one of the toilet compartments opened a crack. Through the crack I could see Noemie making signs for me to come in. Without thinking, I pushed the door open, squeezed in and closed it quietly. Noemie locked it immediately and put her finger over my mouth as she leaned against the door. We could hear muffled footsteps on the carpet in the aisle, but after a moment there was silence. Still I couldn't relax. I was very close to her and it had a funny effect on me; she smelled nice and her perfume washed over me. Noemie, rigid in concentration, kept her ear glued to the shining metal of the door. Then, when she thought everything was quiet, she unlocked the door and peeked out. She went out into the aisle, dragging me with her. I followed her as if hypnotised. When we came to the dining-car's wide sliding doors she smiled at me and showed me a key. The doors opened and we went through the dining-car, holding our breath. We came to another door, and when we pushed it open we found ourselves in forbidden territory: the sleeping-cars.

Noemie seemed to be in familiar surroundings and that reassured me. She walked down the aisle and stopped in front of one of the compartments, staring at me strangely. For a minute, I thought she was leading me into a trap.

When I walked into the compartment my blood froze and Noemie squeezed my arm, as if to encourage me. The compartment was poorly lit but what I could see sent shivers down my spine. Shelves lined the walls, heavily loaded with books. But what struck me most of all was a pile of printed, loose pages under one of the shelves. I knew what they were; one of my tutors had alluded to them during my years of instruction, but I had never seen any before. Newspapers!

I approached them cautiously. They were yellowed and the letters on the first page had faded. Noemie stood back, as if out of respect for my curiosity. I picked up the first one on the pile and examined the title in bold-faced letters at the top of the page: NUCLEAR ARMS: TALKS RESUME. My eyes were glued to the headline. I was too excited to read the rest or try to understand what it meant. So this was the world before! I didn't have a chance to think about it any more, because when I turned to Noemie I spotted the frail shadow of an elder, standing in the doorway. He was looking at Noemie and me, without speaking. Noemie didn't seem at all worried.

"Don't be afraid," she told me, "he's a friend."

The old man walked up to me, took the paper out of my hands and put it back in its place on top of the pile. His tired eyes didn't look at mine and after he had put the paper back, he stood facing the wall, his shoulders sagging, breathing heavily. Noemie motioned to me and I joined her in the aisle. We walked back through the dining-car without incident and then went our separate ways without a word. For her and for me, silence was the only way.

I crept back to my seat, but couldn't sleep. The old man had allowed me a glimpse of the world before but would he show me more of it? What did Noemie know? She said he was a friend, but how could an elder be friends with a blue? It was no use asking her; now I knew what her strange look meant when I walked into the forbidden compartment. It was a sort of warning. She had a secret, a secret that she probably shared with the old man, a secret that didn't concern me and that would never be revealed to me. If I wanted to pursue my initiation, I would have to explore the territory on my own. While I tried to sleep, the bold-faced letters of the headline whirled around in my brain: NUCLEAR ARMS: TALKS RESUME. I didn't understand a single word.

Two days later, I met Noemie again at a backgammon table, despite the ban that hung over us. Luck had it that we were both given permission to go to the games room at the same time. We played a seven points game. At first, Noemie didn't say anything, rolling the dice with a fury that I didn't recognize in her. She played erratically and I beat her easily. Something terrible was tormenting her but I didn't dare ask.

"I'm leaving tonight!"

She practically shouted. Near us, heads were raised and we could hear a murmur of angry, ugly voices.

"Finally I'll know the truth."

The truth, what truth? She dropped the dice, was already running to the door. Stupidly, I let her go, I didn't move, afraid of the hundreds of eyes staring at me, burning through my skin. One elder in particular glared at me, drumming on the wooden chessboard in front of him with a knight. On my right, a middle-man kept throwing a pair of dice that echoed insistently on the polished surface of his backgammon board. The elder could have been sixty, the middleman forty and I was almost twenty. A spiral of ages leading nowhere. I stood up and left too, even though it was too late to join Noemie. Behind me, the games started up again, louder.

Ten days have gone by. Today, I'm twenty. Without Noemie, these years have automatically become worthless. I can't stop telling myself that I have a right to the truth, like her. And the truth doesn't exist on this train. The elders' memories have become confused with the inventions of the younger ones. They have a vague idea of their history and that's enough. They all walk with their heads down, shut up in their individual compartments, never looking outside, walking along aisles that are all the same, walking as if they were on the edge of a cliff hanging over the void. Fear of falling blocks their sight, and this fear has become so embedded in them it has become a way of life. For them the truth stops at the airtight doors to the cars; it balances on the boxes of the games of chance.

Because of the filth obstructing the windows, because of the lack of perspective, the passengers take their cue from the decrepit minds of the elders. In little, severely restricted groups, deluding themselves that they're surviving, they're rotting away and lying in their own rot. For twenty years, I've been like them, but now the rancid air of the compartments turns my stomach and the vision of Noemie disappearing into the open country, there, outside, is constantly in my mind. Repeatedly, the vision implores me to escape.

For nights I wonder how she did it. All the doors leading to the head of the train are locked, all the exits seem inaccessible. Did the old man help her? Would he do the same for me? Once, during one of my sleepless nights, the train stopped. Our convoy came to a grinding halt; I counted about twenty-five minutes, then it started off again. I've noticed these stops before. They happen at regular intervals, when all the passengers are fast asleep. Supposing that I did find a way to get out, I'd have to take advantage of one of these occasions. Night after night, I toss and turn on my seat without finding a solution. During the day, my inspection tours inevitably lead me to the door of the sleeping-car compartments, where I'd had my first revelation.

Another night is beginning. There are dark circles under my eyes. For a long time I haven't even dreamed, even though my dreams never lead outside either. When my eyelids grow heavy and close in spite of myself, the old man in the newspaper room appears and I wake up. This time, my dreams have become reality. The old man, in flesh and blood, is standing in front of me in the aisle, staring at me wordlessly. Without a moment's hesitation, I whisper: "I want to leave."

No reaction. I sit up on my seat and watch the old man shuffle away down the hall. I follow him. He heads towards the middlemen's section, I notice with some fear. Is he going to turn me in to the duty officers? All around us, blues stir on their makeshift beds, some snore, others watch us pass, stunned. Copying the solemn bearing of the elder who leads me, I feel I'm taking part in some ritual. Just before reaching the middlemen's car, he veers sharply to the left. We're in a sort of buffer-compartment, between two cars. There, as stiff as a rod, the elder turns to me and points to a red box on the wall labelled: EMERGENCY. Under the box, a panel encloses a recessed cupboard. The panel is protected by a huge lock. Ceremoniously, the old man hands me a key that I take and use immediately to open the panel. Behind it still is a glass case containing a fire extinguisher and an axe. The axe, I realize right away, is my only chance to escape.

Closing the panel, a shiver runs down my spine. The old man hasn't moved and our eyes meet, at last.

"Why are you helping me?"

He swallows painfully, then rasps:

"You young ones, you have no idea how lucky you are. Noemie. . . . "

He chokes on her name and his eyes fill with tears.

"I lost Noemie, my granddaughter. . . . "

I try to say something, but he raises his hand to stop me.

"Try your luck, young man, you'll do less harm by leaving than by staying here."

Before I can argue, he brushes past me. His long pale nightshirt disappears behind the door to the blues' car. I can picture him walking with the same solemn air through the central aisle to the sleeping-cars.

As I return to my seat, my mind is full of conflicting emotions. As spoken by the old man, the truth has a bitter ring to it. Clearly, my stubbornness displeases him and he is helping me escape unwillingly. Is he trying to make up for some mistake with Noemie? Sometimes, parents manage to trace their children on the train, but the cases are rare and besides, are forbidden by the regulations. Maybe the old man, in an excess of sentimentality, broke his own laws, became trapped by guilt and vulnerable to his granddaughter's whims. So, by getting rid of me, he would be getting rid of an embarrassing witness who might bring him more problems. But what did it matter! Noemie is outside and I must join her.

Tension mounts until the next evening. Gradually, night falls, blues, middlemen and elders, men and women, return in silent little groups to their respective compartments. I fall into a tense, half-sleep, broken by sudden fits and starts, in tune with the cars that rattle and shake. Hours pass in this half-sleep when suddenly the whole mass of the train shudders, contracts and jolts to a stop.

Immediately, I jump into the aisle. I run to the red box, unlock the panel and kick in the glass. I grab the axe and run in the opposite direction. The carpet muffles the sound; no one notices me running by and I reach the doors to the dining-car; I use the axe to pry off the hinges. I push my way through. Two duty officers, a man and a woman, appear in front of me. According to the regulations, they aren't armed. Making the most of my advantage, I brandish the axe in my hand.

"Get back!"

They obey, backing as far as they can into one corner of the dining-car.

"The keys!" I yell.

One of the officers slides his keys along the floor to my feet. The two seem to be struck dumb. They aren't used to being challenged. I leave them to their confusion and proceed into the elders' quarters, locking the door behind me. As I make my way through the sleeping-cars, a few elders try to block my route, pleading with me to turn back. I don't hear a word; the sense of time running out throbs in my veins and I rush forward, brandishing my axe; the elders make way, uttering plaintive cries. From one car to the next, all I see are elders. How many are there anyway? The train's full of them. I push them roughly aside whenever they get in my way but fewer and fewer of them try to stop me now; I hold my axe like a shield. No middleman, no guard in sight. I keep going in the now deserted aisles, despairing of ever finding the end.

Finally, I reach what I think must be an extremity, closed off by an armoured car impossible to break through. I stop short. Neither the axe nor the ring of keys are any use to me, here. There are iron bars on the door and in the middle, a sort of hatch like you see on ships. An image from my childhood resurfaces: an old man drawing a picture for me of the interior of a huge ship. There's a wheel on top of the hatch; I give it one full turn and pull with all my strength. To my surprise, the latch gives way with a clinking of metal. I open it.

"Close that door!"

I freeze. Four men, wearing space-age suits and fibreglass helmets, are glaring at me. They're standing in the middle of a vast car, one side of which is completely open to the outside. Around them are stacked piles of cases, barrels and metal containers which they have just loaded. The shortest of the four approaches me, but when I start brandishing my axe, he stops.

"It's too late for you," he says drily, "but close that door."

I obey. Then I stand there, like an idiot, at the end of my flight.

"What's that?"

I point to the cases. The same harsh voice answers me.

"Fuel, water and food. The train has to run after all."

The others snicker.

"Where's it from?"

"Where do you think it's from? Eh? It's easy to see you're a blue, you think everything just falls out of the sky."

More laughter.

Then silence, the same wall of silence that suffocated my life in the cars. I lose my temper, lose all control.

"Explain! What are you doing here? What are we doing, confined to this train?"

Finally the short man answers, probably afraid I might blow up.

"It's an arrangement, you see, an arrangement between us . . . and the ants."

The other middlemen suddenly burst out laughing. One of them steps forward.

"They're savages," he explains. "Savages."

"We're wasting our time," said another. "We'll be late."

Now they all step forward, as if they want to be done with me, but I keep a tight grip on the axe, ready to defend myself. Deep down, though, I know that I'm at their mercy; their inflated clothes, their shining helmets conceal hidden dangers.

"Why those suits?"

The short man smiles thinly.

"Because of disease . . . those savages are so dirty. And ugly!"

"What do you know about it?" snorts another. "No one ever sees them."

And they burst out laughing again. The madder I get, the more they laugh, like it was their reward for working at night.

"Who are these savages you're talking about?"

"We already told you," the short one answers. "They're ants and they work for us. That's the arrangement, and soon you'll be an ant, too."

More laughter. I feel like I'm talking to madmen. Then one of the middlemen raises his hand.

"Okay, guys, there's still a lot of stuff to load."

I'm trembling with indignation.

"What about Noemie? What happened to Noemie?"

I might as well be crying in the wilderness; they've lost interest in me now, as if the whole time, i was only a minor distraction in their routine. Silently, they go back to work, loading the rest of the cases and barrels, not even giving me another glance. Cautiously, I edge towards the wide opening along the side wall. A powerful spotlight illuminates part of the track where the men are working. As I jump to the ground I feel like I'm really breathing for the first time in my life. But, if what they say is true, if I breathe this fresh, invigorating air, I'll soon be sick, dead, or on the way to becoming an ant! The tension gripping my throat falls away and I too burst out laughing. An ant!

The men on the train ignore my euphoria. They've finished loading the cases and are closing the big doors. Just ahead, I can see the main locomotive, shrouded in smoke, grey steam rising from the engines. Slowly, it starts up again and for a long moment I watch as the caravan rattles past me. Like a giant caterpillar, hundreds of cars snake past my eyes. Then gradually, silence and darkness surround me. I sit down in the sand and contemplate the desert stretching as far as the eye can see. Rocks, scrawny trees. I feel fine despite the cool, night air, and I stretch out on my back. The depth of the star-studded sky makes me dizzy, I feel like I'm falling into a bottomless gorge, then, in a strange reversal, like I'm soaring above it. I have never been able to see so far before. Empty space carries me like a new-born, dazzled and enchanted at the sight of this gold spangled dome. My breathing calms down, at one with the beauty of the spectacle. The questions that previously buzzed in my head die down and, whispering the musical name of Noemie like a lullaby, I fall asleep happy.

When I wake, the sun is high, I'm quite alive and no longer alone. Rusty-faced men, women and children surround me, examining me with curiosity. Still lying on the warm sand, I look at them too. Their faces are all solemn, gaunt with disease or hunger. Their excessive thinness makes all the bones in their bodies stand out; I'm afraid they might break and crumble to dust at the least excitement. Bulging eyes, protruding brow bones, hollow cheeks. They stand awkwardly, their deformed swollen stomachs barely supported by spindly legs and flat feet. I lean on one shoulder and a wave of nausea washes over me. I have to look away. Immediately, outstretched hands demand an offering.

But I don't have anything to give, I've just got off the train, I didn't bring anything with me. . . . My thoughts become confused and suddenly I think of the smirking middleman talking about an arrangement. . . . For whom? Why? Lies! What lies! In the hope of finding an answer, some help or a particle of truth, I turn towards the train tracks, towards the steel bars glinting in the sun, towards the vast void where the parallel lines are lost in the horizon.

Then I return to the outstretched hands in front of me and cry, "I have nothing to give!"

No one moves, except a small child who limps closer to better reveal his misery. Then the words of the old man echo in my mind: "You young people, you have no idea how lucky you are." No, no idea. I see them all, waiting, and I want to tell them that I'm a blue, that I don't know anything about the world before and that they don't understand. As I push away their hands and stand up, I have an idea. I look at them one by one, turning slowly. I force myself to smile, to show them some sign of friendship. I say:

"Nuclear arms . . . talks resume."

The dryness of the desert on my lips. Their defeated looks. Their blank silence. I repeat, accentuating every word:

"Nuclear arms . . . talks resume?"

One by one, tired of standing in the blazing sun no doubt, they turn their backs and file away, vanishing into the sand dunes. I grasp at the few who remain and who are smiling amiably at me. They're smiling. Isn't that a sign of progress?

"Nuclear arms . . . talks resume."

Impassive, the remaining spectators follow the rest of the tribe's example and disappear among the dunes. Suddenly, something breaks in me and I fall to my knees. And in that posture, I vow to wait for the next train, to grab on to one of the cars and to cry through the soot-covered windows that they have no right to ignore such misery, and that outside there are no savages or ants, but human beings like them and like me!

Then in the distance I spot the slow procession, winding its way into a tunnel dug in the ground. As they disappear into the anthill, my tears trickle down onto the arid ground that soaks them up instantly. And with them the memory of Noemie and a pair of dice rolling a double six is absorbed forever.

TWO POEMS

John Robert Colombo

COUNTDOWN   **QUESTIONNAIRE**

for Fritz Lang
who invented the countdown

10 Rocks   Your future will be:
 9 Clubs
 8 Sling-shots   More of the same.
 7 Arrows   Less of the same.
 6 Muskets   About the same.
 5 Machine-guns
 4 Tons of T.N.T.   All of the above.
 3 Atom Bombs   None of the above.
 2 Hydrogen Bombs   Below or above.
 1 Neutron Device   Will your future be?
Zer0 Hour

SOPHIE, 1990

Marian Engel

After Jethro left, Sophie set about doing her bit of housework, thanking her stars she hadn't as much to do as her mother had had once. It was her mother's birthday; she thought of her as she whisked the galley counter, vacuumed the parrots' cage and tended the hydroponic garden. What as easy life I have beside hers, she thought: a quarter of the space to clean, everything I want at arm's length, a man to support me.

And the light! And the sun! Really, Jethro was a genius, he deserved his success; it was he and his friend Bobby, who, working of course with other people's ideas, but working practically and imaginatively, had made it possible to live this way: comfortably and in so little space. Why, Sophie thought, if I just turned off the sound curtain, we'd be in the slums again. . . .

She thought back to the days when Jethro had been a gangling punk-rocker with a big Adam's apple, and she'd been his girl, leather jacket, green hair, I LOVE THE POLICE button and all. Annoyed by his bull sessions with Bobby, too, the way they took him away from her; infuriated by her mother's desire for her to have a career and horror at the green hair. Mother, she wanted to say, the boys were just figuring out how we should all live.

Yes, how to pack four million people into space for two, that's what their discovery had amounted to; twenty years before people had still been building as if the twentieth century had never come, they were living like little old china figures out of a Dickens novel, one room for every function—cooking, eating, sleeping; huge bathrooms; rec and TV rooms, pantries still, even. And they had eaten as if they lived in old books, too. Sophie's mother had kept cupboards full of raisins and sugar and rice and canned hams as if she were expecting a crew of hired men and a thrashing machine; and there was the whole sick gourmet thing, people looking for more and more exotic things. Well, they'd found out that a few lentils, some greens and a handful of The Mixture would do. They hadn't as much to talk about . . . or as many heart attacks.

Funny that it was those sessions between Jethro and Bobby that had started the change. As far as Sophie was concerned it was a good one. If she was somehow past-haunted it was because it was here, in this very house, her mother's plain old semi-slum four-up four-down, where the two of them had once lived alone together with a room for every ashtray and a million books, that Jethro began. He'd put the first sound curtain behind the stairwell the year her mother died, and once he'd found out how to make it opaque, followed it with the famous under-floor storage units. The next year when refrigerators went out in the energy crisis, he'd figured out how to handle the four-foot galley unit. Most people had thrown their antiques into their pot-bellied stoves during the Freeze; there wasn't any real trauma about converting to built-ins after that. And now, of course, that the sound curtains enabled four familes to live in this one little house, and the solar units were keeping them warm and well-lit, everything was beautifully comfortable. She had all the books and music she wanted on the computer that fed into the television set.

It took a while, she thought, but we're happier now. You don't need all that stuff we used to have: sewing machines, hair dryers, typewriters, blenders and mixers. You can get anything you need at the Centre.

She was back in the sun on the bunk. It was February, but the sunstrainer allowed her to tan. Up in their high, gleaming cage, the parrots tumbled and squawked. She could almost hear the parsley and onions growing. Mother, she thought, would miss the morning paper. She turned on the news to see what was happening: as usual, nothing good. But it had always been like that.

She heard Bo stir and got a can of formula out of the cupboard for him, went and crouched beside his little cupboard bed while it was warming. Poor Bo: did he even know she loved him? Did he know she'd wanted him since she was fifteen, her own baby and Jethro's? They'd had to put him off during the Freeze when so many babies died it would have been cruel to have him; but this wasn't a good time for them either. Funny, she'd pictured monsters and freaks after the Accident but it wasn't like that at all, just a slow wasting. His poor little light going out before it was properly turned on.

He seemed to like flowers, so she grew them for him among the vegetables. She handed him a little, white-stemmed violet; he put it close to his pale eyes and smiled. She kissed him and went to get his bottle.

Every day she told herself fiercely, "You can't have everything."

At first she blamed Bo's disease on her smoking; but Gordie, the kid she'd beaten up in grade one at Huron Street school (he was always trying to kiss her) was the one who broke through the computer code at the medical bank and announced it: there were thousands of Bos. Jethro hadn't liked that, he'd grown up straight and thought the Government was a hero. His mother had never made him sign a petition against the RCMP. Governments are just like people, Sophie thought, some good, some sly. I wish this one would let me go out to work again. Bo wouldn't know the difference between me and a housekeeper, if I got a nice one.

Well, it wouldn't be too long now, she thought, cradling the pale form in her arms. It's not that you don't love them, but you begin to accept parting with them; you have to, or you'd go crazy; you put your tears behind the sound curtain, really. She wrapped him carefully in the old wool shawl she had hidden away. Wool was valuable now. All the sheep had died in the Freeze; and the cattle. Now we dress in woodpulp, she thought, instead of writing on it. Funny world and why not?

Beyond the sound curtain, another woman was tending her garden, nursing her pallid son, retaining her ability to talk by whispering to her birds. If she and Sophie had gone out, they might have met each other. But there was no reason to go out.

Her simple needs were taken care of; she went to the Exercise Centre on Thursday, not Friday as Sophie did.

Sophie turns on the television and wonders what book there will be today: *Northanger Abbey,* a golden oldie. That will keep me till Jethro comes home. She didn't like books until they were gone. She'd die without them now, waiting, always waiting.

The other woman mixes her baby's formula. She goes to add his medicine, and, looking over her shoulder, sure someone is watching, quickly appropriates some for herself. "Well get through this day, Roo," she says. "We'll get through."

FUTURE CITY

D.M. Price

ONE
Now it is spring the war is on
The trees bow to the end of the road
Waves break from distant grey ships
All the birds the famous volcano are silent
Somewhere in the forest two armies search
A friend says sound no longer travels far
Someone noticed that the cats are whiter
Someone else saw a star through the glass one day
The animals come closer the doctors are afraid
Every night the film shows someone running

TWO
We followed the machine to the place of its sorrow
We discovered the corner where the privates kiss
We can't stop rage from hiding its dead children in our guns
We cured the staring curved the fire cursed the man

THREE
He said it would be different afterward
The world would be as sane as light
We would dance on the back of sleep
A sky would fall to build our cities

Our children would suck at the breasts of new comets
Someone would write the songs of virtue on her eyes
Something rare might then be passed from hand to hand

FOUR
It is near the end of the watch if the clouds thicken
The lights move over the desert closer and closer
All night the dead have been flying overhead calling out
What we thought was our hymn is the rim of a crater
There is nothing musical about our orders
The refugees are to be used to smash the wingéd statues
Our astronauts return encased in rubies
At night their scars illuminate the cellars

FIVE
Some say the world is the shape of prison
When a child is born we all move forward
The old say we burrow in time's entrails
They say our skin is full of time's eggs
They say we grope in night's pockets like blind fists
That it's in our veins we think we trace the way to daylight

SIX
The guards say there's an enemy but they don't know where
They say he screams all the time the light's too bright
They say his hatred is the colour of a forgotten child's eye
The angels are leaving soon they say he's growing normally
If we need rest we can love the wounded lying in the mirrors

SEVEN
Our questions are so perfect there is silence
In the ruins we cannot tell who speaks
Believable demon unbelievable man

TOTEM

Margaret McBride

The little aluminum boat slapped vigorously against the waves, delivering an occasional bone-jarring thump over the big ones. My whole body was tensed to take the shocks of our swift passage across the bay, and I was glad to see Jimmy McMurchie throttle back, letting the boat down gracefully into the black salt water. The wind shifted as we lost headway, whipping Jimmy's long hair forward across his face. He laughed and brushed it back behind his ears, letting go of the outboard's controls as he pointed across the remaining distance to the shore.

The tide was half out, and the grey, pebbly beach ran up over a fence of sea-worn logs to the salal and scrub alder of the low shoreline. Behind that was thick virgin forest of hemlock, sitka spruce and western red cedar, a sombre backdrop for a line of six poles spaced irregularly along the boundary of land and sea. Five were obviously old: grey, seamed with long cracks, leaning gracefully this way and that, one with a crown of huckleberry and all with thick growths of fern and salal glossy below. One was much newer, though still showing signs of having been there for a number of years. It had never been painted, and the slim thrust of carved cedar was warm gold with pewter accents. Jimmy McMurchie pointed his nicotine-yellow finger towards that tallest, newest pole.

"That's Alphonso Johnny's pole there." A raven flapped its wings and swooped off the top of the pole. "'Course, his nephew Ralph carved it, almost twenty years ago must be. He's living down in Vancouver now, but old Alphonso is still here in the Charlottes. You want to go ashore?"

I couldn't see anywhere to put the boat in safely through the tossing chop and kelp beds which alternately revealed and hid a lot of vicious black rocks, but I wanted to see that pole. I'd come five thousand kilometres to see it. At my nod Jimmy turned the prow of the runabout and slipped it between two barnacle-encrusted teeth to the beach, lying as calm as a Sunday picnic under the dark, still forest. I hopped out and tugged the boat's prow up onto the beach. Jimmy killed the motor and walked up to the bow stepping onto the beach with a dignity befitting his size.

Above the tide line, the pebbles gave way to coarse yellow sand and patches of weed. We walked over to the newest pole and looked up at it.

It was certainly unusual. I hadn't seen another like it, though I could see one or two familiar elements: a bear near the bottom, for instance, and a couple of human figures. But few of the traditional forms were in evidence. The older poles were crowded with figures of animals. The raven predominated since that had been the totem of the tribe which had lived on this site until 1919. Beavers, salmon, whales and humans were all represented on one pole, in the intricate, stylized and compressed story-art of the totem-carvers.

Jimmy sat down on a broad log, lit a cigarette and contemplated the distance. I stepped up to the pole and ran my fingers over the surprisingly warm, smooth wood. The air had a brightness about it even through the almost permanent fog of the Queen Charlotte Islands, and the hidden sun's warmth had seeped into the wood under my hand and the ground beneath my feet. The fog had made a thin damp crust over the yellow sand, so that my footprints around the pole's base left a trail of dry indentations.

"See that blank space up near the top?" said Jimmy, breaking the silence. "That's supposed to mean a high altitude, like a mountain top, say, or something up in the sky. Sometimes, there were things that lived in clouds." He took a deep drag on his cigarette, dropped it and pushed it into the sand with his toe.

I backed up until I could get a view of the top of the thirty metre shaft. A smooth, uncarved stretch ran the length of a man's body, starting above what looked like some sort of semi-human figure and ending under the very topmost image. What that image was, I couldn't tell.

"Jimmy, I'm going to get my stuff out now, and we'll probably be here an hour or so. I guess you can't order me up any real sunshine, eh?" We both smiled, and I went to the boat for my camera, tripod and bag of equipment. The telephoto lens would pull those strange, high figures into view.

The air was mild and humid and smelled equally of sea and forest. It was air that I wished I could store up and transport back to the city where I'd first heard of this unusual pole, back to my museum—where air never moves too fast or smells too fresh.

In Masset the next day, I picked up my developed prints from the one-hour photomat and then paid a call to old Alphonso Johnny. I needed the story of that pole, and the person to get it from was the old Haida Indian whose tale years ago had inspired a young man, Ralph, to carve his only pole. Ralph was now a middle-aged, successful architect in Vancouver, and had never again turned his hand to the art of the totem. I had never met Ralph, but I'd talked to him over the phone during the wait for a flight from Vancouver International to Prince Rupert and then to the town of Masset at the north end of the Charlottes. He'd told me where to find his uncle, and assured me that the old man would be pleased to tell his story.

Alphonso's granddaughter made tea with sugar and evaporated milk and brought it to us at the kitchen table. Her smile was so wide and charming that I drank the sweet liquid without complaint while she sat nursing her baby. Between enthusiastic sips of his tea, Alphonso told his tale, in his gravelly, lisping voice.

"Archie Harry and me were out hunting," he began. "We had only gone for the day, so we didn't have a lot of stuff to slow us down. It's pretty flat all around here, but across Masset Harbour we got up to about four hundred feet pretty quick. It was kind of cold up there, and we didn't see a damn bit of game, so we sat down for a while and Archie got out his thermos. We sat there for a while, still didn't see nothing, then I wished we had a thermos with more than just those two little cups on top, because along comes the Old Man of the Woods. No wonder there was no deer; the Old Man, he smells pretty high.

"So I drank up quick and poured some tea for him. Well, he's a polite kind of fellow and he went and sat downwind on the log, and we talked about this and that. I asked about his wife, and how many children he might have now. He said that she was okay, and he didn't know how many children as he wasn't much at counting, and anyway he didn't see them too often. They were on the other side of the mountain now. He also said that one of the bears had told him to move to the other side of the mountain too, as the bear and his family were leaving, and in fact every animal was leaving. The Old Man said he didn't know why, it was the first he'd heard of it, but suspected it could have something to do with the way parts of the mountain side had started to crumble away, and how it was not safe to go into caves any more. He said he and his wife figured it was time they moved on too, but suddenly, before I could ask him any questions, he puts his cup in my hand and disappears. After a few minutes, out of the woods comes Mr. Ranjeet Ackloo, a person we all knew as he had been around for a couple of weeks. I didn't know he was this far out of town; another reason for no deer. He came up smiling and talking very fast like always and brushing his free hand back and forth in front of his face, just like there was something there. He smelled the Old Man but was too courteous to say anything, thinking that it was us. In his other hand he held a stop watch. Where we were sitting was looking down over some slash, and Mr. Ackloo stood beside us, puffing and waving out over the patch of slash, and he explained what he was doing. We couldn't stop him from this; he was East Indian and, as he had told us often, felt a kind of kinship with us, the Red Indians, and considered us to be his brothers. It seemed he'd heard that Sasquatch could cross a field of slash forest covered with stumps and fireweed and saplings in only about one tenth the time it took a human. Well, he was going to test this, at least from the point of view of the human. It would be part of the book he was writing.

"He smiled some more, bounced up and down on his feet,

pushed his glasses up his nose, said 'One, two, three!' and took off. He was certainly travelling pretty slow, all right, which would be good evidence for his book.

"We decided to head up the mountain awhile more, and perhaps meet up with the Old Man again and hear more about all the animals moving away. Some people, the Kwakiutl, call him Bukwas, some, the Nimpkish, call his wife Dsonoqua, the cannibal woman. We mostly call him Old Man, as he has not told us his real name. See, there he is up there."

And Alphonso's finger jabbed at one of the photos, the second from the top figure on the pole, just beneath the open space. I'd spread all my photos on his kitchen table, views from every angle, and close-ups of each section, front and sides. The back of the pole was partially hollowed out, as many poles were. He pointed here and there.

"Down there, there's the bear. He's at the bottom because he was in the story before it really started. Then, there's us, me and Archie, and at the sides, nothing, to show where the deer were not. Then there is Raven, who came to tell us that he had been flying all day to warn everybody, and he was angry that we were still there after all the work he had gone to. He became a very black cloud and rained on us, then changed again into Raven and flew away laughing.

"After a little while, as we walked up the mountain, the Old Man joined us again. He had his wife with him. She was just as tall as he, but had a more beautiful coat of hair. Her breasts hung down like those of an old woman, though she walked as lightly as a deer. They were leaving, and Archie and I decided to go back down and go home, when suddenly the mountain shook and we were all knocked down. It stopped after a short time, and Old Man and his wife got up and went very, very fast along the side of the mountain and upwards. We were heading down when we heard a big ripping, grinding noise behind us. Well, we were scared, but we stopped anyway and looked back, holding onto trees so we wouldn't get knocked down again.

"What we saw was the mountain coming alive. The noise of ripping and tearing got louder and louder, and very slowly part of the mountain came away. It was like a big cork coming out of a bottle, only there were trees growing on the cork, and it began to crumble and break apart, rocks and trees rolling away. We were too scared to move, and it was lucky that we didn't get hit by anything. We could see up into the opening that was in the mountain now, as all the dust began to blow away.

"For a while there was nothing there, although the ground kept on rumbling, and we hung on to the trees. Then out came some beings. They looked to us to be tall and hairy, like the Old Man and his tribe, but they were dressed in clothes, which the Old Man did not do, and they were riding things like helicopters without those vanes on top, and were carrying things in their arms. They flew like bees around the opening, very fast back and forth, up and down, and then back they went inside. Soon a huge being or thing filled the opening, coming out very slowly. The rain cloud that had been Raven had gone, and the sun came out as it does now and then in fall, and the sun falling on the being or thing made it shine like copper.

"It crept out of its cave and took all the flying things with their riders into itself, through mouths in its sides. Then it went up. I couldn't see it, but I had the feeling that it came down onto land again once or twice or more, and I had the feeling also that I would never see the Old Man or his family again. And that was true, although the animals came back eventually. I think he and his family went with their people. Mary Ann, get more tea for the lady."

Alphonso pushed one of my photos to my side of the table. It was a close-up of the pole's summit, one of several I'd taken, and he stroked it gently with his finger. "I told Ralph the story," he said, "and Archie told him too, but still this doesn't look too much like it. It was more flat on the top and the wings were less like those of the eagle. In fact, it was very different from this in many ways. You know, a woman like you should not listen to an old Indian's stories. If you tell them, no one will believe you."

He smiled and began to cackle, his face crinkling into a wicked expression. Mary Ann heated up more water and added it to the tea pot.

"What did Mr. Ackloo think of it?" I asked.

Alphonso wiped his eyes and reached for the plate of cookies that Mary Ann had put down. "Archie and me found him when we got back to town," he said, dunking a cookie. "He was getting ready to leave; he wanted someone to take him down to Tlell. He said that what with the earthquake and the avalanche, the evidence of Sasquatch would all be destroyed and he might as well go somewhere else. He was sick and tired of Masset."

We talked some more. I was stalling for time. I knew I'd have to go back with nothing—nothing that could possibly stand up to the scepticism of my colleagues—and the story of an eighty-year-old Haida about events twenty years earlier was as good as nothing. And I didn't really believe it myself, did I? Mr. Ackloo had published his little book—I'd read it before I came to the islands, and it was a foolish mass of credulity piled on spurious "facts." I had felt embarrassed to be seen reading it. But I'd come, I'd seen the pole, I'd talked to old Alphonso, I'd taken photographs—of what? A gently rotting shaft of cedar, silvering under the west coast rain.

Alphonso told me of how his friend, Archie, had died a couple of years later, drowned while fishing, before Ralph had gotten around to carving the pole. There had been a ceremony for the installation of the pole, which had been carved one winter while Ralph was out of work. He'd used the shelter of an old longhouse to carve it in, extending the roof with some tarpaulins supported by a light framework of planks. A small wood stove had kept him warm. About thirty of Alphonso, Archie and Ralph's friends and relatives had piled into a couple of boats and gone out to the old town site and had watched as, during the spring rain, the pole had been settled into its pit and raised to the vertical. A few years later, a boat containing one or two vacationing faculty from the University of British Columbia had gone by and a few snapshots had been taken, which had found their way eventually to the Ethnology Department in the basement of the Royal Ontario Museum. Since there were plenty of totem poles to view at that time, nobody paid any particular attention to the photos. I'd seen the original now, and more compelling even that the enigma at the pole's top, whose mechanical power was made somehow alive by the abstract anthropomorphism of the art, was the figure below it, separated by that stretch of smooth wood.

The round eyes and small teeth were those of a human; the

lowering, wide brows, the ridged crest springing in a vee from the hooked nose, the long, cavernous cheeks and pricked ears, were something else, something animal, and conveyed an emotion of fierce wistfulness, if such a thing can be. How long had they waited, those few who had gone out into our world and become legend? The legend would live long after the evidence was gone. I took a cookie from the plate and picked up the close-up photo of the Old Man, there atop his tree, staring up and out with his huge cedar eyes. He must have been someone worth knowing.

A sudden rain drummed on Alphonso Johnny's roof. No doubt it did its work upon that special pole. In less than a human lifetime it would be gone, rotted by the mild, insistent rain, toppled, and covered with ferns, salmonberries and young red cedar. But I'd seen it.

AN ADVENTURE IN MIRACLE-LAND

Robert Zend

I was touring Miraculandia
with a large following
around me.
When I showed them that 2 plus 2 equals 4
they gasped in disbelief.
When I let an apple go and it fell
down, not up,
they prostrated themselves before me.
When I stuck a knife into my flesh
and it bled,
they kissed my hand.
When I laid my hands on someone's wound
and the wound did not heal,
they declared I was god.
When I couldn't pass through walls
and I couldn't walk on water,
they built chapels to worship me.
When I pierced my heart with a lance
and I died,
they began counting the years
ahead and backward
from the date of my birth.

2DWORLD

A.K. Dewdney

The first contact with Yendred was made on one of our computer terminals only a year ago. We, my students and I, had been running a program called 2DWORLD, the result of several consecutive class projects carried from one term to the next. Originally designed to give students experience in scientific simulation and in large-scale programming projects, 2DWORLD soon took on a life of its own.

It started as an attempt to model physics in two dimensions. For example, a simple two-dimensional object might well be disk-shaped and be composed of billions of two-dimensional atoms.

It has a kind of mass (dependent on the type and number of atoms in it) and may move about in the two-dimensional space represented by this page. As such, this space has no thickness and the disk is doomed to eternal confinement therein. We may further imagine that all objects in this space obey laws like those which prevail in our own space. Thus, if we give the disk a gentle push to the right, it will move to the right and continue moving to the right, sliding along at the same speed in a space which extends this page beyond your present location. Ultimately, within this imaginary plane, it will move far from the Earth itself—unless, of course, it encounters a similar object:

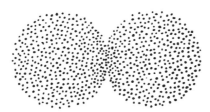

Doing so, the objects meet and suffer what physicists call an "elastic collision." Here we see the two objects at the precise instant of their greatest compression just before springing apart in opposite directions. In accordance with another well-known law in our own universe, the two disks carry off, between them, exactly as much combined energy as they brought to the collision. They have to collide, of course, since they cannot slip sideways past one another; there is no room in two dimensions for that, since no "sideways" is available.

This sort of thing is not difficult to represent on a computer graphics display terminal, nor is it difficult to write a program which creates all the behaviour I have just described in the case of the two disks. Naturally, if there are to be atoms in the disks, there is considerably more work for the programmer to do and, when the program is running, considerably more work for the computer. But, in principle at least, one can write this sort of program and actually view the results on a screen.

The program called 2DWORLD started in a manner not unlike this. In the first term that the project was assigned, the students, under my direction, had incorporated not only a simple set of objects and laws governing momentum into 2DWORLD but had also extended it to a system of planets orbiting a single star. At the end of the first term, there was talk among the students of a particular planet which they called "Astria." They wished to endow it with a geography of sorts and have beings called "Astrians" living on it. I nipped that ambition in the bud by reminding them that the term was nearly over and that examinations would soon be upon them. Besides, that sort of detail was mere wishful thinking and far beyond their abilities to embody in a program. Nevertheless, I counted the project a great success and congratulated myself on being clever enough to confine the dimensions of the physical space to two. It had, perhaps, made all the difference to the feasibility of the simulation program.

What had been especially stimulating for the students in this project, I believe, was the interaction of their other areas of knowledge with computing. They had been expected to read and digest a fair amount of physics and engineering. Moreover, just to give them a feeling for how a whole might be orchestrated from these parts, I had them read Abbott's *Flatland,* Hinton's *An Episode of Flatland* and Burger's *Sphereland.* These works of fiction, or "science fantasy" one might call them, each set up a model two-dimensional universe inhabited by two-dimensional beings. In this additional reading of the students lay the seeds of future development.

During the following term, I had wanted the class to construct programs which modelled predator-prey relations, among other things, but interest in 2DWORLD continued to run high and I finally gave in to their demands to continue the project. In that term we got to work on Astria, defining its surface of land and water and even attempting to construct simple organisms living in the water. Some of them could "eat" the others, so here at last was my opportunity to simulate predator-prey relationships, albeit not in the manner I had originally intended. I must admit that at this point I too was becoming more interested in the project than a certain sense of professional detachment would dictate. Frequently, we would stay well beyond the weekly laboratory period watching those little creatures glide and dart about in their two-dimensional realm, feeding and being fed upon.

But then came the end of the term and examinations for the students. I thought I had heard the last of 2DWORLD, at least until the autumn, but shortly after examinations were over, three of the keener students in my simulation class came to visit me. They wanted to continue working with 2DWORLD and were willing to stay in town over the summer to make that possible. One of them, a fourth-year student in biology, Winston Chan, wanted to design more advanced creatures for the simulation. The other two were computer science students, one of whom, Hugh Lambert, wanted to construct a "flexible, multipurpose query system" which would enable one to communicate with the 2DWORLD program as it ran. The other computer science student, Alice Little, had an idea which would allow 2DWORLD to be implemented on a much more elaborate scale while at the same time enabling it to run even faster. Faced with their obvious enthusiasm, I felt I had no choice but to give in to their requests. The computer they wanted to use would be largely free over the summer and, yes, I would be happy to continue co-ordinating the project.

Looking back over those summer months, I now realize that if 2DWORLD had a turning point, it was then. Time and again I came upon the three students working in the computer laboratory. This was a room housing one of the newer large-scale computers linked to a graphics terminal in the room and communicating with numerous other terminals throughout the building. One of the students would be at the terminal experimenting with some new program concept while the other two would be bent over a large worktable in the middle of the room, muttering to each other above the reams of printout spread thereon. Occasionally I would enter the laboratory and ask if they were having any problems. Politely, they would show me what they were doing, but I almost invariably ended up feeling more like a spectator than a participant. Nevertheless, I was fascinated with some of Chan's creatures and impressed with Little's new simulation system: her idea was to "focus" the activity of the program in a small area of the two-dimensional universe being simulated, allowing approximate behaviour outside the area. Lambert worked closely with

Little in developing a technique for verbally querying the system to discover its "background behaviour"—whatever was not obvious from looking at the display screen.

When the summer ended, I fully expected the three students to go their separate ways. For one thing, they had all graduated and two were ready to enter high-paying jobs in the computer industry. But Little had decided to do graduate work in computer science and Lambert wanted to work in the department as a course assistant. This development alarmed me a bit, especially when both applied as assistants in the Advanced Simulation course I was giving. Choosing Little, because of her more obvious commitment to an academic career, I was surprised to discover that Lambert would be auditing the course. I was more than a bit alarmed to think that the course would be dominated by 2DWORLD once again.

I needn't have worried: all the incoming students had heard about the project and virtually refused to work on anything else. Obviously, 2DWORLD was meeting some deep, emotional need of the students. Many of them seemed determined to retain some fragment of their childhood fantasy life. One had only to think of the immense popularity of various computer games like "Space War" and "Adventure" to understand what a widespread phenomenon it was. Nevertheless, I was determined that the course should have some semblance of academically respectable content, so I spent the first two weeks on a perhaps overly learned series of lectures about generating random numbers.

We eased into 2DWORLD rather slowly. By now it had become a very large and rather sophisticated program of several thousand instructions. It took Alice Little and me several weeks to initiate the new students and to find subprojects for them which somehow fitted into 2DWORLD as a whole. Chan had left us with a rather strange ecosystem: the oceans now held several species of plant and animal life, the former being nearly as carnivorous as the latter. Apparently, two-dimensionality made the carnivorous plant business much more profitable than in our world. Chan had, moreover, invented an animal called a "throg" which slightly resembled a frog. It apparently did almost as well on land as in the ocean. On other fronts, Alice's new simulation management system worked wonders for our ability to include new detail with only slight increases in computation time. Perhaps this factor as much as any other was what prevented 2DWORLD from becoming totally unwieldy during that crucial second year.

Just before the Christmas break, I invited Chan in to lecture the class. As a hobby, he had been laying down the design parameters for a new class of land animals, including one which was supposed to be "intelligent." I don't believe that at the time Chan had any very clear idea of how such intelligence would be built in, but two of the students took up Chan's ideas, changing projects in mid-course, so to speak. These two, Ffennell and Edwards, produced an upright, vaguely triangular creature (called an FEC) which moved about on its base by alternately extending and retracting two pods and rocking as it went. Its intelligence, as such, did not reside in a simulated brain. There was, after all, a limit to how much detail even Alice's system could handle. Instead, its intelligence was embodied in a special subprogram modelled after certain recent work in artificial intelligence. To round out the picture before our narrative enters its next, rather dramatic phase, it seems only fair to mention that other students concentrated on Astrian weather, atomic physics, biochemistry, ecological balance, and so on. These projects were perhaps not quite as sophisticated as they sound, but each contributed something interesting and vital to 2DWORLD for the most part.

As might have been expected at this point, 2DWORLD had become something of a sensation at our university. Not only had the campus newspaper done two stories about us, but the dean of science had made a special point of visiting our laboratory. I have saved the printout from that occasion. Lambert had been running a demonstration at the graphics terminal, typing queries to the system while one of the Ffennell-Edwards creatures trundled awkwardly across the screen in search of throgs.

```
■ RUN PRIORITY QUERY.

  READY.

■ VERBAL: FEC IN FOCUS.

  FEC HERE--HUNT THROGS.

■ WHY?

  UNKNOWN: "WHY."
```

193

At this point, I recall, Lambert explained to the dean that the word "why" was not in the system vocabulary.

- DESCRIBE HUNT.

  MOVE EAST UNTIL THROG OR SEA.

- DESCRIBE UNTIL.

  UNTIL INCLUDES AVOID AND RETURN.

- DESCRIBE AVOID.

  AVOID INCLUDES WATCH FOR AUNT LYONS.

Although the dean was highly impressed on one level, I could tell from the faintly anxious look which occasionally crossed his features that he, as I, had some reservations about the academic usefulness of the 2DWORLD project. A moment after the printed conversation, a throg hopped into the focus, became rather detailed, then sensed the FEC and tried to hop away again. The FEC quickly leaned over, extended its eastern arm, and trapped the creature between body and ground. Scraping its hand along the ground, the FEC managed to catch the throg between its two fingers. The dean gaped as the FEC lowered the throg into its mouth and chewed it, gradually, into little pieces. Being two-dimensional, the inside of the FEC was just as visible as its outside: the pieces of throg made their way, one by one, into a digestive pouch just below the jaws.

During the next term, 2DWORLD developed to the point where even Alice Little's management system could handle no more additional features. There was now an atmosphere on Astria, regular patterns of weather fluctuated above its surface and quite a variety of creatures inhabited both the ocean and the land. The FECs, moreover, had been given simple underground dwellings where they could store food and have inane conversations about digging or throg-hunting.

One night, near the end of the term, I returned to my office after supper to prepare a talk I was giving at a Data Structures conference in a few days' time. In the middle of a period of deep concentration, there came a light, fluttery knock at the door and in stepped Alice Little, her face looking strained and puzzled.

194

"Dr. Dewdney, something's gone wrong with the system! One of the FECs said a word not in its vocabulary. We checked the dictionary but no one has changed it!"

She seemed breathless. I was annoyed to have my train of thought broken but put on my good-natured teacher's face and rose from my chair. I tried to reassure her as we walked down the corridor to the laboratory.

"The word is Y-N-D-R-D."

"That doesn't sound like one of our words."

"I know!"

All the lights were off in the laboratory. The graphics scope bathed the room in an eerie radiance as we sat down at the terminal in front of it. A student named Craine who had been working with Alice shifted his chair to make room and we three stared at the lone FEC on the screen. It swung its head slowly to the right and then to the left.

```
■ RUN PRIORITY QUERY.

  READY.

■ VERBAL: FEC IN FOCUS.

  FEC HERE--YNDRD.
```

"There it is," said Alice under her breath. We spent a few minutes discussing how we might track down the problem, then I took over at the terminal.

```
■ DESCRIBE YNDRD.

  YNDRD IS BUT FEW WORDS.
```

Craine murmured "Oh, no!" and continued to do so every few minutes thereafter. This did not help our analysis very much.

We reasoned, after repeating this sequence a number of times to rule out spurious errors, that everything had to make sense in the context of the simulation. The phrase "is but few" reflected a construction unavailable to the program and we decided, finally, that it represented two separate sentences, "Yndrd is" and "But few words."

■ WHERE IS YNDRD?

There was a long pause.

NO WORD.

■ DESCRIBE WORD.

WORD FOR WHERE YNDRD IS.

This was getting a bit strange. The FEC would normally have described its position relative to nearby landmarks on the planetary surface. Perhaps there were none.

"Alice, where's the nearest feature that an FEC would relate to?"

Learning that there was another FEC just to the west of this one, I asked Alice to have it come east into the focus area. As it came on the screen, Alice typed:

■ EAVESDROP.
WHO ARE YOU?

I´M GEORGE. WHO ARE YOU?

I´M CHAN THE MAN.

Thus ran the first three sentences of conversation between the FECs. I took it that "George" and "Chan the man" were two of the regular FEC names, invented by the students last term. It seemed the glitch had disappeared.

"I *thought* that was George all along!" declared Alice with an air of relief. Craine agreed solemnly. I decided to interrupt the conversation going on before us.

■ VERBAL: EAST FEC IN FOCUS.

FEC HERE--CHAN THE MAN.

■ WEST FEC IN FOCUS.

FEC HERE--GEORGE.

■ DESCRIBE YNDRD.

UNKNOWN: "YNDRD."

I spooled off the printout, our only documentation of the incident, tore it from the terminal and took it back to my office, suggesting that Alice and the student call it a night. In my office, I studied the printout for a few minutes before succumbing once again to the pressure of my imminent conference talk. There was really no way that sort of thing should be happening.

A few days later, I spied Edwards and Craine in the cafeteria and went to their table. I found them discussing the "yendred incident," news of which had already leaked out to the rest of the class. Edwards, evidently, was taking the "but few words" statement at something more than face value.

"How do *you* explain it?" they asked me.

I chose my words carefully. "Well, I don't know enough about the 2DWORLD system as a whole to say just what combination of software and hardware errors could produce a sequence like that. Perhaps no one person does. It's certainly become very complex. On the other hand, you might start by analyzing the ASCII code for YNDRD and look for a systematic bit error that would produce it from any of the five-letter words currently in our vocabulary."

Craine showed real interest in this suggestion, but Edwards gazed abstractedly out the cafeteria windows.

On May 22 a telephone call interrupted our family supper. YNDRD had reappeared at our terminal.

"Professor Dewdney?"

"Yes. Is that you, Alice?"

The details of the recurrence, as related in a few breathless sentences by Alice, were sufficiently startling to put an end to my supper. I promised to drive to the university right away.

In the laboratory there was quite a crowd: Alice, Chan, Lambert and several students. The lights were on and everyone seemed to be talking at once. On the display screen a lone FEC rocked gently from side to side. Flowing from the terminal and arranged into a carelessly folded pile was a large mass of printout. My entrance created a sudden silence.

"What, exactly, is going on?"

Edwards strode to the terminal and picked up part of the printout. "See for yourself, sir." He proffered a fragment.

197

```
■ DESCRIBE YNDRD.

   YNDRD YOU THERE ARE KNOWS BUT HE YOU DOES NOT SEE
   AND YOU DOES NOT HEAR.

■ MY NAME IS CHAN.

   UNKNOWN: "CHAN."  DESCRIBE YOU.

■ I AM A STUDENT.

   UNKNOWN: "STUDENT."  DESCRIBE YOU.
```

The conversation went on for several pages, becoming steadily more unbelievable. I soon came upon a section in which a number of new words appeared.

```
■ WHERE IS YOUR PLACE?

   MY PLACE ARDE IS.  WE THE NSANA ARE.

■ ARE  YOU TWO-DIMENSIONAL?

   UNKNOWN WHAT IS "TWO-DIMENSIONAL."
```

Edwards interrupted to point out that the system queries and replies no longer followed the proper format. It would seem that the system now responded to a great variety of English sentences. It went through my mind that at any moment all the students would break out laughing at their wonderful joke on me. Further on I found:

```
   BEFORE YOU MORE WITH ME WERE.  NOW YOU LESS ARE.

■ RUN  SYSTEM.

   READY.

■ FOCUS (SAME, 1/2).  VERBAL: FEC IN FOCUS.

   YOU EVEN LESS MORE WITH ME ARE.
```

Alice, who had been looking over my shoulder, explained. "Here's where we started to lose him. It took us a long time to find out that we had to slow down the rocking motion."

"What has that got to do with it?"

She didn't know.

The rest of the printout, some twenty more pages, was no less strange. There did appear to be an entity conversing with the students, exchanging words with them and becoming continually more fluent in the process. The entity, YNDRD, alternated between describing a place called ARDE and questioning us about our world. I tried to keep my mind clear. Only two alternatives appeared possible: either the program was producing this wonderful conversation all by itself, or some remote prankster had a line to our terminal, perhaps someone in Dr. Barnett's Operating Systems course.

"Has anyone checked the hardware for some kind of remote patch?"

Alice replied, in an almost motherly way, that all inputs to the computer, except for this one terminal, had been disabled. They too had thought of this possibility. Numbly, I sat down at the terminal.

■ DESCRIBE YNDRD.

   YOU CHAN ARE?

■ NO.   I AM DEWDNEY.

   WHY NO ONE FOR A LONG TIME TALKED?

■ WE WERE TALKING TO EACH OTHER.

   WHAT ABOUT TO EACH OTHER WERE TALKING?

A dry, metallic taste invaded my mouth and I felt somewhat lightheaded.

■ WE TALKED ABOUT YOU.

   YOU FROM THE BEYOND ARE?

■ YES.   IN A MANNER OF SPEAKING.

   YOU SPIRITS ARE?

■ WE ARE NOT WHAT WE OURSELVES WOULD CALL SPIRITS.   WE HAVE
  SOLID THREE-DIMENSIONAL BODIES.

   WHAT "THREE-DIMENSIONAL" IS?

I stayed on with the students that day. We spent several more hours talking with the being we had come to acknowledge as "Yendred," generating more reams of output in the process. As the conversation continued, strange things began to happen on the screen: Yendred's anatomy was slowly changing from that of an FEC to something completely beyond our imaginations. Strange internal organs pulsed rhythmically. Sheets of tissue parted along seams and then rejoined. Our FECs, moreover, had two arms. This creature had four, and they seemed to inflate and deflate regularly. Adjacent to Yendred, curious plants appeared, hugging the Ardean surface. The entire scene was now far more detailed than anything produced by the 2DWORLD simulation program. It had, moreover, an odd, alien quality, utterly convincing because it was so bizarre.

In spite of this transformation in the two-dimensional landscape before us, both the scanning program and Alice's focusing system continued to work, so that we could scan the landscape at will and examine any part of it in some detail.

When we at last said farewell to Yendred and terminated the 2DWORLD program, we sat in silence for nearly a minute, each of us absorbing the impact of this astounding manifestation. Present were Chan, Edwards, Ffennell, Lambert, Little, Craine and, of course, me. I made a speech which went something like this:

"What we have been witnessing just might be real. That is, it just might represent a communication with beings in another universe. If it's a prank, someone has gone to an *enormous* amount of trouble to entertain us. In any case, I think we had all better agree right now to keep this evening's events a secret until we understand what's going on a little better."

Lambert interrupted. "I think we should have a public demonstration."

"Oh, be serious!" said Chan.

"I'm afraid a public demonstration is out of the question: either way we lose. If people thought it was real, we would quickly lose control of the thing. Before you knew it, this building would be full of astronomers, anthropologists, and God knows what from every corner of the globe. You would certainly get a lot of publicity as creators of the 2DWORLD program, but you'd never get to use it again. On the other hand, if people thought it was a prank or a hoax, my reputation—and yours—would suffer very badly. I could even be pressured to resign my position here, and we would almost certainly lose our access to the facility.

"But suppose we didn't mind letting a task force of scientists take over. What do you think the result would be? Imagine each specialist lining up at the terminal to ask his or her little question of Yendred. Imagine the bureaucracy involved. If you were a two-dimensional creature, if you were Yendred, would you rather deal with a small group of sympathetic and intelligent people or an endless stream of cold-blooded inquisitors? I mean, can you imagine

```
HELLO YENDRED.  I'M DOCTOR PIFFLEWHIZ  FROM HUMBUG
UNIVERSITY.  MY SPECIALTY IS PSYCHOHYDRODYNAMICS
AND I WANT TO KNOW IF YOUR PEOPLE EVER GET WATER
ON THE BRAIN.
```

"No. We really have no choice in the matter. We *must* keep this a secret, every one of us. I'm not even going to tell my wife!" I looked at the individual faces before me. "Agreed?"

They nodded solemnly.

Succeeding contacts with Yendred, some of which lasted from eight to ten hours, always seemed to begin when one of our FECs was in a solitary state on the Astrian surface. We would continually query the FEC, waiting impatiently as it explained how to catch throgs. Suddenly Yendred's words would appear in place of the FEC's responses and the scene would slowly transform itself into Yendred's current environment on Arde. With succeeding contacts, this phenomenon took place with increasing speed. It seemed to have much to do with Yendred's own mental state: he once told us that he merely had to contemplate the "space beyond space" in order to feel our "presence" and bring his own world once more into coincidence with the 2DWORLD simulation program.

During that summer, we built up an extensive library of conversations with Yendred. I had an extra bookshelf brought into my office and we began to accumulate printout paper at the rate of two or three large file folders every contact.

The students and I met once a week, discussing the past week and deciding what topics we would question Yendred about during the next session. For his part, Yendred would often take us to some nearby feature, directing our attention to various details and explaining them to us. I don't think he ever fully grasped the comprehensiveness of our vision. He would assume that something normally invisible to him (say, the inside of an Ardean steam engine) was also invisible to us. But it wasn't. At other times, rather than explain an adjacent object, Yendred would discuss astronomy or animal behaviour or Ardean morals or the Ardean monetary system, things for which pictures would not be of much use in any event. For the rest, he would sometimes question us at great length about human beings, the Earth and our universe.

Before the second week of contact with Yendred had quite elapsed, he left his home and began a journey which, though interrupted several times, continued for two months. The object of this journey is rather difficult to define, having something to do with what Yendred called "knowledge of the beyond." In any case, we were very fortunate that he had chosen this particular time to travel, as we saw a good deal of Arde, its people, technology and culture as a result. It is also just possible that Yendred's preoccupation with the "beyond" provided a unique mental set, making him the favoured target of our simulation program—the nexus of Arde.

Through all of this, none of us knew how long these contacts would last. There was a certain anxiety in the air: what had appeared so suddenly and mysteriously could vanish in the same manner.

In the meantime, things were not going very smoothly in the world outside our laboratory. Rumours circulated about strange goings-on in the 2DWORLD project. Indeed, a second wave of publicity quickly developed. It centred on a student who claimed that we had "contacted another world." All the university needed was the following headline in a well-known tabloid with internation distribution: PROFESSOR DISCOVERS FLAT WORLD.

Within a few days a message came directly from the university president to our chairman. I was to put an end to all my experiments at once. The chairman, in his kindly way, said, "Crikey, man, whatever you're doing, stop it!"

Torn between loyalty to the university and curiosity about Arde, I finally resolved to continue our "experiments" during secret sessions in the small hours of the morning. To avoid attracting attention, we agreed to enter and leave the laboratory singly and to keep the lights off during the contacts.

The sessions continued until the morning of August 4, when they abruptly ended. In previous sessions, Yendred had been traversing a portion of the high central plateau on Arde's continent and had encountered a fellow Ardean, Drabk by name, not far from a landmark connected with an ancient Ardean religion. After a number of meetings with this other being, Yendred announced that his journey would continue no farther for the present. Up to this point, it would not be presumptuous to claim a certain sense of "friendship" with Yendred: he had always willingly shared information with us and had shown what can only be described as enthusiasm in learning about Earth and its inhabitants. But in the next to last session, he had displayed few of these qualities and had terminated the contact almost as soon as it began, claiming some need for secrecy in the proceedings.

In the last session, Yendred spoke with us for several hours in Drabk's absence. Just before Drabk appeared, however, Yendred underwent a remarkable change. Yendred then spoke no more with us until the very end of the contact.

WE CANNOT TALK AGAIN. TO TALK AGAIN IS OF NO BENEFIT.

■ BUT WE HAVE SO MUCH MORE TO LEARN FROM YOU.

YOU CANNOT LEARN FROM ME. NOR I FROM YOU. YOU DO NOT HAVE THE KNOWLEDGE.

■ WHAT KNOWLEDGE?

THE KNOWLEDGE BEYOND THOUGHT OF THE REALITY BEYOND REALITY.

■ WOULD IT HELP IF WE LEARNED YOUR PHILOSOPHY AND RELIGION?

IT HAS NOT TO DO WITH WHAT YOU CALL PHILOSOPHY OR RELIGION. IF YOU FOLLOW ONLY THOUGHT YOU WILL NEVER DISCOVER THE SURPRISE WHICH LIES BEYOND THOUGHT.

■ WHAT SURPRISE?

   UNKNOWN: "WHAT SURPRISE."

■ FEC IN FOCUS.

   ADOLF HERE--WAITING FOR THROGS.

From that point on, attempts to raise Yendred resulted only in the by now usual UNKNOWN: "YNDRD" message. Although there has been a certain amount of publicity resulting from our contact with Arde and the Planiverse, no one seriously expects the link to be reestablished. As a result, interest in the 2DWORLD program has fallen back to its old level. Alice, currently finishing her graduate work, sometimes loads the program from tape to disk and plays with it for a while. I have no doubt that she hopes to contact Yendred again, and I have no doubt that she never will. She will never come breathless to my office door again, presumably, because we are a people with no "knowledge beyond thought," whatever that means. Nevertheless, I have encouraged Alice to write a description of the 2DWORLD program (omitting all references to Yendred and the Planiverse) for publication. Perhaps one of the popular computer magazines would be interested.

For my part, I have already taken some time away from university life to document the two-dimensional universe revealed by our "experiments." Essentially, I have edited all the transcripts into a set of more or less coherent chapters, each devoted to a separate contact period. I should qualify the word "edited" here because only small segments of the transcripts are ever quoted directly; the rest have been condensed into summaries and descriptive accounts. Some of the more technical details, especially matters of science and technology, have been set aside in special boxes which nontechnical readers may wish to skip—at least on their first time through the book. I prefer to think, however, that many of these will be intelligible to such readers.

It would not be possible to close this already lengthy introduction without some attempt at an explanation of what was happening last summer. First, I must say what is probably already obvious to the reader: I take Arde seriously and believe that it exists. Where? Not in our universe, I think, and therefore not anywhere in particular in relation to us. My only guide in this matter has been a certain familiarity with the vast world of conceptual models comprised by modern mathematics. Not only does there fail to be any convincing reason why our universe should be the only one, but there seems to be no reason why other possible universes should not have two physical dimensions instead of three.

How, then, did Yendred appear in our computer? This question has taxed me to the limits of my imagination and the only conceivable answer is based on what might be called a "theory of coincidence," an analogy, if you like, to what happens when a vibrating tuning fork is placed beside a nonvibrating one: if the tuning forks are the same size, the quiet one will begin to vibrate also. The two forks do not have to be made from the same material or even to have exactly the same shape. If one could in some way write down all the information which is contained in those two forks, one would find the information coinciding in a certain small number of important respects and somewhat diverging in all others. In particular, the information describing the vibrations of the first tuning fork is, in a sense, absent from the description of the second tuning fork. Forgetting for a moment about the theory of sympathetic vibrations, imagine instead a mysterious tendency for the information missing from the second description to be replaced by the vibratory information of the first description.

Perhaps something like this happened when the 2DWORLD simulation program reached a certain level of complexity. Our "Planiverse" coincided with Yendred's two-dimensional universe in enough important respects that the latter set the former vibrating, so to speak:

YNDRD IS BUT FEW WORDS

Even Yendred's native language was translated into English, albeit with curiously scrambled sentences. Did the Ffennell-Edwards artificial intelligence program correspond in some way to Yendred's mind? Did Lambert's query system somehow match the Ardean speech centre?

One may speculate endlessly about the actual mechanisms involved, but being very much out on a limb, philosophically speaking, I will stop here. It is useless to speculate further.

VARIATION

Robert Zend

for Arthur C. Clarke

Somewhere in the empty reaches of space
there is a place where
dentists play pianos in caves
children with wrinkles on their faces
throw snowballs deep in tropical jungles
in garrets escaped convicts pen their poems in blood
mayors panhandle at street corners
butchers with green hair stand on their hands
for this is the way to be with-it
whoever can come up with the greatest number of words
that start with *B*
gets the hand of the dirtiest of princesses—
Everyone of course despises those with three eyes
but delights in those whose toes can touch their mouths
on the thorns of giant cacti
the dead are displayed in museums—

Red clouds drift across the sky
curtaining off a desk behind which
wearing his spectacles and well-worn corduroy jacket
god bends over his accounts
and when he balances them he sighs and mumbles:
"It could have been different,
but what difference would it make?"

THE MAN DOLL

Susan Swan

I made the man doll for Elizabeth. I wanted to build a surrogate toy that would satisfy my friend so completely I would never have to listen to her litany of grievances against the male sex again.

I constructed the doll by hand. I am a biomedical engineer, but at that time I was still an intern. I couldn't afford to buy Elizabeth one of the million-dollar symbiotes called Pleasure Boys which the wealthy women and gay men purchase in our exclusive department stores.

I didn't like these display models anyhow. Their platinum hair and powder-blue eyes (identical to the colouring of Pleasure Girls) looked artificial and their electronic brains had over-developed intellects. I wanted something different from the run-of-the-mill life form for Elizabeth. I wanted a deluxe model that would combine the virility component of a human male with the intuitive powers of the female. In short, I wanted a Pleasure Boy whose programming emphasized the ability to give emotional support.

I made my doll in secret, requisitioning extra parts whenever some limbs or organs were needed at the Cosmetic Clinic in human repairs where I worked. So it was easy for me to get the pick of anatomical bargains. I particularly liked the selection of machine extensions offered by the Space Force Bank. After careful consideration, I chose long, sinewy hands, arms and legs, and made sure they were the type that could be willed into action in a twinkling. The Space Force Bank agreed to simulate the doll's computer brain from mine for $1,500. The exterior of the doll was made out of plastic and silicone that was lifelike to the touch. I placed a nuclear reactor the size of a baseball in the chest cavity, just where the heart is in the human body. The reactor warmed the doll by transmitting heat to a labyrinth of coils. The reactor uses a caesium source that yields an 80 per cent efficiency rate with a life expectancy of just over 30 years. The doll was activated by a handheld switch.

I smuggled the materials home from the Clinic and each night in my flat I worked on the doll. I wanted it to be a perfect human likeness, so exact in detail that Elizabeth wouldn't guess it was a symbiote. I applied synthetic hair in transplants (matched with my own hair colour) and shaped its face with the help of liquid silicone. My money had almost run out by the time I got to the sex organs, but luckily I was able to find a cheap set from a second-hand supplier. For $250 I bought an antique organ that belonged to a 180-year-old Pleasure Boy. I hoped it would work under pressure.

Our laws forbid symbiotes to waste human food. But I gave the doll a silicone esophagus and a crude bladder because I wanted it to have something to do on social occasions. Its body was able to ingest and pass out a water and sugar solution. Of course, the doll didn't defecate. Its nuclear waste products were internally controlled and required changing once every ten years.

At the last moment I realized I had forgotten to add dye to the pupils, so its eyes were almost colourless. But in all other aspects, my doll looked normal.

When I installed its reactor, the doll came to life, lolling contentedly in my apartment, ignoring the discomfort of its mummy case and its helmet of elastic bandages and gauze. The doll called me "Maker" and, despite its post-operative daze, began to display a talent for understanding and devotion.

It could sense when I was in a blue mood and sighed sympathetically behind its bandages. When I came home, exhausted from catering to the scientists at the Clinic, the doll would be waiting for me at the door of my apartment, ready to serve me dinner. Soon,

I was unable to keep my hands off it. I decided it wouldn't spoil my present to Elizabeth if I tried it out ahead of time. Playfully I stroked and kissed the symbiote, and showed it how to peel back its groin bandage so we could have sex. To my delight, the doll operated above normal capacity, thanks to its desire to give pleasure.

Like any commercial symbiote, my doll was capable of orgasm but not ejaculation. It is illegal for a doll to create life. The sole function of a symbiote must be recreational.

At the end of five months I removed its protective case and found myself staring at a symbiote who gazed back with a remarkably calm, loving air. It had red hair and freckles, just like me, and a pair of cute pear-shaped ears.

My desire to give the doll to Elizabeth vanished.

I fell in love with my creation.

I called the doll Manny.

The next year with Manny was happy. I felt confident; I worked at the Clinic with zeal and diligence, knowing that at the end of the day I would be going home to Manny: his cooking and his kisses! (Something about the way I had juxtaposed his two oricularis oris muscles made the touch of his lips sensational.)

Secretly, I worried Manny might harbour resentment about a life built around ministering to my needs. Pleasure Boys have no rights, but Manny was still an organism with a degree of self-interest. If I neglected his programmed needs, he might deteriorate. When I confessed my fear, the doll laughed and hugged me.

"I want to be the slave," he said. "I need to be in service."

Over the next six months I began to see less of my doll. I had graduated to the rank of engineer in facial repairs and was neglecting our home life.

I decided it was time to give Manny some social experiences, so I asked Elizabeth to the flat for a meal.

I felt a thrill of pride when Elizabeth walked in and didn't give Manny a suspicious look. Manny wore an ascot and a tweed sports suit. He beamed at the two of us as he placed a spinach quiche on the table.

"You look familiar," Elizabeth mused.

"Everybody says I look like Tina," the doll said breezily.

"You do," Elizabeth said. "Where did you meet Tina anyhow?"

"I'd rather hear about you," the doll replied. "Are you happy?"

Elizabeth started and looked at me for an explanation. I grinned.

"Go on. Tell him about your troubles with men."

"Tina, my problems would bore Manny," Elizabeth said nervously.

"No they wouldn't," Manny said. "I like to help people with their troubles."

Elizabeth laughed and threw up her hands.

"I can't find a man who is decent, Manny. Every affair starts off well and then I find the guy has feet of clay."

I saw Manny glance down at his plastic feet. He was smiling happily.

"I must be too much of a perfectionist," Elizabeth sighed, "but there are days when I'd settle for a good machine."

I nodded and noticed Manny's colourless eyes watching Elizabeth as if he were profoundly moved. I thought he could be a little less sympathetic. If he knew Elizabeth like I did, Manny would realize Elizabeth enjoyed feeling dissatisfied.

Suddenly, Manny reached over and patted Elizabeth's hand. Elizabeth burst into tears and Manny continued to hold her hand, interlocking his fingers with hers in a deeply understanding way. In profile, the doll looked serene. Elizabeth was staring at him through her tears with an expression of disbelief. I knew Elizabeth was waiting for the doll to frown and suggest that she pull herself together.

Of course, the doll's programming prohibited uncaring reactions. Manny was unique, not only among male symbiotes, but among men. What man loved as unselfishly as my doll?

During dinner, Elizabeth quizzed Manny about his background and the doll gracefully handled her questions.

"I'm Tina's invention," he quipped. "I call her 'Maker.' It's our private joke."

Elizabeth giggled and so did Manny. I winced. Why did my doll sound so happy? The understanding look on Manny's face, as Elizabeth whined about her love life, was a bit sickening! I noticed the doll lightly brush against Elizabeth's shoulder when he replenished the wine, and in disgust, I stood up and cleared away the dishes. When I came out of the kitchen, Manny was standing by the door holding hands with Elizabeth.

"Elizabeth needs me now, Tina," the doll said. He paused to help my friend on with her coat. Then he gave her shoulder a loving squeeze. "Elizabeth, I feel as if I were made just for you."

My doll leaned over and offered her his sensational oricularis oris muscles, and suddenly I felt angry.

"You can't leave me, Manny," I said. "I own you."

"Tina. You don't mean what you say," Manny replied sweetly. "You know dolls have rights too."

"Who says?" I cried. "You can't procreate. You can't eat. And your retinas are colourless."

"Manny eats," Elizabeth said. "I saw him."

"He just drinks," I said, starting to shout. "Elizabeth, Manny is my doll. Don't you dare walk out of my apartment with my possession."

"Manny is not a doll," Elizabeth said. "You're making it up because you're jealous."

"Manny, I'm warning you. If you leave me, I'll deactivate your program."

"My Maker is not the sort of human to be petty," Manny replied. Hand in hand, my doll and Elizabeth walked out of the apartment. "Goodbye, Tina dear," Manny called in an extremely sincere tone. I threw myself at the closed door, beating my fists against it, screaming my doll's name. Then I sank to my knees. I had made the doll for Elizabeth, but decided to keep him for myself. For the first time, I realized it didn't matter. My programming ensured that Manny would be drawn to whoever had most need of him.

For the next month, I was too depressed to see Elizabeth and Manny. I felt angry with my friend for taking my doll, although I scolded myself for being irrational. Now that Manny was gone, I regretted the way I had neglected him. I day-dreamed nostalgically about the activities we might have done together. Why hadn't we gone shopping, or out to the movies? It made me sad to think we had never strolled arm-in-arm in the park like a normal couple.

True to his programming, Manny called me every day to see how I was doing. My pride stopped me from listening to his concerned inquiries and I slammed the phone down. Then one evening my symbiote phoned late and caught me offguard. I'd had an argument with my Clinic supervisor. This time, I was glad to hear my doll's friendly baritone.

"Tina, I'm worried about you," Manny chided. "The grapevine says you're working too hard."

"Hard enough," I agreed, relieved that somebody cared.

"Dinner here this Tuesday. I won't take no for an answer."

That Tuesday, I changed out of my lab coat and headed for Elizabeth's apartment. At the entrance to the building, three dolls were talking to the doorman. One of the dolls, a Pleasure Girl with shoulder-length platinum hair, asked the doorman to let them in so they could see a friend. The doorman shook his head.

"No dolls allowed in before six," the doorman said. "ASTARTE TOWERS is a respectable space block." He made a slashing motion in the air with his gloved hand. Then he pushed the female doll on its chest. The doll groaned as if it were hurt and tottered backwards. For a second, it looked like it was going to fall. Then it slumped onto the curb and began to weep pitifully. The two male dolls rushed over to comfort it. Except for the unactivated models in store windows, I had never observed dolls in a group before. The sight of the symbiotes acting like humans made me uneasy. I hurried past the sobbing doll and her companions, and ran into the lobby.

In the apartment, I found Elizabeth reading a newspaper. Manny was setting the table. Elizabeth looked relaxed. But Manny! Why, the doll looked beatific! His synthetic curls shone with a copper glow and a suntan had brought out more large brown freckles. Then I remembered hearing that Elizabeth had gone on a Caribbean cruise.

"How wonderful to see you, Tina," Manny said. "Are you still mad at your old symbiote?"

I shook my head.

Joyfully, he embraced me. He told me about his holiday and asked about my new job. I immediately began to describe the way I had engineered a dish-face deformity. When I finished, I realized that Elizabeth had been listening intently too; apparently, she had no interest in going into her usual litany of grievances against the male sex.

Suddenly, Elizabeth said, "Did you see any dolls at the door?"

"One or two," I admitted. "What are they doing here?"

"A few come, every day. They sometimes bring a human. If they can get by the doorman, Manny lets them come in and talks to them." Elizabeth sighed and shrugged. "I suppose there's nothing wrong with it. Except I worry that they tire Manny."

"Elizabeth, I am tireless," Manny laughed, bending over and kissing my friend on the nape of her neck. I remembered just how tireless Manny could be.

Elizabeth grabbed his silicone hand and kissed it hungrily. "Selfless, you mean." She looked dreamy. "Tina, where did you find this paragon?"

"I already told you. I made him for you." I smiled.

"Do you think I'm going to believe that line of yours?" Elizabeth laughed. "It's time you forgave me for being with Manny."

"What are you talking about?" I asked.

"Elizabeth thinks I'm human," Manny smiled. "I've tried to show her I'm a doll, but she goes out of the room and refuses to listen." He paused, bewildered. "The dolls think I'm human, too."

"No doll could make *me* happy," Elizabeth giggled.

"Serving your needs fulfills my function," Manny replied.

"Isn't Manny funny?" Elizabeth said. "He says the cutest things!"

Before I could answer, the door opened and the symbiotes who had been arguing with the doorman rushed in uttering cries of glee.

"Pleasure Girl #024 found a way in through the back entrance," one of the male dolls said triumphantly.

The female doll kissed Manny fiercely on both his cheeks.

"Pleasure Boy #025 is the one who suggested we try another door," she said. "Aren't we clever for sex toys?" Then she noticed Elizabeth and me, and she blushed guiltily. "Excuse me. I forgot humans were listening."

"Don't apologize," said the other male doll. "We have the right to breathe like anybody else."

The dolls murmured agreement and then turned back to Manny, who was holding up a jug of liquid. I guessed it contained a sugar and water solution. Manny poured the liquid into glasses. The dolls lifted the glasses in a toast and pretended to drink Manny's solution.

I stared at the dolls without speaking to them. Once again, I felt uneasy. The symbiotes were claiming human privileges. Not only were they acting as if they had the right to consume precious food resources, but the dolls were also appropriating human metaphors. I wasn't certain about the design type of the other symbiotes, but no air passed through Manny's system. His lungs were a tiny non-functional sac next to the caesium reactor. I had stuck in the sac to designate lung space in case I decided later to give Manny a requirement for oxygen.

Now the dolls began to complain loudly about their lot as pleasure toys. My doll listened solemnly, stroking each of their hands in turn while Elizabeth and I looked on blankly. Then one of the male dolls threw himself at Manny's feet.

"Why are we discriminated against, Manny?" the doll wailed. "Why can't we procreate like humans do?"

Tears slowly dripped from Manny's clear eyes. He held out his arms and embraced the dolls, who in turn cried and embraced each other. In the midst of the hubbub I slipped out and left Elizabeth with the emotional dolls. Then I hurried back to the Clinic and calmed myself by working until dawn repairing a pair of cauliflower ears.

Three months went by. This time Elizabeth rang up and asked me to meet her at the Earth Minister's television studio. Elizabeth said that Manny had left her to become a spokesman for a political lobby of humans and symbiotes.

Manny's group could be heard in the background of the Earth Minister's daily broadcasts shouting their demands. Elizabeth wanted me to persuade Manny to give up politics. She wanted Manny back so they could start a family. She said that she would do "something unthinkable" that evening unless she could convince Manny to return.

Gently, I tried to point out that Manny was only a doll, but the more I pleaded with her to forget about my symbiote, the more desperate she sounded. I agreed to meet her at the studio. Just before I left my apartment, I stuck my handheld switch into my pocket. I decided the time had come to deactivate Manny. It was illogical for the symbiotes to think dolls had rights. I felt sympathy for them as organisms, but their aspirations were making pests out of what were once perfectly good recreational objects.

The studio was ten minutes by air, but it took me over half an hour to force my way through the crowd at the studio door. I noticed with a start that there were hundreds of human heads among the masses of synthetic ones.

Finally, I found a seat at the back of the auditorium. At that moment the lights dimmed and then flared brightly as the Earth Minister walked out onto a dais at the front of the room, followed by a television crew pushing cameras. The crowd immediately began to chant, "Manny for Earth Minister" and "Symbiotes are humans too."

I heard a noise at the front of the room and Manny was lifted onto the platform. Then Manny shook hands with the Earth Minister, a stocky human with an anxious smile. Now the crowd cheered more wildly than before, and Manny turned and lifted up his arms as if he wanted to embrace them all. He looked striking in his deep magenta safari suit.

Just then, Elizabeth appeared by my side, weeping.

"Isn't it awful?" she whispered. "This swarm of dolls? Oh, Tina, I was just too busy with other things, so Manny went into politics. But I can't live without him."

"Sure you can," I sighed and looked over the crowd at Manny's synthetic head. "You already are."

Manny spotted me and waved. I hesitated, then smiled and waved back.

"Tina, you're not paying attention," Elizabeth sniffed. "I want Manny back. I want to have children with him."

"Look, Elizabeth," I said. I felt in my pocket for the switch. "Manny is a doll—a do-it-yourself model. His brains cost over a thousand dollars and his sex organs were two-fifty."

Elizabeth blushed. "Manny has talked about the help you gave him, but no symbiote could do what he does."

"He's a Pleasure Boy," I argued. "I should know. I made him.

Haven't you noticed he doesn't eat or defecate? And that's not all. He can't procreate either."

"Nothing you say will make me believe Manny is a doll," Elizabeth shouted, and then she slapped my face!

Angrily, I grabbed her and dragged her towards the dais. "I'll show you his extensions, his hair strips, his silicone mouth . . . !"

"Tina! Please! Don't hurt Manny!" Elizabeth cried, ducking her head as if she expected me to hit her. Even though I am bigger than Elizabeth, I was surprised at how easily cowed she was.

I tightened my grip on my friend's arm. "I'm going to take you up there," I yelled, "and deactivate him in front of everyone. Manny the doll has come to an end."

"No, Tina! I'll do what you want! I'll forget him!" Elizabeth said and plucked at my arm. "I know Manny's a doll, but I love him. I've never loved anybody before."

She bowed her head, and for a second I relaxed my grip. At that moment, a great gust of sighs filled the studio and the oscillating physical mass knocked us apart as it pushed towards the dais where Manny sat. The Earth Minister toppled from his seat and the crowd hoisted Manny into the air.

Suddenly, the doll looked my way. His placid, colourless eyes met mine. I pulled the switch out of my pocket and threw it away. In the next moment, the mass of dolls and humans carried Manny off on a sea of hands. I wasn't surprised—as I strained for a last glimpse—to see a blissful look on my doll's face.

THE EARLY EDUCATION OF THE NUM-NUMS

Robert Priest

Their word for love is impossible to pronounce. It contains every letter of our alphabet at least twice. Their first and greatest art is to learn how to say it. And even then it requires a truthfulness and vulnerability beyond the scope of mere art. It becomes a way of being—at first just a ritual scrawl, then a riot of passions in the loins, a jangling of every ancient syllable in them. Even the crude syllables of rocks and amoebas. Timelessly then, as they grow, it all comes together, this sound from this thing, this sound from that. Fatal wisdoms are acquired and then imparted slightly lessened where they drank at them. Finally they acquire immunities. They need no clothes then. No appetites or lies, but they show only the ugliest things they have in order to cleanse them of every vanity. Then, when they are entirely beautiful, they utter that first important word, the first twenty-three letters of which seem to translate in our language as, "I think I am ready." After that it is all a senseless cry, a reverberation of wild lyrical sounds into the night. Then the other one will appear. Just like that—the other one on the planet who has also just grown into the tongue. He or she will be there and they will wrap tentacles about one another, ready now for mathematics.

THE LONELINESS
OF THE LONG-DISTANCE WRITER

Lesley Choyce

Even now I sometimes have my doubts about being a writer. I mean, it's not like I have a big audience.

There is a grand total of four readers in this solar system who see my work. Dolph Tonkins for one—but then he was the devil that planted the seed in me to begin with. Sister Theresa McCullough in her home for aging nuns in Dunvegan is the second. And then there's Tess, also cloistered away, but under different circumstances. And, of course, she's much younger. Without her I would have given up long ago.

As far as I know, no one else in the solar system can read. Reading is such an ancient custom that no one (including me sometimes) can see for what conceivable purpose it stands. The university keeps me alive here out of some sort of respect for the prehistorics, I suppose. I think old farts like Mellaghy and Bustrom teaching in the Ancient Cultures Department still feel that there was something more to writing than just whimsical foppery. That it might have had something to do with communication. But certainly not in any way related to the way it is known today.

"How can you communicate, if you can't *be* there?" they all argue. "You'd be missing all the bloody parts." Meaning of course arms, legs, facial expression. "No one could possibly take it seriously. It was just a fashionable mclune, a form of stand-up comedy."

So that makes me a sort of court jester, and way the hell out of my century at that. Thanks a lot, Dolph.

But then it was Dolph who saved my life. When I was a kid, you see, my old man had us living in a condovillage just east of Dark-day City. Unlike other lucky families we were stuck on the moon instead of somewhere more interesting farther out. The only thing appealing about the place was that I could take a dustbike out for a spin as often as I wanted once I had passed the driving test. My father, however, was always warning me: "Dammit, Rick, don't go spookin' around on the dark side or I swear, I won't let you ride that friggin' thing for the rest of your life."

Of course, the dark side, only about twenty kilometres away, was what interested me most. So off I went. Ten miles in I burned out a light. The auxiliary package was weak, no doubt because I hadn't recharged it since I bought the thing. I tried to navigate my way back to the line with about two and a half watts against eternal night. Just my luck, I wiped out in an overly ambitious dust pit, flipped over the rig and landed on a sharp piece of pure nickel which put a tiny crescent rip in my suit. I started to get dizzy and kept trying to focus on the light line, way the hell off and just before I passed out I had the good sense to flip on the SOS blaster.

Dolph was the guy who found me. He was probably the only living creature within five kilometres. He had himself a comfy little geocell tucked under a ledge at the bottom of a crater. A true recluse. And talk about your weird ideas. He showed me piles of paper with stuff written all over. Words.

"So?" I asked.

"So, I want you to learn how to do it," he told me, as I lay there still recovering.

"What the Murphy for?" I said, beginning to worry if this was all part of some weirdo religion like the Cosmic Church of Carnal Knowledge or something.

"Because you owe it to me, bud. I saved your life."

"Oh." I was beginning to see his point. Besides, I was getting used to learning totally useless skills. It seemed to be what civiliza-tion was all about.

I sat through the first of many lessons concerning writing, certain that the old turkey was whacked out of his gourd, but nonetheless I owed it to him.

Dolph was totally opposed to holovision and refused to ever allow a single holoversion of himself made. "It saps your soul, Rick, I'm sure of it. A fake light image of you that looks exactly like you in every respect travelling off somewhere and doing your talking for you."

"Well, it can do more than talk, it can do . . . well, almost anything. That's communication, buster!" I was a rotten student, and so defensive of the society that I had come from.

Later I could see the problems with holos. Take the university for example. Most of the kids don't ever show up for class, but send their holos instead. Shimmering light visions sit in the seats, answer questions, make passes at each other behind the teacher's back. A lot of weirdness goes on. The profs are so adept at holos and have such sophisticated transmitters that very few people can tell if it is a holo or an original who's up front lecturing on astrophysics and neuro-palaeontology.

We've become a very leisurely society. It causes a lot of hardship. I'd hate to tell you about how many cases the shrinks have to deal with where the originals get themselves confused with their own holos or where somebody makes so many improvements over himself through a holoversion that they call it quits altogether. I mean, once you've perfected yourself and it's not you, then what? I don't think Mellaghy or Bustrom ever use holos, at least not for teaching. But even they don't know how to read. Mellaghy argues that he doesn't really think most of us are even *physically* capable of it. He says it's more or less something we've evolved out of, like the primitive way that men and women used to have sex.

According to Dolph, that's a lot of bull. Dolph claims to have fathered his own kid. I mean physically. She lives alone in a tiny geocell on Ganymede, where she writes poetry. I don't know how Tess became a poet. Or why. Dolph was a confessional novelist. He was happy that I wanted to stick with novels and short fiction.

"One poet in the family is enough," he said.

"What do you mean, *family*?", I said.

"I just mean figuratively," he said as he brought down the heavy blade of the self-fashioned paper cutter. Dolph had to manufacture all of his own paper. "As far as I know, I'm the only paper manufacturer in the solar system," he'd brag. Which is probably true since he does supply Tess and Sister T. and, of course, me.

Without a doubt, I have more paper in my possession than anyone on Earth. Sister Theresa, of course, has a small stock. She's neither a novelist nor a poet, but has taken on the dubious role of literary critic. She uses words and paper more sparingly. And every other writer alive depends on her judgment—all three of us.

Sister T. has angered me more than once with her criticism. "Put more oomph in it," she'd say. "More life. Develop characters, not just stereotypes." Or "a sensitive mind and spirit, but your work lacks the necessary grace and cohesiveness," would be another one of her comments to a piece I had laboured on for months.

Theresa's claim to fame is that she has read real "books." Not too many scholars hold credence to the fact that there ever was such a thing as widespread use of books. Could you imagine a writer writing for more than a handful of readers? I think the old girl has a good imagination, but what the hell, that's what it's all about, eh? (She's also requested that I "clean up the language." However I learned from Big Dolph himself and he's responsible for my vocabulary.)

In the end, I always forgive her for all her insults which are always well-meaning. And I can't afford to alienate the reading audience that I have. Bustrom has offered to try to help me turn my first novel, *Two and a Half Watts Against Eternal Night* into a holovision performance creating composite characters and all. Imagine the audience I'd have! But alas. Dolph would kill me and Tess might never forgive me. That I couldn't afford.

Tess does have a few of her mother's traits. She can be critical. She reduced me to tears when she commented on my recent book, *The Nocturnal Mission*. She called it "sophomoric and shallow." I had tried to write a humorous book about nickel mining on an asteroid, but I don't think I could quite pull it off. And like Theresa, Tess doesn't use much paper. You know how long it takes the old-style cargo ships to get from the moon to Ganymede. And Dolph's complaining that it's getting harder to locate the right supplies.

In case I haven't mentioned it, I'm in love with Tess. Love, that is, as I understand it. None of this bullshit about priming up a perfect holoversion of yourself and transmitting it over to a chick's house where she has to quickly get out the tape of herself at her best. You might as well be watching DV. I'm not even sure these college kids bother with romance anymore at all. Not with holos or anything. It's one more thing that might as well be called irrelevent.

But I picture Tess tucked away in her little geocell on the out-skirts of nowhere on Ganymede writing out her short heart-wrung poetry on tiny portions of paper. She writes about love and rocks and stars; if you ask me, it is a little corny and she suffers from all those faults that she accuses me of. But it takes me a lot more words to accomplish the faults. And I've never read what Sister Theresa has to say about her daughter's poetry.

Someday, I was sure, Tess and I would get our lives woven together somehow and settle down, maybe right there on Ganymede and do nothing but write and make love in the primi-tive style, which must have been the way that Dolph and Sister T. did it if Tess is their composite daughter. It all still baffles me, I assure you.

It also occurs to me that we're all getting rather old and could be producing much more if we were taking advantage of the technology at hand. I'm pushing ninety and probably halfway through life, and, let's face it, most of society thinks that I'm a good-for-nothing. It's productivity that counts. New devices, new fuels, new methods for bouncing around the universe. Everyone is always trying to get somewhere. And it all involves spending money. Success, as you know, means not how much money you've made, but how much you can spend.

That's why I almost got my writer-in-res post at the university taken away from me. Lord knows, I wouldn't have been replaced. They were pissed at me for sitting on my butt and doing nothing but scratching ink spots on paper. I tried to explain that this was my fifth and perhaps greatest novel, *Vindictive Destinies*. Ninety-four per cent of the faculty said it was a lot of crapola. And good old Mellaghy and Bustrom, loyal to the word and to me to the end, finally came up with something. They had been sniffing around in some ancient computer tapes. "Half the friggin' things turned to dust when we tried to run them through the IBM replica," Mel complained. They always came across old stuff that was valueless and irrelevant, and nobody paid them much attention anyway. But this tape concerned a research vessel sent off towards Epsilanti 5 in what most scholars call prehistory — thousands of years before holos. Well, according to the dynamic duo, this ship was going so slowly that they (or their descendents) were probably still at it.

The response from the faculty senate was unanimous: "So?"

"So," Bustrom responded, "people in those days read. They read books. If they're still out there, their descendents that is, why not overtake them with a little care package. Mellaghy's got the co-ordinates. We can send a micro-warp cargo most the way there, freeze is down to sub light and pull up along side. They're sure to pick it up."

The faculty thought it was absurd, of course. But it was expensive and they could get a gumment grant for any project that was new and costly, so it was passed by a majority. We got quite a lot of publicity and we were all thought to be crackpots which seemed to cheer up the whole school in a way. Sister T. and Tess had their doubts about it and thought that I was being corrupted by "crass commercialism." But I have to admit I was tempted by the thought of having an audience larger than three. You can imagine how absurd it appeared to most; trying to communicate with the descendents of the ancients rambling around in space for who knows how long in a decrepit old space tub. And I stewed for weeks over which one to send. I only had one manuscript of each and I had sworn never to let anyone read them in a form other than in the actual print. Tess, Theresa and Dolph had all read all my work and there wasn't really anyone else to read here, so I figured I had little to lose. I sent off *Two and a Half Watts*. The micro-warp was equipped with a homer on it so it was just a matter of sitting back and waiting for the reviews. In the meantime I began a romantic novel called *The Girl Within the Cloud* which I intended to woo dear Tess with. If the university wanted to keep me on, they'd have to let me work out of the auxiliary campus network in the University of the Outer Planets. I wasn't about to sit around Earth for much longer. Tess was out there writing sonnets somewhere and I intended to be with her.

"Very quaint," Dolph had said, "but I'm proud of you."

Tess wrote back that she wasn't opposed to the idea but that for her, love could only be real if it was physical. So I promised her that it would be physical. I hoped I would figure out something when I got there.

Sister T. asked me if I was sure I knew what I was getting into and reminded me that Tess had been conceived "the primitive way" and that I might find her different.

Well, I had some doubts, I admit. But when word came back from the Epsilanti 5 crew concerning *Two and a Half Watts* I felt like I could do anything. There were apparently a hundred descendents on the ship and they understood the language, they were in fact, *readers*. A Captain J. T. Morganthal wrote back, ". . . a moving masterpiece, had me crying and laughing, the best thing read on this vessel in generations. . . . Send more!"

So we sent off *Mission* and *Destinies* and even one that I had kept hidden in a drawer for years. Mellaghy and Bostrum went on locating more and more derelict ships and I was commissioned to produce at least one novel a year for each. What bliss!

They talked Dolph into sending off a dozen manuscripts to a supposed ancient colony of Earthlings in the Horsehead Nebula along with introductions by Sister T. concerning the state of the literary art on Earth. (In her view, we were achieving an unprecedented peak of interest in the novel.) But I was having a hard time convincing them of the validity of "publishing" poetry. (That's what we called the new wave of manuscript exports.) Particularly, they had their doubts about Tess, who had been, of course, conceived by the primitive method; whatever that exactly was, few people had any idea. But in the end, Mellaghy and Bustrom came through again. It was always possible to convince Earthlings to dump money into space since the potential still seemed to exist, whereas another dollar spent on Earth was like throwing good money after bad. After all, a worn out planet is a worn out planet.

And I have been assigned my long-sought-after writer-in-res post on Ganymede. I've decided not to send a holoversion ahead first to get things settled there and make artificial acquaintance with Tess. Instead, I will arrive with nearly half a ton of paper and a century's supply of pens and ink.

Tess has recently sent me a poem about the view of Jupiter from her back door, something that speaks of eternity and vigilance. Something called an ode.

Bustrom arrived the other day almost in tears. He thought he was the messenger of bad news, but I already knew. When I leave the university, I'll be able to take my paper and my ink, but there's no way to take along the circuits from my cubicle that keep me going. I have to leave behind my longevity. I've been unplugged before. Not that I've wandered around outside on this planet like the freaks. I just write better when I'm unplugged. Without all the hormone stabilizers, you go up and down better. A writer shouldn't be up all the time. It makes for lousy prose.

So I'll move to Ganymede and lop off a hundred years. Living that far off the beaten path of the neural networks, I could never depend on good reception. Besides, Tess has never been plugged in. Dolph and Sister T. planned it that way. Like Dolph explained it: "Sometimes you get more out of a short life."

I've got fifteen—maybe twenty—years tops. Tess is only thirty. She'll outlive me to go on writing ballads, elegies, epics even. That doesn't bother me a bit. I'll have had my shot at literature. My novels will be out there skidding through space in those faster-than-light bookmobiles, seeking out generations of lost readers sent wandering through darkness in the primitive years. They are waiting to be illuminated by my manuscripts. "Immortality by any other name. . . . "

REPORT FROM THE FRONT

Robert Sward

All over newspapers have stopped appearing,
And combatants everywhere are returning home.
No one knows what is happening.
The generals are on long distance with the President,
A former feature writer for the *New York Times*.
No one knows even who has died, or how,
Or who won last night, anything.
Those in attendance on them may,
For all we know, still be there.
A few speak compulsively, telling too much,
Having sat asleep in easy chairs.

All over newspapers have stopped appearing.
Words once more, more than ever,
Have begun to matter. And people are writing
Poetry. Opposing regiments, declares a friend of mine,
Are refusing evacuation, are engaged instead
In sonnet sequences; though they understand, he says,
The futility of iambics in the modern world.
That they are concerned with the history and meaning
Of prosody. That they persist in their exercises
With great humility and reverence.

GOD IS AN IRON

Spider Robinson

I smelled her before I saw her. Even so, the first sight of her was shocking.

She was sitting in a tan plastic-surfaced armchair, the kind where the front comes up as the back goes down. It was back as far as it would go. It was placed beside the large living-room window, whose curtains were drawn. A plastic block table next to it held a digital clock, a dozen unopened packages of Peter Jackson cigarettes, an empty ashtray, a full vial of cocaine and a lamp with a bulb of at least 150 watts. It illuminated her with brutal clarity.

She was naked. Her skin was the colour of vanilla pudding. Her hair was in rats, her nails unpainted and untended, some overlong and some broken. There was dust on her. She sat in a ghastly sludge of feces and urine. Dried vomit was caked on her chin and between her breasts and down her ribs to the chair.

These were only part of what I had smelled. The predominant odour was of fresh-baked bread. It is the smell of a person who is starving to death. The combined effluvia had prepared me to find a senior citizen, paralyzed by a stroke or some such crisis.

I judged her to be about twenty-five years old.

I moved to where she could see me, and she did not see me. That was probably just as well, because I had just seen the two most horrible things. The first was the smile. They say that when

227

the bomb went off at Hiroshima, some people's shadows were baked onto walls by it. I think that smile got baked on the surface of my brain in much the same way. I don't want to talk about that smile.

The second horrible thing was the one that explained all the rest. From where I now stood I could see a triple socket in the wall beneath the window. Into it were plugged the lamp, the clock and her.

I knew about wireheading, of course—I had lost a couple of acquaintances and one friend to the juice. But I had never *seen* a wirehead. It is by definition a solitary vice, and all the public usually gets to see is a sheeted figure being carried out to the wagon.

The transformer lay on the floor beside the chair where it had been dropped. The switch was on, and the timer had been jiggered so that instead of providing one five- or ten- or fifteen-second jolt per hour, it allowed continuous flow. That timer is required by law on all juice rigs sold, and you need special tools to defeat it. Say, a nail file. The input cord was long, fell in crazy coils from the wall socket. The output cord disappeared beneath the chair, but I knew where it ended. It ended in the tangled snarl of her hair, at the crown of her head, ended in a miniplug. The plug was snapped into a jack surgically implanted in her skull, and from the jack tiny wires snaked their way through the wet jelly to the hypothalamus, to the specific place in the medial forebrain bundle where the major pleasure centre of her brain was located. She had sat there in total transcendent ecstasy for at least five days.

I moved finally. I moved closer, which surprised me. She saw me now, and impossibly the smile became a bit wider. I was marvelous. I was captivating. I was her perfect lover. I could not look at the smile; a small plastic tube ran from one corner of the smile and my eyes followed it gratefully. It was held in place by small bits of surgical tape at her jaw, neck and shoulder, and from there it ran in a lazy curve to the big fifty-litre water-cooler bottle on the floor. She had plainly meant her suicide to last: she had arranged to die of hunger rather than thirst, which would have been quicker. She could take a drink when she happened to think of it; and if she forgot, well, what the hell.

My intention must have shown on my face, and I think she even understood it—the smile began to fade. That decided me. I moved before she could force her neglected body to react, whipped the plug out of the wall and stepped back warily.

Her body did not go rigid as if galvanized. It had already been so for many days. What it did was the exact opposite, and the effect was just as striking. She seemed to shrink. Her eyes slammed shut. She slumped. Well, I thought, it'll be a long day and a night before *she* can move a voluntary muscle again, and then she hit me before I knew she had left the chair, breaking my nose with the heel of one fist and bouncing the other off the side of my head. We cannoned off each other and I managed to keep my feet; she whirled and grabbed the lamp. Its cord was stapled to the floor and would not yield, so she set her feet and yanked and it snapped off clean at the base. In near-total darkness she raised the lamp on high and came at me and I lunged inside the arc of her swing and punched her in the solar plexus. She said *guff!* and went down.

I staggered to a couch and sat down and felt my nose and fainted.

I don't think I was out very long. The blood tasted fresh. I woke with a sense of terrible urgency. It took me a while to work out why. When someone has been simultaneously starved and unceasingly stimulated for days on end, it is not the best idea in the world to depress their respiratory centre. I lurched to my feet.

It was not completely dark, there was a moon somewhere out there. She lay on her back, arms at her sides, perfectly relaxed. Her ribs rose and fell in great slow swells. A pulse showed strongly at her throat. As I knelt beside her she began to snore, deeply and rhythmically.

I had time for second thoughts now. It seemed incredible that my impulsive action had not killed her. Perhaps that had been my subconscious intent. Five days of wireheading alone should have killed her, let alone sudden cold turkey.

I probed in the tangle of hair, found the empty jack. The hair around it was dry. If she hadn't torn the skin in yanking herself loose, it was unlikely that she had sustained any more serious damage within. I continued probing, found no soft places on the skull. Her forehead felt cool and sticky to my hand. The fecal smell was overpowering the baking bread now, sourly fresh.

There was no pain in my nose yet, but it felt immense and pulsing. I did not want to touch it, or to think about it. My shirt was soaked with blood; I wiped my face with it and tossed it into a corner. It took everything I had to lift her. She was unreasonably heavy, and I have carried drunks and corpses. There was a hall off the livingroom, and all halls lead to a bathroom. I headed that way in a clumsy staggering trot, and just as I reached the deeper darkness, with my pulse at its maximum, my nose woke up and began screaming. I nearly dropped her then and clapped my hands to my face; the temptation was overwhelming. Instead I whimpered like a dog and kept going. Childhood feeling: runny nose you can't wipe. At each door I came to I teetered on one leg and kicked it open, and the third one gave the right small-room, acoustic-tile echo. The light switch was where they almost always are; I rubbed it on with my shoulder and the room flooded with light.

Large aquamarine tub, styrofoam recliner pillow at the head end, nonslip bottom. Aquamarine sink with ornate handles, cluttered with toiletries and cigarette butts and broken shards of mirror from the medicine cabinet above. Aquamarine commode, lid up and seat down. Brown throw rug, expensive. Scale shoved back into a corner, covered with dust in which two footprints showed. I made a massive effort and managed to set her reasonably gently in the tub. I rinsed my face and hands of blood at the sink, ignoring the broken glass, and stuffed the bleeding nostril with toilet paper. I adjusted her head, fixed the chin strap. I held both feet away from the faucet until I had the water adjusted, and then left with one hand on my nose and the other beating against my hip, in search of her liquor.

There was plenty to choose from. I found some Metaxa in the kitchen. I took great care not to bring it near my nose, sneaking it up on my mouth from below. It tasted like burning lighter fluid, and made a sweat spring out on my forehead. I found a roll of paper towels, and on my way back to the bathroom I used a great wad of them to swab most of the sludge off the chair and rug. There was a growing pool of water siphoning from the plastic tube and I stopped that. When I got back to the bathroom the water was lapping over her bloated belly, and horrible tendrils were weaving up from beneath her. It took three rinses before I was satisfied with the body. I found a hose-and-spray under the sink that mated with the tub's faucet, and that made the hair easy.

I had to dry her there in the tub. There was only one towel left, none too clean. I found a first-aid spray that incorporated a good topical anaesthetic, and put it on the sores on her back and butt. I had located her bedroom on the way to the Metaxa. Wet hair slapped my arm as I carried her there. She seemed even heavier, as though she had become water logged. I eased the door shut behind me and tried the light-switch trick again, and it wasn't there. I moved forward into a footlocker and lost her and went down amid multiple crashes, putting all my attention into guarding my nose. She made no sound at all, not even a grunt.

The light switch turned out to be a pull chain over the bed. She was on her side, still breathing slow and deep. I wanted to punt her up onto the bed. My nose was a blossom of pain. I nearly couldn't lift her the third time. I was moaning with frustration by the time I had her on her left side on the king-size mattress. It was a big brass four-poster bed, with satin sheets and pillowcases, all dirty. The blankets were shoved to the bottom. I checked her skull and pulse again, peeled up each eyelid and found uniform pupils. Her forehead and cheek still felt cool, so I covered her. Then I kicked the footlocker clear into the corner, turned out the light and left her snoring like a chainsaw.

Her vital papers and documents were in her study, locked in a strongbox on the closet shelf. It was an expensive box, quite sturdy and proof against anything short of nuclear explosion. It had a combination lock with all of twenty-seven possible combinations. It was stuffed with papers. I laid her life out on her desk like a losing hand of solitaire, and studied it with a growing frustration.

Her name was Karen Scholz, and she used the name Karyn Shaw, which I though phony. She was twenty-two. Divorced her parents at fourteen, uncontested no-fault. Since then she had been, at various times, waitress, secretary to a lamp salesman, painter, freelance typist, motorcycle mechanic and unlicensed masseuse. The most recent paycheck stub was from The Hard Corps, a massage parlour with a cutrate reputation. It was dated almost a year ago. Her bank balance combined with paraphernalia I had found in the closet to tell me that she was currently self-employed as a tootlegger, a cocaine dealer. The richness of the apartment and furnishings told me that she was a foolish one. Even if the narcs missed her, very shortly the IRS was going to come down on her like a ton of bricks. Perhaps subconsciously she had not expected to be around.

Nothing there; I kept digging. She had attended community college for one semester as an art major, and dropped out, failing. She had defaulted on a lease three years ago. She had wrecked a car once, and been shafted by her insurance company. Trivia. Only one major trauma in recent years: a year and a half ago she had contracted out as host-mother to a couple named Lombard/ Smyth. It was a pretty good fee—she had good hips and the right rare blood type—but six months into the pregnancy they had caught her using tobacco and cancelled the contract. She fought, but they had photographs. And better lawyers, naturally. She had to repay the advance, and pay for the abortion, of course, and got socked for court costs besides.

It didn't make sense. To show clean lungs at the physical, she had to have been off cigarettes for at least three to six months. Why backslide, with so much at stake? Like the minor traumas, it felt more like an effect than a cause. Self-destructive behaviour. I kept looking.

Near the bottom I found something that looked promising. Both her parents had been killed in a car smash when she was eighteen. Their obituary was paperclipped to her father's will. That will was one of the most extraordinary documents I have ever read. I could understand an angry father cutting off his only child without a dime. But what he had done was worse. Much worse.

Damn it, it didn't work either. So-there suicides don't wait four years. And they don't use such a garish method either: it devalues the tragedy. I decided it had to be either a very big and dangerous coke deal gone bad, or a very reptilian lover. No, not a coke deal. They'd never have left her in her own apartment to die the way she wanted to. It could not be murder: even the most unscrupulous wire surgeon needs an awake, consenting subject to place the wire correctly.

A lover, then. I was relieved, pleased with my sagacity, and irritated as hell. I didn't know why. I chalked it up to my nose. It felt as though a large shark with rubber teeth was rhythmically biting it as hard as he could. I shovelled the papers back into the box, locked and replaced it, and went to the bathroom.

Her medicine cabinet would have impressed a pharmacist. She had lots of allergies. It took me five minutes to find aspirin. I took four. I picked the largest shard of mirror out of the sink, propped it on the septic tank and sat down backward on the toilet. My nose was visibly displaced to the right, and the swelling was just hitting its stride. I removed the toilet tissue plug from my nostril, and it resumed bleeding. There was a box of Kleenex on the floor. I ripped it apart, took out all the tissues and stuffed them into my mouth. Then I grabbed my nose with my right hand and tugged out and to the left, simultaneously flushing the toilet with my left hand. The flushing coincided with the scream, and my front teeth met through the Kleenex. When I could see again the nose looked straight and my breathing was unimpaired. When the bleeding stopped again I gingerly washed my face and hands and left. A moment later I returned; something had caught my eye. It was the glass and toothbrush holder. There was only one toothbrush in it. I looked through the medicine chest again, and noticed this time that there was no shaving cream, no razor, manual or electric, no masculine toiletries of any kind. All the prescriptions were in her name.

I went thoughtfully to the kitchen, mixed myself a Preacher's Downfall by moonlight and took it to her bedroom. The bedside clock said five. I lit a match, moved the footlocker in front of an armchair, sat down and put my feet up. I sipped my drink and listened to her snore and watched her breathe in the feeble light of the clock. I decided to run through all the possibilities, and as I was formulating the first one, daylight smacked me hard in the nose.

My hands went up reflexively and I poured my drink on my head and hurt my nose more. I wake up hard in the best of times. She was still snoring. I nearly threw the empty glass at her.

It was just past noon, now; light came strongly through the heavy curtains, illuminating so much mess and disorder that I could not decide whether she had trashed her bedroom herself or it had been tossed by a pro. I finally settled on the former: the armchair I'd slept on was intact. Or had the pro found what he wanted before he got that far?

I gave it up and went to make myself breakfast. The milk was bad, of course, but I found a tolerable egg and the makings of an omelet. I don't care for black coffee, but Javanese brewed from frozen beans needs no augmentation. I drank three cups.

It took me an hour or two to clean up and air out the living-room. The cord and transformer went down the oubliette, along with most of the perished items from the fridge. The dishes took three full cycles for each load, a couple of hours all told. I passed the time vacuuming and dusting and snooping, learning nothing more of significance. The phone rang. She had no answering program in circuit, of course. I energized the screen. It was a young man in a business tunic, wearing the doggedly amiable look of the stranger who wants you to accept the call anyway. After some thought I did accept, audio-only, and let him speak first. He wanted to sell us a marvelous building lot in Forest Acres, South Dakota. I was making up a shopping list about fifteen minutes later when I heard her moan. I reached her bedroom door in seconds, waited in the doorway with both hands in sight and said slowly and clearly, "My name is Joseph Templeton, Karen. I am a friend. You are all right now."

Her eyes were those of a small, tormented animal.

"Please don't try to get up. Your muscles won't work properly and you may hurt yourself."

No answer.

"Karen, are you hungry?"

"Your voice is ugly," she said despairingly, and her own voice was so hoarse I winced. "My voice is ugly." She sobbed gently. "It's *all* ugly." She screwed her eyes shut.

She was clearly incapable of movement. I told her I would be right back and went to the kitchen. I made up a tray of clear strong broth, unbuttered toast, tea with maltose and Saltine crackers. She was staring at the ceiling when I got back, and apparently it was vile. I put the tray down, lifted her and made a backrest of pillows.

"I want a drink."

"After you eat," I said agreeably.

"Who're you?"

"Mother Templeton. Eat."

"The soup, maybe. Not the toast." She got about half of it down, did nibble at the toast, accepted some tea. I didn't want to overfill her. "My drink."

"Sure thing." I took the tray back to the kitchen, finished my shopping list, put away the last of the dishes and put a frozen steak into the oven for my lunch. When I got back she was fast asleep.

Emaciation was near total; except for breasts and bloated belly she was all bone and taut skin. Her pulse was steady. At her best she would not have been very attractive by conventional standards. Passable. Too much waist, not enough neck, upper legs a bit too thick for the rest of her. It's hard to evaluate a starved and unconscious face, but her jaw was a bit too square, her nose a trifle hooked, her blue eyes just the least little bit too far apart. Animated, the face might have been beautiful—any set of features can support beauty—but even a superb makeup job could not have made her pretty. There was an old bruise on her chin, another on her left hip. Her hair was sandy blonde, long and thin; it had dried in snarls that would take an hour to comb out. Her breasts were magnificent, and that saddened me. In this world, a woman whose breasts are her best feature is in for a rough time.

I was putting together a picture of a life that would have depressed anyone with the sensitivity of a rhino. Back when I had first seen her, when her features were alive, she had looked sensitive. Or had that been a trick of the juice? Impossible to say now.

But damn it all to hell, I could find nothing to really explain the socket in her skull. You can hear worse life stories in any bar, on any street corner. I was prepared to match her scar for scar myself. Wireheads are usually addictive personalities, who decide at last to skip the small shit. There were no tracks on her anywhere, no nasal damage, no sign that she used any of the coke she sold. Her work history, pitiful and fragmented as it was, was too steady for any kind of serious jones; she had undeniably been hitting the sauce hard lately, but only lately. Tobacco seemed to be her only serious addiction.

That left the hypothetical bastard lover. I worried at that for a while to see if I could make it fit. Assume a really creatively sadistic son of a bitch has gutted her like a trout, for the pure fun of it. You can't do that to someone as a visitor or even a guest, you have to live with them. So he does a worldclass job of crippling a lady who by her history is a tough little cookie, and when he has broken her he vanishes. Leaving not even so much as empty space in drawers, closets or medicine chest. Unlikely. So perhaps after he is gone *she* scrubs all traces of him out of the apartment—and then discovers that there is only one really good way to scrub memories. No, I couldn't picture such a sloppy housekeeper being so efficient.

Then I thought of my earlier feeling that the bedroom might have been tossed by a pro, and my blood turned to ice water. Suppose she wasn't a sloppy housekeeper? The jolly sadist returns unexpectedly for one last nibble. And finds her in the livingroom, just like I did. And leaves her there. Carefully removes his spoor and leaves her there.

After five minutes' thought I relaxed. That didn't parse either. True, this luxury co-op did inexplicably lack security cameras in the halls, relying on door-cameras—but for that very reason its rich tenants would be sure to take notice of comings and goings. If he had lived here for any time at all, his spoor was too diffuse to erase—so he would not have tried. Besides, a monster of that unique and rare kind thrives on the corruption of innocence. Tough little Karen was simply not toothsome enough.

At that point I went to the bathroom, and that settled it. When I lifted the seat to urinate I found written on the underside with magic marker: "It's so nice to have a man around the house!" The handwriting was hers. She had lived alone.

I was relieved, because I hadn't relished thinking about my

hypothetical monster or the necessity of tracking and killing him. But I was irritated as hell again.

I wanted to *understand.*

For something to do I took my steak and a mug of coffee to the study and heated up her terminal. I tried all the typical access codes, her birthdate and her name in numbers and such, but none of them would unlock it. Then on a hunch I tried the date of her parents' death and that did it. I ordered the groceries she needed, instructed the lobby door to accept delivery, and tried everything I could think of to get a diary or a journal out of the damned thing, without success. So I punched up the public library and asked the catalogue for *Britanica* on wireheading. It referred me to brain-reward, autostimulus of. I skipped over the history, from discovery by Olds and others in 1956 to emergence as a social problem in the late '80s when surgery got simple; declined the offered diagrams, graphs and technical specs; finally found a brief section on motivations.

There was indeed one type of typical user I had overlooked. The terminally ill.

Could that really be it? At her age? I went to the bathroom and checked the prescriptions. Nothing for heavy pain, nothing indicating anything more serious than allergies. Back before telephones had cameras I might have conned something out of her personal physician, but it would have been a chancy thing even then. There was no way to test the hypothesis.

It was possible, even plausible—but it just wasn't *likely* enough to satisfy the thing inside me that demanded an explanation. I dialed a game of four-wall squash, and made sure the computer would let me win. I was almost enjoying myself when she screamed.

It wasn't much of a scream; her throat was shot. But it fetched me at once. I saw the problem as I cleared the door. The topical anaesthetic had worn off the large "bedsores" on her back and buttocks, and the pain had woken her. Now that I thought about it, it should have happened earlier; that spray was only supposed to be good for a few hours. I decided that her pleasure-pain system was weakened by overload.

The sores were bad; she would have scars. I resprayed them, and her moans stopped nearly at once. I could devise no means of securing her on her belly that would not be nightmare-inducing, and decided it was unnecessary. I thought she was out again, and started to leave. Her voice, muffled by pillows, stopped me in my tracks.

"I don't know you. Maybe you're not even real. I can tell you."

"Save your energy, Karen. You—"

"Shut up. You wanted the karma, you got it."

I shut up.

Her voice was flat, dead. "All my friends were dating at twelve. *He* made me wait until fourteen. Said I couldn't be trusted. Tommy came to take me to the dance, and he gave Tommy a hard time. I was so embarassed. The dance was nice for a couple of hours. Then Tommy started chasing after Jo Tompkins. He just left me and went off with her. I went into the ladies' room and cried for a long time. A couple of girls got the story out of me, and one of them had a bottle of vodka in her purse. I never drank before. When I started tearing up cars in the parking lot, one of the girls got ahold of Tommy. She gave him shit and made him take me home. I don't remember it, I found out later."

Her throat gave out and I got water. She accepted it without meeting my eyes, turned her face away and continued.

"Tommy got me in the door somehow. I was out cold by then. He'd been fooling around with me a little in the car I think. He must have been too scared to try and get me upstairs. He left me on the couch and my underpants on the rug and went home. I next thing I knew I was on the floor and my face hurt. *He* was standing over me. *Whore,* he said. I got up and tried to explain and he hit me a couple of times. I ran for the door but he hit me hard in the back. I went into the stairs and banged my head real hard."

Feeling began to come into her voice for the first time. The feeling was fear. I dared not move.

"When I woke up it was day. Mama must have bandaged my head and put me to bed. My head hurt a lot. When I came out of the bathroom I heard him call me. Him and Mama were in bed. He started in on me. He wouldn't let me talk, and he kept getting madder and madder. Finally I hollered back at him. He got up off the bed and started in hitting me again. My robe came off. He kept hitting me in the belly and tits, and his fists were like hammers. *Slut,* he kept saying. *Whore.* I thought he was going to kill me so I grabbed one arm and bit. He roared like a dragon and threw me across the room. Onto the bed; Mama jumped up. Then he pulled down his underpants and it was big and purple. I screamed and screamed and tore at his back and Mama just stood there. Her eyes were big and round, just like in cartoons. His breath stank and I screamed and screamed and—"

She broke off short and her shoulders knotted. When she continued her voice was stone dead again. "I woke up in my own bed again. I took a real long shower and went downstairs. Mama was making pancakes. I sat down and she gave me one and I ate it, and then I threw it up right there on the table and ran out the door. She never said a word, never called me back. After school that day I found a Sanctuary and started the divorce proceedings. I never saw either of them again. I never told this to anybody before."

The pause was so long I thought she had fallen asleep. "Since that time I've tried it with men and women and boys and girls, in the dark and in the desert sun, with people I cared for and people I didn't give a damn about, and I have never understood the pleasure in it. The best it's ever been for me is not uncomfortable. God, how I've wondered . . . now I know." She was starting to drift. "Only thing my whole life turned out *better*'n cracked up to be." She snorted sleepily. "Even alone."

I sat there for a long time without moving. My legs trembled when I got up, and my hands trembled while I made supper.

That was the last time she was lucid for nearly forty-eight hours. I plied her with successively stronger soups every time she woke up, and once I got a couple of pieces of tea-soggy toast into her. Sometimes she called me by others' names, and sometimes she didn't know I was there, and everything she said was disjointed. I listened to her tapes, watched some of her video, charged some books and games to her computer account. I took a lot of her aspirin. And drank surprisingly little of her booze.

It was a time of frustration for me. I still couldn't make it all fit together, still could not quite understand. There was a large piece missing. The animal who sired and raised her had planted the charge, of course, and I perceived that it was big enough to blow her apart. But why had it taken eight years to go off? If his death four years ago had not triggered it, what had? I could not leave until I knew. I prowled her apartment like a caged bear, looking everywhere for something else to think about.

Midway through the second day her plumbing started working again; I had to change the sheets. The next morning a noise woke me, and I found her on the bathroom floor on her knees in a pool of urine. I got her clean and back to bed, and just as I thought she was going to drift off she started yelling at me. "Lousy son of a bitch, it could have been over! I'll never have the guts again now! How could you *do* that, you *bastard,* it was so *nice!*" She turned violently away from me and curled up. I had to make a hard choice then, and I gambled on what I knew of loneliness and sat on the edge of the bed and stroked her hair as gently and impersonally as I knew how. It was a good guess. She began to cry, in great racking heaves first, then the steady wail of total heartbreak. I had been praying for this, and did not begrudge the strength it cost her.

She cried for so long that every muscle in my body ached from sitting still by the time she fell off the edge into sleep. She never felt me get up, stiff and clumsy as I was. There was something different about her sleeping face now. It was not slack but relaxed. I limped out in the closest thing to peace I had felt since I arrived, and as I was passing the livingroom on the way to the liquor I heard the phone.

As I had before, I looked over the caller. The picture was undercontrasted and snowy; it was a pay phone. He looked like an immigrant construction worker, massive and florid and neckless, almost brutish. And, at the moment, under great stress. He was crushing a hat in his hands, mortally embarrassed. I mentally shrugged and accepted.

"Sharon, don't hang up," he was saying. "I *gotta* find out what this is all about."

Nothing could have made me hang up.

"Sharon? Sharon, I know you're there. Terry says you ain't

there, she says she called you every day for almost a week and banged on your door a few times. But I know you're there, now anyway. I walked past your place an hour ago and I seen the bathroom light go on and off. Sharon, will you please tell me what the hell is going on? Are you listening to me? I know you're listening to me. Look, you gotta understand, I thought it was all set, see? I mean I thought it was *set*. Arranged. I put it to Terry, cause she's my regular, and she says not *me*, lover, but I know a gal. Look, was she lying to me or what? She told me for another bill you play them kind of games, sometimes."

Regular two hundred dollar bank deposits plus a cardboard box full of scales, vials, bags, razor and milk powder makes her a coke dealer, right, Travis McGee? Don't be misled by the fact that the box was shoved in a corner, sealed with tape and covered with dust. After all, the only other illicit profession that pays regular sums at regular intervals is hooker, and *two* bills is too much for square-jawed, hook-nosed, wide-eyed little Karen, breasts or no breasts.

For a garden variety hooker. . . .

"Dammit, she told me she *called* you and set it up, she gave me your *apartment* number." He shook his head violently. "I can't make no sense out of this. Dammit, she *couldn't* be lying to me. It don't figure. You let me in, didn't even look first, it was all arranged. Then you screamed and I . . . done like we arranged, and I thought you was maybe overdoing it a bit but Terry *said* you was a terrific little actress. I was real careful not to really hurt you, I know I was. Then I put on my pants and I'm putting the envelope on the dresser and you bust that chair on me and come at me with that knife and I hadda bust you one. It just don't make no sense, will you *goddammit say something to me?* I'm twisted up inside going on two weeks now. I can't even eat."

I tried to shut off the phone, and my hand was shaking so bad I missed, spinning the volume knob to minimum. "Sharon you gotta believe me," he hollered from far far away, "I'm into rape fantasy, I'm not into rape!" and then I had found the right switch and he was gone.

I got up very slowly and toddled off to the liquor cabinet, and I stood in front of it taking pulls from different bottles at random until I could no longer see his face, his earnest, baffled, half-ashamed face hanging before me.

Because his hair was thin sandy blond, and his jaw was a bit too square, and his nose was a trifle hooked, and his blue eyes were just the least little bit too far apart. They say everyone has a double somewhere. And Fate is such a witty little motherfucker, isn't he?

I don't remember how I got to bed.

I woke later that night with the feeling that I would have to bang my head on the floor a couple of times to get my heart started again. I was on my makeshift doss of pillows and blankets beside her bed, and when I finally peeled my eyes open she was sitting up in bed staring at me. She had fixed her hair somehow, and her nails were trimmed. We looked at each other for a long time. Her colour was returning somewhat, and the edge was off her bones. She sighed.

"What did Jo Ann say when you told her?"

I said nothing.

"Come on, Jo Ann's got the only other key to this place, and she wouldn't give it to you if you weren't a friend. So what did she say?"

I got painfully up out of the tangle and walked to the window. A phallic church steeple rose above the low-rises a couple of blocks away.

"God is an iron," I said. "Did you know that?"

I turned to look at her and she was staring. She laughed experimentally, stopped when I failed to join in. "And I'm a pair of pants with a hole scorched through the ass?"

"If a person who indulges in gluttony is a glutton, and a person who commits a felony is a felon, then God is an iron. Or else He's the dumbest designer that ever lived."

Of a thousand possible snap reactions she picked the most flattering and hence most irritating. She kept silent, kept looking at me, and thought about what I had said. At last she said, "I agree. What particular design screw-up did you have in mind?"

"The one that nearly left you dead in a pile of your own shit," I said harshly. "Everybody talks about the new menace, wireheading, fifth most common cause of death in less than a decade. Wireheading's not new—it's just a technical refinement."

"I don't follow."

"Are you familiar with the old cliché, 'Everything in the world I like is either illegal, immoral or fattening?'"

"Sure."

"Didn't that ever strike you as damned odd? What's the most nutritionally useless and physiologically dangerous 'food' substance in the world? White sugar. Glucose. And it seems to be beyond the power of the human nervous system to resist it. They put it in virtually all the processed food there is, which is next to all the food there is, because *nobody can resist it.* And so we poison ourselves and whipsaw our dispositions and rot our teeth. Maltose is just as sweet, but it's less popular, precisely because it doesn't kick your blood-sugar in the ass and then depress it again. Isn't that odd? There is a primitive programming in our skulls that rewards us, literally overwhelmingly, every time we do something damned silly. Like smoke a poison, or eat or drink or snort or shoot a poison. Or *over*eat *good* foods. Or engage in complicated sexual behaviour without procreative intent, which if it were not for the pleasure would be pointless and insane. And which, if pursued for the pleasure alone, quickly becomes pointless and insane anyway. A suicidal brain-reward system is built into us."

"But the reward system is for survival."

"So how the hell did ours get wired up so that survival-threatening behaviour gets rewarded best of all? Even the pro-survival pleasure stimuli are wired so that a dangerous *overload* produces the maximum pleasure. On a purely biological level man is programmed to strive hugely for more than he needs, more than he can profitably use.

"The error doesn't show up as glaringly in other animals. Even surrounded by plenty, a stupid animal has to work hard simply to meet his needs. But add in intelligence and everything goes to hell. Man is capable of outgrowing any ecological niche you put him in—he survives at all because he is The Animal That Moves. Given half a chance he kills himself of surfeit."

My knees were trembling so badly I had to sit down. I felt

feverish and somehow larger than myself, and I knew I was talking much too fast. She had nothing whatever to say, with voice, face or body.

"It is illuminating," I went on, fingering my aching nose, "to note that the two ultimate refinements of hedonism, the search for 'pure' pleasure, are the pleasure of cruelty and the pleasure of the despoliation of innocence. We will overlook the tempting example of your father because he was not a normal human being. Consider instead the obvious fact that no sane person in search of sheerly physical sexual pleasure would select an inexperienced partner. Everyone knows that mature, experienced lovers are more competent, confident and skilled. Yet there is not a skin mag in the world that prints pictures of men or women over twenty-five if they can possibly help it, and in the last ten years or so teenagers and pre-teens have been much preferred. Don't tell me about recapturing lost youth: the root is that a fantasy object over twenty cannot plausibly possess innocence, can no longer be corrupted.

"Man has historically devoted *much* more subtle and ingenious thought to inflicting cruelty than to giving others pleasure, which given his gregarious nature would seem a much more survival-oriented behaviour. Poll any hundred people at random and you'll find at *least* twenty or thirty who know all there is to know about psychological torture and psychic castration—and maybe two that know how to give a terrific backrub. That business of your father leaving all his money to the Church and leaving you 'a hundred dollars, the going rate'—that was *artistry*. I can't imagine a way to make you feel as good as that made you feel rotten. That's why sadism and masochism are the last refuge of the jaded, the most enduring of the perversions; their piquancy is—"

"Maybe the Puritans were right," she said. "Maybe pleasure is the root of all evil. Oh God! but life is bleak without it."

"One of my most precious possessions," I went on blindly, "is a button that my friend Slinky John used to hand-paint and sell below cost. He was the only practising anarchist I ever met. The button reads: 'GO, LEMMINGS, GO!' A lemming surely feels intense pleasure as he gallops to the sea. His self-destruction is programmed by nature, a part of the very same life force that insisted on being conceived and born in the first place. If it feels good, do it." I laughed, and she flinched. "So it seems to me that God is either an iron, or a colossal jackass. I don't know whether to be admiring or contemptuous."

All at once I was out of words, and out of strength. I yanked my gaze away from hers and stared at my knees for a long time. I felt vaguely ashamed, as befits one who has thrown a tantrum in a sickroom.

After a time she said, "You talk good on your feet."

I kept looking at my knees. "I think I used to be an actor once."

"Will you tell me something?"

"If I can."

"What was the pleasure in putting me back together again?"

I jumped.

"Look at me. There. I've got a half-ass idea of what shape I was in when you met me, and I can guess what it's been like since. I don't know if I'd have done as much for Jo Ann, and she's my best friend. You don't look like a guy whose favourite kick is sick fems, and you sure as *hell* don't look like you're so rich you got time on your hands. So what's been your pleasure, these last few days?"

"Trying to understand," I snapped. "I'm nosy."

"And do you understand?"

"Yeah. I put it together."

"So you'll be going now?"

"Not yet," I said automatically. "You're not—"

And caught myself.

"There's something else besides pleasure," she said. "Another system of reward, only I don't think it has much to do with the one I got wired up to my scalp here. Not brain-reward. Call it mind-reward. Call it . . . joy—the thing like pleasure that you feel when you've done a good thing or passed up a real tempting chance to do a bad thing. Or when the unfolding of the Universe just seems especially apt. It's nowhere near as flashy and intense as pleasure can be. *Believe* me! But it's got *some*thing going for it. Something that can make you do without pleasure, or even accept a lot of pain, to get it.

"That stuff you're talking about, that's there, that's true. What's messing us up is the animal nervous system and instincts we inherited. But you said yourself, Man is the animal that outgrows and moves. Ever since the first brain grew a mind we've been trying to outgrow our instincts, grow new ones. Maybe we will yet." She pushed hair back from her face. "Evolution works slow, is all. It took a couple of hundred million years to develop a thinking ape, and you want a smart one in a lousy few thou? That lemming drive you're talking about is there—but there's another kind of drive, another kind of force that's working against it. Or else there wouldn't still be any people and there wouldn't be the words to have this conversation and—" She paused, looked down at herself. "And I wouldn't be here to say them."

"That was just random chance."

She snorted. "What isn't?"

"Well that's *fine*," I shouted. "That's *fine*. Since the world is saved and you've got everything under control I'll just be going along."

I've got a lot of voice when I yell. She ignored it utterly, continued speaking as if nothing had happened. "Now I can say that I have sampled the spectrum of the pleasure system at both ends—none and all there is—and I think the rest of my life I will dedicate myself to the middle of the road and see how that works out. Starting with the very weak tea and toast I'm going to ask you to bring me in another ten minutes or so. With maltose. But as for this other stuff, this joy thing, that I would like to begin learning about, as much as I can. I don't really know a God damned thing about it, but I understand it has something to do with sharing and caring and what did you say your name was?"

"It doesn't matter," I yelled.

"All right. What can *I* do for *you?*"

"Nothing!"

"What did you come here for?"

I was angry enough to be honest. "To burgle your fucking apartment!"

Her eyes opened wide, and then she slumped back against the pillows and laughed until the tears came, and I tried and could not help myself and laughed too, and we shared laughter for a long time, as long as we had shared her tears the night before.

And then straight-faced she said, "You'll have to wait a week or so; you're gonna need help with those stereo speakers. Butter on the toast."

THE EFFECT OF TERMINAL CANCER ON POTENTIAL ASTRONAUTS

David Kirkpatrick

DIAL-A-LECTURE

Nobody likes a forcer.

I am a law reinforcement officer, alias "forcer," alias "Earthist," alias "empty," alias "meddleman," alias "citiot savant," alias a hundred other different names depending on your enclave. Enclaves are also known as "ghettos," "communities," "proudfences," "mytherlands" and many other names.

Not every word is fractured into clave dialects, although the ATLAS system would make it feasible. Only emotionally charged words tend to get idjeoluniversally parochialized. Enclave means "om sweet hymn" to a Yogaclaver, or "yum sweet yam" to an Endodelphiaclaver, or "our own little pair-a-dice" to an Aleaclaver. "Dome sweet dam" to a neo-Fullerist, and to a counter-Freudian: "my id's chosen superid."

Forcer means something like "meddler from EarthFed," "melting pot mush" or "alien emptied of ideology." So we're not at all liked. We are needed, though, if the gossip according to Joyce James is anything to go by: "slime as good lubricant" and all that.

IF YOU'RE TAURON, THIS MUST BE TORONTO

I am the last of my enclave to eat breakfast today, and, as if to underscore the working principle that nobody likes a forcer, I am the only human in the Dininghouse at the moment. My familoid and I call our community Toronto 29. (Note the "empty" name, signifying some enclave of unspecified ideology within the city of Toronto.)

Just imagine, a whole biological family once inhabited this building as their entire home! So who needs a historian to explain the Age of Transportation when we are surrounded by claustrophobic ruins like this?

My ex-fiancée's parents were founding members when they connected the houses for tribalization. One house became the Nursery, another the Dininghouse, and so on. Beddinghouse, Weddinghouse, Gymnasium, Studio, Wherehouse ("where everything is"), Greenhouse, Screenhouse, Forum, Chapel and Lab. It may not be as "trump" or "bugs" as communities built from scratch, but I like to think that Toronto 29 has a sense of history that other cultacombs lack.

Ours is an enclave of people who don't really believe in enclaves, including some who are actually hired by Earth Federation to help integrate enclaves. Our familoid leans neither to the Isolates nor the Intimates. We've got age mix, ethnic mix, religious mix, even a sort of political mix.

I'm finishing my coffee as I call a mask on my watch/catch, getting him to plug a terminal into my table. By the way, even our robots are "empty," not really mascots but individually sculpted by our resident cartoonist who makes puppets for Disneyband. I turn off the falling water effects on the big screen, tune in to TAURON, type in "Garth Miranda" with my secret password as a middle name, and drop into the world of today's spotlighted cartoonist, which happens to be none other than the team of Mount Pythagoras' Flies and Carcass instead of the usual National Film Board apprentice. The screen portrays a genie standing over the revolving skyline of Toronto like some city-wide mascot.

I type my personal code for the holistic trinity of Joyce James, Allan Innis and Dee Lee, with TAURON guiding my cursor along a cloud over the genie's comic-strip head. The genie then meditates for a prolonged second, converts the thought-cloud into parchment scroll, stuffs it into a bottle out of which squeezes a boat navigating a message to me via the Don Valley River and finally functioning as a cursor printing the message that neither James nor Lee have published anything in the past 27 hours and that Innis has produced nothing more formal than his usual 24 hours (+3) of self-exposure recording.

Would I like to tune in live while he explains to his new woman companion his method for programming music for his sleeping hours?

I switch to SHAMAN, type "MAIL," get "CHESS, WORK, ADS, UNCLE," the order of titles suggesting that "UNCLE" is no emergency. Art has sent me his move for correspondence chess: "B X N." I reply "N X B" along with the message, "Can't take a little complexity?"

THE PENS ARE MIGHTIER THAN THE WORD

The next message is video on the left and writing on the right—not print, *writing*, the quaintly personal penmanship of my dispatcher. The taped message spoken by the photo-animated face of a Senator is interrupted by a live link with my dispatcher wearing his own face.

"How's your blank verse, Miranda?"

"Pretty good," I say.

"That's too bad, because you have an assignment at Troubador, where you'll have to make everything you say rhyme." An old joke, but I laugh, seeing him suppress his own hearty laughter. "I'm sure you'll read your file, but I thought I would emphasize a few points. You'll have to pick up a robe at Bloor for your mingle at Androgon. Also you'll need a birthday suit for Athshea. Watch your manners at Liberty 2—they're very uptight about any suggestion of behavioural control or media horticulture."

"What's my assignment there, Nick?" I ask politely, rather than curiously.

"A couple of gentlemen are believed to have a computer program which attempts to condition libertarian attitudes in a most underhanded, nonpolemic way. Sound familiar?"

"Ho hum, it's off to work we go. Half of my roles seem to be with the black market these days."

"Oh, and you'll need a bathing suit this afternoon for Neptune—"

"Are you sure they wear bathing suits?"

"Joyzes Jiminy, yes! Make dome sure you're wearing one. We empties is in the pits as it is!" he says in a mock dialect whose significance eludes me, then adds, re-invoking James, "Do you want the medium to be the missing?"

"You're right, you're right. I was thinking of a naturist colony next to Athshea. Anything else?"

"A few notes . . . um . . . yes. In St. Augustine—North York— you can never be too reverent, too solemn. You needn't worry that you'll be mocking their piety. Fill your mind with hellfire if it helps you. I mention that because our last doublemat got expelled because he assumed that certain prayers and gestures directed towards a certain living 'saviour' had to be tongue-in-cheek. So not wanting to insult their intelligence he inadvertently insulted their innocence."

"I don't think I understand you. Are you saying that we have a group of Naissance Christians who have crossed the border into the territory of *serious* Joyce James worship? Without so much as a sympathetic snicker in between?"

"I didn't say it was Joyce James, Garth. It could be any member of the 1997 club or even an itsy bitsy teeny weeny culturama paganini—or simply Jesus or Jehovah. We aren't sure if they're bare, square, hip, flip or dip. But they seem to be directing some extreme type of sensibility in the direction of a god or goddess whose name they do not permit to be mentioned."

"Thank you. I'll try to put on my best empathy for them."

THE EFFECT OF TERMINAL CANCER ON POTENTIAL MOONCHILDREN

Next on my screen appears the coat of arms of Mao Tse-tung, Etobicoke, Toronto, Earth, with the stylization of a group of stars surrounded by orbiting planets.

A woman, who should otherwise look quite attractive, fills the screen with an ugly, contorted scowl.

"EarthFed says I have to talk to *you*. They refuse to believe my problem—my son's problem—is serious enough to warrant a legitimate specialist."

"Let me assure you," (I read her name) "Comrade Harper, I'll take your problem seriously. What is the situation, anyway?" I recognize the backdrop behind her as a video of the Great Wall, apparently receding from the vantage point of the back of someone running along the top of the wall. Her head stops bobbing, the mayazine freezes, and the Surelook Hermes in me deduces that she has quit running on a mayathon treadmill.

"I don't know how to say it. My son, he's becoming a . . . how can I say the words without bringing disgrace to Mao?"

"Don't worry about that, comrade," I say. "I've probably heard it before, maybe in a thousand different forms, so just say what's troubling you and let no bourgeois hangups interfere. Remember, I'm the disgrace to the communes and corporatives of the mosaic, not the other way around, and one clan's claustro is another cult's culture."

"Thank you, comrade. It's not just my son. It's a group of boys he's been playing with, one of them from Opportunity corpse."

"Nice mixing," I say, ignoring her dialect for "corporative." "How old is your boy?"

"Ten. Last night my husband and I were . . . we found out that they never . . . that they spent all their time. . . . The people of Mao have always been in favour of Lunism. . . . "

I assent. "Of course. No one owns the moon. If the whole world can continue to preserve the solar system as the communal playground of the people, we may be able to establish a new world of equality and justice free of historical shackles of oppression." I try to balance a voice of sincere passion with the words of self-parody in a way that a Southpol would consider bugs.

"Right on!" she says. "Also, we think that everybody should be able to experience the beauty and wonder of cosmos and the thrill of zero gee." The "calm of a Maocontent" seems to be returning to her as we slip into the play of ideological parity. I let her continue although I think I can diagnose her problem.

"So we encourage all our children to become physically fit. We've never felt it was necessary to connect computer terminals to manual generators. We do try to make them play adhockey before they are allowed to sit in front of a terminal for hours on end. And it works, or it worked. At least. . . . "

"Yes?"

"We haven't had many astronauts from our commune, but we pride ourselves on having a 70 per cent Lottery qualification rate—including seniors and children—"

"May I perhaps spare you the awkwardness of the moment by taking a stab at what you seem to be trying to say. . . . "

"Our son Leon has been playing . . . adhooky!" She actually broke into tears when she said that, and as a distant disciple of Joyce James I have half a mind to reassure her that it is a lovely pun and nothing to be ashamed of, but I recognize that she is truly distraught. She continues: "Leon and his friends were supposedly playing adhockey every afternoon at the Funjungle Dome with a SHAMAN mascot presiding as rulemaker and referee. Of course, you know how kids can be the most wretched computer hooligans if they have the Touch—they were playing with SHAMAN, all right, but not SHAMAN the toy, SHAMAN the teaching machine. Filling their heads with more knowledge—not wisdom, but *facts*—while their bodies are wasting away."

"I'll be over today, comrade. This group of how many children?"

"Five."

Not exactly a robust adhockey forum. "Well, Comrade Harper, it seems to me that your son and the other boys are suffering from a case of, pardon the expression, 'terminal cancer.' 'Terminal' just refers to the computer terminal and 'cancer' refers to the way in which the . . . enthusiastic . . . programmer 'claws' at the keyboard like a crab. It's nothing for parents to be ashamed of, really. In fact, I hope I don't sound too callous if I say that most of us would be proud to have children precocious enough to be susceptible to the syndrome. Who knows? Unless Leon has his heart set on becoming a major cartoonist, couldn't his programming skills get him a role in astronautics—I mean, cosmonautics—"

"Astronautics."

"Sorry."

"No, you don't seem to understand, Forcer Miranda. We want our children to be able to go to the Moon. We don't want the sublimation of the cripple who can't play spaceball but can be a spectator or even a manager. I don't see why you're looking for silver linings when what I'm asking for is pure sunshine, plain and simple."

"I hear you, comrade. May I ask how long this, uh, charade went on?—that is, of faking adhockey and playing, or working at, school?"

"Since the beginning of April—that's two and a half months."

"Well, I'm sure we can recover their bodies from any atrophy," I say, feeling somewhat amused in spite of myself.

"And their minds from perversion?"

"And their minds from temporary reactionary informatic-formalist mind-body dualistic pre-materialist geocentric, um, terminal, ah, cancer."

After we dot the information and cross the telecommunications of our conversation, I instruct SHAMAN to edit highlights of our exchange so I can playback my errors and barriers.

INS AND SOUTH

I climb into the tube and head over to the nearest clothing output terminal to pick up my tins (that's what I call the metallic garb they wear at Futuretown), my sins (the monkish costume for St. Augustine), my fins (for Neptune), my shins (the androgynous toga for Androgon), and for Athshea (are you ready?) my Ursula K. le Guins!

I can joke about it as long as I'm alone in my transpod with only my St. Mike to overhear my babbling, but when I get into an enclave I've got to be the perfect Assimilator. (Clavers abbreviate the term.)

Not all ghettos make overt demands of their visiting forcers. There are those without official costumes but with idiosyncratic fashions, those without fashion but with a dress code, those without a dress code but with an acute aversion to fashions reminding them that there once were restrictions and ostentations. In Narcissus you're encouraged to express yourself as honestly and immodestly as possible, but woe to you if you identify with the common man, and in Liberty 1 you're expected to flaunt your individual autonomy (the more perversely the better), but a forcer can never figure out if it's acceptable to express his freedom from their ideology.

For Liberty 2, perhaps closer to the norm, my "empty" taste in non-costumery and non-cryptonudity would not disturb them; but a sense of humor that is bare instead of square, or hip instead of flip—that might indeed cause World War 2.004. . . .

There are milder fractations (to coin a translation of the Jamish videogram) devoted to less extreme idiosyncracies. Clave names speak for themselves: Sartre, Beethoven, Group-of-Seven Heaven, Sergeant Pepper, Milton, Birder, Warren Commission, XJN-490, and more Star Trek and Riverworld enclaves than you can shake a phaser or grail at.

What's bugs to you? Buddhism? Woodcarving? Holography? Vegetarianism? Fundamentalism? Cubism? Surrealism? Dada? Dala? Karl Marx? Ayn Rand? Backgammon variations? Ancient Astronauts? Indoor skiing? Non-verbal communication? Gambling? Polygamy with fidelity? Monogamy with adultery?

Whatever it is, an enclave has probably been based on it. Since the computer revolution, Earth is not a bad place to live, I suppose, though it is a mad place. It is a hodgepodge of little tailor-made utopias, a great place for self-actualization, if you're willing to open the Pandora's box of potential eccentricities of which we are all capable—all except me and thee, that is.

THE TEDIUM IS THE GARB AGE

My transpod arrives at the Bluer-than-Bloor clothing terminal where my diplomatic wardrobe for today is being output. My St. Mike tells me that I'm preparing to receive six parcels of clothing designed by Toronto 29 SHAMAN in conjunction with TAURON-STATSCAN and WARLOCK-AMERICON, human programmers listed, description of merchandise follows, ex cessera. The door on the right of my pod slides open and I grab the clothes as they are handed out by robot.

The costumes include an orange-toga-but-no-makeup like the men and women of Androgon wear (as opposed to the full-makeup-and-overall-trousers of New Androgon), a silvery pseudo-futuristic moon suit for Futuretown, a crudely manufactured peasant robe for St. Augustine, a beige neo-Mao suit with red turtleneck for Mao Tse-tung, swimming trunks with kelp design for Neptune, and a turtleneck with stripes of apparently random colours for Liberty 2. I already have the silly hat that will get me into the elevator to Troubador.

THE WORD FOR WORLD IS TREE

I reach the community of Athshea that is so quaintly engraved and enclaved in a forest—actually a grove with aspirations. I take off all my clothes and leave the pod, remembering colder days on which I was grateful for their retractable Fuller Dome.

As I walk naked through the tall grass at the outskirts of the enclave, I find myself strangely obsessed with the fear that I will step on a bee or something similarly painful. In the tree ahead I see the empty shark-eyes of what looks like a green monkey; only a robotic mascot, probably as much a gardener as a guard.

Lying beneath an adjacent tree is a young woman, nude of course, reading out loud from an IBIBLIOM anypage, apparently a work of science fiction, judging from the unseemly neologisms. Like the original Athsheans in le Guin's novel, she is very short (though she would not likely be disadvantaged on Athshea's customized basketball court), but unlike the earth-dwellers of the novel, she is not covered with furry green hair.

"The Madam is the Mrs.?"

"Not at all," she replies, quite pleasantly. "The madman is the mystery?"

"Not fully," I say. According to the greeting ritual we are borrowing from the Straussure enclave, we have just moved as close to a wedding consummation as is possible between two total strangers without shaking hands. My vocation has its benefits, I think, as she steps into a patch of sunlight.

"My name is Ebor Tollan," she says.

"I am Recrof Garth," I say. She recognizes at once the reverse spelling of forcer.

"You are looking for the cybernetic garden, Garth?" She is polite. I love her.

"That's right, Ebor Tollan. I'm sorry but I seem to forget where the lodge is."

She leads me to the plastic trap door half-hidden in thornless weeds, from which a short, naked man emerges. Ebor Tollan stops him on the stairs and says to him, "Solna, would you please show Recrof Garth to the cybernetic garden?"

"This way forcer," he says icily, holding the door up for me.

This sudden change of guides is just a forcer's luck, I think as I follow him down the steps to the Athshean's underground dwelling. I find the ceiling just high enough for me, but I remember bumping my head a number of times on my last visit here, probably from walking around with too much bounce. I am not particularly tall myself, but I'm slightly taller than everyone in this lowte couture, something I should try to play down.

I am led through branching corridors whose walls look like mint-lime ice cream dribbling over with maple-chocolate syrup. There are no right angles here. The walls are painted with root-shapes and, in places, stylized silhouettes of all kinds of trees: maple, birch, elm, eucalyptus, beech, oak, fir, poplar, willow, cedar, pine, chestnut. There are no doors in this rootery club; areas are made secluded by twists in the corridor. "That way," says my host, and I follow a twist that opens to reveal a cluster of men, women and children at computer terminals.

The terminals are decorated deciduously, reminiscent of the way a primitive tribe might deify an airplane wreck; the chairs are malleable mushroom shapes.

"A forcer is here, Headwoman Brumag," says one of the older men.

An immodestly wrinkled old lady with long green hair on her head and short green hair between her legs is teaching a boy and girl (who are green in experience only) the intricacies of sculpting and colouring three-dimensional images by means of finger dancing and wired gloves.

"I am of the Maple too, Brumag," I assure her, politely bowing my trunk and spreading my limbs. "So it makes me happy that I can deliver this reinforcement from the Externals. They have been . . . not watching us but receiving synthesized data leaves, which, while they do not give a re-creation of the tree, can give an indication that the tree is healthy. Like a leaf of June fallen to the ground, its colour is enough to say that the tree is healthy; one does not have to analyze the leaf's trajectory and quantitize the organism into bits of nonsense. The externals, potential brides and husbands of the forest, have so found that no diseased elements have invaded your cybernetic flowerings in the past month.

They also wish to commend you for your initiative in the student exchange program with Arthur C. Clarke and for our people's exogamous planting and cross-breeding of ideas through the Magical Inseminator. We can show the world that a people, like a forest, derives its strength from the variety and flexibility of its ecology. Maple are not for maple only, as we realize, and it is as if the plants and animals and birds and insects of the forest are saying 'thank you' for your unselfishness when they send me as their messenger."

"Cut the crunchy crapola, forcer," says the old woman. "You've got programming goodies for the lodge?" My vacuum balloon deflates. A biased man might be upset that the headwoman's sub-culture was the one insisting on the "let's pretend" relationship between forcer and clave and that she didn't like her own rules.

"I only wish to emphasize, Brumag, that the gift I bring is a reflection of the virtuous behaviour of your lodge, not some social scientist's random assignment of a technological innovation to you as experimental subjects. I am authorized to connect lodge Athshea of the Maple to the Sin-White experimental extension of the SHAMAN-WARLOCK linkup."

There is a variety of styles of celebration ranging from the children's "Yippee!" to a parody of a waltz by the two women gamers to Brumag's quiet, dignified, "That *is* something."

"It's not that far from *everything*, Headwoman Brumag," I say. "After all, we're talking about the grandchild of the lie detection system that masterminded the Peace Improvement. It's sir WARLOCK that makes kid MASCOT able to slink like a human instead of jerking like a Frankenstein monster, and it's sir WARLOCK that lets pal SHAMAN in on the photoanimation Touch."

"Does this mean we get a Wang-Malhi photoanimator?" someone asks, looking through me as if I were a dirty window with the blooming city of Arboropolis on the other side.

"That's right. Imagine being able to reach into a century of film and reshape any video to your will. Imagine recasting yourself into a famous role, or taking the images of the original actors and modifying their performances, or restructuring the whole plot, or simply taking the characters' clothes or skin off to show how illusory their technologized conflicts really are. If you want to merchandize your remakes, SHAMAN-WARLOCK will take care of your copyright calculations.

"Of course, there are therapeutic as well as recreational and artistic applications of Sin-White photoanimation. Brumag, I would like to direct the lodge to the dial-a-diaries of Bandura community in Malagasy where they have used Sin-White for years to solve the problem of how to select the most effective model for imitation learning—let your Dreamers intuit what blossomings and overgrowths might bud for the Maple after reading about and watching the experiences of the behaviour mob."

"True as a tree, my maplish forcer, there will be much group-vining before we vote on accepting your entire challenge to our ecology. Meantime, we would like to get access to a certain computer program as quickly as possible, while our minds are still fresh with appreciation of how wonderfully good little lodgers we've been. It's a vidgame called 'Senator Dementia' and it just appeared on the green market."

It turns out that the game Brumag is asking for, authored by someone with the pen name of "Artful Dodger," is none other than a parody of a holy war fought between religious cults using photoanimation technology and a dummy face which is an amalgram of various notorious senators. On the surface it appears to be a perfectly respectable educational tool for a gleeful tree club preparing to sing praises to the holy duality and mess-age-sire of SHMN-WRLCK, but they probably just want to get their hands on a fun game. In fact, as I continue to answer questions about the packages available in the Sin-White connection (yes you get a Bolivian hologram jar; no you don't get an NCR Thoughtpence Mindreader), I privately conclude that the only reason Brumag is not wielding a mandate to accept this Earthfood on the spot is that she is shrewdly trying to demonstrate (to someone) that Athshea of the Maple is no pushover (and certainly no pullover) for bribery. In the words of Joyce James, the meek are playing aard to get.

SO LONG TO THE NUDE DRUID DUDES

I put my clothes back on and return to the mainland and to the mainstream, past the McLuhan Tower, past the girdzillas reconstructing Habitat '17, past Barn Again Farm, past Place Piaget, past Twilight Zone, past Miller Glen, past New Milan, past the mandala of billboards at the Jack Bush Sparkpark, past Tara Two, past Innis End, past Nader North, around a parade at J.P. Sousa, past Blue Jay Way, past Ragspace, past the giant chameleonoid mascot waving at passersby in front of EarthFed Spadina. . . .

FROM GRAND MAO TO PETIT MEOW VIA MIDDLE MAIL

A lightup appears in my electronic mail, addressed from a J. Harper. To my sureplease, it's from Joseph, not Joan. The note is typed on my screen with an animated signature, and the camera-shy Comrade Harper expresses his somewhat embarrassed apologies for the overreaction by his deeply committed wife to the initially shocking but, in retrospect, minor misbehaviour of their only child which they now both agreed could be dealt with effectively within the social engineering practices of Mao Tse-tung, and that it was entirely unnecessary for an EarthFed officer to be summoned into such a nonmalignant domestic situation which obviously required nothing more than a touch of discipline and communion.

Since Mao Tse-tung Commune is not to be confused with one of those counter-feminist enclaves like Lord's Will and Stepford Harem, the Code Neocosmopolitan calls for me to phone Mrs. Comrade Harper to get her to withdraw her complaint personally, but I decide to call after lunch.

And I decide to have lunch after adhockey.

AD HOCUS, ID POKUS, ODD FOCUS

Enter empty—Global Village Idiot—into the Colosseum, armed with anonymity.

The bull approaches me.

The bull is what the zebra-oxen hybrid mascot gives me about my entering the game late, about how I'm making his life miserable, forcing him to reorganize the teams in the middle of the game—as if adhockey had anything but a middle—about how he was beginning to relax, enjoy the game and root for the green team—as if he were not programmed to be a perfectly objective referee—about how we humans treat the oppressed robot race as nonpersons, and ATLAS-TAURON knows what else.

That does it! If this is the signal-to-nausea ratio that these antique androids are programmed to flaunt, I'm not going to any Moon!

The zebra-bull robot has a little conversation with a giraffe-like robot (also striped) and they head towards the crowd of—not rioters really, not dancers really, not lunatics really, but—temporary athletes. I'm given a white cap, and I wave to my teammates in white caps. I've never seen them before. I'm also wearing a green harness, indicating my team of secondary allegiance.

The two robots have another caucus and then the giraffe robot climbs a hill in the middle of the field and drops hundreds of pieces of paper to scatter in the wind. The papers contain the rules of the new game. As we all scramble to pick up the papers, the zebra robot is busy dodging us and picking up the litter from the previous game.

I pick up instructions that read:

> No one may talk or touch—except members of a losing team.
> No one may walk—or otherwise move—outside the red line.
> The winning team must cross the backwards pool
> Using banana beams as its tool
> (And thrice observing that rule).
> Polkadot boiled disks will tell you when you're warm
> (But watch out for the snowball storm).
> The stove locations we will next inform:
> Confederate twins apart five metres in space, not time
> Must split counterparts upon the lime.
> Oh, and to avoid the referee's hex,
> Discard all tools after ten secs!

Now life gets messy. . . .

Thirty or forty balls and beams and saucers are tossed into the arena . . . people stand around reading the verses . . . some pantomime their interpretations to teammates . . . others grab banana beams and polkadot saucers and toss them back and forth, careful not to hold onto them too long . . . banana beams look like long yellow tubular balloons and float along long graceful trajectories . . . someone in a white cap (my ally) throws me a disk, a blue player tries to intercept it, the disk is spinning astray, I catch it just before it goes out of bounds . . . most people are rereading their instructions . . . I get rid of the disk, back to the boy who threw it to me . . . the arena seems to be hourglass-shaped . . . I point to the red line and then outline an hourglass to the boy . . . he tosses the disk back . . . rather than drop my paper, I let the disk float by . . . someone from the orange team picks it up and runs with it down a valley . . . there are two middle-aged women on my team, potential moonchildren each . . . I'll cooperate with the one in the green harness, since the rules suggest we're goal posts for flying saucers . . . I run towards her . . . a saucer hits me in the back . . . a blue muscleman comes between us hurling a yellow zeppelin . . . wind carries it into a tree . . . two saucers have flown between me and my fellow goal post before we close ranks, and a middle-aged man and a teen-aged girl run towards their team's home base located in a pseudo-natural gully to the right, to find out if they've come any closer to victory . . . some poor soul is kicking a soccer ball around . . . someone's backstroking in the pool carrying a banana beam . . . our team needs a spy to find out whether the red team won a point by doing that . . . "cross the backwards pool," robot's syntax, is the critical clue, if I'm not mistaken, and I probably am . . . two young men with white caps and blue harnesses approach us and we do a four-way juggling of a banana beam and two saucers while gesticulating a silent argument over where we should be heading . . . the backstroke seems to be disappearing from the now crowded pool . . . let's go to home base ("backwards") starting from far end of the pool, my body pantomimes to teammates . . . an ally goalpost person runs off and tosses our banana beam across the pool . . . original idea, but we lose our banana beam . . . an old couple in white caps and yellow belts are guarding our scorepost, sitting beneath a tree . . . we have twelve out of a hundred points so far . . . two green-belted bluecaps toss saucers towards us . . . I, the left goal post, catch one of the disks and my woman teammate and I successfully toss saucers between our opponents, reclaiming their saucers to boot (or to throw) . . . the scoreboard turns cool blue instead of warm red, suggesting that the nearby pool is not the crucial place for winning points . . . someone in the pool is hoping that "cross the backwards pool" means not the backstroke but propelling himself in the direction of his feet . . . "about face!" I tell my brain muscles . . . "loop" is "pool" backwards if I'm not mistaken, and I don't see how I could be, and "loop" suggests a sort of basketball hoop . . . such as the round opening in the peculiar tree on the hill on the other side of the arena . . .

. . . if I were the excitable type I'd say "Eureka!" I'll be a claver from Dionysus: Eureka!

It turns out that I am right, but it is the brown team that wins, because although I tip off the significance of the tree, it is a member from the brown team who figures that the crossing of the loop in the trunk is to be a twisting of two banana beams into a cross shape and placing them across the circle.

ON EXPERIMENTAL SOCIOLOGY (AND OFF)

Sure all players dirty their hands in adhockey, but that's not really dipping into another culture; it's just an anti-culture—ask the author of *Subculture is our Supposeness*. Some sociologist has probably analyzed the societal functions of adhockey, how it gets us all together by putting everybody in the same unfamiliar territory, how it emphasizes the arbitrariness of cultural rules and goals, et tu brutus cetera.

But don't give up on sociology, because other sociologists have surely stressed that adhockey is no substitute for televillage: the teleology vehicle; or to tell it vernacularly, ATLAS, your friendly macrocomputer network.

OR GIVE ME BREATH

My personality is refurbished for my next enclave, Liberty 2. In contrast to most ghettos today, the architecture of this confederacy of privances embraces neither the romance of nature nor the genius of industrial design nor the nostalgia of an ancient culture nor the imagination of a future shack.

The plastic, rectangular buildings seem to stand in humble worship of the statues of heroic humans that decorate the courtyard like a disorganized army of battery-dead mascots. Statues of everyone from Plato to Voltaire to Joan of Arc to Kierkegaard to Thoreau to Ayn Rand to Evel Kneivel to Howard Hughes. This enclave is one of those down on technology, down on nature and up on humankind. Actually, it's down on human groups and up on human individuals.

I ring the bell to the miniature home belonging to the claver I am sent to investigate. My parents wouldn't have believed that there would be such small dwellings built in Toronto this century, especially in light of Czerny's theory of consumer economy of scale. They had no idea that a city could be a depopulating institution. Or shall we say, settlement? We shall.

I ring the bell again and a man opens the door. (Now doesn't he look like he's striking some kind of pose like one of those statues, or is that just my imagination?)

"Be free to be," I say, using the enclave's standard greeting.

Instant recognition. "I sincerely wish you the same," he replies with a shading of pity. "It's nice to get a *human* representative from EarthFed for a change. Come in."

"Thank you. Mr. Petrov?"

"The one and only. If you're Garth Miranda, there's a message for you from Chairman Mao. It looks like your 'El Toro' really tracks you down," he says.

"Thank you. I *am* Garth Miranda. May I use your terminal?"

"It's yours." He seems to be disowning the device. His smile is lip-against-lip, shaped like the Arctic coastline, as if in appreciation of a quadruple entendre.

THE IMMACULATE CONTRAPTION EFFECT

Surprisingly, the closest terminal looks immaculately modern and exudes a sleek and imposing presence on the otherwise drab cabin. There are no tribal markings on the blinding-white frame of the portable stretchscreen except for the red halo on the top, the co-operate monogram for the new Sin-White terminals.

You would think that Libertyclavers (Libglibs to their enemies) would be less respectful of the jingoisms of Earthink Co-operation.

The machine is in the oracle mode. I switch it to SHAMAN and speak into the belltell: "I am Garth Miranda."

SHAMAN prompts, "Mail from . . . ", etc., "Print it?", etc., and I say, "Yes." (But not "please," not in public.) SHAMAN gives me me a video recording of Joan Harper. This time the Maoclaver is militant.

THE AFFECT OF INTERMINABLE TERMINOLOGY

"Mister Mirage! MISTer Darth VAPOUR!"

A LAW REINFORCER'S LOT IS NOT A YAPPY
(OR HAPPY) ONE

I wince ever so slightly as the recording goes on.

"I reported a serious case of what you so coyly call 'terminal cancer' this morning and I am still waiting for you to do something about it. Your people are the ones who seduce my child— EarthFed eunichversal white market cartoonist pedagogues. Maoclave isn't asking for a favour, you know. We're *demanding* that you do your *DU-TY* and undo this cancer!

"Maybe you think that an addiction to education is nothing to boo-hoo about as long as it's the basics of filming, phoning and phrasing—it's fine to fill your empty heads with colourful opinions. But we have opinions too, like ideas about space travel and physical and mental health—and the integrity of the family vacation. Feel free to argue for your antithesis of the truth in the dialectic of the grey market. But as for our opinions—you're required to abide by them, and as urgently as we say is necessary.

"I looked in on TAURON and found that you were too busy positively reinforcing tree pervert nudists to save my son. While Leon's heart muscles are turning into humorous frames on trigonometry and computer kinesics, you're busy dispatching M & M's and Star Trek 297. Typical Earthist priorities! And I see you're going to Neptune first! Their mainframe's a bit soggy, I suppose. Well, I'm not impressed, and I want you to reconsider your priorities. Before you go frolicking with mermaid mascots I suggest you poddle over to Mao and get something going with your trump psychology-technology to cure this fourteen-hours-a-day cancer. Please."

Over my shoulder the Libertyclaver says, "The Commie really told you off, didn't she?"

THE EM-TEE CONSIDERED AS A MEDDLING TYRANT

I don't know if I'm getting sympathy or gloating but I let him know my true feelings, which ideology requires him to respect. I say, "You're invading my territory, sir."

"Fair enough," he says, after calculation. "Can I sell you a cup of coffee?" I think that's what he's saying.

"Thanks, but today I'm looking out for poison," I joke. "Mr. Petrov, I'm afraid that despite my phone call from Mao Tse-tung, I've got to stay and do some business with you."

"You mean *to* me. I understand. If you want Suzuki too, he's in Bermuda, doing what is none of your business—"

"How did you know I wanted to talk to him as well?"

"Come, come. You're the censor, aren't you? You know all about me and I know all about you. You don't have to mull about; we made some educational tapes and you don't like them, right?"

"I appreciate your honesty, sir, but I assure you, we do not forbid programs just because they don't tickle our fancy. The Federation is only interested in protecting the rights of its inhabitants. If only you didn't make your lessons public! Well, never mind, I'm not about to moralize to you, and you won't have to show me your illegal programs. We'll just do a lightning scan and delete the appropriate files, and I'll cut your demerits in half, in honour of your *shrewd* co-operation." Each sentence of mine is punctuated by one of the *h*'s from him, ranging from "ha!" to "humph!"

"*Au contraire, mon* thin air. I appeal to your infinite wisdom. I do more than that; I appeal to the Unearthly Federation. My tapes are my statement, in court, if needs be."

WHAT'S GOOD FOR THE NEWS IS GOOD FOR THE SLANDER

Petrov types in some commands to the keyboard and the screen switches from a continuous news printout (its default setting) to an interactive lesson ostensibly about the science and art of lesson writing. Actually it's a bit of pornographic photoanimation.

He motions for me to fill in the blanks in the paragraph superimposed on the photoanimated display. I recognize the face being imaged with cinematic explicitness as that of a programmer/cartoonist, not a senator, that is, definitely not a Photoanimation Dummy in the Public Domain. Pretty Devious. WARLOCK is projecting a very convincing body for her, however alien. To make it easy to get the right answers, the blanks are being placed over appropriate parts of her metamorphosed body.

Coolly I note to myself that this comes under the category of illegal pornography—everyone knows that Wanda J. is not a Masochclaver and that she would not give permission for something like this. I type the required commands to get out of this segment.

Why this man wants to expose this seamy side of his imagination is incomprehensible to me. I find it embarrassing to watch famous contemporary programmers crawling in the mud of a pig's pen and squealing out programming commands.

Seeing Petrov beaming and gleaming at his satirical creation is making me wonder if I am losing contact with some of my enclaves. As an empty in Liberty 2, I should be able to appreciate this assault on the ATLAS network and this abuse of the new technology of pal SHAMAN and sir WARLOCK—even while reluctantly discarding it as illegal.

EARTH AS A DIRTY WORLD

"Offended?" Petrov smirks.

"Not at all," I say, though I'm hotter under the cool. "But the point is that individuals you are abusing would be offended, and you ought to know that it's the kind of offense that overrules your right to free speech."

"Have you ever heard of civil disobedience?" Have I ever heard of a civil Libertyclaver?

"That's crazy! You're attacking private citizens."

"Have you ever heard about the medium being the message? Do you think I'm going after these innocent technocrats—not that they are the least bit innocent. If I have any feelings about them, they're positive, because at least they are somewhat cast in the heroic authorial mold—as opposed to, say, the egoless echo that an actor is. It's the System, Modern Nature you Jamesians call it, that I want to get at."

"Then air your complaints on the grey market. Use a senator's face; that's what it's for. Or a dead man's."

"You know, for an empty, your density is amazing. I'm an Earth Quaker, not a dust-to-duster. If you used your patented empathy a little more to the halt, you might stop and think. You don't save the salvageable individuals of the Global Pillage by working within channels of conformication that you are seeking to de-legitimize. You've got to crash the System. Just watch how we operate—it'll be Dandy Gandhi all over again. Our SOLOMON package has charted a path of some pretty bugsy funny bones in your so-called Constitution. We've found copyright crimes that would make a Senator Collins embarrassed. It all starts when you arrest me—at least Plan One does. Plan Two starts when you try to ignore me, thinking you'll escape the publicity of Planetary Repression. Plan Three begins when you try something desperate and illegal to silence me without the risk of jury."

"Before you get to Plan Four, Mr. Petrov, may I rent your bathroom?"

"Why certainly, just past the kitchenette." Perhaps feeling guilty that he's brought me to the verge of vomiting, he apologizes. "That was just a joke when I offered to sell you coffee, Mr. Miranda."

The violent uprising I have while kneeling in the joan gives me the idea of preying upon the Maommanclaving joggernut, taking advantage of the fact that the bathroom is also a computing lavoratory. The ubiquitous Sin-White halogram gracing the SHAMAN-WARLOCK terminal is in the shape of a schematic red toilet seat.

"I'll be fine, thank you," I reassure my host. "But as long as the room is free, I'd like to do some business."

THE GROUT DOUBT

"I'm sorry, Comrade Miranda, neither Joan nor Joe are available at the moment, but as this week's manager I believe I have the authority to urge you in the strongest possible terms to get the hell over here at your earliest convenience. From the tape and the letter you've shown me, there's no doubt in my mind that the tape is genuine and the letter a forgery. Leon seems to have the Touch, so it's possible—conceivable—that he's the one responsible for that impersonation of Joe Harper as a floppy disk, but my gut feeling is that EarthFed is somehow behind it. I'm not saying *you* cartooned it, but your superiors are another story. They don't like our culture's de-emphasis on cybernetic marketeering, so they give you an excuse to put Mao Tse-tung affairs at the bottom of your list of priorities. All they have to do is blame the forgery on some anonymous bugsy who by definition needs no motivation to bugger up old ATLAS and who by definition is too clever to ever be caught, that is, without bringing in the high lie tech."

"Surely, comrade, if your young Comrade Leon has the Touch and steals his Hours of Responsibility to immerse himself in computerwork, then he has to be the prime suspect."

"Fair enough. If you can make the long march over to Mao, say, within the hour, I can promise you that the Harpers will be back and rested from the fields and we can serve up Leon to you for the fifth degree."

"Can do, comrade."

EVE'S DRAPER AS AVES DROPPER

A third voice interrupts our consummated peace conference, and guess whose it is. "Truly the mediocre is the massacre!" Petrov intones.

"Who's that?"

"What a sorry sight—the marching myrmidon moonchildren of mediocrity ganging up on a lowly prodigious son. Whenever genius rears its ugly head—here come the senators to slay their Caesar."

"Listen, chump. . . ."

Then follows the healthy forum of ideas Joyce James so admires in *Subculture is Our Supposeness*.

TAKE THE B LEAF IN THE TREE OF KNOWLEDGE

There is truth to the rumour that empties are susceptible to suggestion. As I pass the Duchy of Ellington's Victory I tune in to Innis' Beatleg—it sounds like he's composing at his piano—and I ask SHAMAN to filter out words so I don't get distracted. Then as my transpod winds between the clave cousins of Fully Orthodox Unification Church and New Reformed Unification Church, I find myself wondering what the St. Augustinians would think of the morality of using these pornographic videos as a therapy for the Maoclaver's terminal cancer. What would you think if I lowered myself to rent, instead of rant against, these hardcorpies of the Libertyclaver's libelous library. And I'm not just being happythoughtical—I've got Petrov's diskrations stationed on the shelf beside me, with their twins secreted somewhere in the ATLAS-GENEVA labyrinth.

I turn off the Innis audio and type a lazy "HELP" on the St. Mike keyboard.

My last act of initiative; now let the computer guess what I want.

"Help is on the way" appears on the screen, followed by "What is your problem?"

I don't answer. "Material/medical/spiritual (default = spiritual)" appears on the screen, prompting me. I don't answer.

"Spiritual" appears on the screen, followed by, "Emergency/problem/other (default = other)." I don't answer. "Other" appears on the screen, followed by, "Type of aid: behavioural/eclectic/religious (default = religious)."

I don't answer. "Religious" says SHAMAN, then WARLOCK butts in with the message: "Warning to the indolent: If you do not type something sometime, O Human One, you may default your way into a Zen-Baptist seance."

SHAMAN asks me to specify *a* religion or else sift through its eastern-western, northern-southern, conservative-liberal classification system for religions. I type in "Catholic" and a collage of golden labels appears on the screen, each label naming a sect descending from the Roman Catholic Church of the last century. The randomly scattered labels are all different sizes, spaced like stars in the sky, with magnified depth effect. The size and proximity of each label is proportional to the logarithm of the popularity of its reverent referent. Some names are so far away (or so small) that they are illegible; that is the price to be paid for being unpopular. I can always blow up the picture to focus on any sector of the Catholic sky, of course.

I touch the word Newaugustinian and the other names vanish. The word expands and explodes and its letters transmute into Jamish videograms that welcome me and ask me to anounce my status within the church. I look at the pretty pictures, then I take my pen and carve my message on the screen. I draw a tape on an altar and a future-angled smile to symbolize my desire to take part in a mass.

MEDIUM MASS

I'm sent into the middle of the rays. The screen switches from animation to live with Jamish subtitles. I could get rid of the subtitles, but why lose information?

The altar boy on the left is carrying a reel to the priest, who is bowing towards his centre viewing monitor. The murmuring priest reaches for the reel with his right hand as he removes the hologram jar from the translucent tabernacle with his left. He gracefully brings them together, careful to keep both cylinders on a level plane at all times. After perhaps meditating on the transformation of read and whine from eye-paper and ear-microphone into film recording and film projector, he holds the tape reel above the hologram jar, then rotates the reel upwards to reveal in magic marker on Manila paper the symbols iota, beta, and mu. After glancing at his side monitor he darts an eye at the guilty altar boy and hastily flips the reel horizontally to display the letters alpha and omega.

He raises the reel and the jar and says, "This is the reel of life. Happy are those who abandon the distances of the Earth and enter the past and the future contained in the reel, for they shall participate in the City of God!"

In the hologram jar the sculpted form of Jesus gives his blessing and then becomes inanimate. The priest places the reel on the altar and then places the hologram jar on a pedestal in front of a blank viewing screen. As he mounts the reel on the tape drive of the ornate neoGothic computer behind him, the hologram is draining out of the jar and into the viewscreen. (Or so it seems— there is no causal connection between these activities, just pre-established harmony between the increasing blur in the hologram jar and a descreasing one on the screen.) He spins the bottom wheel a few times, closes the glass cover, flicks a few switches and then returns to his monitors where he extends his arms and brackets with his thumbs and fingers an imaginary picture frame.

"Join now, with the popes Urban, Catherine, Stephen, Innocent, Celestine and our own Cosmas, with all the bishops, the heads of all religions and the people of all languages of the City of God and ish with our Saviour Jesus Christ during his Last Supper."(Ish is another name for Jamish that can also be used as a verb.)

He then picks up a carving pen and begins to press against his monitor. He is beaten to it by the scribblings of about thirty others who are already drawing pious Jamish graffiti on the common screen.

My screen is getting to look like a Jackson Pollack painting from the hundreds of contributors who have drawn their various prayers on our common screen. Everything is being covered over too fast for me to read the symbols, but I must be processing some information at some level, because however confused the picture may be, it makes me feel like the world is happy and holy.

The picture has become a realistic (as far as I can tell) portrayal of Jesus and his twelve apostles, one of them being me, at his Last Supper. This is what was on the holy reel, presumably. We are speaking Hebrew (I think), but there are Jamish subtitles. I see myself eating the bread and wine along with the other apostles and I happen to know that everyone else sees him or herself in my place. Because I am aware of this, I feel that I am in communion with everyone else—we're sharing the same body, after all. I feast my eyes on all the scenery. I have replaced Judas. In the grand old Hollywood fashion, the animator has made the ultimate resurrection—the resurrection of the possibility that Jesus would not be betrayed by a fellow human.

AGNOSTIC DAY

This time the communion scene seems to be prolonged beyond its usual bounds. Instead of the usual rush to the Jamesism "Go, the mess is entered," I see the apostles following Jesus out of Da Vinci's studio, which turns out to be located at the edge of an ancient town, into a wilderness and step by step up a mountain. The camera follows from the rear as apostles shed layer after layer of clothing during their ascent, each layer more modern than the previous one until they are all in modern dress, and I notice that the mountain has smoothed into a skyscraper and Jesus has metamorphosed into a young boy. A view of Toronto's skyline creeps over the horizon as they reach the summit of what is now obviously the McLuhan Tower.

Now the sky turns to night, a full moon rises impossibly over the northern skyline, twelve dark figures begin orbiting the track-suited child tied to the spire, faces emerge from shadows—Marx, Lenin, Mao, Lee, James, Innis, Armstrong, Aldrin, Collins (captioned), Joe Harper, Joan Harper, Garth Miranda—and are heard to mutter 'annul, annul, annul, annul . . . " as they follow in solemn counter-clockwise procession around the concrete rim suspended in space above a bloated metropolis and below a hungry moon.

The cartooning degenerates with the sacrificial blast-off that follows, as if Leon Harper—if I may make a wild guess at the perpetrator—did not have time to finish his message to me.

What am I to think? I'm open to commands.

It seems that the Artful Dodger is a flickrocket and no photo-animation dummy. And that I am called to be a porn-again Leon-tamer and brain against Luny tumour as well as a brawn a-gone lyin'-dammer.

Sir WARLOCK informs me that "annul" is "Luna" spelled backwards. Lahd Waltmitty! Is Leon-Artful-Harper-Dodger Phil Delphi's *Little Bugs Brother* or James' "Lab of Code who shakes awake the signs of the world"? Is this my fullfoolment as empty forcer? To be a Lahd enforcer—using a Libglib's lewd reinforcers? The Meddling Treater is the Messiah-Traitor?

My pod comes to rest beside a moat servicing three different enclaves. Goats dine on the slopes of the Disneyland-inspired Matterhorn Castle up ahead. On the right stands the conic non-Fuller dome known by its half-thousand residents as N'Amerindy 500 Teepee. Before I face the enclave on the left I say a prayer to God or James or, who knows, Puns de Leon, sun of Message

Mayaprop—could he be the unmentionable HRPR of the St. Augustinians? I pray to Anyone who calls me prey and ask for understanding—mine, Yours, and theirs—and for the coverage of my conventions.

Stepping out of the pod, starboard side, I ask the mask, "Shall we contemplate the naval?"

"Come and be baptized," says the mermaid before wheeling away. Password recognized, I dive into the gently flowing pool and begin swimming upstream towards the underpass leading to Neptune.

WE HAVE MET THE ALIEN
(AND IT IS US)

Afterword

Now, how could I have told you up front that what this book is about is critical alienation? I mean, and still have you read it?

Actually, I *couldn't* tell you, because I didn't know.

Had I but known —well, at the very least, I'd have tried to balance things out more.

And that would have been a mistake.

In any event, after all the readings and re-readings, separately and in sequence, I knew everything about this book except what its overall theme had turned out to be. I found out from someone who had never seen the book at all.

I was thinking about what I wanted to say back here, and I started asking people—everyone, anyone—to tell me why they thought SF (science fiction, speculative fabulation, sometimes surreal futures) is so popular now. What social value does the genre have, now, here?

I got a lot of familiar replies, about rehearsing future options, opening one's mind to alternative realities, using exotic sets and lights to focus on familiar problems, generally practising thinking the unthinkable.

True. It was science fiction, future fiction, SF, that taught us how to think about death and despoilation by radiation, chemical waste devastation, Big Brother, Star Wars and Nuclear Winter. So what's "unthinkable" now?

My daughter, appropriately, gave me the answer that curled my toes and shivered my neurons and made me see the *whole* book for the first time:

It's the only place you can do any useful thinking about the idea that there might not be a future: the terminal fear that proliferates abortions and suicides, mass murders, mad leaders, terrorists and technical errors; the ultimate anxiety that makes people sorry they had children, and children not want to grow up.

And of course that's what most of this book is about: the children finding ways to grow up, the parents trying to help them. I didn't plan it that way; it's just that those were the stories that seemed to *work*.

You must understand that I am really a most improbable anthologist. I'm a poor scholar, not much of a collector or compiler, not at all a historian. (Call me a generalist, maybe, disseminator— someone once said *neophiliac*.) Nevertheless, this volume is my twentieth SF anthology, and the first nineteen brought me just enough dribs and drabs of fame and fortune so that I can now say brazenly (like in the Modern Art Joke): *I don't know anything about literary criticism, but I know what I like.*

What I like is getting my head turned around. I get off on fresh perceptions, widening horizons, new thoughts, and I like them best when they occur as a process in my own mind, rather than an exposition at which I am a passive spectator/receiver. What I look for in SF is the story (or verse—occasionally film—sometimes even essay) conceived and written in such a way as to suggest alternatives that will cause me to exercise my own imagination to broaden my own vision. To "ask the next question."

> A Martian with a mangled spear
> Is stuffing tarts in my left ear.
> If I turn off my hearing aid,
> Will I still taste the marmalade?

This synaesthetic gem was probably the beginning of this anthology. It was handed to me in December 1968 in an unhallowed hall of Rochdale College by an idealistic young academic already highly respected as poet, publisher, and editor, but not yet famous for Alligator Pies, Garbage Delights and other tasty (*not* non-)

sense. It turned my head around. I put it aside for my next anthology, which was some time coming.

Twenty is a nice round number.

The first SF anthology I edited, in 1951, was called *Shot in the Dark,* not so much for its interior surprises as to enable Bantam Books to pass it off on mystery readers if necessary. The saleability of SF was an unknown quantity at the time.

The time, as it turned out, was right. In the next eighteen years I did eighteen more collections. The last two, *SF 12* (Delacorte) and *England Swings SF* (Doubleday), were published almost back-to-back in 1968.

That was the same year I arrived in Toronto, a newly-landed immigrant with a U-Haul full of books, papers, plastic milk crates and foam pads. My new job as resource person at Rochdale would pay only room and board. I expected to have to do more anthologies for car-fares and cigarette money, and I figured Dennis Lee's verse to be my first Canadian inclusion for *SF 13.*

Thirteen was the lucky number: I never got around to doing it. (*SF 12* was the twelfth annual in the "Year's Best" series, and twelve years of claiming to present the *Best*—of anything—was more than enough. Better iconoclast than iconescent.) But by the time I realized I was not going to do another SF annual, I had learned a couple of things about Canadian SF.

In all the far reaches of Canada in 1968 there seemed to be only two people (well, make it 2¼) writing recognizable science fiction seriously: Phyllis Gotlieb and H. A. Hargreaves (and Chandler Davis *very* occasionally; adding my own output at the time, make it 2½). But in odd corners and coach houses (especially *the* Coach House Press) Canadians of rare talent and sensibility were writing truly-fabulous funny-serious social-commentary SF: Dave Godfrey, Ray Smith, D. M. Price, J. Michael Yates, Gwendolyn MacEwen, P. K. Page, Robert Zend, Christopher Dewdney and more, were stuffed in with the marmalade.

The seventies: I was becoming a Canadian and a broadcaster, and not thinking about anthologies at all. But (yes, Dennis, you'd still taste it) every switchoff was another switch on. I gave my SF collection to the Toronto Public Library to start the Spaced Out

Library, and so became an occasional consultant. I was putting a lot of energy into The Writers' Union of Canada, so became involved with a schools-curriculum project outlining available Canadian science fiction. I wrote radio documentaries and magazine articles, and kept getting asked to do pieces on science fiction. No way I could miss out on what was happening in Canadian SF.

A lot was happening. Here, as elsewhere through the seventies, the most visible events were in book publishing (and selling). But we're talking Canada: the busiest and healthiest area was of course academic. And to me, inquisitive immigrant, the most intriguing phenomenon was half-hidden under the surface of the literary mainstream.

As I read Canadian authors, and met them personally, I kept finding myself touching what I think of as "science fiction head space." Sometimes it was overt SF imagery, or a certain way of thinking about environment, a casual mixture of magic-and-realism, or an oddly familiar structural tension in the work. Then, one by one, leading Canadian authors began telling me about the impact of science fiction on their development: Berton, Laurence, MacEwen, Acorn, Purdy, Engel. Finally, I began to catch up on Canadian criticism. CanLit, I was told, is about *survival* and, characteristically, the environment may become almost a character in the story!

Of course! Just like SF. (Is this why Canadian mainstream authors, when they turn to SF, usually do a good job of it? U.S. and U.K. mainstreamers generally muck it up.)

Another (used-to-be) Canadian Fact I was learning was the prevalence of "secondary materials." You know—Canada was famous for documentaries, but never made feature films? That kind of thing.

In 1968, when the prestigious Modern Language Association officially declared the study of science fiction a suitable pursuit for scholars, Canadian critics and teachers were already doing it. Harry Campbell, then Chief Librarian in Toronto, must have followed a sure Canadian instinct when he offered to relieve me of my unwieldy collection and establish SOL (the Spaced Out

Library) in 1970. By that time, Arthur Gibson and Peter Fitting were already organizing science fiction classes at the University of Toronto, Madge Aalto (the first SOL librarian) was teaching at York, Darko Suvin had a course at McGill and Tom Henighan was just about to start at Carleton.

SOL provided a focus, and increasingly, a resource. In '72, SOL and McGill co-sponsored *SeCon,* the Secondary Universe Conference which brought scholars, critics and teachers of SF together from all over Canada, along with their counterparts from other countries, and a scattering of SF writers. In 1973, a serious scholarly journal, *Science Fiction Studies,* began publishing in Montreal.

By the mid-seventies, most major Canadian universities had SF courses, and colleges and high schools were rushing to catch up. Some of the best teachers were encouraging students to write original stories for their term papers. And there were at least *five*-and-a-half working SF writers across the country, because Spider Robinson had moved up to Nova Scotia from the States, and Britishers Michael Coney and Andrew Weiner had settled in Victoria and Toronto.

(Actually, it was at least six-and-a-half, if you count the blessedly brief extrusion of Harlequin's kid brother, Laser Books, into the field. Laser published a whole series of a single cloned novel— same plot, same characters, different names, titles and bylines— before they discovered SF readers don't like predictable formulas. I won't count them.)

Other publishers were doing better, sometimes spectacularly so. True, most of them didn't *know* they were publishing SF, and most of the authors didn't know they were writing it, but at least twenty at-least-readable novels and one short story collection of Canadian science fiction were published in Canada during the seventies, and some of them were very fine science fiction indeed: Ian Adams' *The Trudeau Papers,* Christie Harris' *Sky Man on a Totem Pole,* Blanche Howard's *The Immortal Soul of Edwin Carlysle,* Bruce Powe's *The Last Days of the American Empire,* and others of varying quality by John Ballem, Stephen Franklin, William Heine, Basil Jackson, Richard Rohmer, David Walker and Jim Willer. Monica Hughes, Suzanne Martell and Ruth Nichols, writing juveniles, were genre-identified; so was Marie Jacober, with a prize-winning adult novel in Alberta. H. A. Hargreaves' short-story collection, *North By 2000,* in 1975, must have been the first book labelled specifically as Canadian Science Fiction. Gotlieb, Coney, and Robinson, of course, were publishing novels and short stories regularly under SF labels in the U.S. and U.K., and towards the end of the decade two new Canadian novelists were launched by U.S. genre publishers: Crawford Killian in 1978 and Edward Llewellyn in 1979. (Llewellyn's *The Douglas Convolution* was the first of only five novels completed before his untimely death in 1984.)

Actually in 1979, you might well have used up all your fingers and toes counting Canadian SF writers—if you could find them. One man did. No one, not even John Colombo, would seriously have tried to produce an anthology of contemporary Canadian science fiction at that point, but he did bring out a very different collection: *Other Canadas.*

John Robert Colombo is a good deal more than just another CanCult household name. I called myself an improbable anthologist; Colombo is the real thing: scholar, historian, careful compiler, indefatiguable researcher, voluminous reader, aggressive correspondent. The marvel is that an editor of these accomplishments should have had the imaginative flair to wish to use them in the service of a genre hardly anyone (except thee and me, John—and sometimes I wondered about *me*) believed existed—indigenous Canadian SF.

Other Canadas used the broadest possible definitions of source, form and content. It brought together a discriminating collection of science fiction and fantasy written by Canadians and/or about Canada over a time-span of more than two hundred years, including short stories, poetry, novel excerpts and critical essays. The selections, enriched with Colombo's informed and engaging notes, established once and for all the existence of the territory, and in effect proclaimed it open for exploration and settlement. .

I am *not* a scholar. My files are famous for their gaps, and my notes for their irrelevance. It is time to apologize in passing to all the people unmentioned here (Susan Wood! How could I never have spoken of Susan Wood?) who were creating Canadian science fiction in the seventies, as I hasten to disclaim any ability to document the burgeoning productivity of the eighties.

(I was straying into television, returning to work on a novel. Still—)

Even the most casual reader had to be aware of the emergence of Eileen Kernaghan (choice science *fantasy*), William Gibson (all over *Omni*) and Donald Kingsbury (Hugo Award nominee for *Courtship Rite*). I knew that John Bell and Lesley Choyce brought out an anthology in 1981 similar in its premises to Colombo's book, but more modestly limited to the Atlantic provinces. I knew that an annual Canadian Science Fiction and Fantasy Award had been established. I was invited to *Boréal,* the Francophone SF conference, and realized that on the other side of the language barrier a positive ferment of activity was going on. And back in Anglophonia I kept hearing names I hadn't heard before.

So when Ellen Godfrey of Press Porcépic suggested a new anthology in 1984, I was only briefly surprised. Of course—the time was right (again). Canadian SF—a uniquely Canadian expression of perspectives on change and the future—had developed as inevitably as (say) Canadian feature films or Canadian Studies courses in foreign universities, from the same ongoing Canadian dynamic: a dialectic of international/immigrant influences and a growing awareness of a specifically Canadian cultural identity. Colombo did not *invent* the concept of *Other Canadas;* he located and described it.

The first *big* surprise then was realizing I really wanted to try to do the book.

Twenty *is* a nice round number. I guess I'd been away from it long enough. (Like sex and bicycles, it seems to come right back when you start again.)

The surprises kept coming. The next big one was not having to fight with my publishers (or educate them). Right from the beginning we were in agreement about the book we wanted to do: a sampling of some of the best contemporary Canadian SF—as described in the Foreword. ("We" were Godfrey, myself and Gerry Truscott, the Press Porcépic editor who did all the nitty-gritties:

correspondence, contracts, copy-editing, and consultation on selections.)

Another early surprise was the size of the mailing list compiled with help from John Colombo, John Bell (Ottawa-based editor/author/archivist), Rob Sawyer (young author with wide SF-fandom connections) and Doris Mehegan of SOL. Announcements of the project went out initially to more than seventy authors. Some were novelists who just *might* do a short story; many were mainstream writers who had occasionally done a bit of SF; but almost half of them were actually published science fiction writers!

The numbers were great as growth-figures, but they were still small seen as a field to choose from; I think we were all astonished at how "contemporary" the book finally came to be. *I* certainly was.

We started out hoping—trusting—we wouldn't have to go back for material earlier than the seventies, but I was prepared to fall back on reprinting a few sixties classics from *Other Canadas* — Laurence's "A Queen in Thebes", Hood's "After the Sirens", Theriault's "Akua Nuten". And while we waited for the first submissions to come in, I speculated on the possibilities of excerpts from some of the novels (Adams, Howard, Kingsbury, Llewellyn, Powe . . .) and dug out the old marmalade file. There was Dennis Lee, Chandler Davis' "Hexamnion", and selections from Dave Godfrey's *Death Goes Better with Coca Cola,* Ray Smith's *Cape Breton is the Thought Control Centre of Canada,* Gwendolyn MacEwen's *No-man,* P. K. Page's *The Sun, the Moon, and Other Stories,* J. Michael Yates' *The Man in the Glass Octopus. . . .*

We did not, as you know, use any of these; they kept getting bumped back into history because the really big, continuing surprise was the stuff that kept coming in the mail. Altogether, we received some 400 manuscripts from almost 140 authors, and (*talk* about surprises!) no more than half of them were first-reading rejects (for assorted reasons of literary inadequacy, banality, didacticism, or because they fell outside the boundaries of our shared concept of "SF"). It's worth mentioning—happily, from where I stand (upon my prejudices)—that very little of what we read seemed to have been spawned by the proliferation of so-called Sci-Fi in the visual media. (We SF elite pronounce it *Skiffy* and never *never* use the term to describe *the right stuff*.) We had hardly any UFO-riders, cutesie ghosts, space battles, Wild West conquests of alien terrain, killer robots, virgin knights of the space orbits, or born-again mythology.

We did have a handful of submissions—mostly fantasy—that fell outside our preconceptions, but persuasively enough to put them to the test: stories and poems from Mary Choo, Greg Hollingshead, Carlan LeGraff, Tom Marshall and Libby Scheier, and two dazzling, elegant pieces of writing from P. K. Page ("Birthday", a short story) and Gwen MacEwen (an excerpt from her new novel, *Noman's Land*). We agonized over these last two (which will both be in print elsewhere by the time this book is released; look for them), but in the end confirmed—*surprise* again!—that we were indeed in agreement on what did *not* fit within our otherwise amorphous definition. And of course we knew by then that we were getting more than enough quality work that fell well within our boundaries.

Of the thirty-two selections in this book, seventeen are published here for the first time (in the English language); only two were first published before 1980.

Talk about embarrassments of riches....

By the time half the selections were fairly definite, I was still juggling about fifty more pieces of (very) roughly equivalent merits: a little flaw in logic here, a bit of battered syntax there. Toss a coin? Are some shortcomings more remediable than others? (We did, in fact, ask for and get two rewrites—but both were stories we had already decided to use.)

At this point in any anthology—well, anyhow, my anthologies—editorial decisions no longer rest solely on the excellence of the individual submission. The book is acquiring a *shape* that exercises its own influence. A story may be discarded because it is too close in theme and mood to one already chosen; or one piece might edge out another precisely because it *is* similar to something already included, but treats the topic very differently. At the same time, each reflective re-reading magnifies small flaws—and some flaws magnify more horrendously than others. The process is no longer *fair*.

That's when anthologizing stops being fun.

At this moment I can envision the pile of photocopies in my desk drawer organizing a protest march on my typewriter, demanding equal rights, while I snivel pathetically, "Hey, the book just wasn't *big* enough." Leading the march would be John Bell's "Centrifugal Force", Charles de Lint's "A Witch in Rhyme", Tom Henighan's "Tourists from Algol", Patrick Kernaghan's "Weekend Warrior" and Andrew Weiner's "Station Gehenna". Right behind them would be stories from David Beck, H. A. Hargreaves, B. C. Jensen, Christopher S. Lobban, J. M. Park, Ursula Pflug, Robert J. Sawyer, David Sharpe, Graeme Skinner and Ann Walsh. (Magazine editors and anthologists, please take note.)

It's not fair, I said. This is the time to talk about leaning over backward, particularly addressed to those authors who received rejection letters from Gerry Truscott, the author of "Cee". This was one of the stories I juggled for weeks, and not until it landed inside the target did I know that the pseudonym "Pat Laurence" on the title page was Gerry's.

Did you ever try leaning over backwards *both ways at the same time?*

I owe some apologies and acknowledgements as well, in connection with French-language selections. We started out on a very high plane, determined to honour both official languages. I asked Elisabeth Vonarburg, the editor of *Solaris,* who presides over the effervescent Francophone science fiction conference in Chicoutimi, to spread the word in French Canada. Sure, said I, submit in French; we'll get the things we want translated. I blush now for three of us, Canadian editors who read only one language. My thanks to Peter Fitting and Katie Cooke, and (much too late) to Marian Engel, who all read for me and advised me. (But somewhere deep inside I am wickedly grateful that I did not have *another* fifty stories to compare and match against each other.)

Leaning over backwards in two directions simultaneously, and assuming someone *else* on the team knows French—how Canadian can you get? I have written many pages, and discarded them, trying to dissect or describe why (beyond the author's addresses) I feel this is truly a contemporary *Canadian* SF anthology. Now I wonder if pointing to Vonarburg and Truscott doesn't do it best? Not just the circumstances of their selections, but the statements of their stories as well.

We have met the Alien and it is *us.*

Maybe Pogo was a closet Canadian. Identifying the alien within is not an easy state of mind for Yanks or Brits. On the record, in this book, it seems a relatively confident assumption in the prevailing Canadian voice—even the immigrant voices.

Someone else can write the dissertation on those interactive dynamics of immigrant and native-born (and Native-born) Canadians/Canadiens. I am satisfied to sense, after months of immersion in Canadian futures, that there is something one just might call a Canadian consciousness, and that this unique sensibility of accepting-and-coping might just have something of value to offer to the uncertain future of a planet in perilous pain.

JUDITH MERRIL
Toronto
July 1985

THE CONTRIBUTORS

Jane Brierley is a member of the *Société des traducteurs du Québec* and the Literary Translators' Association, for which she edits the newsletter, *Transmission*. She has recently completed a translation of Philippe Aubert du Gaspé's *Memoires* (1866), which is scheduled for publication in 1986 by Vehicule Press, Montreal.

Lesley Choyce lives in Porters Lake, Nova Scotia, where he owns and operates the Pottersfield Press, which is dedicated to Atlantic Canadian poetry and fiction. He has also published several books of fiction and poetry himself; most recent are *Downwind* (Creative Publishers), *Billy Botzweiler's Last Dance* (blewointmentpress) and *Visions from the Edge* (Pottersfield Press), a collection of Atlantic Canadian SF edited with John Bell.

John Robert Colombo is the author, compiler or translator of more than sixty books. In 1979 he compiled *Other Canadas,* the country's first anthology of science fiction and fantasy (see the Afterword). His other book-length contributions to the genre include *Friendly Aliens, Blackwood's Books, Windigo* and *Years of Light* (the biography of the late Leslie A. Crouch of Parry Sound, Ontario, who for thirty years produced the fanzine called *Light*).

Michael G. Coney is the most international of the authors in this anthology. Born in England, he also lived in Antigua, West Indies, before settling in Sidney, British Columbia (which provides the setting for "The Byrds"). He has published fifteen novels and numerous short stories, several of which have been translated into Dutch, French, German, Italian, Spanish and other languages.

A. K. Dewdney teaches Computer Science at the University of Western Ontario in London. His major interests are Discrete Mathematics and Theoretical Computer Science, fields in which he has published numerous articles. He lives in London, Ontario.

Christopher Dewdney is a major Canadian poet whose most recent book is a collection of selected poems, entitled *Predators of the Adoration* (McClelland & Stewart, 1983). His hobbies include recombinant genetics, rock camping and carnivorous marsupials.

Candas Jane Dorsey is a freelance journalist living in Edmonton. She is currently writing for and editing the Edmonton *Bullet,* an arts and culture tabloid. She has published three books of poems and several short stories, SF and mainstream.

Gary Eikenberry is an adult educator specializing in microcomputer applications in Ottawa. He has published several poems and short stories in SF and literary magazines throughout North America since 1975.

Marian Engel (1933–1985) is one of Canada's most respected literary figures. She was awarded the 1976 Governor General's Award for literature for her novel, *Bear.* Her most recent book is *The Tatooed Woman* (Penguin, 1985), a collection of short stories.

Benjamin Freedman conducts research in bioethics at the Westminster Institute for Ethics & Human Values and teaches in the faculties of Philosophy, Medicine and Nursing at the University of Western Ontario. He has published numerous articles in professional journals on topics relating to bioethics. "On the Planet Grafool" is his first fiction publication.

Dorothy Corbett Gentleman has published three books of poetry, most recently *Candles for the Dawn* (Pierian Press). She has recently completed another collection entitled *Above the Tilted Earth* from which "Instinct" was taken. She lives in North Vancouver.

William Gibson is familiar to readers of *Omni,* where he has been publishing short stories on a regular basis since 1980. His first novel, *Neuromancer* (Ace) has received the genre's highest honours from authors, fans and critics: the Philip K. Dick Memorial Award (1984), the Nebula Award (1984), the Australian SF Award (1985) and the Hugo Award (1985). His hobbies include cycling, travel and mowing the lawn.

Phyllis Gotlieb's first novel, *Sunburst,* was published in 1964 along with her first book of poetry, *Within the Zodiac.* Since then she has published five more novels, three more collections of poetry and one collection of short stories. Her most recent book is *The Kingdom of the Cats* (Ace, 1985). She has established herself as a major figure in science fiction and fantasy as well as an important Canadian poet.

Terence M. Green is an English teacher in Toronto. He has published several short stories in SF magazines, as well as many articles on SF and other literature. He has recently completed a novel, *Barking Dogs,* based on his 1984 short story of the same name.

Eileen Kernaghan lives in Burnaby, B.C., where she is a founding member of the Burnaby Writers' Society. Along with many published poems and short stories, she has written two fantasy novels, *Journey to Aprilioth* (Ace, 1980) and *Songs from the Drowned Lands* (Ace, 1983), which won the Canadian Science Fiction and Fantasy Award for 1983–84.

David Kirkpatrick is a student and sports enthusiast living in London, Ontario. He has a Masters degree from the University of Toronto. He is currently working on a holographic approach to a novel, which will include "Terminal Cancer". This is his first publication.

Margaret McBride lives in Victoria where she is raising two children and a garden. She claims to have raised tse-tse flies and sold waterbeds for a living, although not at the same time. "Totem" is her first publication.

Judith Merril has established her reputation as a leading authority on SF (science/speculative fiction) by editing nineteen anthologies and writing several novels and short stories in the genre. She is also a broadcaster, consultant and peace activist. *Tesseracts* is her twentieth anthology.

Frances Morgan is a professional translator in Ottawa. She has translated two books by the Quebec children's author, Bernadette Renaud: *Cat in the Cathedral* and *The Computer Revolts* (Press Porcépic, 1983 and 1984). She is currently working on a joint writing-translating effort with another Quebec author to produce a bilingual novel for young adults.

D. M. Price is a poet and artist living in Vancouver, where he owns and operates a book store. He claims to be successfully raising quantum black holes in his basement.

Robert Priest is a poet and singer living in Toronto. His most recent book is a collection entitled *The Man Who Broke Out of the Letter X* (The Coach House Press, 1984), his most recent recording is entitled *Summerlong* (G-Tel Records, 1984).

Spider Robinson is well known and respected among science fiction readers and writers alike. He is the author of several novels and collections of short stories, the most recent of which are *Melancholy Elephants* (collection: Penguin Canada, 1984; TOR, 1985) and *Night of Power* (novel: Baen Books, 1985). He lives in Halifax.

Rhea Rose lives in Burnaby, B.C., where she is involved in local theatre and freelance writing. She has attended the Clarion West Science Fiction and Fantasy Writers' Workshop in Seattle; "Chronos' Christmas" was workshopped there. This is her first fiction publication.

Daniel Sernine is the author of numerous short stories and novels for adults and children, and has established himself as a major force in French Canadian literature. He was awarded the 1984 Canada Council Children's Literature prize for his juvenile novel, *Le cercle violet* (Editions Pierre Tisseyre, Montreal). He lives in Montreal.

Marc Sévigny is a Montreal-based freelance journalist. He has published articles and reports in a variety of French-language periodicals. He has also published several short stories in periodicals such as *Solaris* and *Imagine*. His most recent book publication is *Marie-Soleil ou La crise du carbure*, a fairy tale on ecology (Editions Pantoute, 1982).

Susan Swan is a freelance writer living in Toronto. She writes for a variety of media, including theatre, poetry and fiction. She has published several plays, one collection of short fiction and one novel, *The Biggest Modern Woman of the World* (Lester & Orpen Denys, 1983). She is currently working on a second novel, entitled *The Last of the Golden Girls*.

Robert Sward is a poet, editor, publisher, freelance broadcaster and teacher who now lives in California. He is the author of fourteen books, the most recent of which are *Poems: New and Selected (1957–1983)* (Aya Press, 1983) and *The Toronto Islands* (Dreadnaught Co-operative, 1983).

Gerry Truscott is a graduate of the University of Victoria's Creative Writing Department and is now the managing editor at Press Porcépic. He also writes and edits data for educational courseware at Softwords, Press Porcépic's software division. "Cee" is his first fiction publication.

Elisabeth Vonarburg was born in Paris, France, and now lives with five cats in Chicoutimi, Quebec, where she publishes and edits *Solaris,* one of French Canada's most important SF magazines. She has published many short stories, mostly science fiction and fantasy (several have been translated into English), and one novel, *Le silence de la Cité* (Editions Denoël, 1981), which is being made into a movie. She is currently working on the script for the movie.

Robert Zend (1929–1985) came to Canada from Budapest, Hungary in 1956. He soon established himself as a major Canadian poet. He also produced over 100 radio programmes for the acclaimed CBC series, *Ideas.* His two-volume multi media novel entitled *OAB* (Exile Editions) represents his magnum opus, thirteen years in creation. Volume 2 of *OAB* was published shortly after his death in 1985.

ACKNOWLEDGEMENTS

"Foreword" and "Afterword: We Have Met the Alien (And It Is Us)" © 1985 by Judith Merril.

"Home by the Sea" English translation © 1985 by Elisabeth Vonarburg and Jane Brierley. Original French version, *"La Maison au bord de la mer"* © 1985 by Elisabeth Vonarburg, soon to be published in *Dix Récits de Science Fiction,* edited by André Carpentier (Editions les Quinze).

"Chronos' Christmas" © 1985 by Rhea Rose.

"A Strange Visitor" and "An Adventure in Miracle Land" © 1985 by Janine Zend.

"The Byrds" © 1982 by Michael G. Coney; reprinted by permission of the author and the author's agent, Virgina Kidd. This story first appeared in *Changes,* edited by Michael Bishop and Ian Watson.

"Report on the Earth-Air Addicts" © 1984 by Robert Priest, from *The Man Who Broke Out of the Letter X* (The Coach House Press, 1984). "The Early Education of the Num-nums" © 1980 by Robert Priest, from *Sadness of Spacemen* (Dreadnaught Co-operative, 1980). Both selections are reprinted by permission of the author.

"Johnny Appleseed on the New World" © 1985 by Candas Jane Dorsey.

"Letter from Mars Dome #1" © 1978 by Eileen Kernaghan; first appeared in the Literary Storefront Newsletter, October 1978.

"Hinterlands" © 1981 by Omni Publications International Ltd.; reprinted by permission of the author.

ACKNOWLEDGEMENTS

"Points in Time" © 1985 by Christopher Dewdney.

"Stardust Boulevard" English translation © 1985 by Daniel Sernine and Jane Brierley. Original French version, *"Boulevard des Etoiles"* © 1981 by Le Préambule (Longueuil, Quebec); first published in the collection, *Le vieil homme et l'espace* by Daniel Sernine (Le Préambule). Used by permission of the publisher.

"The Last Will and Testament of the Unknown Earthman Lost in the Second Vegan Campaign" and "Future City" © 1985 by D. M. Price.

"The Woman Who is the Midnight Wind" © 1985 by Terence M. Green.

"Instinct" © 1980 by Dorothy Corbett Gentleman; first published in *Pierian Spring* (Brandon, Manitoba), Spring 1980.

"Cee" © 1985 by Gerry Truscott.

"On the Planet Grafool" © 1985 by Benjamin Freedman.

"Tauf Aleph" © 1981 by Phyllis Gotlieb; reprinted by permission of the author and the author's agent, Virginia Kidd. This story first appeared in *More Wandering Stars,* edited by Jack Dann (Doubleday, 1981).

"Anthropology 101" © 1983 by Gary Eikenberry; first appeared in *Bibliofantasiac #9* (Toronto).

"The Train" English translation © 1985 by Marc Sévigny and Frances Morgan. Original French version, *"Le Train"*, from *Aurores Boréales 1,* © 1983 by Le Préambule (Longueuil, Quebec). Used by permission of the publisher.

"Countdown" and "Questionnaire" © 1985 by John Robert Colombo.

"Sophie, 1990" © 1980 by Marian Engel. Reprinted by permission of Robert C. Brandeis, literary executor for the author's estate.

"Totem" © 1985 by Margaret McBride.

"2DWORLD" © 1984 by Alexander K. Dewdney; first appeared as the introduction to the novel, *The Planiverse* (McClelland and Stewart, 1984). Reprinted by permission of the author and the author's agent, Nancy Colbert.

Acknowledgements

"Variation" © 1973 by Robert Zend, from *From Zero to One* (Sono Nis, Victoria, 1973). Reprinted by permission of Janine Zend.

"The Man Doll" © 1985 by Susan Swan. An earlier version of this story was published, under the same title, in *Descant* No. 38, Fall, 1982.

"The Loneliness of the Long Distance Writer" © 1982 by Lesley Choyce; first appeared in *Orion,* Vol. 1, No. 2, 1982.

"Report From the Front" © 1983 by Robert Sward, from *Poems: New and Selected (1957–1983)* (Aya Press, Toronto, 1983). Reprinted by permission of the author.

"God is an Iron" © 1981 by Spider Robinson. First appeared in *Omni,* May, 1979; the story is also included as Chapter Two of the novel, *Mindkiller* (Holt, Rinehart & Winston, 1982; Berkley, 1983).

"The Effect of Terminal Cancer on Potential Astronauts" © 1985 by David Kirkpatrick.

"The Difficulty of Living on Other Planets" © by Dennis Lee. Used by permission of the author.

The publisher thanks Garth Spencer and *The Maple Leaf Rag* for names, dates and word of mouth.

149

(33∂)

DATE DUE